BLACK POWER

Black Power

Dean Baxter

Dedicated to all the little ones who ran with a towel
as a cape.

PROLOGUE

Philadelphia, Pennsylvania, May 10, 1985, 7:00 a.m. EST.

On a beautiful Philadelphia day in May 1985, two cultures clashed, and a burgeoning David would be crushed by an ancient Goliath, created centuries before, to kill him.

The police surrounded them in concentric circles. From the sky, they looked like a target with the fortified house at the center. They had sharpshooters on the outer ring and a mixture of crack shots and machine gunners on the middle ring, and the explosive specialists occupied the closest ring. The police filled the immediate area of the house with CS gas as the fire department sprayed the house with four separate deluge hoses, raising the area's humidity and obscuring the vision of the presumed armed men in the roof fortification.

The house sheltered sixteen people, half of whom cowered in the basement. Sharp *anger* and general fear boiled in the house, and there was nowhere to go.

They called themselves Progress. The exhaustion of hiding and skulking in the shadows of society wore on them, so they decided not to hide. The abilities they manifested were limited and insignificant in the grand scheme of things. But more people feared what they could do than those who accepted them.

Being helpful in the neighborhood used to be enough; however, over the last decade or so, as Black people created their own working-class communities, they glimpsed what many perceived as a light at the end of a nearly 400-year-long tunnel of horrors. Anything that disrupted the freedom boat, held together by their forebears' blood, sweat, and flesh, proved antithetical to their survival.

This hope-fulfilled generation excised any subgroup that might make Black people any more of an outsider than they already were. Even if that subgroup made things move or grow. Some of the more conservative pastors even preached whole sermons against the witchcraft of the Outsiders. The side eyes and whispers spread swiftly. They did what any good American would do when someone disturbed the peace. They called the police, and the anonymous calls trickled in at first, then, as the months passed, poured in. Soon, larger and more dangerous predators took notice of the small Philadelphia community.

A few hours before smoke and blood marred the morning, a young girl named Sunrose opened her golden eyes. She greeted the morning with a smile that was bright and infectious. She immediately detected the tumultuous emotions in the house. Tumultuous was a new word she learned, and she loved the images it conjured in her mind. She looked down at her hands, where a pink swirl of raw, psionic energy formed in the palm of her young hand. Sunrose giggled to herself, and one of the rushing adults saw her manifestation. She stopped and smiled at the young girl.

"That's beautiful, Sunrose, impressive control. You're showing incredible growth. Go catch up with the other children and have breakfast." Ramona stood up, gave Sunrose a smile haloed by thick black locks, and faded into the house's bustle.

Sunrose, being the obedient seven-year-old, sprinted happily to the dining area, which turned out to be empty.

She stopped and instinctively reached out with her mind to find her siblings. They were all downstairs having breakfast; their familiar emotes bright to her inner eye. Phasing through the floor easily, she dropped onto the table, startling everyone eating. One of her tiny feet landed in someone's oatmeal, it squished warmly between her toes, and she laughed at the sensation. However, giggles turned to tears as the others yelled and screamed at her. Someone grabbed her roughly from the table. Why was everyone so angry?

Sunrose sat and ate her food in silence, listening to the older kids speculate on what was happening. They waved their arms and clenched their fists, but they did not eat. Realizing all at once that they weren't hungry, they started cleaning. Sunrose helped as best she could. When she expressed excitement about going outside to play with the animals, the adults told her there would be no outside today. She was sad at first until they were told they could play with the new puppies that had been born a week or so ago. That was fun.

As the morning progressed, Sunrose heard the big people yelling more and more, on loudspeakers like they were talking to someone outside. She figured the neighbors were yelling mean things again. Then a sharp stab of fear lanced her little heart, and an awful feeling of dread about the day darted through her mind. Dread was one of her spelling words, and she knew what it meant.

The sound of the air being zippered apart shattered the quiet. An adult appeared before the children. She spread her hands to expand the comforting aura that came from her. Her name was Josie, and she told them it was just a recording to scare the bad people away. However, as she spoke these comforting words, the "someone" returned fire, and the comfort coming from her was gone. The very real bullets slammed into the house over and over. Sunrose tried to make herself as small as possible as the air above her was shredded.

The shooting stopped for a moment.

Sunrose heard footsteps on the porch of the house. Josie and the children were huddled in the basement's corner. The silence was a suffocating blanket. Sunrose yearned to investigate, but Josie told her it wasn't safe. She complied without hesitation. She was drilled with the lessons of when compliance was proper, at home with family, and when it was bad, with the White supremacy power structure. Sunrose knew what all of that meant; she was a very bright child and had a near-genius-level intellect, yet she had never lost the innocence of childhood. She calmed her breathing and stretched out her mind.

She touched the waning life force of the wood that the house was built from and the tiny creatures that lived in the walls. She took control of a simple little pincher bug and ran to the outside of the house, using the knowledge that the tiny creature had gathered as a map. She was aware that the bug could never interpret the information independently, but it was a tool for Sunrose.

She made it to the front of the house and saw soldiers in black uniforms and shiny armor on their shoulders, thighs, and shins. Sunrose saw one of the men place what looked like a giant candy bar wrapped in some weird paper right in front of the house's door. The mean man turned around and casually walked away. He had seemed so cautious before, but now he had a smirk on his face.

Progress was, at its core, a peaceful group. They had no reason to teach children about explosives or weaponry, but they would learn a terrible lesson today.

Because the pincher bug had very terrible vision, Sunrose used the life force of the tiny creature to change its eyesight gently, to be more beneficial to her on this reconnaissance mission. It would change back once she released the twist of the life force.

Once the army man rejoined his buddies, they jogged away as quietly as they could. Sunrose turned back to the package and realized there was a small timer on it. The numbers read:

:06s

She stared at the clock in bewilderment.

:05s

Was it an automatic door knocker?

:04s

No, that was dumb. Did the adults only have so long to open the box? Oh no, she had to tell Josie the men left a package at the door that needed to be opened right away!

:03s

Sunrose popped back into herself. "Um, excuse me, Josie, the army man, left a package on the doorstep for us."

:02s

"The army man left what?" Josie said, whirling to face Sunrose. Sunrose flashed her a mental picture.

:01s

"BOMB!" Josie screamed.

:00s

The explosion ripped through the front of the house. The front door all but disintegrated, and pieces of it embedded themselves in some of the house's occupants. The explosion destroyed part of the basement, and the porch collapsed into the hole made by the explosion.

Within a few seconds of this explosion, a barrage of bullets filled the front of the house. Josie put up a barrier to protect the children, and Sunrose reinforced it. They both knew it would not hold.

The huddled group had been on the far side of the basement when the collapse happened.

Sunrose heard the grunts and moans of injured people and started to look up, but Josie refocused her.

"Sunrose! Listen to me. I don't think I can hold it for long. You have to get the kids out of here, someone..." Her voice trailed off, and Josie slowly lowered her hands.

"Okay, they stopped shooting. Run, children!" Josie gasped, and the children dashed through the smoke, unusually silent, though terror gripped their tiny hearts.

Sunrose did not cry.

As Josie led the kids to apparent safety, a helicopter hovered over the barricaded house. The order had come from very high up and was the death knell of the officials' careers delivering the command.

Two men flew in this helicopter. The pilot, Lieutenant Frank Howell, believed he was doing God's work and following reasonable orders. The other man was not visible to Lieutenant Howell. This man had dark skin and a small, tight afro. He wore a black, well-fitting suit and very sensible shoes. If Lieutenant Howell had been aware of the dark-skinned man, he would have noticed a strange metal collar. It had a small hole and a solid red light. The shadowy Black man cast a simple localized illusion that anyone watching or recording would see what he wanted them to see. The pilot held out his hand and dropped a satchel. The shadow man in the black suit leaped from the helicopter to the roof of the house. Once on the roof, any need for deception no longer existed.

"Who the hell are you?" a voice called out as the man stood to his full height. The shadow man knew he only had a few seconds to begin his mission before his controller outside would doubt his efficacy.

The shadowy, Black man with the tight afro, black suit, and tie, and sensible shoes exploded. The man who challenged the intruder and several others in the immediate area vaporized instantly.

Josie led the children upstairs to the rear of the house. The explosion from the roof knocked them all to the floor. They got up and sprinted for the back of the house to the exit when the shooting, at the front of the house, started again.

Sunrose did not scream.

The collapsed rubble on the front of the house provided some cover and deflected many rounds of bullets. The smoke and dust obscured Sunrose's vision. The little yellow dress she had on became badly torn somewhere along the way, and it hung on her by just a few threads. However, she saw that the others around her fared no better: some were naked, the violence having blown their clothes from their bodies.

Sunrose did not cry.

It seemed to take forever to reach the back door. It was so smoky, and hot bullets whizzed over her head. Sunrose realized that there must be a fire somewhere.

Oh no, the puppies! She thought.

Suddenly, she could see the light outside streaming through the smoke.

Sunrose saw Ramona come out of the backroom and see the group of frightened children. Ramona picked up one child and ran for the door, calling for the others to hurry.

Panic tried to choke her.

As Ramona turned to usher the rest of the children and Josie out of the burning house, more bullets tore into the door she had been holding open. Sunrose heard the pops of the guns, and they sounded like firecrackers. The bangs were coming from both sides of the alley. They were trapped.

Sunrose refused to panic.

Then, with a great groaning noise, the burning upper floors collapsed and crashed onto the terrified group, and Ramona disappeared from Sunrose's sight.

No one screamed; they did not have time.

Sunrose tried to open her eyes and had to shake her head because dirt covered her eyes. She tried to move her left hand to clear her face. Something heavy pinned her wrists. She tried to cry out for help but just choked on more dirt. She could have phased her hands through whatever was blocking her, but she remembered her lessons in an emergency.

Always assess the situation before *you use your abilities.*

Sunrose shook her head more vigorously this time and was able to open her eyes.

For a split second, she was happy to see Josie's face smiling at her. The other half of that second, she bit her lip, struggling not to scream.

It seemed Josie's body had turned to stone, and she was holding the weight of the building on her back. Beams of wood had pierced through her body, but ironically, they helped keep the rubble from crushing her. Josie was clearly dead, but she had used whatever energy she had left to protect the child. Sunrose could see the final grief-stricken grimace frozen on the stone face; she bit back tears. The young girl's bright mind bent to the problem at hand.

Sunrose looked at her pinned hands and saw that Josie's stone hand had pinned her left wrist while her right was under some debris. She phased her arm and went under Josie's hand.

"Thank you," she said, bringing her right hand out to touch the cold face. Sunrose could not sense her family's life force at all. She was morbidly thankful she could not see what happened to her loved ones.

Still no tears, just their sting.

After looking around, she knew she could not crawl out of here, but maybe she could phase through the rubble and crawl out.

Always assess the situation before *you use your abilities.*

The crumbling rubble groaned around her, and she could hear the unmistakable sound of burning wood.

Someone had attacked them. Sunrose recalled the army man she saw at the front door planting that small bomb and walking away with smug satisfaction.

She had no idea who was left or what would happen to her after getting out of this. She was a seven-year-old girl on her own. However, she was not helpless.

Sunrose dove into the dirt she was lying on.

Sunrose Alkebulan did not cry.

Philadelphia, Pennsylvania, May 10, 1985, 5:10 p.m. EST.

A long, black, unmarked car came to a stop just outside the yellow tape. There were no official markings on the vehicle, but people steered clear of the car instinctively.

"You know what to do, Sam," one of the men said to the other.

The rear passenger door opened coach-style; it was a small mercy. A tall, dark-skinned man emerged from the car; it seemed he had to unfold himself to get out. He was identical to the man who exploded on the roof earlier, but this man wore casual attire as if he had been walking through the neighborhood and just happened to come upon the scene.

As he made his way through the crowd, he touched as many people as he could. When the time came, and these people tried to describe what happened here, all of them would say these people had been terrorizing the neighborhood for months.

Someone had to do something.

It's a shame it had to come to all of this.

All the violence was unnecessary.

All they had to do was comply.

They should have just given up, and no one would have died.

Even as their own homes burned.

He gave all of this to them like a mental virus. The suggestion didn't last long, but the belief in it did. When he finished his work, he returned to the car; there was a soft clicking sound as the collar light turned from red to green. The older White man in the car put the key in Sam's pocket.

"Don't lose that," he said. He turned around, and they drove away.

BOOK ONE

The Book of Akhet

CHAPTER 1

"I am the Consequence of White Supremacy."

Emperor Okoro, the Gilded Embare.

San Jose, California, February 15, Present Day, 9:50 a.m. PST.

My dad taught me that in life, you are either coming out of a storm cloud or going into one. To me, that means, instead of being afraid of the storm, you appreciate the calm.

Today marked the calm before the most significant storm cloud of my life.

My name is Scipio Harelson; I'm a seventeen-year-old 6'5" 225-pound young Black male. I'm a long way from the cute little chocolate-skinned Black boy people found harmless when I was five or six. I tend to walk around with a smile on my face and a song in my heart to offset my physique's perceived 'scariness.'

I am a martial artist: I worked hard to be in shape and skilled at what I do. I had two big days ahead of me. One was happening tomorrow, a full-contact martial arts tournament. All the big scouts would be there. The second was my third-degree black belt test. I prepared for this test day and night. I ate, slept, and woke up with the test on my mind. I worried about being ready. I feared I would forget my forms - oh God, the bricks ... why had I said I could break ten?

Oh man, I was graduating later this year. I wondered if I would have time to work before or during my Olympic Development Program. Someone had signed me up for the ODP for martial arts, and when I say someone, I mean my teacher and mentor, Adrian Lake, or Coach. That's who I was going to see; we planned to spar today to get ready for the tourney.

I was so deep in thought about everything starting in my life that I did not notice the officer approaching me from behind.

"Stop!" he yelled as he grabbed my arm.

I spun to see who grabbed me, my arm coiling for a blow or a block.

"Don't," he said; his hand dropped to the butt of his gun as he stepped back. I realized the person grabbing me was a police officer. My hands shot up, and the worries in my head fell away.

"Sorry, Sir," I said. My heart thundered in my chest. Prickly heat crawled up the back of my neck and scalp.

The officer examined me suspiciously. "Where are you headed? I haven't seen you around here before." His blue eyes squinted as he spoke.

His words struck me as weird. I have been walking or running to the studio for at least five years. All the store owners and employees in the area knew me. I knew Mrs. Ngyuen from the Great Wok. Her oldest son had recently died of cancer, and we spoke at length of her memories of him. I am a superb listener, and my shoulders are the perfect size to cry on for her. She cried a lot. I knew Mr. Achebe, who owned the local market store; he always had a bottle of water or juice for me. There was Ms. Rhodes and the ladies at the Rat's Nest. She has a weird sense of humor. This flashed through my head in a second.

His badge bounced frantically on his uniform. "Are you deaf?" the officer barked.

"No, Sir." I tried to calm my heart.

"You don't know where you are going?" he cocked his head to the side as if he was aiming.

"Yes, Sir, I know where I am going." My dad's calm voice came to me, reminding me:

Keep your hands visible.

Be extra courteous.

Don't raise your voice.

Obey every command.

Do not resist in any way.

Survive the encounter.

"Let me see your ID," he commanded. He didn't move; he just stared at me, eyes squinting.

"Sir, my ID is in my bag. Can I get it?" Keeping my hands up, I pointed and nodded at my bag.

"Sure. Take it slow," the officer said, taking a deep breath as I unslung my pack.

I moved very slowly and deliberately.

Two years ago, a massive shoot-out called The Chicago Massacre happened over an entire weekend. During a protest, someone shot at the police. The police, of course, returned fire, and a massive gun battle ensued. Seven officers and nine civilians died. The following weekend, the Governor empowered the state police to search all the houses and people in the neighborhood. They did, with violent gusto. Gunfights became constant as the Black and White citizens boiled over at the Gestapo treatment.

I remember watching the horror unfold. My dad and mom were very concerned. The violence against law enforcement angered the police all over the country, and they were downright terrified now. Some police force captain said, "The best defense is a strong offense," and the cops all over America took that to heart.

My heart pounded, and my palms sweated so badly as I reached into the bag. Was this the time I'd get shot? I avoided gangs and places where gang members hung out. I got good grades because I worked hard. I did all the right things not to get shot. I was not wearing anything that would be considered thuggish. The police have stopped me enough times for me to know all the ways not to look sus. My parents taught me to be respectful and polite.

Yet, here I was about to get shot for doing what I was told to do. I found my wallet and made sure to pull it out slowly. It was a bright green folded wallet my mom got for me a couple of years ago. She did not want it ever to be confused for a gun, so she bought the brightest one she could find. Usually, I hated to carry the green monstrosity. Today, I was glad to have it, and I thanked my mom for being so thoughtful. I pulled the wallet out slowly.

"What the hell is that?" The officer chuckled; his eyes widened in amusement.

"My wallet, Sir." I tried to open my wallet, but my hands shook. I fumbled it and nearly dropped the wallet. I did not know if I was scared or angry.

The cop took a step back. I wondered what this was like for him. He does not know me from any other stranger. However, he chose to see my skin tone as a threat. If I were him, I would at least be nervous, stopping people for any reason. He was probably terrified. I did not want to add any more tension to this already stressful situation.

"Sorry," I said sheepishly.

I thought about how this must look to the people driving by. My cheeks flushed, and I felt the heat of the blood rushing to them. I was glad my skin was dark so he could not see me blush.

He probably thought I was a criminal. I pulled out my California ID and handed it to him.

"Wait here," he said as he turned and walked to his patrol car. I figured he must not be too scared because he turned his back on me.

With my hands still in the air, I waited for him to run my ID. I knew he would not find anything. I knew Coach was going to at least poke his head out of the door to see where I was soon.

It dawned on me that I did not know this officer. Coach also served as the city police department's defensive tactics instructor, and for years, I was his faithful companion. I had a chance to meet most, if not all, of the officers on the force. My parents had been all for it. They hoped it would slow down or stop the police from harassing me as I got older. It worked a little bit, I suppose. It had been a unique opportunity afforded by my parents' friendship with Coach. However, these last two years, Coach has been dedicated to helping me train for the ODP, so he missed meeting the recruits of several previous classes.

My parents truly wanted me to be safe; I had two strict curfew times, one if I was walking and one if I had a ride. The former was before sundown, and the latter was no later than eleven p.m. I didn't complain, even though it was frustrating to have to cut my nights short. I understood their fear. The police have stopped me eleven times in my life. Each time has been scary and humiliating. Usually, I "fit the description," but sometimes, they said I was just suspicious.

The officer was only in his car for a minute when I heard sirens coming from all directions. I didn't think my heart could beat any faster.

A wild thought came into my mind.

Run! Fly away!

I knew if I did, I would not live, and it would be my fault. So, I pushed the alien thought away and stood there with my hands up, hoping to survive the encounter.

The officer poked his head out of his cruiser. "You can put your hands down!" he shouted. His eyes were blinking rapidly.

Trap!

The word and the image of a mousetrap appeared in my mind. The thought was not mine.

I can't explain it, but I listened.

"I'm fine, Sir, thank you," I responded, just loud enough for him to hear me. He stared at me for a moment, then he shrugged his shoulders and ducked back into his cruiser.

Another cruiser came screeching and bouncing into the parking lot. The new officer brought his SUV around to box me in. With no expression, the officer calmly walked up to me. I recognized him immediately. I saw him in line at the Great Wok, and we nodded to each other as he had been in one of Coach's D.T. classes.

He walked up to me, put my arms down, spun me around, and slammed me up against the nearby wall. There was no recognition in his eyes.

"Stop resisting," he ordered, pushing me harder into the wall. I tried to relax my arms more.

This was it; this was how I was going to die.

"Sir, why am I being detained?"

"You fit the description," he growled.

I turned my head, and to my surprise, one officer had turned into ten. I felt the cold cuffs on my wrists and heard them ratchet closed. "Sir, I was just on my way to my martial arts class; it's right there, just a few doors down. My coach is there, and he can vouch for me. His name is Adrian Lake." I hoped his name would jog the officer's memory. It didn't.

He roughly turned me to his car and pushed me toward it. I could not believe this was happening to me, again. I had not done anything wrong. I was just going to train for my big day tomorrow. I knew if I got into the back of the cruiser, I would never be seen again. It was an absolute certainty to me. My legs stopped moving; I did not want to die.

"Sir, why are you arresting me?" I shouted. I tried to dig my heels into the concrete to no avail.

"Stop resisting!" he responded. He was on my right side, leading me to the cruiser. He put his left leg in front of both of mine and pushed. I pitched forward, and he slammed me on the hood of the cruiser. My breath left my lungs in a huff. Before I knew it, punches pummeled me.

"Stop resisting!"

"Stop re-fucking-sisting!"

"Stop resisting!"

"Stop re-fucking-sisting!"

"Stop resisting!" was all I could hear. I clenched my teeth, tucked my chin, and tried to raise my shoulders. Then a baton hit me on the back of the legs. I did not fall. Then the strike came again, and I wasn't sure if I could keep standing. If I fell, I was dead. They had trapped me between two impossible choices.

"Hey! What the hell is going on here?" Coach's voice cut through all the yelling and roiling confusion.

I couldn't see him, but his presence was a godsend. Coach was 5'8" and 160 pounds of pure death. Adrian Lake has been my mentor, coach, and friend for eight years. We met when I was nine, and he became a family friend. He and my dad served in the Navy, not at the same time, but it bonded them. He and my mom were fast friends as well. Her calming spirit and energy leveled his near-manic need to wander and made them all fun to be around. When the three of them got together, they were hilarious.

All those years ago, I wanted to be a ninja and wouldn't take logic as an answer. My parents took me to the local karate school and signed me up. At the time, Adrian was the head instructor. The owner at the time did a team-building exercise with the students and their families. My parents and Adrian became friends, which was terrific for me because I got extra lessons at my house. I got good, good enough to compete.

I knew little about Adrian's background, except that he had been in Afghanistan for a couple of tours. He has a photographic memory and was faster than any fighter I have ever seen. Sparring with him always proved to be a new lesson.

All the blows stopped; it was a miracle. The officers still pressed me on the hood with their forearms.

"Do you know this man?" one of the officers shouted.

"He is a child, and yes, I do know him. He is my student."

My head was being pressed into the hood of the car. I was facing away from the conversing adults. People had crowded around the eight police cars and two police motorcycles, most of them filming with their cell phones. Great! I saw Ms. Rhodes and Mr. Achebe looking concerned and angry at the same time.

"Well, he fit the description of a robbery suspect. Someone hit the thrift store up the road," I heard the officer say.

"No, they didn't," Coach responded matter-of-factly.

"What?" The officer was taken aback.

"There was no call to 911, no radio call to respond to a 211, 211A, 211S, 243, 245, 415, 417. There wasn't even a 507 call. So, I'll ask again. What the hell is going on here?"

I could feel the hesitation emanating from the police officer. "Are you a lawyer or something? Do you have a police scanner?"

I didn't hear a response from Coach. I assumed he was standing there with his hands casually at his sides, with his eyebrows up. He was probably standing just out of reach of the officer and far enough away that he did not have to look up into the officer's eyes.

"Coach Lake?" the officer asked as if waking from a fog. There was a beat, then the weight on me was released, and I was out of the handcuffs.

I stood up and rubbed my wrists. I snatched up my bag. The first officer appeared before me.

"Here," he said flatly.

I jumped at the sound of his voice. I hated myself for that flinch. "Thanks," I returned, taking the card from him.

I turned and walked to the studio, my head hung low and tears burning my eyes.

Thanks? I clenched my jaw so tight I thought my teeth would shatter.

I heard Coach come in five minutes later. I sat in the middle of the padded floor meditating, trying to calm my raging heart.

"What are you doing?" he asked.

"You like that question," I responded.

"It serves me well enough."

"It served you well outside. Thank you." My nose burned. I breathed.

"You're welcome, but you still haven't answered my question."

"I'm meditating, calming myself down." I breathed in for four, out for four, and held for four. My mind was still racing over the altercation. Why did I flinch? Thanks? This wasn't my first time being stopped. I should have kicked that cop's ass! Then I'd be dead.

"No, you are not; you're beating yourself up," the words came quietly, but they stung, and I shot to my feet.

"What should I be doing? Flailing my arms and screaming?" I swung my arms and turned around to face him.

"No," Coach stated simply.

"What?" I was so confused. I just wanted to disappear. I felt small and angry.

"Focus," he spoke in a normal tone as he raised his finger.

"You have control over your own mind. You can respond any way you want. You can choose healthy or harmful, or anywhere in between. However, you may not eat it. You may not swallow it and hide it away; you must spend it." His voice was quiet and intense.

Tears welled in my eyes and spilled down my cheeks.

"Why are you crying?"

"Because I'm fucking pissed!" I screamed at him. That relieved some pressure.

"What can you do about the anger?"

"Nothing."

The thought of the police officers beating me for being afraid angered me again.

"What can you do with the anger?"

"Use it," I muttered.

"Good," then Coach was directly in front of me, hitting me in the stomach.

Well, he tried to. I dropped my arm and absorbed the punch out of reflex. I pushed him away from me, and he came at me again.

After thirty minutes of off-and-on sparring, I was able to submit Coach three out of four times. It was a record for me. We were both tired and sweaty. I started looking for my shirt. It had come off somewhere along the way.

"Do you feel better?" Coach inquired. He smoothed the wrinkles from his gi and retied his black belt.

"Yes, I do," I half lied. The embarrassment of the encounter was still with me, but the Anger seemed to have dissipated during our sparring.

"Good. You are lucky you have that tournament tomorrow, or we would be sparring with combatives next." A dangerous smile creased his brown face, and a twinkle sparked in his dark eyes. In addition to standard martial arts like Taekwondo, Kali, Jeet Kune Do, and Brazilian Jiu-Jitsu, Adrian taught me modern military combatives. The combative arts taught me about aggression and efficiency in an actual fight. I learned rapidly about the difference between fighting for points and fighting to live.

"Thank you," I said, relieved. "I don't think I could take getting beat up three times today," Coach's eyes stopped smiling.

"You'll be alright; just take a cold bath tonight, and you should be good as new in the morning."

He patted me on the back after I slipped my shirt on.

"Do you have a ride home?" Coach inquired. He tried to ask casually, but I could tell it worried him that I would try to walk home.

"Yes, Sir. Ian will be here to pick me up soon."

I looked out of the big front windows and saw the lights of Ian's parents' car pulling up to the studio's parking spaces.

"I think that's him now," I said.

I was grabbing my bag and heading for the door when Coach stopped me.

"Hey! You better be on time tomorrow. You are the first match."

His reminder sent chills over my skin and brought a smile to my face. "I won't be late. Thanks again, Coach." I smiled and headed out the door.

"No problem, kid," I heard him say before the door closed.

CHAPTER 2

San Jose, California, February 16, 1:02 p.m. PST.

I was so late. I ran to the gym, my bag banging against my leg. Ugh, I was so late!

I pulled the doors open and almost ran over my best friend, Ian Henderson. We grew up together in our cozy little California suburb. We have been through everything together.

Ian is White, which of course got us teased with that oldie but goodie. "Hey, you guys are like Ebony and Ivory!"

"There you are!" he half-shouted at me. "I've been texting you. Why didn't you answer me?"

"Dude, I forgot my Global. I totally overslept. I got here as fast as I could. I had to ride my bike because my parents weren't at home," I said as we walked into the gym. We came to a junction.

"Okay. Okay, just get in the locker room and get changed; you're up next," Ian broke off and jogged into the competition area of the gym.

I knew I had a little bit of time, but I ran anyway. Coach would not be happy; I was so late.

I came into the locker room half expecting him to be standing there staring at me with disapproval, but he was not there. I changed rapidly and went out to the main area and found Coach.

So here I was, I made it to the county finals and was likely going to the state competition. Coach Adrian was standing near the mat, watching for me. He waved me over when he saw me come into the gym. When I got there, he said, "Nice of you to join us. Did you get lost?"

"No, Sir," I answered, slightly out of breath.

I did not add that I had to ride my bike because my parents just left me at home, to go who knew where.

"I've got a surprise for you, Scip," he said, pointing up into the bleachers.

Sitting in the bleachers were my parents, waving and smiling at me. I felt my heart leap in my chest, and I got nervous. I did not want to lose in front of them. Just then, the announcer called my name:

"Scipio Harelson!"

"Don't worry," Adrian said. "Just go out there and do your best. Keep moving; target don't be a target," he was looking at me with coach eyes. The intensity level was off the charts.

"Yes, Sir." My head bobbed in understanding as I put in my mouthpiece and fastened on my head, hand, and foot-gear. I knew I had size on the guy, but I still felt small walking onto the big mat. My confidence returned when I actually stood on the big blue cushions.

I took that first step up to the line, and my head felt like it was going to explode. I felt like the entire crowd in the gymnasium was screaming in my head. I blinked my eyes, shook my head, and focused on the match. It stopped just as suddenly as it started.

I stepped to the line, the referee bowed us in, and the match started.

My opponent came at me like a whirlwind, striking and kicking as fast as he could. At first, all I could do was move back. Then something strange happened. I could see his next move, I could see him set up the kick, but I could also see where it was going to land. I was confused by what I was seeing. When I saw my own face, my feet tangled, and I fell. The referee stopped the match and awarded points because I took a glancing front kick. Because I fell, it looked worse than it genuinely was.

I went back to the line, and the referee started the match again. He came at me with a roundhouse followed by a vicious wheel kick. It was an excellent combination, but I saw him do it. Well, I felt him prepare each strike. It felt alien and familiar at the same time.

I sidestepped the roundhouse and swept his foot out from under him, just as he gave a tiny hop to set up the wheel kick.

He crashed to his back, feet flailing in the air.

The surprise on his face was apparent. Just then, that screaming headache came back, and the world went red, then black.

I could hear screams coming from far away as worried voices gathered around me.

I tried to open my eyes, but someone had decided to shine a laser into them. I squeezed my eyelids closed to avoid the light and pain.

All I could do was grit my teeth and moan. I tried to raise my hands to my face, but they would not move. That is when the panic crept in. I did not know what was happening; at first, I thought my opponent had hit me, broken my neck, and paralyzed me. But I couldn't remember the blow. My breathing increased as the panic dug its horrible claws into me. I tried to listen to the people around me, trying to hear what they were saying, but there was too much voice overlap.

Then it happened again. The world made a nauseating turn, and I could see myself from the outside. A tsunami of panic rushed over and through me. Was I dead and floating away? I was not getting any higher, and I was looking at other people bending over me. Wait. What? I saw myself. Then I was looking at my parents. After that, the world dropped into a half-spin, and the paramedics rushed over to me. Wait, not me, someone close to me. I could see myself lying on my back, but then I was backing away, making room for the EMTs. I was close again, next to one of the EMTs.

This all happened so fast. I didn't have time to think and figure out what was happening. The pain was there again as one of the EMTs shined a bright light in my eyes. That pain was too much; I retreated into the darkness and silence.

San Jose, California, February 16, 1:32 p.m. PST

One second, Ian Henderson had been about to watch his best friend win an easy match, and the next, he was running down the bleacher steps in a full-blown panic.

He was the third person to get to him. Scipio's dad was already there, but he hadn't touched his son; his hands were just hovering over him like he wanted desperately to fix him, but was stopped because he didn't know what was wrong. Ian had seen that Scipio wasn't hit; he just spurted blood from his nose and fell back. Having sparred with him many times, Ian knew his friend's moves like the back of his own hand, yet he could not beat Scipio. Ian instantly knew this was something worse. Adrian was kneeling there as well, and he straightened Scipio's limp body; it seemed like he thought Scip had been hit, or he at least was acting like it. Blood covered the lower half of Scipio's face.

Ian and Scipio had been friends since they were in third grade. He could remember how they met, clear as day. He hoped this wouldn't be the last day they knew each other.

San Jose, California, May 25, nine years ago, 9:45 a.m. PST.

Ian was a normal young Caucasian male, a cute tow-headed boy with bright blue eyes. The young man had no idea that anyone else's world was anything less than his own. He had the best parents; they weren't too strict and were pretty relaxed about most things. He was a pretty good kid, too; he liked to make his dad laugh and get hugs from his mom.

Ian was so happy about his birthday; he was about to turn eight years old, only two years away from double digits. He was also excited to invite his friends to his house.

Ian's birthday was in early May, so he was usually one of the younger students in his class and the smallest. On this day, his size did him no favors. The three boys were much bigger than Ian. He had seen them around the school; they were all fourth graders and, for some reason, were demanding that they be invited to his party. He hadn't known their names at the time, but he would learn them over the school year. The leader and meanest was Tim; Ian remembered thinking it was an old-fashioned name like a grandpa's name.

Hey, Grandpa Tim! He had thought.

The instigator was named Mal. Ian couldn't remember what it was short for.

The Peanut Gallery of the group was named Gunner. Ian's Mema said the Peanut Gallery was full of people who always had something to say, especially if it was mean.

The boys had chased him way out into the grass field. The closest Campus Supervisor was too far away to help before they hurt him.

Ian's mom told him that he could only invite four because this was his first party with friends. He had his heart set on asking Jessica for sure. The other three were his buddies, Ben, Mike, and Howie. So, he couldn't invite them even if he wanted to.

"C'mon, Ian Bean, let us come to your party. We wanna see what you get for your birthday," Tim said. The other two boys started chanting Ian Bean. They were trying to rhyme Ian with Bean. It wasn't working.

The three boys closed around him, and his back was against the fence. He tried to yell for help, but his throat was dry from running from these bullies.

"I can't," was all he could croak out.

"Wrong answer, bitch!" The word stung Ian: he had never heard that word in real life. Sure, he heard it in a movie, but never from an actual person, especially not directed at him.

Then, to add salt to the wound, the foul-mouthed boy punched him in the stomach. It seemed to happen in slow motion for Ian. His bright blue eyes widened at the foul word, and then he saw the boy's right hand ball into a fist.

It was shaped like a box. Ian wondered if that was why they called boxing boxing.

Then the fist was rammed into his stomach, and all the air in his lungs disappeared. Ian's legs folded at once. He reached out to grab anything as he fell.

You broke my spine; the least you can do is catch me, Ian thought as he fell.

The other boys were laughing hysterically.

"I think you punched a fart out of him," Gunner said.

They laughed harder.

"Kick him in the stomach; maybe he'll shit himself," Mal said.

Ian was still trying to catch his breath from the punch in the stomach and couldn't ball himself up. He saw Tim's foot pull back to kick him. Again, it was in slow motion, but he vanished. Sunlight replaced the space Tim's body had been filling.

Ian heard a quick scream and an "Oof!" in the distance.

He then heard a grunt and a growl; then Mal disappeared too. He heard a sickening wet crunching, and Mal's scream intensified.

Ian tried to look up, but the sun was in his eyes. All he could see was a tall black silhouette pushing Gunner to the ground. Then a two-toned brown hand was offered to him. Ian reached up and grabbed it. He was pulled to his feet easily and looked at his rescuer clearly for the first time.

He was a dark-skinned boy with big golden-brown eyes and a bright, white, wide, toothy grin.

"Are you alright?" Ian's rescuer's voice was light and cheerful. "Thank you," was all Ian could wheeze out.

Suddenly, there was a whistle from the Campus Supervisor, but the dark-skinned boy tried to ignore it. Ian saw his eyes dart in the direction of the whistle, though.

"Are you okay?" he asked again.

"Yeah," Ian was getting his wind back.

Ian secretly thought that when he was out in the wide world of school, he was indeed on his own, and that thought laid a seed of terror that was rushing to sprout during this encounter. Then this guy showed up and stamped that terrible seed out by stopping these bullies.

"Good. I saw those guys chasing you, and I came to see if you were okay. Why were they beating you up?" Ian's eyes filled with tears as an idea sprang into his mind.

"What's your name?" Ian asked in a rush, ignoring his savior's question.

The Campus Supervisor had arrived and was yelling at the brown-skinned boy; she grabbed his arm. The other three boys were on the ground, and Mal was crying hysterically.

"Skipio Harelson, what in God's name did you do to these poor boys?" the Campus Supervisor asked. Her face was flushed, and she was out of breath. Ian raised his hand and waved it frantically at the adult.

"What is it, Ian? Did Skipio try to beat you up, too?" She gave Skipio's arm a rough shake.

"No, no, no, no," Ian's words spilled out. "He was helping me! Th...these boys were trying to make me invite them to my party, but I didn't want to because they're mean. That one hit me and knocked me down." Ian had said, waggling his finger at the large brown-haired boy. "Then, then this guy, Skipio, came and saved me."

The Campus Supervisor looked around and saw Mal's broken arm.

"Oh, my goodness! You broke this boy's arm!" she screamed at Skipio, letting go of him and rushing to Mal's aid.

The Campus Supervisor turned to Skipio and spoke to him in a way Ian had never heard before.

"Get your bl... behind to the principal's office, now!"

There was so much venom in her voice.

Ian figured it was Skipio's first day because he had never seen him before, but if it was his first day, why was she talking to him like she hated him? The look on the Campus Supervisor's face frightened Ian, and he decided he would try to repay Skipio for saving him.

"I can take him, Mrs. Rogers," Ian offered.

"Okay, you be careful, Ian; I'll have someone there waiting for you." She comforted Mal and then called on her walkie-talkie to get someone to meet up with them. Mal's arm was bent at an acute angle just above his wrist.

Ian and Skipio started walking to the office.

"My name is Scipio, not Skipio," he said, "Like a sip of water."

"Oh... okay, my name is Ian; nice to meet you, Scipio." Ian's mom would have been so proud of his manners. "Thanks again for saving me back there." Ian felt like he was in a movie, and the hero of the story had just swooped in to save his life.

"No problem. I don't like to see people get bullied. I guess this isn't the best foot forward like my mom wanted me to do."

"You made a good impression on me. Hey, want to come to my birthday party this Saturday?" he said, completing his idea from earlier.

"Sure! If I'm not grounded. I didn't mean to break that boy's arm. It looked pretty bad."

"Hey, I got your back; I'll be your witness," Ian said, placing his tiny hand on Scipio's shoulder.

San Jose, California, February 16, present, 1:02 p.m. PST

Ian placed his hand on Mr. Harelson's shoulder as the big man stood up. Mrs. Harelson made it to the mat and pushed her way through the crowd. Scipio's mom was a force to be reckoned with on a good day.

"Get away from him!" she shouted, and the small crowd of officials that had formed simultaneously took three steps back. She did not move Adrian away but maneuvered to the other side of Scipio.

Before she touched him, Adrian said, "I don't know what happened, but he's breathing. They'll put him into a neck restraint." Freakishly, as he spoke, one of the EMTs produced a neck brace, but Beverly Harelson did not move.

Paul Harelson gently pulled her to her feet and helped her step aside. "Bev, let them work."

To Ian, it was the gentlest use of force he had ever seen. Beverly buried her face in Paul's chest when she couldn't see Scipio anymore. Ian was still watching over his friend; he did not let the crowd push him away. They secured his head and shoulders and carefully rolled him onto the backboard. Then they lifted him and put him on the gurney that was standing nearby. The EMTs rolled Scipio to the ambulance and put him in. Ian stood with the Harelsons, watching them work.

"Come on, guys, let's get to the car," Paul said.

The end of the story floated to the surface of Ian's memory as they raced to the hospital.

Scipio got suspended for three days, but he was invited to come to Ian's birthday party. Scipio told him his parents said it's never wrong to do what is right. They only lived a couple of blocks from each other, and their parents were cordial to each other at first and eventually became friends. It wasn't long until the boys were having sleep-overs and finally were inseparable as they cemented their friendship.

Ian heard people around town calling them Ebony and Ivory, but Scipio always seemed to miss them saying it. He accepted that Ian had heard it, but he would just shrug and say, "Oh man, I didn't hear them; I must have been lost in thought." Scipio was a good guy.

Please let him be okay, Ian prayed.

Interlude 1

I knew I was dreaming; I had to be. I was high above a lush, fertile land. Everything was green and alive. I could feel my body moving perfectly; my arms, my legs, and my pounding heart felt like worlds colliding over and over. There was singing all around me and through me. However, I could not understand the words. I turned to look up and was surprised to see the night sky filled with so many stars that I could not make out familiar constellations. How was this possible? The ground was so bright and clear that I couldn't even see shadows.

The singing continued: a fervent sound coursing through me. It was everywhere, but it also had an origin. I flew to it; my curiosity peaked to bursting. The thread of sound led me to a small grove of trees, the likes of which I had never seen. Trunks thick with age and radiant wisdom that I could taste. What was happening to me?

In this copse of ancient trees was a group of naked humanoids covered in coarse black fur. Their deep-set eyes turned up to me as I descended to them. As I maneuvered my body to land on my feet, I caught a glimpse of what was most certainly not my feet or legs. They were covered in the same black hair as the group of hominids I was floating down to. My feet seemed to have their own opposable thumbs. I recoiled violently at the sight of them and jerked myself awake.

CHAPTER 3

San Jose, California, March 9, 12:00 p.m. PST.

I tried to sit up in my bed, expecting to be soaked with sweat and have the acrid taste of fear in my mouth, but all I felt was peace. There was a lingering pink sound in my mind. *Shhh, peace...*

When I opened my eyes, I realized I was in a hospital, and the world looked familiar again. Machines beeped and whirred nearby. I could not move my head, but I sensed my mom sitting next to my bed. She stared at me with so much worry on her face that it broke my heart. I tried to say something light like, "Hey, Mom, how ya doing?" but all that came out was a hoarse croak.

She leaped to her feet, tears streaming from her eyes.

"Baby! My baby, Mama is here!" She blanketed my face with kisses, tears, and snot. I tried to move my head away and tell her to stop, but it would not move.

"Shh! Shh! Be still, the nurses and doctors are on their way. Don't move. They're worried you have a spinal injury." That stopped me. I moved my fingers, and relief washed over me. I tried to lift my arm, and it did not move. A bottomless panic swept over me with blinding irrationality.

"Mom, what happened?" I heard the panic in my own voice. I'm sure she heard it as well.

"Well, Baby, they're not sure. They think your opponent may have hit you just right to break your neck."

"What!" I tried to shout, "The guy was never even close." I tried to console my mom with my eyes because I could not move my arms.

"Mom, why can't I move my arms?" I pulled at the restraints holding me down.

"*Mom*! Why can't I move my arms?" Just then, my dad walked into the room and assessed the situation.

"Son, you're okay, just relax," he said, and I stopped struggling.

"Honey, you were convulsing, and for your own safety, they restrained you." As Mom was saying this, she was busily unhooking the restraints.

"Beverly, wait, let the doctors check him out. He's fine; just let them do their job."

My mom wheeled on him; her face was a mask of rage fueled by a mother's concern. "This is my son, and I will not leave him tied to some hospital bed like a crazy person."

The emotion and power in her voice would have sent anyone else reeling. Not my dad; he stood there looking her in the eyes, just as calm as you please. He had his eyebrows up, which meant this was one of those moments when he would not be moved. Paul Harelson was the only person I knew that could do that.

"Bev, hon, they will do it." That was all he said, and resignation replaced the flames in Mom's eyes.

She exhaled and started for the door. "Well, I'm going to get the doctor!"

Just as she said that, the doctor and a nurse walked into the room. My dad had to shuffle aside and then make his way to my mom. He caught my eye and winked.

I instantly felt better.

San Jose, California, March 12, 4:35 p.m. PST.

I stayed in the hospital for a couple of days while they ran test after test. I learned a long time ago that patience was truly a virtue.

Adrian came to see me once. He was so uncomfortable it was painful to watch. We talked for a while, and then he abruptly had to go, but I chalked it up to him being uneasy in hospitals. He told me to call him if I saw anyone strange hanging around my room or if someone seemed to stare at me too long. He would not explain past that warning.

The headaches kept happening, but the pain was less each time. I did, however, begin to hear what I thought were *voices.*

On the last day in the hospital, while I waited for what was to be my final MRI before I went home, I decided to listen to the *voices.* What I heard fascinated me, but it did not frighten me.

I could *hear* the tech and the nurse talking. Well, not quite talking. I mean, I heard that, too, but I also heard what they were going to say before they said it. Sometimes, it was edited like they wanted to say more, but they only said half of what they actually thought. The possibility of me losing my mind was a horrible prospect. However, it fascinated me because:

I could fuckin' read people's minds.

As I was wheeled back to my room, I stretched out, looking for other minds to *listen* in on. I *heard* a lot of worried and frightened people. I figured this was normal since I was in a hospital. I shut everything out because the flow was getting a little too much to handle. I thought it was weird; I could do it so easily. All the stories about people with telepathy... *wait, telepathy? Am I saying I have telepathy?*

It should be easy to prove, but to just acknowledge it to myself was breathtaking. According to all the stories and movies, I should have been overwhelmed by all the mental noise flying around me, but I wasn't. I was able to just turn them off at will. I realized I could focus on one person and listen to just them. I discovered if I concentrated hard, I could go deeper than surface thoughts and see people's secrets. That made me uncomfortable, so I cut that short, too.

I was wondering what kind of telepathy this was going to be like. Was I just going to be able to hear thoughts, or could I talk to people? Was this just the beginning?

When they wheeled me into the room, my parents greeted me with hugs and kisses. A darkness I had not noticed surrounded me, and their presence banished it.

The nurse who rolled me into the room was thinking about her boyfriend and how she was a little bit afraid of him.

It sounds like I adjusted to this fast, but I never understood the whole *woe is me* thoughts in movies of heroes that get powers. I always felt they should embrace them and do good. So, when I got home, I started to study. I looked into every iteration of telepathy: movies, comic books, even the Wikipedia of superpowers.

My parents were glad to have me home, and they made everything normal for me. Three days after I got out of the hospital, Ian came by. It astonished me that it took him this long.

I was on the computer when he burst into my room. He was always trying to catch me doing something. I knew he was coming before he knocked. His mind was almost an open book to me. I turned around to stare at him just as he burst in.

"Whoa, creepy much!" he was startled, his joke dying behind his eyes.

"What?" I asked, looking at him innocently.

He shook his head, clearing his mind.

"Dude, your convalescence spread around the school like a fire." Prickly feet of embarrassment crawled from the front of my scalp to the base of my neck.

"The good news is: said rehabilitation got us invited to a party, and guess who is going to be there?" I read his mind before I could stop myself. Diana's name brought an unbidden smile to my face.

"Yeah, you know what I'm going to say. Your girl is going to be there," he was poking me.

"Stop," I said, my smile still plastered on my face.

Ian's eyes brightened. "Dude, I have a surprise, c'mon!" This time, I was fast enough to stay out of his head.

We went outside into the bright sunlight. There was a strange silver car parked at the curb. It was clean and in excellent condition, but obviously old. Ian walked up to it, looking back at me with pride.

"You like?" he said, his left hand caressing the top of the car. "It's a Supra; my parents surprised me this morning after," he paused for dramatic effect, "*I passed my driving test*!" he shouted jubilantly. "Get your party clothes on, and let's go in style!"

CHAPTER 4

San Francisco, California, January 3, 2014, 7:50 a.m. PST.

The dark-haired man walked up to the reflective glass doors of the towering building. Massive letters hovered near the top of the tower; they read The SOTIR Group. The man paused for just a moment to make sure he looked right. He smiled to himself, knowing he carried his 190 pounds well on his six-foot frame. He opened the doors with a smile of confidence on his face. He walked up to the security desk. His blue eyes gleamed with pleasure.

"Alexander Lamb, I have an interview with Dr. Gordon." His voice didn't go up at the end of the sentence as he heard most sheeple do, and he took pride in that. His dad taught him to walk straight and talk straight. It pleased Alexander to see that the security guard behind the counter was brown-haired with bright green eyes.

"Mr. Lamb, welcome." He handed him a visitor's badge and told him to have a seat; someone would be out soon to see him.

Five minutes later, a tall tubby man with a graying beard and a tweed jacket came to collect him.

"Alexander, hello, it's good to see you made it. I'm Dr. Gordon. You don't mind if I call you Alexander, do you?"

"Not at all," Alex said. Dr. Gordon has a rapid, breathy air about him.

"Good," Dr. Gordon said.

They shook hands and walked deeper into the building. They took an elevator up quite high. On the way up, Alex thought back to how he ended up in this plush elevator.

Three months ago, Alex Lamb was at the end of his rope. Alex applied for the police academy and was rejected. He felt that it was because he was *too* smart. As he lay on his bed in his mother's basement, he stared at a painting he had done of a warrior angel. He had given up.

He planned to load his Colt LE6920SOCOMII, which he bought secondhand, and go drop a few mud people. The Colt was in excellent condition. He would do his part to cleanse this great country. He would go out in a blaze of glory and be remembered for all time.

"Alex!" his mom had called from upstairs; you got mail." She cackled at her own joke. Whatever it had been. Alex didn't move or speak. Maybe she would shut up if he just ignored her. She had smashed his daydream.

"It's a big package from someone called the SOTIR Group." His mom squawked. Alex lay there for a few seconds more when the memory crashed into him. One of his friends online talked about the SOTIR Group and how they were looking for armed security agents. Alex's dad had taught him to be respectful of guns and the awesome power you wield when you hold one.

He missed his dad; he had been taken too soon.

Alex followed the link his friend had given him on a whim. He had been sure he was going to get into the police academy. His test scores would be the highest they had ever seen. Alex Lamb had a near-photographic memory, and he read the entire study guide for the entrance exam several times. When he took the test, he recognized the material and breezed through it easily.

Had they rejected him, too? If so, why would they send a big package to tell him he didn't get it? Alex got out of bed quickly and went upstairs to retrieve the package.

"He's alive!" his mom exclaimed when he emerged from the basement.

"Hey, Ma," Alex replied, "where's the pack..." The package was a large manila folder with the SOTIR Group name and logo all over it. Alex picked it up and started to retreat to the basement, but his mother stood in his way.

"Open it! I wanna see, too."

Alex sighed and set the package back on the table and opened it. He had no idea what to expect.

On the forty-eighth floor, the stainless-steel doors slid open, and they stepped out of the elevator car onto a plush red carpet.

"This way." Dr. Gordon gestured, and Alex followed him to a well-furnished office. As Alex followed Dr. Gordon, he returned to his memory of getting the application; maybe there was something that could help him in this third and final interview.

After his mother saw it was just a stack of papers to be read and filled out, she lost interest and returned to watching TV. Alex took the papers back to his basement room and laid them out on his bed.

At the age of 24, Alex Lamb was back in his mother's house as he clawed his way back to his feet. He had become tired of the rat race of corporate America and decided he still had time to follow his dream to become a police officer. The reality was that he had been laid off and took the opportunity to follow his dream.

When he was first extricated from the never-ending scramble for the few crumbs corporate deigned to let fall from their mahogany tables, Alex gathered certifications like playing cards. He felt he was too old for the military; besides, he didn't want to get brainwashed in boot camp. One of the things he picked up was his armed guard card. It opened several doors for him, and he was able to get a few jobs as an armed guard. However, he found he hated the small jobs guarding places like pot dispensaries or banks. Both were places of gluttony and greed.

Now, here he was, out of savings and out of options. Alex sat down at his desk and dug into the papers.

The more he read, the more he liked the SOTIR Group. They were a philanthropic company, and they did God's work all over the world. The Group was looking for a few good men to be security and was willing to train and house the candidates.

There seemed to be two career paths available: support and tactical. On a whim, Alex checked the tactical box. Of course, most people would check this box, but Alex was sure he could pass whatever test there was. There would be three interviews to determine if he was worthy of representing the SOTIR Group's name. The paperwork was ambiguous at best on the details of the job. Alex chalked it up to not being able to predict every situation perfectly and the legal team not wanting the company to get sued somehow.

Dr. Gordon sat heavily in his chair behind his desk.

"Have a seat, Alexander." As Alex sat down, Dr. Gordon's facial expression became serious.

"Alexander," he said gravely. "I want to impress upon you the nature of this interview. This is the final step before we hire you."

Alex just stared at him.

Clearing his throat, Dr. Gordon continued, "Well, okay. Do you have a problem with killing in self-defense?"

"No," he responded instantly but in a measured voice. *Why was that the first question?*

"Good. Do you have a problem following orders when you do not completely understand the reasoning behind them?"

"Well, that depends. Do I trust the person giving the order?"

"Hmm, good question. How about no? This person just presents you with authorization to be able to give the order."

"Then yes, I have a problem following ambiguous orders with no clear reasoning," Alex knew this was a deal-breaker; most of these corporate types wanted blind allegiance. The need to ask questions and get straight answers was lost; sheeple these days just follow blindly.

"Good, good, I have one more..." Just then, Dr. Gordon's phone rang, and he immediately picked it up. Until that moment, Alex hadn't realized there was a second phone on the large desk. It was big and gaudily red. How had he missed it?

Wow, he picked the phone up before the ring was over. Alex wondered who could be on the other end. After the first interview, Alex began to suspect this was some kind of government contracting job. However, by the second "interview," he realized this company was doing more than helping people eat.

All the other candidates looked like him. The rhetoric they talked about was something he had been researching ever since he was laid off to make room for a person of color to be hired. The adventurer in him wanted to see where this job went. Would he get the chance to shoot at those brown bastards?

"Yes, Sir, right away, Sir," he hung the phone up and motioned to a blank wall.

Alex looked in that direction, then back at Dr. Gordon, confused. Then a door seemed to appear mysteriously, the cedar paneled wall swung open. Alex got up hesitantly and walked to the newly revealed entrance.

The room he looked into was well-lit, and there was a salt and pepper-haired man, mostly salt, hanging from a bar by the back of his knees, doing hanging sit-ups.

When Alex walked in, the door closed quietly. The younger man just stood there, waiting for the gentleman to finish his set. Sweat dripped from him and pooled on the floor beneath him. He didn't count out loud, so when he curled up the last time and swung down, it seemed abrupt. He wasn't winded at all. The man toweled himself off and shook Alexander's hand.

"Nice to meet you, Alex. I can call you Alex, right?" All Alex could do was nod his head. This man's presence was immense, and it filled the office.

"Good, good, sit down," he gestured to a chair, much like Dr. Gordon had. *No, that wasn't right. Dr. Gordon had done it the way this man had.*

As he moved to sit down, he glanced around the room and saw, to his surprise, a tall Black man standing in the rear of the gigantic office. At first, he thought he was a statue, but he smiled at him. Alex jumped, the only crack in his outward calm.

The man behind the desk laughed.

"Don't mind, Sam. He's an old friend and confidant." His smile was brilliant and disarming.

"If you haven't guessed already, I'm Robert Cross, and this is my think tank."

Alex had recognized him as soon as he was right-side up. The man was tremendous; he had to be at least 6'4"- 250, 260 pounds of mostly muscle. He was older, but he seemed to be fighting- and winning- the battle of the bulge. All Alex could do was nod his head. This was *The* Robert Cross, owner of the Trillion Dollar Cross Tower, being built here in San Francisco and a hero to all the right-minded thinkers in America.

Cross pressed forward. "I called you in here because your answer to the second question, in conjunction with the first, intrigued me. So, you are willing to kill just as long as you understand why *or* trust the person giving the order?"

"Yes, Sir," Alex said as his inner composure returned to him.

"Good, good. What if it were the other way around? What if *you* were giving the order, and someone refused because they didn't trust you or understand why?"

"Well, Sir," Alex said, clearing his throat. "I would hope that the person I was giving the order to trusted me. If the person was someone I didn't know, I would do what needed to be done myself."

"Good," the older man said, clearly pleased.

"You understand what we are fighting for, don't you?" His eyes seemed to burn through Alex.

"Y... yes," he stuttered, trying to get the words out as fast as possible. "We are fighting to reclaim our country and our heritage."

Cross laughed heartily. "No, son, we are fighting for something much more basic than that: we are fighting for our right to exist. You see, in this world, we are the minority and always have been. We are explorers and conquerors by nature. However, everywhere we sailed, we only met brown people. We were the first to explore this entire planet on sheer will and ingenuity, and not once did we find anyone with features like ours. Our fair skin, desire, and ability to rule were nowhere to be found," Cross paused and walked around his enormous desk. "We were a rarity, and the knowledge filled us with the holy realization that we were more valuable because of our small numbers. Only we could bring order to the chaos and savagery we encountered, so we did."

Cross enthralled Alex; the former statesman's words rang so true in his heart that he could only wonder how he had missed such a fundamental truth.

"We taught them to live in a roofed dwelling, to speak our language, and to worship our gods. We brought them out of the Stone Age and gave them a modern life of comfort and ease, and how do they repay us? By trying to exterminate us. There are less than 800 million White people in the world right now, and we are an endangered species. They tried to breed us out of existence. Now, they are trying to cause a new type of White extinction. These Black bastards have begun to show signs of abilities that make armies of trained soldiers seem ineffective at best. When they begin to learn they are not alone, they will band together and come for us. So, you see, we have to kill them and stop this mutation from spreading."

Alex looked nervously back at Sam, standing there in the corner, watching them both.

Cross chuckled, "Don't worry about Sam. He's been with me from the beginning. Well, he's been with my family for as long as I can remember. He doesn't care either way, so don't worry about him. I have a good feeling about you. I am rarely wrong. You will start ASAP. Come to this address tomorrow. Come with purpose in your heart and a strong will."

Cross handed Alex a business card. At first, the card was blank, but soon, golden numbers and letters formed on the face of the card. It was an address in a city Alex was unfamiliar with.

Alex got the feeling of dismissal almost immediately. He stood and found Sam standing at his elbow, guiding him to the door. He looked back, and Robert Cross was deep in his work as if he had never been there. *Such focus*, Alex thought, *I'll do well to match that.*

Northern California, January 4, 2014, 7:30 a.m. EST.

Alex arrived at what looked like a farmhouse, sitting in the middle of nowhere. He saw no other cars; he was thirty minutes early, just in case. No CP time here. He got out of the car, walked up to the large doors, and looked around. As he inspected the area, a voice startled him.

"Are you Alexander Lamb?" The voice was androgynous. There was no emotion either. Nevertheless, he answered with as much controlled confidence as he could.

"Yes, I am," the doors opened slowly.

"Go in, sit down, and buckle up." Alex was confused, but he entered and found a chair sitting in the middle of the room with, to Alex's surprise, a seat belt. He walked over, sat down, and buckled up as he was told. As the belt clicked, the floor of the room dropped so fast it took his breath away. He opened his eyes after a couple of seconds when he realized the dropping had not stopped.

"Ah, there you are, Mr. Lamb. I feared you had passed out from the sudden drop. Not uncommon at all," the voice was coming from the wall facing him; there was an androgynous face on the giant screen. They had a nice enough look about them: youthful, plump cheeks, their eyes were green, and they had the ghost of a pleasant smile on their face. Short auburn hair adorned their head.

"How deep are we going?" Alex asked.

"Oh, not deep at all; it only feels that way. My name is Minerva. I will be your guide and, hopefully, in the future, your friend. The elevator will stop soon, and several men in surgical masks will get on. They will begin our intake procedure. They will check for diseases and give you vaccinations and whatnot. Don't worry; these are not full of mercury." The face had a pleasant smile.

Alex saw something was wrong with this person's face; it wasn't exactly real. Just as he was coming to that conclusion, the elevator stopped abruptly. Doors on either side of him opened, and men in surgical masks rushed in just as Minerva said they would. The chair he was sitting in unfolded, leaving him on his back. Before he knew what was happening, the men strapped him to the chair, turned gurney, and started poking him with needles. Alex winced. Minerva appeared on the ceiling now.

"Don't worry, Alex. May I call you Alex? They will just take some blood and give you some shots. You'll be fine. We need to make sure you are who you say you are. Facial recognition can only go so far. Have you ever had a genetic assay done on you? It's quite fascinating; you will learn so much about yourself, and so will we." Alex realized as Minerva was talking that they/it was a computer-generated face, a very good one.

"Alex, you are surprisingly calm. Most new hires are in at least wary annoyance at this point."

"I'm not worried. I know if you wanted to kill me, you would have already. Besides, you warned me of this, so why should I be? For a program, you are forgetful."

"Ah, so you noticed I'm not human. Everyone does eventually, but you were quicker than most who have come through here. I, however, am more than a *program*. I am an A.I., which means I am parsecs away from a program." Minerva smiled, and it seemed genuine, even for an Artificial Intelligence. "Well, let's get started, shall we?"

Darkness enveloped Alex, and he dreamed of needles and sharp instruments. He dreamed of a world that was sane and good and White.

Interlude 2

I was dreaming again, and I knew it. I was moving through trees at an incredible pace. As before, I felt the pull of the thread, only now it was a string, strong with time and wisdom, I could feel it at the base of my skull. It thrummed with age.

I tried to focus on my surroundings. There were trees with impossible branches. They were feet around, and were we chasing... something? Something big and furry. I felt myself hoot in excitement! The sound was startling, but I was able to hold on to the dream.

"Good little Mfalme, you have gotten better. Now watch and learn." *The voice came from outside of me.*

Suddenly, I felt other minds in my head with me. They were telling me where they were and where I should turn the massive beast. I hooted on cue. The minds were clear as day to me; it was not a language per se but more like a clear and concise idea. I could put faces to different opinions. I

*knew who they were by the way they made me feel. There
was a whoop heard in my head and outside of it. There was
a tremendous crash, and we all started hooting together. My
pulse pounded in my ears. My blood seemed on fire, and I was
pushed out of the dream.*

"No!" I screamed.

"No, little Mfalme, this is not for you. Not yet."

CHAPTER 5

West San Jose, California, March 12, Present Day, 9:00 p.m. PST.

We pulled into the long driveway of the house, and we could already hear the music.

"Scip! Man, wake up and wipe that drool off your chin; you look gross!" Ian laughed as he elbowed me awake.

"I'm up, dude!" I was annoyed about being pushed from the dream, but I checked my face just in case.

"Dude, how do you do that?" Ian asked as we got out of the car to let the valet park it.

"Do what? Be this badass?" I said, and Ian laughed hard.

"No, I mean, fall asleep in a car so fast. We weren't even on the main street, and you were already out like a light."

Ian seemed genuinely curious.

"I don't know; it's a gift, I guess. How do you *not* fall asleep?" I countered.

"Well, that's why you don't have a license. You'd fall asleep during the driving test." We were laughing as we approached the enormous house.

Then Ian said, "Oh shit, Scip, there she is!"

I followed his gaze to Diana, looking fine as she could be. I have known Diana since fourth grade. She was a shy little girl. Her big hazel eyes were wide and trusting behind her glasses. She kept pushing her chestnut hair out of her face.

On her first day, Ian and I were the first ones to talk to her. We became fast friends. At the time, I didn't know how other girls could be so mean to other girls they consider a threat. During one recess period, I came out of the bathroom and went to find Ian and Diana. When I found them, Diana was crying, and Ian was sitting next to her on the lunch table benches. I rushed to her side. Ian explained that some girls were teasing her about her glasses. I stalked off, determined to make them apologize for hurting Diana's feelings.

The clique of three girls, on any other day, would have had me shaking in my shoes, but today, I was *angry,* and none of that mattered. I lit into them. I yelled and called them all kinds of names. I never cussed at them because I did not want the smoke from my parents. They tried to defend themselves from my tirade, but I was too *angry* to care. It was like I knew stuff about them I could not have known. Looking back, I heard a voice in my mind that was not my own. When I returned to my friends, Diana had stopped crying, but her cheeks were flushed and dirty from wiping tears away. I used my shirt to wipe the dirt and tears away. When I finished wiping, she looked up at me, and there was something in her eyes I did not understand, but my heart leaped. I think that was when I fell in deep like with her. I was too afraid to jeopardize our friendship to ever ask her to be my girlfriend. When Ian realized how I felt, he was no help at all. He was always trying to get us alone together.

In sixth grade, it only got worse. Diana started dating other boys in the class, but never me. Our friendship stayed steady, and I told myself I was happy. Now, in high school, I came into my own physically, but I never genuinely was attracted to anyone else; it was always Diana.

Ian tried to get me to notice all the other girls looking at me, or he heard about wanting to date me, but they had no pull. It had to be her. We texted all the time. Today would be the day I would talk to her about my feelings. I would explain how our friendship should be more, and how I would never hurt her like those other guys had done. I felt good and confident that no matter her reaction, I would be okay, but I also was daydreaming about all the fun we would have together after we got married. Oh man, I was so nervous, but my brush with death taught me to seize the day.

She was with someone, someone I had never seen before.

Her skin was dark brown and shone even at night, her eyes were the color of a golden sunset, and her hair was curly and black like the night sky in my dreams, full of shining stars and infinite possibility; it seemed to leap from her head, reaching for life. My heart skipped a beat. She was tall, maybe 5'10", and strong like time herself had sculpted her. She looked like she was a dancer and a casual weightlifter. Two ends came together to complete a spiritual circle. My heart and mind aligned.

CLICK!

My heart skipped another beat. The Mystery Girl was laughing at something Diana said, and her smile lit her whole being up. I was mesmerized.

"Scipio Octavius Harelson! Dude!" Ian hit me in the shoulder.

I turned. "What, dude?"

"Dude, you were staring so hard at Diana that I thought your eyes were going to fall out of your head."

I was dazed. I didn't know what Ian was talking about; the new girl had my full attention.

"Dude, what has got you so messed up?"

Then he looked and saw what I saw. "Oh man, who is that?" "I don't know but aim to find out," I said.

Suddenly, Diana didn't seem so scary. The memories of my nervousness around her seemed absurd.

"Scip..." but I was already walking up the long path to the house. It felt like I blinked, and I was right next to them.

"Hi, Diana." She jumped.

"Scip! I didn't see you walk up. How are you doing? Where's your other half?" her voice was climbing in volume as she got closer to the house.

Who's your friend?" I asked. Her eyes widened a bit at the abrupt change, but I didn't care; she was just an obstacle.

"Oh, this is Saphronia; she's an exchange student from Cape Verde, and she is staying with us." She stepped to the side so Saphronia and I could see each other. Saphronia smiled, and my heart leaped in my chest. I rolled her name around in my head: Saphro-nia.

"Hi, nice to meet you." Her voice was clear and strong, like a sunrise.

She had an accent I had never heard before. She stuck out her hand for a handshake, and I took it.

"H.... Hi, nice to meet you as well. My name is..." My mind was reeling. It seemed like I knew this girl. My own name slipped from my head. She was familiar to me, but at the same time, I had no idea who she was. There was something about her eyes that called to me.

"This is Scipio. I like to call him my sippy cup. Isn't that right, Sippy Cup?"

I was mortified, but Saphronia and I never lost eye contact; I could not look away. Diana had not called me that in years. In fact, the last time I heard it was in fifth grade. Fifteen minutes ago, I would have been on cloud nine to hear her call me that, but now I was just pissed off. I tore my gaze away from Saphronia to look at Diana.

I laughed courteously and said, "No, you haven't called me that in years, Didi."

I focused my attention back on Saphronia, "People call me Scip for short. It's a pleasure to meet you." I reached my hand out for a shake.

Where was all of this coming from? Our eyes remained locked. I was content to get lost in the golden pools, and I felt completely comfortable talking to her, even with Diana acting salty and calling me by my old nickname. She barely gave me the time of day these days.

Just then, Ian ran up and grabbed my arm, physically tearing me away from Saphronia's gaze.

"What the hell, man!" he was visibly upset and out of breath.

Diana took the break in the obvious magic that was happening to walk off with Saphronia.

"See you guys inside!" she called over her shoulder, guiding Saphronia inside.

I could still smell the shea butter she used. I turned to Ian. "What is wrong with you?"

Ian gaped at me.

"Me? *Me?* What the *hell* is wrong with you? Do you even know what you just did?" Ian asked, exasperated.

"Dude, what the hell are you talking about?" I was getting exasperated.

"Dude, you just teleported or something!"

Ian's eyes were as wide as saucers.

I pulled him aside. I did not want anyone to start thinking he was crazy, so I laughed when I responded. "Ian, what the hell are you talking about? I ran over here to meet that girl, Saphronia." Oh man, even her name was special.

Ian was shaking his head.

"You were staring so hard at her, I thought your eyes were going to pop out of your head. Then, poof, you were gone. You had me fucked up! There was a whump sound right after you left, and then I saw you standing halfway to the girls. Then you were gone again. Then you were standing next to Diana just as relaxed as you please."

My eyes widened as well.

"Ian, what the heck are you talking about? I ran over there! I didn't disappear and... teleport or whatever."

I was incredulous.

"Yes, the fuck you did! I saw it with my own two eyes. Did you drink a potion or get bit by a radioactive magician? And why is this the first I hear of your superpowers?"

I looked at him at a loss.

"I don't know, man; I was still figuring things out."

Ian's brow furrowed in confusion. "This isn't the first time you teleported?"

"No, it's the first time; it's just not the only thing I can do," I said, defeated.

Impossibly, Ian's eyes doubled in size.

"What? What else can you do?"

"Well, so far, I can..." I concentrated for a moment. I saw a blue glow when I closed my eyes.

When I had it, I opened my eyes.

"You were thinking, *'Holy shit, my friend has powers! I wonder if it was something he ate; I wonder if I'll get powers.'*"

Ian's face went white as a sheet. "You read my mind! Holy shit, Scip!"

His voice was loud, very loud, but luckily, the music coming from the house was also loud.

"Shut up!" I said, gripping his arm and moving toward the front door.

"Dude, what the heck are you doing?" I growled.

"Sorry, sorry," he said. "I wasn't trying to blow your cover, but you just read my mind. How am I supposed to react?"

"We can talk about it later, I promise," I said, turning him toward the front door and the party. "Right now, let's go in." I had read enough comic books in my life to know that once you could read minds, you could push them as well. So, I pushed him with my mind.

Ian's entire demeanor changed, and he just nodded his head and strode into the house.

I would think about that later, I told myself. Right now, I wanted to find Saphronia. I looked around but did not see her. I pushed and shoved my way to the kitchen, hoping to catch sight of her and to get a break from the crowd. I wondered if she experienced the same CLICK I did.

I felt a light tap on my shoulder and turned to see Saphronia walking into the kitchen close behind me.

"Hey," I said in surprise, "I was looking for you." Ugh. I mentally facepalmed. *Creepy much,* I thought to myself.

To my surprise, Saphronia smiled.

"I was looking for you, too. You are a fascinating boy," she said. Her accent was terrific, and it gave me goosebumps. "I would like to get to know you better."

"Uh, me too," I said clumsily.

This was going well.

"Can we leave this place?" she asked with a small smile accenting her face.

"Sure, let's go for a walk outside," I said and mentally facepalmed myself again.

Where else would we walk? Dummy.

"Do not be so hard on yourself, Scipio. I would be flustered if I met me, too."

"Wait, what?"

"Oh, nothing. Let's go."

We wove our way out of the party, somehow ending up in the backyard. Kids played in the pool and laughed while others sat on the grass, talking and just hanging out.

We left the backyard through the gate, walked down to the sidewalk, and turned left. My dad, who was a lefty like me, or me like him, whatever, always said when in doubt, go left, so left it was.

I asked Saphronia where she was from, and without missing a beat, she said, "Wakanda."

At first, my mind ground to a halt, but when she couldn't hold in her laughter, I knew she was kidding.

I started laughing, too.

Probably a little too hard, but it was funny. Saphronia said she was from Cabo Verde, a small group of islands off the coast of West Africa. I told her I had never heard of that place, and she told me I wasn't unique. She used *"unique"* in everyday parlance. How hot was that?

We walked and talked. When I told her about my training, she asked to see some of my moves, and I was happy to oblige. I showed her some basic forms, and she clapped for me. A goofy smile appeared on my face.

Then she showed me what she knew. She had an expert grasp of combatives, and she was scary... and hot.

Her body was lithe, and her moves were crisp. I was impressed. I invited her to our studio to meet Adrian, and she accepted.

I told her about my recent match and how I passed out... and I left out the new parts about hearing other people's thoughts.

She seemed genuinely interested and concerned. I told her I was all better. We talked about where she was from and how different it was here. I was intrigued by her description of her home. I wanted to see it for myself.

We walked and talked, sharing and listening to each other. Saphronia totally enraptured me. After what seemed like only a few minutes, my Global rang; when I checked it, I saw it was Ian calling. I tapped the earpiece and answered the call.

"What's up, bro?" I asked casually.

"Where the heck are you, Scipio?" Ian sounded pissed.

"Dude, what's wrong? I just went for a walk. Did something happen?" I was genuinely worried.

"Yeah! You ditched me! Where have you been? I haven't seen you in hours!" Yep, he was pissed but kind of overreacting.

"Dude," I laughed, "we've only been gone for what?" I looked at my Global to check the time. Two hours had passed.

"Ian, I'm so sorry; I didn't realize how long we had been gone." Just then, Saphronia touched my arm.

I looked at her, and she seemed worried.

"I have to go back. Diana is looking for me," she whispered. "Are we far away from the party?"

I looked around to get my bearings, and my heart skipped when I realized where we were.

"Dude, we are like three miles away. Can you come to pick us up?"

"Yeah, I'll be right there," he sounded defeated.

I sent him our location after he hung up.

Saphronia was looking at me with raised eyebrows. Oh man, was she gorgeous!

"Ian is on his way," I said.

"Is he a good friend of yours?" she asked.

"Yeah, he's my best friend: we've known each other for years. Since we were very young, like seven or eight years old."

We found a place to sit and wait for Ian. I was getting nervous sitting out like this so late at night. I had completely lost track of time and place, which was very uncharacteristic of me. As we talked, I kept looking around, and my nervousness must have shown.

"Are we in a bad part of town?" Saphronia asked. "You keep looking around like a gang is going to show up."

"That's close to the truth," I responded.

I looked left and saw a car turn left onto the street we were on, and I looked right and saw the same thing. I hoped one of the pair of headlights was Ian. I jumped as a bright, white light illuminated everything around us. I instinctively turned to look at the bright beam and covered my eyes reflexively. Red and blue lights joined the bright white searchlight, and a whoop came from the source.

Saphronia and I stood up without thinking. My knees felt weak with dread. The police car stopped ten feet away from us, its blinding bright lights washing all details from the world.

The other car stopped across the street; it had to be Ian. Two officers got out of the cruiser and walked over to us, both of their hands resting ominously on their sidearms.

"You kids are out kinda late, aren't you?" one of them asked. Saphronia didn't move, but I could sense her tension. I spoke up.

"Sorry, officer, we were on a first date and really hit it off. We lost track of time," I explained. I hoped Saphronia didn't mind me embellishing our situation.

One of them laughed and said, "Oh, I see this is a pre-baby momma moment."

I still could not see their faces or exactly where they were because of the light, but I realized I could sense where they were just by focusing on their thoughts.

Hmmm, that's a nice piece of young ass.

The thought appeared in my mind like a rancid piece of meat. It made me sick and angry at the same time. The fear I felt was washed away by a wave of familiar *anger*. It was a living, breathing thing, clearing space in my mind. The world sharpened, and I was filled with clarity.

"What did you just say?" I said, surging to my feet. The challenge in my voice was evident and surprising. I felt the surprise flare from them, but it was replaced by twisted amusement and eager anticipation for violence.

"What did you just say, son?" The cop with the rancid thought stepped up to me, his breath hot and forced through his nose. He was as tall as I was and muscular with a broad, angular face. His brow was furrowed in anger, and his cheeks were still in the process of flushing. I thought I would stand my ground, but my legs took a step back on their own, the ghost of the earlier fear asserting itself briefly.

"I thought I heard you say something," I said in a small voice. The cop turned and looked at Saphronia, but still spoke to me.

"That's what I thought," he said as he turned his full attention to Saphronia.

"Hey, young lady, do your parents know you are out so late with this homeboy?" His head gestured toward me as he spoke.

He was invading her personal space, and I was about to say something when the other officer took me by the arm and said, "Come with me, let's check you out," he ordered, walking me over to the cruiser and pushing me up against the hood.

This cop was a little shorter than me, and he didn't like that I kept looking over him to see what was going on with Saphronia.

"You're a big one. What's your name, son?" the officer asked.

"Scipio Harelson," I said. "I'd like to call my parents if you wouldn't mind, Sir." I glanced over his head again to see if Saphronia was alright.

"Oh, parents plural? You got a daddy, too?" the officer mocked. "We don't need to call them; we're doing just fine. Don't worry about your little girlfriend over there. My partner will take good care of her. Maybe I will, too, when he's done."

My eyes dropped to his when he said the last part.

"What?" I could feel the *anger* rising to assert itself. It was like an explosion in my chest, spreading to my arms and legs and then my head.

I tried to stare holes into his head.

"Turn around, hands on the hood, and spread your legs. Let's make sure you aren't armed."

He tried to spin me around, but I didn't budge. I was staring at him with unabashed, living *anger*. As worried as I had been about the cops showing up, I still could not believe this was actually happening. I could see the other officer pushing Saphronia up against a nearby tree outside of the splash of light. He was way too close to her, and I heard something about frisking her. What happened next transpired so fast that I barely remember what exactly occurred.

My cop's hands moved so quickly that I felt them before I knew what was happening. His hands gripped my neck with a crushing force. We were hip to hip, and he was trying to break my posture by lifting me off my feet or hitting me up against the police cruiser. His hands were enormous; I could feel the fingertips of both his hands pinching the skin on the back of my neck.

I did not bend. Instead, I flexed my neck and growled at him. Spittle flew between my clenched teeth.

"Stop resisting!" he growled at me. His breath was hot with fear, and his voice broke.

I heard Saphronia yell, *Get off of me!*

Something old and dangerous sprang across the bridge in my soul and burst into flames in my mind. The angry flame spread through me in an instant.

CHAPTER 6

"While the Goddess of Suffering took me in her arms, often threatening to crush me, my will to resistance grew, and in the end, this will was victorious."

-Adolf Hitler

Somewhere in San Francisco, April 4, 2015, 6:00 a.m. EST.

Alex pushed himself off the floor, launching his body at his opponent. The speed at which he moved was astonishing. He covered a twenty-meter distance in less than a second. His opponent and teacher sidestepped him with ease and tripped him. Alex hit the mat, and his momentum carried him several meters.

"Alexander, speed is good, but you are dealing with thoughts, and thoughts will always be faster than your movement."

Alex came at him again; this time, his own speed was his downfall; he ran directly into his teacher's fist. It was a perfect strike to the solar plexus. His breath left him, and he collapsed to his knees, or at least he tried to. He hung in a fetal position on his teacher's fist. The teacher let him fall, and Alex vomited.

"We are done for the day," the teacher said with contempt. "Clean up my mat, then go get assessed."

"Yes, teacher," Alex snapped his answer as he had been instructed to do. He ran to the nearby closet, grabbed cleaning supplies, and got to work.

He let his mind drift back to a year ago, when he woke up from whatever they had done to him.

Somewhere in California, March 1, 2014, 6:00 p.m. EST.

Alex lay on the gurney, blood still dripping from the open wounds all over his body. The microsurgery had been successful. The doctors were still programming his nano-machines. His wounds remained open to demonstrate that the nano-machines were indeed working. Alex experienced immense pain, but he remained silent. Without warning, a voice cut through the pain. He recognized Robert Cross's voice.

"Stay strong, young Alexander. Your ordeal is nearly finished. If you survive this, you will be a god among men. You have passed every test, and now you are passing through the final gate. Greatness and hope stand on the other side. Not just for you but for your people. Hold fast, son, do not give in to weakness."

The words rang in Alexander's ears. *He believed, he believed.*

The pain began to subside; he felt the wounds closing, but the itching started to build to intolerable levels.

"It itches!" The words forced their way out of his mouth, his clenched teeth unable to hold them back. His arms and legs began to flail uncontrollably. There was a flurry of movement and typing, and the terrible sensation began to fade. His mind blanked and then went dark.

In another room nearby, Robert Cross returned to his seat to watch the procedure. He had been here for everyone. He held each man's hand as they lay dying or, on the rarer occasions, as they survived. He gave the same practiced speech at the same exact moment. He believed in what he was saying, so much so that the speech became a mantra for himself. He said these words when he had a tough order to give or a choice to make. The sacrifices these brave men and women were making would ensure the continuation of the White race. They would help defend a Holy Minority from an inhuman adversary. He sat, watched, and encouraged out of pure reverence for them and their determination to see a better tomorrow. He also wanted to know when they had perfected the process so he could go through the enhancement himself.

Somewhere in California, April 4, 2015, 5:50 p.m. EST.

Once Alex had cleaned up his vomit and disinfected the whole 1000 square foot mat, the sun had gone down, and his training was over. It was a day wasted because of his weakness. He only had ninety days to become proficient enough to join the primary group of recruits. If not, he wasn't sure what would happen. Would they kill him, or would he just try again? He had no idea. That line of thinking was moot, anyway. He would pass, and he would excel. While his body failed him today, he learned something about his new body. He learned about belief in himself and his abilities. He realized they needed to align for him to be effective, and he learned what it feels like when they are not aligned. All valuable lessons he could put into practice immediately. Alex found his rack and fell into it.

He awoke the following day, gathering his soap and towel, he showered and dressed in his grey gi for another day of training.

He won four out of his five matches. Two of them were fatal moves. Because of the nano-machines, the trainees he *killed* quickly recovered from their mortal injuries. In the match, he lost; he felt the sting of a mortal blow for the first time. His opponent kicked him in the back, breaking his spinal

column and severing his spinal cord. His legs buckled, and he fell awkwardly, all feeling in his chest and legs gone. They dragged him off the mat and arranged him so his body would heal properly. He could only gasp. Within a few minutes, he could move his toes and felt his chest moving. It was a surreal experience for the young man; he had only broken one other bone in his life as a child.

Alex resumed his training and pushed himself even harder. His body was better than 100%, and he felt no residual pain. At the end of his training, he reviewed what lessons he could glean beyond the obvious physical training. He learned the pain of severe injury, what he would one day inflict upon others. He understood what mercy was. He learned to kill out of mercy instead of without it. The lessons reminded him he was in no less of a war for his Race, and the struggle allowed for anything to preserve that Race. He said the words that saved him all those days ago.

"Stay strong, young Alexander. Your ordeal is nearly finished. If you survive this, you will be a god among men. You have passed every test, and now you are passing through the final gate. Greatness and hope stand on the other side.

Not just for you but for your people. Hold fast, son, do not give in to weakness."

The words rang in Alexander's ears. *He believed, and he believed again.*

Interlude 3

I was falling or sliding down a tube. It was made of the same string I had seen before. There was light beneath me. As I neared it, I could see greens and browns. The end of the tube I was in yawned before me, and then I really was falling. There was a group of hominids below me, and even from the angle, I saw they looked familiar somehow. I realized I was falling directly toward a specific one. Then I was standing in a clearing in a jungle, the humidity was heavy on my body. I was looking at another group of hominids. They were hooting and jumping about. All but one. It seemed we were in a staring contest. It had its teeth bared in an unspoken challenge. I could see it was a male, and I knew I was female. I bared my own teeth and stood up, showing my full height. I could sense my clan behind me; I could hear their emotions; they were utterly still with rage and fear. This must be some kind of territorial dispute. While staring at my opponent, I could sense what he was about to do. I motioned behind me to move my troop to the right of me. They obeyed.

My rival saw an opening and leaped at me, powerful arms raised above his head and his fists clenched into tight boxes of hate. How dare a female challenge him this way? I stepped aside, and as he passed, I hit him across the back with a heavy club I had in my left hand. The sound of his ribs breaking was loud and clear. He rolled over, ready to attack again despite the injury and the pain it was causing him. I hit him with the club again, breaking his upheld arm. He screamed and fell back, trying to crawl away. I ignored his scream and hit him again and again. His blood splashed my face, and I screamed harder. Eventually, the club broke, and I had nothing else to hit him with. My mind reached out and grabbed his body. He was curled up in a fetal position. I pictured him spreading like an eagle, and I forced his legs and his arms straight. I screamed again, and all four of his limbs flew away from his torso. His head remained in place, and with the power of my mind, I crushed it, driving it back into his torso. His body exploded, showering both groups with blood and bone.

Not all enemies can be reasoned with.

CHAPTER 7

San Jose, California, March 13, 9:30 a.m. PST.

I woke with a start, the dream so fresh in my mind I could still feel the wetness of the blood. A scream was falling back down my throat. I cleared it and took a deep breath. Then the real world came rushing in all at once. The police would be here soon, asking what happened to their men.

After everything that happened, we drove off as calmly as we could. Saphronia and I did not have to say anything to Ian. He just drove us home, stopping first at Diana's house to drop Saphronia off. We exchanged quiet goodbyes and furtive glances at each other. Then to my house. The car ride was silent until the very end. I got out and turned back.

"I'll see you tomorrow, Ian. Maybe we will have time to talk before, you know," I was so shaken I could not even say the words. I went to the door, knowing I had one more thing to do, and I was unsure how.

It was twelve-thirty a.m. when I opened the door, and my parents were sitting on the couch waiting for me. I stopped in front of them and waited for the hammer to fall.

"I'm sure your Global died, and you couldn't call us. We'll talk about it later today. Your mom and I are glad you are home." With that, he put his arm around my mom; they climbed the stairs and disappeared into their bedroom.

I stood there in shock and disbelief. *What had just happened?* Eventually, I trudged upstairs and into my room. I vaguely noticed there was no blood on me whatsoever as I started to undress for bed. I stopped when I thought of the police kicking down my door and marching me out of the house in my boxers. I left my clothes on and fell on the bed. I don't even remember falling asleep.

I snapped back to the present; my waking mind was already anxious and trying to spin out of control. I sat there on my bed, waiting for life to catch up to me. My parents, the cops, or Ian and Saphronia. One of them would come and get me and change my life in some way. If the police came, would I just go with them without a fight? My life experience has taught me that the police could be dangerous and unhinged in typical situations. How would they act if they came for me because I killed two of their own? I hoped if I did not resist, they would leave my family and friends alone. I should have told my parents everything last night, but I could not even talk with Ian about it, and he was there! What was I supposed to say, "Hey Mom and Dad, I think I killed two police officers yesterday, and I'm not sure how I did it?" That sounded insane. All I could do was wait.

I took a deep breath and sent my mind out to see who was home. I had seen and read about this ability in countless movies and books. I realized this was probably why I was not afraid of these new abilities I seemed to be getting. In every story, the person gifted with powers was always scared of them and wished they would go away. Not me, I always thought, man, if I got powers, I would do this or that, but I would not be afraid, and I wasn't. At least not for myself. My friends and family were another deal entirely, but at the same time, they had always taught me that knowledge is power. So maybe telling the people I cared about what was happening to me was the best thing to do.

I was so confused.

Everything was happening so fast; my life was turning into one of the sci-fi stories I loved so much. I had lost focus and was back inside my own head.

"Right," I said aloud.

"Focus," I said, and took a deep breath. My cheeks puffed out when I blew it out; I was centered and focused, just like in my physical training. It was interesting that all of this was happening at the end of my training and school year. Adrian had been the one to introduce me to combatives two years ago when I had won my first competition. It was a small local one, but it was a decisive point win for me. Later that week, he sat me down over coffee and told me a little about what he had done in the military. Mostly his preparation and combative fighting style, and how it had helped him be a better and more effective fighter. He asked me if I wanted to learn what he was telling me about. Of course, I said yes. The little kid in me still wanted to be a ninja. So, we started training, and it was hard even for me. We trained five days a week after school and after my normal martial arts class. I promptly learned the difference between martial arts and combat. Before long, I was sore, cramping, and loving every minute of it. For a little while, I considered going into the military, but Adrian strongly discouraged me.

Wait, I'm supposed to be focusing. My mind had wandered again.

"Dammit!" I breathed and shook myself. "One more time, focus," I said, cheering myself on. I closed my eyes and focused on pushing my senses out from myself. It worked almost immediately; I moved from my room down the hall

and into my parents' room. I was a tiny hummingbird dart-
ing through the house. The bedroom was empty. However,
a glint or a shine caught my eye. It was below me. Rather,
they were below me, in the kitchen. As soon as I saw them,
I knew them as my parents. Their identities were as clear
as day, and I moved directly to them, passing through the
floor like it was air. I saw them standing there talking about
me. For a second, something garbled it. I concentrated
harder, and I could make out what they were talking about.
They worried I had started using drugs, but at the same
time, they knew I would never do that. I could see and feel
the confusion radiating from them. It felt hot and uncomfortable. I thought I could dig into their minds if I wanted
to. I stopped before temptation could take hold of me. I
started to snap back to my body and resolved to tell them
everything.

A blinding golden light caught my attention. It was walking up to the front door. I could sense a lesser glow existing
next to the other light, and I recognized it. The smaller
brightness was male; it was Ian, but who was he with? I
looked harder but could not see past the golden light. In
fact, the light pushed me back. I retreated to my body and
got myself changed as fast as I could. I was reaching for
the door of my bedroom when my mom called me to come
downstairs.

"Ian and a friend are here to see you."

A friend? Who could... Was it Saphronia?

Almost as if on cue, my mom says, "Her name is Saphronia. Oh, honey, that is such a beautiful name." I could hear
my mom gushing. She was a geek about names. I came
down the stairs into the living room, and there they all
were. Except I could see a faint glow around Saphronia.
It seemed golden. I came down the stairs and saw her,

Saphronia, and a great weight lifted from my shoulders. My mom conspicuously but politely left us to talk. I looked back at her as she walked to the kitchen, perplexed. I shook my head and turned around to Saphronia, staring at me with her eyebrows raised.

"Well, are you going to tell me what that was last night and why the police are not here arresting us?" she was speaking in a harsh whisper.

"Yeah, man, what and *how* did you do what you did?" Ian's eyes were saucers.

"Ian, man, I don't know what you are talking about. I barely remember last night." I rubbed my face in frustration.

"You don't remember anything? Like what you did to those cops? Dude, I'm as surprised as Saphronia that the police are not here!" I stared at my best friend in disbelief. Until this moment, last night had been hazy. I remember getting seriously angry about that cop manhandling Saphronia. After that, it was just gray.

Ian found the remote for the television and started scrolling through the news channels.

On one of the local news stations, there was a story of a pair of police officers in a fatal car crash. The screen showed a scene of what must have been controlled chaos. There were flashing lights, a big coroner's van, and a mangled police car with yellow tape around the whole area. The broadcaster was saying, "The police cruiser somehow lost control and hit a massive oak tree head-on, and the officers were not wearing their seatbelts and crashed through the windshield, striking another tree each. The initial reports suggest they were responding to a call and were about to exit the vehicle when they lost control and crashed."

Ian turned off the TV.

"That was a bad idea," he quipped.

"Why are they lying?" My stomach was somewhere near my feet. I walked over to the window next to our front door and peeked through the blinds. I half expected to see cop cars and SWAT teams outside, but it was just a typical quiet morning on our street. No strange vehicles or people.

"Why are they lying?" I muttered, thinking to myself.

Either they were trying to trick me and were out there waiting for me, or they truly thought it was an accident. The two cops who were harassing us must not have called in the stop when they rolled up on us. Which means they were up to no good. This thought did my heart some good because I didn't mean to kill those men. I was just so *angry*. When I turned around to face my friends, they were smiling at me.

"What?" The word came through the smile that appeared on my face. Both of their smiles grew into goofy grins.

"I have a surprise for you!" Ian said. I raised my eyebrows. "Oh really?"

"Yeah," he grinned.

"Yes, he does!" Saphronia agreed in her dulcet voice.

Dulcet? Oh boy, Scipio, you got it bad.

"Dude, I taped the whole thing!"

"What!" Heat filled my chest.

"You taped us getting messed up by the police? You just watched?" I was trying to keep my voice down so my parents would not get suspicious.

"C'mon, man, what could I do? They have guns and badges that let them use those guns with impunity. My little martial arts wouldn't have helped one bit!" he bit back.

I opened my mouth to say something and just closed it. My dad taught me to know when to stop talking. He always said men get themselves into more trouble because they don't know how to just shut up.

Saphronia was looking very concerned. So, I tried to move things along.

I said, "Let's see it. Have you seen it, Saphronia?" A twinge of jealousy poked me in the heart.

"No, he just told me about the recording as we were walking up to your door."

"Before I show it to you, just know it's really weird."

I was still stuck on the fact that they came here together.

"Wait," I said, "before you show me, you guys came here together?"

There was an abrupt stop to the momentum of the moment.

Have you ever been in a conversation, and someone says something so non-sequitur that it kills the conversation? Yeah, that was this moment.

"Dude? No! What are you talking about?" Ian was looking at me like my head had turned into an octopus.

"She must have got dropped off; she was walking up as I pulled up," Ian said.

Saphronia did not say a word; she just stared at me with a look of disappointment and defiance. *Try me*, came to my mind loud and clear.

I rethought my words. My heart and my head seemed to connect for the first time. I know next to nothing about Saphronia, which meant I had more to learn.

"Dude. Sorry," I said, completely wanting to fall through the floor. The video was no longer scary; it was welcome.

"Just show me the video." We all linked our devices up, and I watched as the encounter unfolded.

CHAPTER 8

San Jose, California, March 12, 12:05 a.m. PST.

Ian arrived just as the police blasted us with the light. The beam was bright and made every aspect of the encounter vivid. From Ian's vantage point, I noticed that the colored lights on top of the squad car were on and making lazy blue and red circles in their clear cages. I saw us standing there, terror freezing us in place. I saw myself step forward and in front of Saphronia, but I did not remember doing that.

"Look at you being all badass and protective," Ian commented on the video. Ian is the best-best friend. We watched as the cops took way too many liberties with our rights. Then, the situation took a horrible turn.

As I watched the video, the memory of the confrontation became clear. I saw the cop's hands move to my throat, and I remembered thinking how fast it had happened. However, as I watched, it seemed slow and obvious. Saphronia's protesting screams seemed strangely muffled. He had not been that far away, and the cop did not have his hand on her mouth as far as I could see.

"Ian, can you go back to the beginning?" I didn't elaborate on why. "No problem," he slid the dot back to the beginning.

Hmmm, that's a nice piece *of young black booty.*

The thought appeared in my mind like a rancid piece of meat. It made me sick and angry at the same time. The fear I felt was washed away by familiar *anger*. It was a living, breathing thing, clearing space in my mind. The world sharpened, and I was filled with clarity.

"What did you just say?" The challenge in my voice was clear and surprising. I felt the surprise flare from them, but it was replaced by twisted amusement and eager anticipation for violence. They swaggered up to us.

"What did you just say, son?" the officer, with the rancid thought, asked me. He stepped up to me and into the cone of light, his breath hot and forced through his nose. He was as tall as I was and muscular with a broad, angular face. He furrowed his brow in anger, and his cheeks were still in the process of flushing.

I thought I would stand my ground, but my legs took a step back on their own. The ghost of the earlier fear asserted itself briefly. "I thought I heard you say something," I said in a small voice.

He looked at Saphronia but still spoke to me, "That's what I thought." he turned his full attention to Saphronia.

My stomach tightened in anger at my cowardice. What could I do? They have guns, and everyone knows guns win over *karate* every time, but I had to do something.

I retrieved my lost territory.

"Hey, young lady, do your parents know you are out so late with this homeboy?" His head gestured toward me as he spoke. He was invading her personal space, and I was about to say something when the other officer dragged me away by the arm and said, "Come with me, let's check you out." He walked me over to the cruiser and pushed me up against the hood. I almost lost my footing, but I managed to stay up. I stood up to my full height.

This officer was a little shorter than me, and he didn't like that I kept looking over him to see what was going on with Saphronia.

"What's your name, son?"

"Scipio Harelson," I blurted. "I'd like to call my parents if you wouldn't mind, Sir." I glanced over his head again. Seeing if Saphronia was alright, she was not.

All at once, my father's voice came into my mind.

Keep your hands visible.

Be extra courteous.

Don't raise your voice.

Obey every command.

Do not resist *in any way.*

Survive *the encounter.*

"Oh, *parents'* plural? You got a daddy, too?" the officer mocked. "We don't need to call them; we're doing just fine," he seemed to try to soothe me.

"Don't worry about your little girlfriend over there; my partner will take good care of her. Maybe I will, too, when he's done."

All my combative training left my mind as more adrenaline was dumped into my system.

Be extra courteous.

"Don't worry about your little girlfriend over there; my partner will take good care of her. Maybe I will, too, when he's done."

Breathe in, one-two-three-four.

Don't raise your voice. "... worry about your little girlfriend over there; my partner will take good care of her. Maybe I will, too, when he's done."

Hold for one-two-three-four.

Obey every command.

"... little girlfriend over there, my partner will take good care of her. Maybe I will, too, when he's done."

Exhale for one-two-three-four.

Do not resist in any way.

"... my partner will take good care of her. Maybe I will, too, when he's done."

Hold for one-two-three-four.

Survive the encounter.

"Maybe I will, too, when he's done."

I felt like an infant in the hands of someone who cared nothing for me. We were not safe, and it was very apparent. I know that sounds like an obvious *statement*, but when you realize deep in your soul that death is very close, it changes everything. Coach taught me to use combat breathing to calm myself. He gave homework on how to breathe this way.

"... Maybe I will, too, when he's done."

My eyes dropped to his.

"What!" The former *anger* rose to assert itself. It was like a slow explosion in my chest, spreading to my arms and legs and then my head.

Keep your hands visible.

Be extra courteous.

Don't raise your voice.

Obey every command.

Do not resist in any way.

Survive the encounter.

"Maybe I will, too, when he's done."

I wasn't doing any of those things.

My body felt cold and hot simultaneously; my vision centered on this *man* standing before me. A quake started deep in my core, and my father's voice was lost in the rumble.

I assessed my opponent. He was shorter than me by about half a head. He had green eyes and brown hair peeking from under his hat that had a gold badge on it. He had an aquiline nose over a wide mouth and a small chin. I could see his teeth were small and square. I noticed his neck was muscular, which hinted that he was stronger than he looked.

He wore a well-fitting bulletproof vest over his tactical shirt. The armor had several pouches with extra clips and a radio. I also saw a tear gas grenade in one pouch, and for some reason, alarm bells blared in my mind. I could still see his belt, which meant he was not too close. He had several utility gadgets on his belt. I even saw a folding knife, and then my eyes found his gun behind his right hand.

That was the danger, my mind said over and over.

I must have been staring hard at his gun because he said, "Are you thinking of taking my gun?"

He stepped forward and said, "Turn around, put your hands on the hood, and spread your legs. Let's make sure you aren't armed." He tried to spin me around, but I did not budge. I was staring at him with unabashed living *anger.* My lessons about what to do when a police officer confronts you were strangely quiet. In fact, the breadth and depth of this *anger* overshadowed the entire emotion of fear. Earlier, I worried about the cops showing up, but talking with Saphronia had been well worth the risk. However, seeing her threatened awakened something old in me.

Stories of young Black men being beaten or shot for much less flooded my mind as fear gave one last push to save my life.

It failed.

I could see the other officer pushing Saphronia up against a nearby tree outside of the splash of the cops' searchlight. His hips were way too close to hers, and I heard something about frisking her extra carefully.

Something in me opened. A gate or a bridge, a connection to my ancestral past, I'm not sure. I felt and remembered a proverb Adrian taught me long ago.

The lion's power lies in our fear of him.

I knew something. *I was the lion*, and these men were only pretenders. I knew I could protect us. I *knew* I could stop this.

The next part happened so fast that I barely remember what occurred exactly; watching it helped me fill in some gaps I had.

My cop's hands moved so rapidly that I felt them before I knew what was happening. His hands gripped my neck with a crushing force. We were hip to hip, and he was trying to break my posture by lifting me off my feet or hitting me up against the police cruiser. His hands were enormous; I could feel his fingertips pinching the skin on the back of my neck.

I did not bend. Instead, I flexed my neck and growled at him. Spittle flew between my clenched teeth.

"Stop re-fucking-sisting!" he growled at me. His breath was hot with fear, and his voice broke.

I heard Saphronia yell, *"Get off of me!"* and something old and dangerous sprang across the bridge in my soul and burst into flames in my mind. For an instant, that ancient helplessness swallowed me. I could see Saphronia naked and chained to the brown earth. Her body was open to the world, and European men took turns at her. I was behind flat iron bars bolted together by hate. I gripped them until my hands bled; I screamed until I could taste blood in every ragged breath. The pale men with pale eyes looked at me with smug victory.

That is what swallowed me. I was trapped and defeated.

Suddenly, the doors to the cages swung open as if they had never been locked. I burst from the cell, my brothers beside me.

That is what leaped across the bridge. The flames of an old unresolved rage burned through me and ignited the living *anger*. The blaze spread through me in an instant.

In the video, I could see that my eyes flashed a reddish color. It was only for a second, but it was unmistakable. I looked up from the video, and Ian looked at me with his eyebrows up, his young forehead wrinkled in acknowledgment. Saphronia did not look away; she was watching very carefully; her fingers covered her mouth.

Both of Officer Friendly's hands were around my neck, choking me. His arms were slightly off my chest, and his elbows were not bent all the way. I used my right arm and scooped under both of his arms. I turned my shoulder, tucked my chin, and broke his grip on my throat. I tried to get fancy and spin around and elbow him in the back of the head, but my feet got tangled up. I stumbled forward into the light of the cruiser. My arms waved wildly, and I was able to regain my balance.

I noticed my clothes were moving weirdly. They were billowing like the wind was coming out of me.

I used my hand to keep on my feet and spun myself to face the cop. He was rushing at me, trying to tackle me high like a bear hug. I stepped to my left and grabbed his vest as he stumbled by and threw him to the ground. He rolled five or six feet and slammed into a car. Thankfully, the car alarm did not go off.

"Holy shit!" I heard Ian say from behind the camera.

I could not believe what I was watching. I glanced nervously at the others, but the video enthralled them. What the hell had I been thinking? I remember feeling so *angry* and powerful. I went back to watching the video because this was the part that was extremely hazy for me.

The cop yelled when he hit the car, and his partner turned to see what was happening. Seeing his partner on the ground sent him into a fear-filled panic. I heard Saphronia scream, "Gun!" and I turned to see a muzzle flash, then the massive sound of the tiny explosions sending death into me. I defensively closed my eyes and raised my hands, trying ineffectually to ward off death.

Sixteen rounds.

The way Ian was filming, my back was to him, and you could not see what was happening to me. All you could see was the flash of the gun firing repeatedly.

Sixteen rounds.

"No, Scipio!" Ian screamed from behind the camera.

Surprisingly, I didn't feel any pain. I opened my eyes when I heard a gasp and a gruff "What the fuck!" A blue light filled my vision; I saw my hands outstretched, trying to ward off the bullets. And just past my hands floating in a beachball-sized blue bubble of, I don't know what, were the bullets. They hung there unmoving. Most of them were going right at me, but at least six were wildly high and would have easily gone into the houses behind me. I remember looking at the cop in the eyes and sharing in the surprise.

"Look out!" Saphronia's warning broke me from the reverie of surprise. My left hand shot up instinctively, and my eyes followed its lead. The cop I had thrown to the ground was already firing his service weapon.

Sixteen more rounds.

I caught these, too. This time, my perception was clearer. I could feel the rounds slamming into the field I was creating. It did not hurt, but I could feel the influx of energy being absorbed into my body.

My senses extended out, and I could sense the beats of all the hearts in the immediate area. I could see the wind moving like a bright stream in the night. I sensed the magazine fall from the cop's gun on my right and felt it hit the ground before I heard it. My body hungrily absorbed the kinetic energy from the empty magazine. I felt it enter me. I felt the *control* of it all. It was like never knowing how to whistle to suddenly being able to whistle complete songs perfectly.

The *anger* was still there, and it asserted itself.

Before the first shooter could continue, I pushed the energy at him, and he looked like he was hit by a semi-truck. He launched into the air and hit the tree he had been pushing Saphronia against. There was a wet crunch.

My arms and legs felt ready to explode from my body. The weight and power of spirits named centuries of endured pain, covered *anger,* and soul-deep hurt flowed through me.

A scream was pulled from my soul's ancestry.

I remember it surprised me because I expected a growl of rage; instead, it was the scream of a million gallons of spilled blood.

The ground around me cracked and sank as if I was carrying the weight of generations of sorrow.

I watched as, in the video, I began glowing so brightly that the Global glitched for a moment. Just before the footage glitched, I saw my eyes; they were glowing, too. I looked at Saphronia when I heard her gasp. Her hand covered her mouth again. I dodged her eyes when I saw her about to return my gaze. I could feel embarrassment crawling with hot, prickly needle feet up my back to my scalp. I concentrated on the video, hoping she had not noticed me.

More shots slammed rapidly into the field I was creating. I turned to the shooter. The man tried to run, and I chased him. I must have been moving too fast because I ran into him almost instantly. The impact launched him into the trunk of another tree twenty feet away. There was another wet crunch as he hit the tree. His body slumped to the ground, leaving a bloody stain on the bark.

The smell of gunpowder and human waste filled the air. I came back to my senses and looked at the violence I had caused.

While I don't remember the actual event, I did not feel bad at this moment.

I told Ian to rewind the video.

"Sure," he said. He must have known I wanted to see the screaming part again because he scrolled right to it.

As I watched the video, I looked for Saphronia in the video. She was standing as if she were fighting a strong wind. A piece of debris I had not seen before was flung directly at her, and there was a flash of golden light, and the debris was gone. She had not even been looking at me. Her focus seemed to be on the houses behind where Ian had been filming.

In the video, I held my hand out to Saphronia, and we ran toward Ian. The video ended as we approached.

I looked up from the video and at Saphronia; she met my gaze, and I almost forgot what I was going to ask.

"Um, what were you looking at there at the end?" I asked.

"I was trying to see if anyone was watching us. I was scared we were getting filmed," she explained.

"I'm sure we are on the cruiser's camera and the cop's body cameras." My heart pounded hard in my chest again.

I felt each thudding beat reverberate and absorb into my body.

"Then why aren't the cops beating down your door right now?" Ian's voice rose a little bit. Then he looked back at the kitchen where my parents were.

"Sorry," he whispered.

"I don't know, Ian, apparently, they covered the whole thing up. I have no idea why they would do that. I don't know what we should do now. I think we should tell my parents. I'm sure they could help us. Somehow, I have powers. What the actual hell is going on?" I was nearing the end of my rope when the doorbell rang.

We all looked at each other first, then at the front door.

I got up, on shaky legs, to open it, thinking the police were on the other side of the door. I was surprised when I opened it. Adrian Lake stood there.

"What's up, kid?" he greeted me nonchalantly.

"Coach! What are you doing here?" I blurted out. My relief was pronounced.

"I'm here to see you guys. I heard you had a rough night last night." I stared at him in utter disbelief.

"Www.... what," I stammered. Coach smiled and walked into the house.

CHAPTER 9

Cleveland, Ohio, July 27, 2018, 12:17 a.m. EST.

The night was unusually warm but dark. There was no moon in the sky, and it was quiet. Alex walked confidently up to the small, well-groomed house and peered inside a window. The house was asleep. He almost whispered the word *Minerva*. That would have activated his onboard A.I., and his little extracurricular field trip would have been a bust. Minerva could have remotely disarmed the house alarm and then used the information from the alarm system and the house wi-fi and their Globals to create a complete and exact map of the house and its occupants. However, it would also record his every move, see what he saw, and record his biochemical reactions.

So, instead, he withdrew a small egg-shaped device from a small sack slung across his shoulder. He knew there was an active alarm, and this device would take care of that. He ran the device over the wall and waited. A green light shone brightly in the darkness, and he put the device back into his sack. He walked around to the side of the house, opened the fence, and crept into the backyard. He was listening intently as he walked to the back door. He knew the door would be locked, and he was strong enough to open it by force, but that would make too much noise. As he came around to the rear of the house, he saw his way in immediately. One of the ground-floor windows was left open.

His gamble had finally paid off.

Several months ago, well before summer, he had sabotaged their air conditioner. The weather had been cold, and the summer seemed a long way away. In the intervening months, he did little things like flattening their tires, causing engine trouble, and other little annoying costs that built up over time. Then he waited for the heat. He knew they would not have the money to fix the air conditioner immediately, and one warm night, they would leave a ground-floor window open. Moving like a shadow's shadow, he watched and checked.

And checked.

And checked.

Until tonight, the window was open, and the downstairs was dark. Alex listened for snoring from the family room, but it was quiet. He cut two small holes in the screen, stuck his fingers into them, and pulled. The screen popped out smoothly with just a small scraping sound. He looked into the darkened room with perfect clarity and leaped in, tucking and rolling as he contacted the floor. His sheer strength made the landing completely silent. He rolled nimbly to his feet and stepped into shadow. He slipped around a bookcase filled with books by lofty men of great thinking. Typical bourgeoisie American Blacks thinking they could relieve their guilt of leaving their people in squalor and abject poverty by reading and promoting elitist garbage masked as uplifting religion. These people were so trapped in the web, killing them would not destabilize the Great Plan. His plan would paint a picture of a disgraced professional. He padded to the den and found the computer terminal. He inserted a small device into one of the ports on the computer. It was a hexagonal hole with the sides sized in such a way as to only fit one way. Only the newer high-end computers had this type of security port. There was a small beep, and Alex pulled the device from the port. When the house was torn apart for evidence, they would find a nasty surprise involving children and animals on this terminal. The doctor's reputation would be ruined. *Salt to the wound,* he thought gleefully. He moved to the stairs, and as he ascended each step, his heart rate increased.

He was silent as a ghost's whisper. He flipped a coin to decide which room to go to first. The parents won the toss. He moved to their room, avoiding the creaks in the floor. It was an old house with a lot of history. He was going to add more.

He knew the door would squeak when he opened it, but he could hear loud snoring coming from the other side. The husband was the threat to be eliminated. He was an operant and, at the very least, comfortable with his powers. Maybe even a Tier Three or Four. The whole family knew and kept the secret tightly guarded, but they also played in the sacrosanct safety of their home. He would toss them around and retrieve things for them from different places in the house. He was dangerous and must be killed first. Thinking back on it now, he knew there never was a choice. Pops had to go first.

He eased the door open, and as expected, it creaked, then the sound was gone. He saw the bodies in the bed reposition themselves, and he saw his target lying on his back. He smiled, reptilian and cold. The cold spread swiftly through his body, followed by jittery anticipation, and the palms of his hands felt clammy.

In one fluid motion, he moved to the side of the bed, drew an eight-inch blade from somewhere on his waist, and placed his left hand tightly over his nose and mouth.

His heart was pounding with excitement, and his mind was flying at a million miles per second. His insides were vibrating.

He thrust the blade into the curve of his neck just under his jawline at about a forty-degree angle, destroying the brain stem and killing the man instantly.

This husband and father of two beautiful children fell limp, and blood bubbled from the wound Alex expertly made. The wife was woken by the wet sound of the wound the dead man made. She rolled toward him and started to say his name.

"Henr...." Her voice trailed off as she saw Alex standing over her husband. She inhaled sharply to belt out an ear-piercing scream, no doubt, but Alex was faster and shot her with a small dart that was tipped with a paralytic toxin. The cry wheezed out of her throat as a dry cough. She flopped back onto the bed, and her terror-filled eyes rolled in her sockets. He sauntered over to her side of the bed and moved her small frame easily into a sitting position.

"Believe you me, your man here got the better end of the deal. You, on the other hand, get to watch me slaughter your children. Sit back and do try to enjoy the performance," Alex said jovially, giving the mammy a wide, toothy grin. He silently skipped out of the room and returned shortly with a young boy of about eight years old. The mother moaned with ineffable grief and horror.

He placed a mask that fit over the boy's nose and mouth. The light on the contraption turned from red to green.

"There we go," he said under his breath.

"I don't want to disturb the neighbors. I'm sure you've annoyed them enough with your jungle music," Alex said pleasantly.

The mother's eyes flashed with anger, but it was ultimately impotent and wasted.

She watched helplessly as her children were brutally ripped from this life and sent screaming into the next. Alex explained to her, as he worked, that every time the little light on the mask turned red, it meant that the kids were screaming.

The mother passed out from shock several times, and Alex gently woke her up each time. He didn't want her to miss the puppet show he was putting on. The children danced and cavorted with such rhythm and grace, a true credit to their race.

The three hours seemed to skip by. The house was quiet now except for his heavy breathing. He was exhausted. He had ejaculated in his pants several times. His balls ached, but he was glad he had worn the adult diaper. He could feel his family jewels sloshing around in the small puddle of semen the diaper could not absorb. He sat down, leaning against the last clean wall. He could feel his body repairing itself; a slight itch ran all throughout his body in waves. His breathing came under control as he surveyed the horror scene he had created. The mother had died of a heart attack or stroke from the extreme trauma of watching her children be butchered and then played with. He had watched as her entire face had gone slack, and her eyes rolled up until just the whites showed. She died from the sheer horror of what he had done to them. This was much more personal than going out in a blaze of *glory* at some dirty old mall that would just close down after the massacre. They would tear it down and build something new, and he would be forgotten forever. But *this* was intimate. He caused the maximum amount of pain at a pinpoint level. It was glorious! He could do this forever.

He stood to his feet shakily at first, but then his strength returned. He walked back to the bed, to the side with the dead father. He looked down at him and withdrew his knife from his belt. He ran the wickedly sharp blade over the man's dead flesh. He savored the moment. He plunged the knife into the soft tissue at the base of his throat and pulled down sharply. He knew the blade wouldn't cut through the sternum, but it would score it and separate the muscle, and that was all he needed. He punched down hard; his fist passed through the breastbone and into the man's chest cavity. He felt around in the still-warm viscera, finding his prize.

Movies make it seem like pulling someone's whole and complete heart out is easy; it's not. The major blood vessels attached to it don't rip perfectly every time; part of the organ could be left dangling from an artery or any number of other versions. The one thing it was was bloody. Alex knew this because he had done it several times before. Some of them were sanctioned, some not, but each one taught him something. His hand grasped the not-quite-cold organ and pulled. Most of it came out with jagged pieces at the top. Alex looked at it for a moment, considering it, then he bit into it. Blood spilled over his fingers and squirted down his throat, trying to choke him as he swallowed instead; he immediately took another bite and another and another and another. Blood dribbled down his arm and around his mouth. He could feel the meat choke down his throat and settle defiantly in his stomach. He burped massively.

"Excuse me," he said sheepishly. He picked his way around the crimson-splattered bed and wrapped the female in the bloody sheet. He leaped over the bed back to the male's side. Alex paused, set an incendiary grenade in the hole in the male's chest, and pulled the pin.

Alex carried the female downstairs. His mood was somber and thoughtful, which warred with his euphoric state. He kept his movements smooth and with little waste.

He strode to the den and threw the computer's CPU out of one of the windows. Alex then went to the kitchen and pulled the stove away from the wall, tearing the gas hose. Gas poured into the house with a hiss. He walked out of the back door and leaped away into the night, the Black woman's body slung over his shoulder.

Several streets away, a white van waited for him. He loaded the female body into the back of the van. In the distance, the night was rocked by a tremendously loud boom. Car alarms began serenading the night. Alex smiled, got in the van, started it, and drove away.

After an hour of driving, he arrived at a compost company called Rueger Compost. He pulled up to the gate, flashed a black badge, and held up one finger. The guard nodded and said, "Go to row one, it's to the left, then take the right-hand lane, then go to the end of the little road. Got it?" His eyebrows raised questioningly.

Alex nodded. The guard continued.

"Drop your refuse to the right of the gate. Someone will take care of it from there. Thank you for your service."

The guard nodded, and the gate opened.

Alex supposed he was grateful for the directions. He had never been to this compost drop before. He pulled up to the right of the gate as he was instructed. Alex opened the door and exited the van, but a young man with sandy blond hair ran up to the van.

"Hey, I got it, don't worry," he said, walking to the back of the van and unloading the refuse.

"Thank you," he said to the young man.

"No problem, do you want the sheet?" the young man asked. Alex shook his head. The lifeless Black body of the woman flopped stiffly to the ground as he pulled the sheet from it. The muscles in her face had returned to some semblance of normalcy, and the mother of a slain family stared defiantly. The young man picked the body up, tossed it over his shoulder, and started climbing stairs Alex had somehow missed. Alex followed.

They climbed up the side of one of the larger compost heaps. Alex noticed the young man was not breathing heavily as he ascended the stairs with the woman's dead weight on his shoulder. *Respirocytes maybe?* They were nano-machines created several years ago to relieve breathing ailments, but they were repurposed for military use. Of course, a black market arose, and the SOTIR Group engineered its own. He approached a hollow in the compost and dropped the body into a hole in the side of the heap. The body fell several feet in, and he began to shovel compost into the hole. The disappearance of this woman would be a big case, all hands on deck, and he would be able to revisit his crime scene. Also, he would be able to interview the relatives and taste their despair. *Oh, this would be amazing!*

Alex knew that in a few weeks, the body would be gone entirely. He drove home to clean up; he had a new school to go to tomorrow, and he had finally made detective.

CHAPTER 10

San Jose, California, March 13, Present Day, 10:30 a.m. PST.

Beverly Danielle Harelson, the mother of Scipio Harelson, was delighted to see Ian and the young Black girl at her door. She had known they were coming after the night her son had been through. She opened the door.

"Hello, Ian, nice to see you. An..."

"Hi, Mrs. Harelson, is Scipio here?"

She let him push past her into the house. When Ian got excited, he sometimes forgot himself.

"Yes, he's upstairs," she said, looking at the young lady. "And your name is?"

"Saphronia, mum," she said in a clear, strong voice.

Beverly smiled. "That is a beautiful accent," Beverly said. "Scipio, come downstairs, son!" Hearing the door open, she continued, "Ian and a friend are here to see you. I'm sorry, honey. Can you tell me your name one more time?" Beverly asked.

"Saphronia," she answered.

"Her name is Saphronia," she announced. "Oh, honey, that is such a beautiful name," Beverly gushed. "One day, you will have to tell me how your parents came up with such a beautiful name. I love names."

Scipio came down the stairs. Beverly noticed the girl was glowing slightly golden. She ignored it and went into the kitchen.

She turned the corner and turned on a communication inhibitor. When she entered the complicated inhibitor field, she spoke to her husband in hushed tones.

"She is here, Paul," she said, "The Ikhawu has arrived."

"I will make the call," Paul responded.

Beverly blinked tears away.

CHAPTER 11

San Francisco, California, July 27, 2018, 7:19 a.m. PST.

Robert Cross sat in his high-backed chair behind his enormous desk. He turned the monitor off. The scene was of a gruesome murder of a Black family by one of his best and most strategically placed operatives. The murder bothered him as much as a waste of any resource would. He didn't want to have to pull Alex from the field, and he knew he wouldn't. Alex was a rare jewel in his arsenal. He was smart, driven, and deadly. In the short time since he was given the nano-machines, he had improved by leaps and bounds. He assimilated into the training rapidly and rose to the top of his class easily. Now that he was in the field as a police officer, he was strategically placed to find these blights in humanity. Officially, he removed six families from the pure human gene pool. Cross knew the number was much higher, closer to forty.

Cross gave him hints of his knowledge. He would credit other teams with the kills, and the teams always toed the line. Of course, they never told the other teams because the accolades and bonuses were so extraordinary, no team would want that particular fall from grace. It was a plan easily executed, but he was absolutely confident Alex heard the news of the kills and the team stories, and he was sure he put two and two together. His time between killings shortened dramatically, and the stories had to come out faster and in better detail. Cross had allowed and often planted mistakes in the details, only things Alex would know.

However, he kept the leash he installed with the nano-machines tight, often reprimanding him for the slightest offense. When he attempted to hack the nano-machines, he was punished mercilessly. Internally, Cross cheered when he saw Alex tried again and successfully hacked the nano-machines. Cross had a private feed from Alex via Minerva and would often *ride* with Alex on his hunts. The man was an artist of terrible effect. The things he perpetrated on his victims were truly horrific; at the same time, they were entertaining and funny. Cross would watch Alex work with burning, unblinking eyes. When he was done, Cross would flop back in his chair, his brow and crotch of his pants both wet. The satisfaction didn't last, but Alex refilled his cup every time, living vicariously through it. It gave him the ability to face the public with honesty and purity. He could relive the images during a speech to rile himself up. The best part was that he was free from even the appearance of guilt.

It helped him in his projection of sincerity. The ability to project earnestness helped him win his seat in the U.S. Senate all those years ago. It helped him become the king-maker he was.

Robert Cross had been the driving force behind two presidents on both sides. He played the government like the corporation it was. He moved people and ideals like checkers. Advancing opposing ideas at different times kept the money flowing. No one suspected him at all. He was wholly insulated through intermediaries and shell compa-nies started by people he had dirt on.

His time on the International Development, Multilateral Institutions and International Economic, Energy, and Environmental Policy subcommittee was very lucrative. He was able to secure permanent contracts with the U.S. government and several of his *subsidiary* companies. When he left Congress, he became a lobbyist for the companies for which he garnered the contracts. Money became a non-issue, so he began to study anything. He had always liked history but never actually dove headlong into it until now, and he discovered something. The history of America has always been about men like him fighting to retain their hard-earned power. The Founding Fathers saw the theft that the crown was perpetrating on them and decided to do something about it.

When the Africans were being enslaved, the Europeans realized the *tribes* were very segregated. None of the groups spoke the same language and often sold people from other ethnic tribes. The slavers purposefully mixed up the tribesmen so they could not plan to avoid mutinies. Some called it a modern-day Tower of Babel. When the mixed cargo arrived in the United States and or the Caribbean, they were often bred together with each other and the already present slaves. Entire ethnic groups that were separated for thousands of years were rejoined through chattel slavery.

The Rejoining caused something strange to happen. After several generations, the offspring were sometimes born *awake,* as they were called. They had abilities that, when manifested, were awe-inspiring and deadly. It became customary to kill the child and their parents as soon as they manifested their abilities. It was treated like cancer in the inventory. A whole page in history was erased in fifty years, except for diaries kept by a select few in obscure entries.

Cross came across the thread of information in a journal of one of his ancestors. A man named Walter Cross had lived in the middle of those horrific days. He had been a young man, and the experience he lived through left an obvious mark on him. According to the diaries, the effect was physical and psychological.

The young boy was a *friend* as far as a young White boy and a young Black boy could have been friends in 1690. The diary tells the story of how the boys got lost in the woods near their home in South Carolina. They got turned around playing *chase the nigger* and didn't know how to get back. Walter tells how they walked for what seemed like hours and ended up coming to a stream. They drank from it and sat by the creek and waited for someone to find them. Walter's father was, by all accounts, an excellent tracker, and he was sure his father would find them soon. Things had gone well, and the boys talked and played as boys would do, never straying too far from the spot they had chosen to wait in. The night seemed to fall like a curtain, and Walter began to worry. The young Black boy was described as shaking with terror, and young Walter was a pillar of calm and resolve. The diary reads that the young Walter Cross tried to use the stars as his ancestors did and navigate their way home. Unfortunately, the young master was a feeble astronomer, and the boys got more turned around than ever.

Current Cross remembered thinking how terrified little Walter must have been, even how worried he had been for his little Black friend, how responsible he must have felt.

South Carolina, British Colony, August 19, 1690, 7:39 p.m.

Walter and the Black boy wandered for what seemed like hours. Their breath became visible in the night air.

Walter describes the sounds of the woods as echoing. "All at once, something would move in the brush and sound so close you could, if you knew where to reach, reach out and grab whatever made the sound. At other times, the sound came from a far way off, it seemed. The trees echoed every distant scratch or squeal from woodland creatures to startling clarity."

The boys were lost.

Then, their nightmare became a reality. A long wail pierced the night. The howl was answered by a growling bark. The boys' terror caused them to bolt. Their day of play caught up with them before the wolves did. Walter fell and was not able to get back to his feet without assistance. The Black boy came back for him and got young Walter to his feet. They had not taken more than a dozen steps before the first of the wolves struck Walter, causing the pair of young men to fall in a tangle of arms and legs.

Screaming with terror, the boys regained their feet and continued to run. Walter had somehow fallen behind the little nigger boy, and the wolf was nipping viciously at his calves.

The second wolf ran headlong into him. The ferocious creatures began tearing at his soft flesh. This next part of Walter's story would cause a lot of controversy. Walter told of a flash of light so bright he thought an angel of God Himself had come down to save him. He blinked and kicked furiously, trying to free himself and see what was happening. Walter could feel the animals pulling less and less at his legs and hear their cries of pain. His right leg was shredded; he could feel the cold of the outside air brushing places he knew he wasn't supposed to. His vision slowly came back to him. At first, his mind could not comprehend the images his blue eyes were relaying.

Tobby stood with his arm extended and his hand splayed open. Three of the wolves hung in mid-air, and two others were just landing roughly several yards away. The three hanging in the air did not hang there for long. The young nigger boy flicked his wrist as simple as you please, and the large predators just flew off into the evening shadows. Walter heard their cries of pain far away from them. Mind you, these were wolves weighing at least thirteen stone each, and he tossed them like driftwood lost in the sea. Walter writes that four more wolves had snuck up and swiftly grabbed him in their teeth and tried to drag him away, but Tobby turned around because of Walter's scream and waved his arm, and the wolves flew away, end over end, one of them striking a nearby tree. Tobby seemed out of breath. His shoulders sagging as if under a great weight, Walter wrote.

The wolves howled in pain and fear. Most of them ran for their lives; however, there was one that couldn't move its hind legs. It cried and whined in pain. It was feebly trying to crawl away; blood trickled from its muzzle. Walter struggled bravely to his feet, wincing in pain; he looked for a rock to put the poor animal out of its misery.

He found a hefty ten-pound rock with a pointed edge and limped over to the wounded wolf.

"I win, you son of a bitch!" his teeth were clenched in hatred. Walter raised the rock and was about to bring it down on the wolf's head when it leaped at him. The razor-sharp teeth sank into his leg right above the knee.

The wolf shook its head wildly, and there was a dry snapping sound and an ear-piercing scream in response. Walter was kicking and beating at the head of the massive predator to no avail. Suddenly, the great beast fell still. The jaws released, and the wolf's carcass floated away. Walter looked around to see how this was happening and saw Tobby standing in the center of the grove with his right arm outstretched, his tattered clothes blowing in an unfelt wind. Then he fell to his knees, exhausted. Walter was so confused he didn't know what kind of witchcraft this was, but little Tobby was dangerous.

Several minutes passed by, and Walter was trying to tend to his wounds when he heard the braying of his father's dogs, and his heart lifted. Walter's father and a mixed group of his friends and his slaves poured into the clearing. James Cross ran to his son.

Seeing his son's bloody leg, the rock next to him, and a passed-out nigglet sent James Cross into a fear-filled rage.

"Did this niggra boy hurt you?" James growled.

"No, Pa twas a pack of wolves. We was playing, and we got lost." Tears welled in his eyes; he wiped them away.

"He saved you?" James' rage was subsiding.

"Yes, Pa, he did, but something was amiss." Walter didn't have the words to explain it.

"What boy, tell me?" James demanded.

Walter looked away from his father and saw the group of niggers his father had brought tending to Tobby; the boy was coming back to the waking world. He looked back at his Pa.

"I am not sure how to explain it, Pa. He had some kind of magic, and he drove off the wolves."

The blood drained from James Cross's face.

"Not in my house!" he muttered as he stood.

"Pa?" Walter questioned.

James Cross walked to where the actual family was tending to his wounds. *Tobby's* family begged James to be allowed to join the search party. Now, they were all conveniently there. The women were tending to young Tobby, patting his little brown head.

James Cross shot Tobby in the head. Blood and gore sprayed all over the ground behind his precious little skull.

Tobby's father leaped from where he had been kneeling, rage and confusion warring in his eyes. *Tobby's* mother and two sisters screamed at the savagery.

"Massa!" James stabbed him in the heart. He dropped with a wheeze coming from his mouth. The women stood up and backed away. James held out his hand, and one of his men put a pistol in it. He raised it to shoot the mammy in the face, but one of the daughters jumped in front of her and took the bullet. She fell dead with a black wound under her left eye. The screaming intensified.

"Run, girl!" the mammy shouted and threw herself at the man she served, toppling to the ground. She was not a very big woman, but she did her best to tie him up to give her baby a chance to run.

In the 1690s, guns were not very accurate past a certain range. Fortunately, Black people were as fast as ever.

The daughter's name was May because she was born in May, and she could run. She was often tasked with carrying missives to the other nearby plantations. When she saw her family members slaughtered in front of her, she froze, but hearing her mother scream at her to run, broke the ice around her legs.

May ran.

"Shoot her!" James screamed from under the mammy, tangling him up. One of his men kicked the mammy from him and shot her in the face.

"Shoot the runaway, you idiots!"

Bullets struck trees all around her, but May ran for her life. That was the last time anyone saw her, as far as Walter Cross knew.

San Francisco, California, July 27, 2018, 7:30 a.m. PST.

Cross found other stories like this and corroborating reports from other witnesses. It had been mind-boggling. Were these Blacks capable of developing superhuman abilities? How come no one seemed to know about this? He was once the Ranking member of the U.S. Senate Intelligence Committee, and this was absolutely new to him. He began to search for current proof of this phenomenon. Luckily, the general population of Blacks did not know of this phenomenon, and it was so rare that it didn't manifest much in the current African American population. So, he thought, as technology improved and Big Brother grew in power and sophistication, he could piece together a theory. They were here, and they were hiding because they knew that if they were to be exposed, they would be exterminated. The entire world would hunt them without mercy. Any slip-up was so few and far between that it was considered a hoax. He had been one of the skeptics until he became a full man.

In 2010, when Cross was sixty years old, his father died a year after discovering this unsettling information. His mother had passed several years earlier from cancer. After his father's funeral, a tall Black man named Sam came to see him in his office.

He had been perplexed when his secretary paged him to inform him of his visitor.

"How can I help you, Mister? Uh, what did you say your last name was?"

"Just Sam, Sir," the man's voice was a deep baritone.

"Well, how can I help you, Sam?" Cross switched to full politician mode, especially when dealing with Blacks; he had convinced whole groups of them to back him politically on more than one occasion.

"Well, Sir, your father sent me. He instructed me to show you something." Sam was stone-calm. His eyes were gentle, and when he talked, only his mouth moved. Still, this was bold and disrespectful; his father hadn't been in the ground for one whole day.

"Uh, Sam, you say, what do you want?" Cross said, letting a little anger creep into his voice.

Tears welled in Sam's eyes.

"I'm sorry, Sir, I was not clear. Please don't be angry," Sam pleaded. "I used to work for your father. He employed my unique abilities."

Cross shot to his feet.

"What did you say? Are you one of them?" he ground the words through his teeth.

For the first time, another part of Sam's face moved. His forehead wrinkled in surprise and shock. Sam reached into the sports jacket he was wearing and produced a small memory stick. Cross had flinched at the movement despite his anger.

"This should explain everything," he held the stick out. Cross looked at it. There were two words on it. DEUS VULT. Cross had seen those words carved roughly on his father's desk but never asked him about them. This was enough for him to take that first step of trust.

"What is this?" Cross asked.

"A message," was all Sam said.

Cross inserted the memory stick and clicked the little icon that came up. The page was filled with files and videos. He clicked the one titled *A1. WATCH THIS FIRST*.

His father came up and started talking.

"Hello, son, this is going to be a lot of information," he began.

Over the next few hours, Cross would learn of his father's real mission in life.

CHAPTER 12

San Francisco, California, July 13, 2010, 7:35 a.m. PST.

The SOTIR Group was a creation of necessity. The first member was James Cross. After the fateful night, he knew he must do something. He was a man of immense means even then. While the extermination of these demonic beings was stalling, James Cross revitalized the cause. In his crusade, he met a man named David Roth, who was the owner of a large southern newspaper company. James and David hit it off immediately. They were often seen together, carousing with women of the night. It was a ruse; they were hunting. They started small, looking for any sign of demonic ability. Maybe a wench knew more than she should have or guessed a little too well. The victims were always Black. Then one day, they met Dr. Edward Berg. Dr. Berg was a tall Swedish man with delicate, skilled hands and a questioning mind. He suggested that they capture the specimens and conduct tests on them. He did not believe in demons, and he surmised there might be a scientific explanation. The three of them formed a cabal they called the Savior Commission. They theorized that the number of operant slaves would become an insurmountable obstacle to the White race if unchecked. These men grew in knowledge and power. They made connections and found allies. As time continued on, they passed their goals and hopes to their children, and every descendant continued the Work.

During slavery, it was easy to acquire specimens, but even those became few and far between. After four generations of the Commission and surviving the United States Civil War, they surmised that it would be better to look to a future where they could act freely.

The now-renamed SOTIR Commission had their hands in every pot imaginable, and they amassed large sums of money to fight the coming emergence of the Negro Problem. Racism was their bread and butter. During the Reconstruction era, they convinced the population of the United States that Negroes were the enemy. They had a hand in promoting the first American movie, "Birth of a Nation." Their prescient insight showed them that movies were the ultimate propaganda machine.

They learned through the World Wars that the Negroes had not been idle either. They came across stories of a worldwide underground railroad. When someone exhibited abilities, they were whisked away often before the SOTIR Commission could get there. The unnamed Underground Resistance became a thorn in the SOTIR Commission's side. As the years ground on, they clashed more often. During the 1920's they clashed openly in the streets and again in the 1960s. Both groups shared a common goal: to stay hidden. The SOTIR Commission found that their adversary was very well-equipped and at times deadly. The SOTIR Commission often met during these tumultuous times. They strategized and considered ideas to win this War. When predictive data came out that the White race would become a minority in the 21st century, they ramped up their war machine. They studied those they had captured and tried to create countermeasures.

They were connected to nearly every United States President and right-minded Congressman. Still, the Resistance had worldwide help. The Enhanced Powered Beings, or EPBs, were moved with near-perfect secrecy. The newly minted SOTIR Group was losing. The age of technology and the advent of Moore's Law brought the SOTIR Group closer to an even playing field. The SOTIR Group found that the Resistance over the years had changed their strategy from outright fighting to a quiet removal of EPBs from the field. However, they did not believe the Resistance was killing them, so they had to be hiding them somewhere. That somewhere would have an army of EPBs, and if they wanted to, they could wipe the White race off the face of the earth. They desperately wanted to find them and kill them first. But how?

Through the centuries, the SOTIR Group cataloged dozens of powers. They saw fire, air, water, and earth controllers. There were telekinetics, speedsters, invisibility, and a theory on magic users. Rarely did they run into a telepath; those were the most dangerous because they were able to see your thoughts before you knew they were in the room. Then, in 1901, there came along Albert Crosby. Albert was a telepath but also terribly addicted to alcohol. There was a moment as he approached inebriation that his head was clear, AND his body relaxed enough for him to use his ability. He "shopped" at white-only stores and dispensed his haul among the negro masses for free. While dangerous, his capture was quite simple. The team the group sent was called Sigma.

Sigma simply waited for him to pass out. They went in, killed the two women in the room with him, and staged the room like a murder scene.

With the damning evidence, they forced him to stay under their thumb voluntarily. They were able to successfully breed Albert and create a family of servants that assisted them. They were all named Sam, male or female.

Albert Crosby had a unique DNA structure. His gene for telepathy was a dominant one, his every offspring was born with some version of the ability and one other ability. One Sam was born with the ability to negate telepathy in a thousand-foot radius. The Group cultivated the ability. The completion and distribution of the Human Genome Project in 2003 and the "rediscovery' of CRISPR in 2012 exploded the boundaries of what they could create. Nonetheless, a boundary remained.

No matter what combination they tried, they could not stitch any ability nucleotide into white DNA. The cell would die, and the donor would suffer a debilitating if not fatal accident. The SOTIR Group lost three brilliant scientists and three unwitting soldiers to the Curse. While slow, they did learn their lesson.

The SOTIR Group constantly strategized on how to kill this theoretical base of EPBs. They were pleasantly surprised with mustard gas during World War One, but the wind manipulators crushed that dream in a decisive battle. Then World War Two brought the advent of the nuclear bomb, and that was considered the best chance to wipe them out in one blow. The SOTIR Group did not care if they were in a city or in a barren wilderness; they would erase them.

As Cross watched video after video, his mind was blown at the war that had been going on right under his nose. How come his father had never told him? He would have gladly joined in the search. Eventually, even that was explained in one of the videos.

In order to protect the family from the ultra-liberal culture they saw emerging, the SOTIR Group decided that only the leader of the family would be involved in the SOTIR Group to insulate the wealth and power they had amassed. If one of them were exposed, they could be cut off, and the family would still be able to replace the member. The discovered member would have to fall on their sword to keep all the secrets. This one rule held the cover of the group intact.

He looked up from the stream of information, and Sam was still there, his eyes never wavering.

In this modern era, Cross learned, the SOTIR Group had its fingers in a great many pots. Millions of people worked for subsidiaries of the Group and never even knew it. White, Black, Latino, Asian, and even Indian people worked for them. The group had weaponized the fight for equality. If someone in their *employ* showed signs of having an ability, they were investigated and removed. They were not always successful, but it was enough to keep going. It seemed the resistance had grown in a similar fashion. Quiet battles between the two sides were waged in empty warehouses, secluded forests, and even in dark alleys.

The videos were over, and Robert Cross was awestruck. The last instruction his father gave was to go to a specific address and provide a code word. He would be let in and accepted. There was something about the last word that grabbed him.

Cross had always been the rich, out-of-touch White boy. His father had taught him that the inhuman races of the world were nothing better than tools to be used for his advancement, but deep down, he craved the friendships these "tools" seemed to foster with each other. He was always made to feel guilty about his family's wealth and privilege in his school career. He hated the feeling of being wrong somehow for what he was born into. He couldn't control the color of his skin or his family having wealth any more than those darkies could. Why should he feel guilty? After everything, he just learned his family was guilty of great atrocities in the name of survival. That thought made him laugh and laugh and laugh.

He *was* the *man* they all had accused him of being. He decided then and there that he would be much worse.

Cross came back to himself and saw Sam calmly looking at him."You can go home, Sam," Cross offered, feeling the old White guilt.

"I am home, Sir; I am yours to do with as you will," the Black man responded.

"You just sat and listened to all that, and you still want to stay?" Cross's eyebrows shot up.

"Yes, Sir, your family has been real good to me and mine. We swore our loyalty to your family and the cause they fight for. I don't wanna see you all get wiped out, and these people are vicious. What kind of terrible world would they bring about if they were able to succeed?" This was a strange shift in the Black man that Cross noticed. He was animated and passionate about helping the Work continue.

"Well, where do you sleep? Where is your family? You can't possibly stay with me 100 percent of the time."

"Sir, I sleep where you tell me to, and as for my family, they are at the address you were given. It is a safe place, and I know they are well taken care of." The animation Sam exhibited before was gone; he was all business. "Okay, then let's go now."

He stood, and nature called him. When he returned from the bathroom, Sam was standing by the door and had something in his hand. Cross looked at the device in his hand.

"What's this?" he asked, genuinely perplexed.

"It is the Master's Key; it controls this collar." Sam opened his shirt lapel. A dull silver collar with no markings save for an LED light, which was bright green.

"What's this for?" Cross had asked all those years ago.

"It is a safety precaution for you, Sir, for your safety and mine. You can activate and deactivate my abilities. The green light means I am in safe mode and cannot use my abilities. However, with either a press of the button on the fob or swiping it in close proximity, the collar may be turned off or on," Sam explained.

"Why would I need this if you are completely loyal?" Cross made the quotation signs.

"Sir, I am completely loyal, but we have had mishaps when encountering stronger telepaths. The collar can render me completely unconscious as well as detonate." Sam's facial expression was completely neutral as he spoke.

Cross's eyebrows shot up. "Oh, okay, wow!" He took a moment to gather himself. He was about to continue out the door, but a strange thought occurred to him.

"If you were constantly by my father's side, why don't I ever remember seeing you? You are a complete stranger to me." Doubt was growing in Cross's mind.

"Excuse me, Sir. That is part of my ability. I can fix it," Sam reached up and touched Cross's temple.

Memories of Sam flooded in. Sam always ushered Cross out when he came to see his father. Often, his father was on a phone call with someone, and Sam would usher him out, wiping his memory of the call and Sam himself.

Cross gasped at the flood of information.

"What the hell!" he steadied himself on a chair.

"You've been there the entire time?"

"Yes, Sir, I was ordered to keep myself hidden." Sam's face was stone.

Robert Cross had always been an adaptable soul; he didn't take these revelations in stride so much as he took them as possibilities, then as fact. In his mind, Sam had connected so many dots he didn't even know he had.

"Thank you," Cross said, wondering why he had said it at all.

San Francisco, California, Present Day, 3:35 p.m. PST.

Robert Cross woke from his nap with the memory still fresh in his mind. All of that seemed like centuries ago. He had seen and been a part of a great many things since that first day all those years ago.

Now, he was watching his best and most vicious operative prepare to become a police detective. He was going to send him to San Francisco, but something was happening in San Jose; he dispatched the police chief to cover the incident with Sam's help. It was reported as an accident, and the two officers were given full honors, but the actual video had been sequestered. The public swallowed the entire story. The real video was useless; it was nothing but static, and somehow, with all the shots fired, no one in the immediate area woke up. It had all the hallmarks of the beginning of a war. The newly emerged usually went on a tear against the police, but they were typically sloppy and promptly taken off the board. Usually by the Resistance, but this time they covered their tracks, and there were also rumblings of the Resistance being in the area. Something didn't smell right to Cross, and he trusted his instincts, hence the transfer of Alex. The young man had been given some upgrades, and Cross was anxious to see them used in the field. He was such a good test subject. He did not complain; he just tried to fulfill his duty, which was why Cross let him pursue his happiness.

CHAPTER 13

West San Jose, California, March 14, 4:00 p.m.
PST.

Alex sat in the old Latina's living room, waiting for the woman to return with some hot chocolate he would not drink. He waited for her to enter the kitchen, then he sprang from his seat, quiet as a ghost, and slipped to the window to look out. He had a perfect view of the park across the street. How had she not been roused by thirty-two gunshots? This was the third of six townhouses that were directly across from the park. There was a sound wall, but these apartments were above the wall. The shots should have at least brought someone to check. This was not an abjectly poor community. Something like that would have been very out of place. It did make the cover story easier since no one heard anything; they could say anything they wanted. He slipped into her guest bedroom and looked out the window, and she had the perfect vantage. He heard her trembling return to the living room and found his seat before she saw him moving about.

"Here you are, dear. Now, what were you asking me?" the ancient lady smiled warmly at Alex. It was always amazing to him the deference he received from people when they knew he was a detective. She was very wrinkled. Alex assumed she was over 100 years old. He was impressed that she was still living by herself.

"I was asking if you heard anything the night of the accident?" he asked tenderly. It was easy being congenial when he needed to be. The thought of breaking her neck skittered through his mind. The dry sound it would make, and her gasping surprise.

Stay on track, Alex, he told himself.

Besides, he was carrying a passenger today. Mr. Cross was observing via his nano-machines. They attached to his optic nerve and relayed a digital picture of what his eyes saw. They also gathered in his hair so Mr. Cross could hear what was being said.

"No, I usually am a very light sleeper, but I guess I must have been tired that night because I didn't hear anything," the old lady said. Alex was glad she didn't have a thick accent; he was horrible with deciphering people's gibberish. He glanced down at his cup of hot chocolate and gently placed it on the coffee table in front of him.

"Thank you, ma'am," he said, standing smoothly. "I'm glad you were not interrupted by the terrible incident." He moved to the door. The ancient-looking lady struggled to stand. Alex watched her, fascinated by her battle. Right when she found her feet, Alex said, "I'll see myself out. Thank you for your help."

He left the apartment abruptly; the smell was starting to irritate him.

He didn't want to go to the rest of the apartments, but he had to do his due diligence. Plus, his ride-along partner was watching.

"Do we know anything about the people that live in these homes?" he said sub-vocally.

"No," the answer was crisp.

"Okay," he said, knocking on the next door.

"Hello, Police," Alex announced.

"Just a sec!" came a soft voice from the other side of the door. Soft feet danced and padded to the door. Several locks were opened, and a woman answered the door.

Alex was awestruck. She was beautiful. She had long brown hair with a hint of curl in it. Her eyes were hazel, and her button nose and rosy cheeks were peppered with freckles. Her lips were full and smiling. Her skin was sun-kissed and perfect.

"Hello," she said. "How can I help you, officer?" Her eyes were bright and intelligent.

"Uh... may I come in?" He was trying to recover from her stunning beauty.

"Can I see a badge?" she asked politely, but Alex heard steel in the question as well.

"Of course," he pulled his new detective badge from his jacket pocket and showed it to her.

"My name is Detective Alex Lamb, and I'm investigating the accident that happened outside your home a couple of nights ago. May I come in and ask you a few questions?" he smiled warmly. She hesitated for a moment.

"Yeah, sure, come on in," and she stood aside to let him in.

Every time.

He already knew the layout of the townhome; it would be the mirror image of the one he had just come from. However, he stood in the doorway and let her lock up before leading him to her spacious living room. Where the old senora next door had a living room packed with couches and plants and knick-knacks, this room was devoid of any furniture. There was a huge mirror on one of the walls and a wooden bar that stretched the length of the mirror. The floor was hardwood and polished to within an inch of its life. Alex whistled as he came into the open space.

"Wow, this is amazing," he said. He was looking at the pictures on the walls. Famous dancers and paintings of dancers. Alex wagged his finger playfully.

"I bet you're a dancer," he said confidently.

The beautiful woman giggled, and Alex's heart fell.

"Alex, your heart rate is increasing. Please stay focused. She is lovely, and you may return and pursue a relationship with her if you so desire, but right now, we need information on the EPBs that may have been here. Ask her name and get on with it," Mr. Cross's order came with a quick white-hot pain in his gums. He nodded his head imperceptibly in obedience.

"I am. How did you guess?" the woman asked playfully.

"I am a detective. I have great powers of deduction," Alex mimed, rubbing his chin.

This time, she laughed. Alex had her at ease, once again marveling at the deference people give to the police.

"Can I have your name?" he asked, and her face darkened just a bit.

"Oh, it's just so I know who I talked to and didn't talk to," he said nervously.

"My name is Mary Dutch," she stated. "Do you need to see my driver's license?"

"No, it's fine. Obviously, I believe you." He had his Global out, and he was taking notes.

"Um, okay, Mary, did you see or hear anything out of the ordinary a couple of nights ago, around midnight?" he asked. It was the standard question.

"Oh, are you talking about that terrible accident that happened? No, I didn't hear anything." She was clear and truthful.

"I am usually up at that hour, but I just moved in, and I was exhausted. I must have slept through quite a noise!"

Mary's eyes sparked and widened at the thought of the accident.

"Were the officers killed, detective?" Her face was grave, and Alex loved her even more.

If I could just preserve her face just like that, maybe in clear epoxy?

"Did you hear or see anything *later* that night?" He feared the pain that could be inflicted through his nano-machines.

"Yes, there was a generator, a tent, and lights. It seemed like there was daylight in the one area down there. At the time, I didn't know what had happened. It was just a loud nuisance. I feel guilty for feeling that way, knowing what happened." Alex felt sympathy for her. It was an unfamiliar sensation.

"No, no, it's understandable. From what I hear, they were found around two-thirty a.m. by an insomniac out for a night walk. I'm sure that he will change his route from now on," he chuckled a little at his last quip, and she did, too.

Oh man, she has a dark side too! Alex thought to himself.

He wanted to find a reason to stay longer and talk to her. Surprisingly, she reached up, standing on her tiptoes. Her long, lithe body stretched to the heavens, for God knew what.

She grabbed a ring in the ceiling and pulled down.

"Oh, you might want to step back," Mary warned as she pulled down what looked like a couch that had been hiding in the ceiling.

"Wow!" Alex said, stepping aside.

"Hey, it's the future. We can have transforming rooms now." Her smile lit up his dark heart.

"Have a seat; I was about to put on some tea when you knocked.

Would you like some?"

"Yes, please!" he answered happily. Mary giggled again, and his heart skipped a beat.

"Okay, I'll be right back!" She seemed to float away into the kitchen.

Alex desperately tried to come up with legitimate questions to keep himself here for a few more minutes.

She returned in a few moments with two cups of tea.

"Would you like sugar or milk?" she asked.

"No, I am fine," he was about to launch into the questions he had come up with when Mary exclaimed.

"Oh no! I have class in a few minutes." She looked truly hurt. "I have a tele-dance class in five minutes."

"Tele-dance class? You teach dance on a computer?" Alex asked, surprised.

"No, I use the holo-emitters." She pointed up to the corners of the room near the ceiling. Small baseball-sized mirrors sat nestled in their corners.

"Wow, those are expensive emitters!" he said.

"You must do pretty good for yourself to be able to afford something like that. Your halo rig looks like it's state of the art," Alex observed.

"Oh, I do very well, Mr. Detective." She shook her head playfully.

"Do you have a card?" she asked as she moved him to the door.

"Why yes, I do!" Alex said a little too excitedly and produced one.

"Okay, how about I call you when I am free, say tomorrow at lunch, and we can talk about this horrible case." She said this so cheerfully, and with such conviction, he couldn't help but go along.

"Okay...I uh, look forward to your call." Then he was outside the door, and it was closed. She was gone just like that.

Robert Cross' voice intruded on his reverie.

"Okay, let's go to the next house. Hopefully, this person had a camera mounted at the perfect angle to see everything that happened." He went to the next home and found no one home. Alex looked around and saw no one. He quickly picked the lock and entered.

The house was typically furnished. It looked like a small working family lived there. There were no holo-emitters in any of the rooms, so they were not telecommuting in any way, it seemed. No cameras were facing the street.

"Well, Boss, I don't see cameras, and since no one is here, there is no one to ask what they saw. Can we go?"

"Obviously, Alex," was the only response.

Alex left the townhouse quietly. He looked to the last home on his list. He knocked on the door and heard it echo through the apartment. Alex took out his Global and checked the address; it was listed for sale.

"Hey, boss..."

"No," was all he got.

"Why not?" Alex asked. "I just moved to San Jose, and I need a place to stay. Plus, this looks like a good place to stay."

"Be honest, Alex. Why do you really want to buy this town house?"

Alex was silent.

"Well?" Mr. Cross pressed.

"Look, sure, I want to get to know Ms. Dutch a little better, but this is also a good starting point, and surveillance of the area may yield a lead in the long term."

There was only a hearty laugh on the other side.

"It's good to see you are still having some normalcy about you, boy!" Mr. Cross chuckled, and Alex eventually joined in.

"Fine, I will make sure you get this place. However, the second I think you are becoming distracted, I will burn this place and everyone that lives here to the ground." The ice in Mr. Cross' voice was palpable.

"Yes, Mr. Cross," was the only available answer.

"Good, let's get you settled in," Mr. Cross said. The cheer returned to his voice.

CHAPTER 14

We were standing in a room that was under my Coach's house. It was bigger than any basement I ever saw, and it was in California. There are typically no basements in a state where there are earthquakes, but here we were. Saphronia and Ian were sitting several feet away, watching Coach and me work out.

"Uh... Coach?" I raised my hand to get his attention.

"What if there is an earthquake while we are down here?"

"There won't be," he was matter-of-fact about it. How could he be so sure? I was starting to feel claustrophobic. The walls, which were very far away, began to close in. I took a deep breath and did some four-count breathing, and the trapped feeling began to pass. I took a deep breath and fixated on Coach. When I looked up, he was staring at me. I stared back.

"As I was saying. You have to find the access in your mind." Coach was in full teaching mode; his hands were clasped behind his back, and he was explaining and telling stories.

"The way you use your powers is the same way you use your body to fight. We don't know what you can or cannot do yet. So today, we will find out."

Yesterday, Coach showed up at my house. At the time, I thought the police were there to arrest me, so I was surprised to see my mentor.

I was so confused; he somehow knew what happened the night before. Then my parents came from the kitchen, and my dad thanked him for coming so fast. My jaw fell to the floor.

San Jose, California, March 13, 10:30 a.m. PST.

"I'm sorry, but what the hell is going on here?" My voice was loud for the space.

"First of all, you better watch your volume and tone, young man!" My mom was stern.

"But you knew this happened to me and didn't say anything?"

"We were under orders, son. My dad was always the peacemaker.

"From whom? What is going on?" The world was coming apart at the seams.

"From me," Adrian said. "It wasn't time, and I wanted to be here to talk to you with your parents."

He was looking at me with such compassion, tears sprang to my eyes.

"What?" was all I could say. I was such a crybaby.

"Sit down, you guys," Adrian gestured to the couch.

"First, I want to say that what is happening to you is relatively normal."

"Relative to who?" Ian asked.

"Good question, Ian. It's normal for people like me who are dispatched to retrieve new Emergents like Scipio."

"So, you were sent here to help me understand my powers?" My mind was working in overdrive.

"But I've known you since I was nine. How did you know I would have powers?"

"Well, that is where it's kind of complicated," Adrian admitted.

I nodded my head as if to say, Go on.

"Well, son, we have a lot to tell you, too," my mom said sadly.

Did I say I was confused?

"What the hell is happening?"

"Scip, just calm down," Adrian said.

I immediately felt better. I knew it was going to be okay, and all I had to do was listen. There had to be a perfectly reasonable explanation for all of this. Right?

My mom was staring at Adrian. I recognized the look of impending doom.

"What?" Adrian shrugged, "It will help," he said.

"Okay, this time," she warned quietly.

"Listen, Scipio, this is going to be a lot of information, and it's going to change your entire world, but it is all the truth. I ...we have never lied to you," he said, pointing to my parents.

The funny thing is, I was perfectly calm. So were Ian and Saphronia. They just sat there listening like this was all something they had heard before.

A paranoid thought started to form in my mind, but it vanished as fast as it began to form. *What was happening to me?*

"The world is a strange place," Adrian began. His voice was gentle, and it was blending into me somehow.

A very well-rendered globe appeared and hung in the air between all of us; small lights flickered to life all over the blue ball. I didn't remember syncing my Global with anyone. The little lights were golden, and they glittered playfully. I stared at the globe, unblinking. A small voice deep inside my mind screamed in alarm. *Whoa!*

"There are eight billion people on this planet. It is estimated that of that number, one percent of one percent of the people have abilities that can slightly affect the physical world. Of that group, it is estimated that only 80k of those people have access to abilities they can control, be it physical, psionic, or what we call magic. Of that small number of people, ninety-five percent of them are of direct African descent. That estimate was from the year you were born. As of today, nearly eighteen years later, the total operant population is 2.5 million, and of that number, 95 percent are of direct African descent, both with a plus or minus of five percent. The percentage never changed."

The feeling of gently falling enveloped me, but I was not surprised.

Adrian's voice seemed to come from everywhere. For a moment, I almost felt force-fed, like the information he was telling us was being pushed down my mental throat, and then it was gone. The globe spun lazily, and lights filled the landmasses. I knew they were people. *How was this happening?*

The lights dwindled to what seemed like a precious few jewels in a vast, dark, and terrifying world. Adrian continued to speak.

"Over the past year, there has been a sharp increase in the number of operant people. We call them Enhanced Powered Beings or EPBs."

The number of lights increased, being spread out around the world. The globe turned slowly before us, and Adrian continued. *Was Adrian controlling it?*

"As in ancient times, Mother Africa was the birthplace of a new page in human evolution. Over the centuries, the Western world abused and used the Motherland to within a proverbial inch of her life, but Africa is strong, and her people are a testament to her strength. The hardships of disease, famine, and impoverishment pushed the human form to adapt and overcome. Emergence has happened and is happening worldwide, but once again, America proves itself peculiar.

"The cruelty and savagery of slavery here in America were the catalyst. In 1808, breeding pens were created, or rather ramped up, when, for all intents and purposes, it became illegal to buy slaves directly from Africa. The northern slave states had an abundance of slaves because of their shift to a less labor-intensive crop. However, the Deep South states transitioned to cotton, which had a shorter turnaround but was significantly more labor-intensive. Not to mention the recent invention of the cotton gin. The plantations needed bodies, and the northern slave states were ready to make a deal. To keep up stock, places like the breeding farms in Richmond, Virginia, and the Eastern shore of Maryland bred the slaves indiscriminately. They would put bags over the heads of both parties so they couldn't recognize each other. This was done on a massive scale.

"However, nature finds a way, and in what we call the Rejoining, the scattered genetic fragments of our powerful foremother were brought together, albeit forcefully. The compelled mixing of the different African ethnicities and under the oppressive conditions of American slavery, formed an unprecedented jewel in humankind. The once desperate human tribes' genetic lineage was once again rejoined, creating a genetic bridge almost directly to the fore-mothers of African heritage, resulting in people like you.

"Fortunately, Gia is not afraid to use trial and error. While you are the chosen repository- we believe- millions of other configurations have been born. This is why there are so many more EPBs.

"It is believed that more is yet to come, but no one knows what the more is. Anything is possible."

The room regained its previous light, and the unearthly globe vanished.

I studied Adrian for a long moment, and he returned my gaze and did not look away. It seemed like he was waiting for me to say something, but I only had one question that kept swimming to the forefront of my brain.

"Who sent you?"

Adrian sighed deeply. I felt as though I had failed some hidden test.

"I am a part of a small group called the Nine Ghana's. We borrowed the name from African history. That's a whole other story. Our Elder is named East, and she sent me. She is a part of the Amanirenan Resistance. To put it bluntly, she sent all of us for you," he said, letting the statement hang in the air like toxic smoke.

I was just staring at Adrian, expecting him to go on. Then I looked around, and everyone had an oddly expectant facial expression except Ian and Saphronia. It took a moment for my mind to catch up to what Adrian was saying.

"Wait, what do you mean us?" I didn't know who else he could have been talking about.

"Sweety, I am so sorry; we love you very much," my mom said.

Usually, in American society, Black people are expected to carry a great deal of trauma and pain without the slightest indication of their misery. We are expected to absorb ridicule and second-hand justice at best and still be sane. If we get *angry*, we are called the angry Black man, labeled dangerous, and reduced to a caricature of our own suffering. I have been beaten by police for no reason, constantly stopped by the same, and made to believe it was my fault for looking suspicious. I was not allowed to get mad and was taught to turn the other cheek if a White person, or any person for that matter, was racist toward me. I tried to be non-threatening to people who assumed my guilt before they could think of a crime I may have committed. However, this was too much for me. Just the suggestion of my life being a lie was overwhelming.

"What does that mean?" I turned to face her. My *anger* was there; I could feel it, but it was contained somehow. I was not screaming at them.

"Well, son, it means we are more of your guardians than we are your parents. We are family. In fact, we are your Aunt and Uncle. The Resistance tasked us with keeping you safe and helping you to explore your abilities if they manifested early. When the school system started targeting you, we sent word to East that we were having trouble protecting you, so they sent Adrian." Mom paused to gather her thoughts, and Adrian jumped in.

"Scipio, I know it all seems like a lot of life-shattering knowledge, but we are not lying, and we genuinely love you." Adrian was trying to calm me, but I felt fine. I could feel I was angry, but I didn't feel out of control. I assumed that part would come later. In the movies, the *hero* is confronted with a piece of life-changing information, and they usually run off, but I didn't feel that way.

"Why?" was the only word I could muster. Adrian took another deep breath.

"Well, you are a Scion of our Mitochondrial Eve. Meaning you are a reconstituted direct descendant of her," Adrian tried to explain.

"What do you mean 'reconstituted'?" I was trying to wrap my head around the reality of the situation and my lack of reaction.

"As far as we can tell, your birth parents had forty percent of her DNA combination each. The more of her DNA you have, the more complete and more operant your ascendency or ascendancies will be," Adrian explained, "You have eighty to ninety percent of her operant DNA chain. When the Rejoining of the tribes happened, a genetic roulette started to happen. It was slow, as nature tends to be, but it was happening, nonetheless. The slave breeding farms sped the process. Eventually, your parents were produced and found each other. Then they made you."

"Also, the closer you get to a pure strain of her DNA, the *more* ascendancies you have available to be operant," my mom added. I looked at all of them; it was like I was full of information and couldn't digest anymore, but I had questions that needed answering.

"First, who were my real parents, and what happened to them? Second, what are ascendancies? And third, why are the police lying about what happened last night?" I pushed for information, but I couldn't form the question I really wanted to ask. The answer would be too much.

Adrian spoke up first.

"We will get to your real parents in a moment. However, your second question is much easier to answer."

Once again, my brain felt invaded with information.

"An ascendency is a specific ability trait that one may have. I always tried to get you to watch sci-fi shows just for this purpose," Adrian attempted to lighten the mood, but I was laser-focused and unsmiling.

"Do you remember a long time ago when you were about twelve or thirteen, and you had to get your blood taken?"

"Yeah?" I was not sure where he was going with this.

"Well, we were able to do a genetic assay on you, and our science team was able to determine that you have access to at least three full ascendancies. So far, from what you have told us, you have some version of kinetic manipulation and telepathy. Unfortunately, your third ascendency has yet to reveal itself. You may have more, but as of now, they are latent, meaning you can't access them."

"Well, how am I supposed to find out what the third one is and if I have more?" I could feel my emotions start to rise and then fall to normal levels. I didn't feel right. It occurred to me that someone was manipulating my emotions. *Could it be Adrian?*

"What ascendancies do you have, Adrian?" I asked pointedly.

"Well, before we get to that, let me answer your third question."

"Why won't you answer my question, Adrian?" I said his name in the most disrespectful way I could.

"I will, Scip; I just want to get to your questions first," Adrian's voice was low and comforting. He was also an expert in de-escalation.

"No, you're not. You are avoiding my questions." It felt like my brain was going to explode. I was pushing against a wall that was somehow blocking my emotions.

"Okay, okay, stop it, Scip, I'll answer your questions."

My mom got up, went to the kitchen, and came back with a glass of water for Adrian. That was it, that was the straw that broke the horse's, camel's, whatever's back.

"Why did you get *him* water, *Mom*?" I jumped to my feet and faced her. I saw Adrian start to get up out of the corner of my eye, but my guardian gestured for him to remain seated.

"You're mad, I know, and I understand. Your father and I love you very much."

"The hell you do!" I yelled.

"Easy, son," was all my uncle said.

I looked directly into his eyes and said, "You aren't even my real father. Why should I do what you say?"

I had always thought I got my temper from my 'dad' because he had an explosive temper, and sometimes he would say something mean because to him, every disagreement was a contest, and he would be damned if he lost. My aunt was so caught up in the heat of the moment that she missed seeing my uncle about to lose his temper.

"I knew your father very well. He was *my* brother, and when the SOTIR Group killed your parents, we did what any family would do; we stepped up. But we had to hide in plain sight because the SOTIR Group never rests." I was in shock! He just said it like it was an everyday occurrence to find out you don't have parents.

"Your real parents were extraordinary operatives. You were their treasure. I remember your mother telling us shortly after you were born that you would be a game-changer in the War." I had never seen my *dad* cry; he was a throwback to stoic men, now tears streamed down his face as he thought of his brother and his wife, my real parents.

"Your parents were true heroes. They didn't believe in hiding from the SOTIR Group or the World. They actively sought to disrupt and destroy any and all of the SOTIR Group's plans. They were very good at their job."

Adrian said, "I trained them as best and as thoroughly as I could. Your dad had a strong expression of his ascendancy. He had a min-max version of pyrokinesis; he could make a tiny flame like a lighter or a massive fireball, but nothing in between. He was a fierce warrior. Your mother was fierce as well; she could heal people, and she had a smidgeon of telepathy. Which is where you get yours from." I just stared at him.

"Dude, what are you talking about?" This was starting to get out of hand. The more they talked, the more confused I got.

I closed my eyes and took a deep breath.

I figured if I could focus on one thing, I could eventually handle the rest. I knew some things for sure. One: No one here ever wanted to or tried to hurt me. Two: As fantastic as this all sounded, I knew what happened the night before actually happened. Three: I needed more information, and my family had the answers.

I opened my eyes and asked, "Who is the SOTIR Group, and why did they kill my real parents?"

"The real answer is they were too disruptive and cost the SOTIR Group substantial sums of money," Adrian answered, "but I suspect they were getting close to something, but I don't know what it was."

"I may have an idea," my *dad* said.

"Your birthday is next week, and something came in the mail for you." My dad had a resigned look in his eyes, "I opened it and read some of the letter."

"Paul?" my mom said sharply.

"What?" I was annoyed he would go through my mail.

"Look, son, it is our job to protect you, and I recognized the handwriting as Jamal's, so I wanted to see it first to make sure it was something you could handle."

"I am not *a* child, nor am I *your* child, so you had no business *opening my mail*!" I screamed the last part of my sentence, and it felt like a relief. It felt good to express my anger. But just as fast as I was able to find a way to express my wrath, the feeling of white-hot anger faded, and I watched it disappear. Someone was controlling my emotions; I could feel it. It was helping me absorb these impossible blows. I locked eyes with Coach Adrian, and I knew.

Coach, can you hear me? I thought loudly at him.

Adrian winced... *Yes, Scip! I hear you. No need to shout.*

Why are you blocking my emotions?

I'm helping, not hurting, trust, trust, trust.

Maybe-Yes-please-don't-LEAVE-me.

Never!

The exchange happened in a fraction of a second, and we were in the real world again.

Coach said, "We will get to that; let me answer your questions." After the mental exchange. I was in a completely different mindset. I understood what needed to happen and knew that the answers I needed only started here.

San Jose, California, March 13, 11:10 a.m. PST.

"I mentioned the SOTIR Group earlier; they are the enemy, to put it simply. They are as old as American slavery. They were started by a man named James Cross, and one of his descendants, Robert Cross, runs the SOTIR Group with two other people, Lilly Roth and Allen Berg."

I interrupted, *"The* Allen Berg, the tech genius?"

"Yes, unfortunately, he makes staying off the grid nearly impossible. Anyway, the SOTIR Group lives in fear of people like us and the extinction of the *White* race. James Cross encountered an operant EPB and decided to begin to hunt them, and they have been doing it ever since. They have their hands in everything and everywhere. They all but control the police."

"Of course, they do. Don't all big, bad guys own the police?" I said, rolling my eyes dramatically.

When Adrian said Allen Berg was a part of this, I almost walked out. It was such a conspiracy theory thing to do; declare the most prominent tech genius in the world is one of the heads of a global cabal to kill Black people with superpowers, except for three crucial things.

One: again, last night had happened. I wasn't going crazy or hallucinating. Ian recorded it. My best friend is brilliant and even tech-savvy, but he is *not* a videographer nor a special effects wizard. What I watched was real. The memories were real.

Two: the mental conversation I just had with Coach was real. Thoughts are pure. They are uncorrupted by speech because the information you are trading has more than words in it. There are emotions and sensations all wrapped up in the message. It was a sixth sense; once I experienced it, I couldn't unknow it. Also, what happened to me in the hospital was real.

Three: This was the most important one. The people in this room are the people I love and trust the most. Well, except for Saphronia, I mean, I do trust her, but I do not really know her. I mean, we just met, but we kind of were in this thing together. I could not leave her out. So yeah, these were the people I loved and trusted, and I do not think they would all get together to lie to me. Why would they? Why something like this? What would they gain by this? Then something occurred to me. What if I'm still in the coma, and this is all the coma? Well then, hell yeah, let's go! The way I saw it, it was a win-win.

Besides, it was safer to accept the evidence before me; if this SOTIR Group was a real threat, then it would be stupid to waste time denying all the things I knew to be true. They already killed my birth parents. If this was the universe where I was on some kind of hero team, let's play it smart. Okay, I was pouring it on there at the end, but I did not want to be the guy who died because I was too busy trying to prove it was all fake. Actually, I didn't want to die at all, but I did want to help people. Probably one of the nobler reasons someone volunteers for military service. Maybe I could do some good in this world. If I was a Scion, then perhaps I had a responsibility.

I trusted my Ancestors.

The room had gone quiet, and the stillness brought me back to the moment.

"Where did you go?" Adrian asked softly.

Shaking my head, I said, "I was making the leap."

I thank you, Coach. I thought at him, and Coach's eyes widened, and he smiled.

"Good, that should make things a lot easier. Thank you for trusting us, Scip."

"You don't have to convince me this SOTIR Group is bad or give me a detailed history lesson. Just tell me why the police are lying and why the news doesn't know."

"Well, Scip, they *are* probably looking for you, the dash-cam footage was probably sent up the chain to them, and they have an idea of what you can do." My heart dropped. I was about to ask a bunch of questions when Saphronia spoke for the first time in a long while.

"There is no dashcam footage."

"And how would you know that?" Adrian wanted to know.

"Because I erased it," Saphronia said.

"What?" Adrian shot to his feet. *Were his hands glowing red a little bit?*

"Wait, wait!" I was yelling, "Coach, what is going on?"

I looked at Saphronia, "What do you mean you erased it? I never saw you go near the cruiser." Saphronia was quiet, but her eyes were locked with mine.

"Scipio, I was sent here to find you."

"By whom?" Coach shouted. There was a deep hum in the room now, and Coach's hands were definitely glowing red.

"Wait, wait," I thundered, "let her answer before you zap her, Coach."

"My mother sent me. She told me a similar story, but I was not as accepting of it as you are, Scipio." Saphronia's eyes remained locked on me. "When I was thirteen, my mother and my Vovo told me I would have to come to California to find a boy that was like me."

"What do you mean like you?" Adrian demanded.

"Well," she started. Saphronia stretched out her hand toward the TV. A transparent bubble appeared around the screen, and it rose into the air. The TV spun slowly in the golden-hued bubble, then settled back down onto the entertainment center.

A breeze caressed my teeth, and I realized my mouth was hanging open.

"What the..." My mind was utterly blown. It was one thing to realize you have abilities, but quite another to see other people have and use them.

The more subtle punch came when I realized she said she was sent here to find *me*. My spirit dipped. I thought we had a connection, but apparently, it was a setup.

"So, you were just trying to get close to me? So, you could, what, kill me?" Oh man, I was taking this hero-of-the-story idea a little far.

Saphronia's eyes pleaded with me. She still was locking eyes with me.

"*No*, Scipio, I really do like you," she clapped her hands over her mouth, and her eyes opened wide!

"Oh, Ancestors!" The words were muffled, but I caught them. She shook her head and simply faded away.

"Saphronia!" I reached out and grabbed where I thought her arm was. She reappeared when I touched her.

"Did I just disappear?" Her clear accent was thicker.

"Yeah," I said, "Where were you going?"

"I was not leaving. When I get embarrassed, I disappear sometimes."

"Don't be embarrassed." I wasn't captivated by her gaze anymore; she was caught in mine. If I had known at the time I was that smooth, I would have said something cooler.

"We are all friends here," the words just fell out of my mouth.

Saphronia nodded her head solemnly, and I was backing away with a goofy smile on my face when Coach roughly pushed me aside.

"Hey!" I blurted out.

"Finish your story, Saphronia," Adrian said in a congenial tone. "You were saying your mother and grandmother sent you here." I could not tell if Coach was being sarcastic or genuine.

Saphronia started off in a small voice.

CHAPTER 15

Under Hollister, California, March 14, 12:05 p.m. PST.

I was jolted out of my memory by hitting the floor and hearing Saphronia and Ian shouting in surprise.

"You need to pay attention. Wherever you were right now was not here, and I made you pay," Coach moved back to his starting spot. I could not figure out how he moved fifteen feet without being seen. I know I was distracted, but I would have at least heard his footsteps.

"How did you do that, Coach? I never saw you coming." "Because you weren't paying attention," he said, smirking at me.

I tilted my head in disbelief.

"Pay attention, and you won't be surprised." I was looking right at Coach, and he just blinked out.

"What?" We were all astonished.

Suddenly, I was catching a kick to the head. My head slammed to the floor. I did not feel dazed or dizzy. Propping myself on my hand, I swept my leg out and kicked Adrian's feet out from under him. Before he hit the mat, he disappeared again.

I felt the air change above me, and heat prickled on my neck. I rolled to the side. Adrian's knee came crashing down where I had been. I rolled up to a crouching position, raised my hand, and imagined a punch coming out of it.

I was aiming for Coach's chest, and the blow hit him just below his sternum. He folded and rolled head over heels twice. I felt a recoil in my body.

"Ohhhhh!" Ian and Saphronia exclaimed together.

I was already running to Coach's side. I could hear him coughing. *Oh man, I killed him!* I expected to see a fist-sized hole in his chest. Instead, he was laughing.

"Good hit, Scip. I didn't see that coming," Coach coughed and sat up. He looked down at his chest, and there was a light singe mark there.

"Looks like you had a little heat on that one."

"I don't know how I did it. I felt like I was pushing a punch toward you, and then it happened."

"Yeah, it's like I was telling you. You must think of your ability as an extension of yourself. You," Adrian gestured to all of us, "we all can affect the world around us in a way other people can't." Coach climbed to his feet noisily.

"Your ability is offensive and defensive." Coach waited for me to catch up.

"How do you know it's defensive?" It perplexed me how he could make an assertion like that. I glanced over to Saphronia and Ian. They both shrugged.

Coach chuckled, "I kicked you to the ground earlier, and your head bounced off the floor. It's not padded like at the studio." I looked down as he was talking. What the heck? I should have been bleeding from a cracked skull, or at least my nose should be bleeding.

"What's going on?" I was baffled.

"It seems you have some kind of resistance or immunity to physical attacks."

"Wait, you kicked me as hard as you could; how did you know I had anything like that?"

Coach just laughed. I stared at him in shock.

"Why are you laughing?" I was more than annoyed.

"Remember when those cops stopped you outside of my studio?"

"Yeah," I replied, wondering where he was going with this.

"What do you think they were hitting you with?" His eyebrows were up; Coach had the worst poker face.

I sagged. "Can you just tell me? I'm tired," I whined.

Coach just shook his head.

"Ugh, I guess their fists and a baton? I mean, it didn't hurt; you have hit me harder than they were. At least it felt that way." I started to see what Coach was getting at.

"They were hitting you with batons, not fists. One of the officers was kicking you in your legs with all his might, and you didn't budge," Coach said, crinkling his chin.

"What?" Again, I glanced at Ian and Saphronia. They looked as surprised as I did.

"I have wanted to test my theory for a while now, but I wasn't sure how or when. Today presented a perfect opportunity to test it."

"Well, I am glad you were right, I guess." This was good information. I had not felt that much pain that day; I assumed they were pushing on me really hard. I hadn't thought about that day until now. So much has happened. I wondered if I was bulletproof. Oh man, I would never have to be afraid of the police again. I could make that difference I wanted to make in the lives of people like me. The wave of excitement I had been riding over the past couple of days lifted me, and I felt I could save the world.

"Okay, Saphronia, your turn." Coach was waving Saphronia over. She stood up meekly at first, but I could see her confidence fill her up as she got closer.

"Thank you, Sir, but I don't need to practice. I know how to use my abilities effectively."

I smiled to myself. *Good luck with that one, Saphronia,* I thought to myself as I went to sit next to Ian.

"Hey, buddy!" I nudged him as I sat. Ian and I had sat in this position many times, watching Coach teach someone else.

"Hey," was all he said.

"What's up, Ian?"

"Nothing, man," he said, and I turned and looked at him.

"Ian, I have known you since forever; I know when something is wrong. What is it?"

He returned my gaze, and I could see hurt in his blue eyes.

"You guys are all going to leave me." Flashes of my mental conversation with Coach came to mind.

Please-don't-leave-me. I had begged in terror.

I put on my best reassuring smile.

"Ian, I don't know about anyone else, but I will not leave you."

"C'mon, man, you got superpowers, and you are going up against an evil cabal of evil." Ian brought his knees to his chest and rested his chin on his crossed arms. I knew this pouting look.

"Dude, c'mon, we are in this together. What if we need an infiltrator or someone to pose as one of the bad guys? You are the perfect candidate."

Ian whipped his head up and looked at me so intensely that I was taken aback.

"I don't think like them, Scipio. I don't hate!" Ian said, clearly offended. Man, I did not mean to insult him.

"I didn't say you did; I was just trying to say you are a valuable member of the team, and I could not imagine this adventure without you." I was trying to show Ian my heart. My friend Ian always stood with me. On the few times I was stopped by the police while he was there, he always stood with me. One time, he even got arrested for jumping on the back of a cop that was wrestling me to the ground for no reason. We were ten, and Ian's dad is well-connected, so nothing actually happened. Except for the cop that threw the ten-year-old blonde-haired blue-eyed boy to the ground, he got fired. Not because he was beating up a ten-year-old Black boy. Ian has always had my back, and I would always have his. The day we met, I was saving him from bullies.

The fire in Ian's eyes lessened. I held out my hand, "We are in this together, promise?"

He grabbed my hand, "Promise." We shook hands the way we had since elementary school.

Having saved my friendship, I turned my attention to Coach and Saphronia, but they were just talking in low tones, and I could not hear everything they were saying.

My mind drifted back to her explanation of why she was there.

San Jose, California, March 13, 11:40 a.m. PST.

Saphronia's voice started soft and timid but rapidly became strong and clear.

"My Vovo is," she shook her head slightly, "*was* a precognitive, meaning she could see the future. When she was younger, she used her ability to get what she wanted, but my Vovo realized the more she used it, the better and clearer the visions got. Over time, she could see further and further, but one day she couldn't see past a certain point in time. She was obviously curious about why this was, and she began to investigate. She was able to pull bits and pieces of information from her visions. She built a picture of an enemy that she could not name but was certain existed. Eventually, she started a family, and she noticed her vision changed a bit. She could see the next day, when she had a daughter, the next day was revealed, and when I was born, she saw another day, farther, and a face of a young man was prominent in her vision. When you were hurt in the tournament, she saw your face in the news and recognized you immediately." Saphronia took a breath, and a glass of water not very mysteriously showed up. My mom believed in the power of water.

"I have been training in one way or another since I was five. My abilities manifested early. I was and still am an adventurous, and some say, headstrong child." Saphronia's face lit up with a smile.

"One day, I climbed to the roof of a neighbor's house, and I lost my footing and fell off. When I came to, I was scared but uninjured. I remember falling and thinking I was going to die, and not knowing what that meant. Apparently, I created a protective field around myself, and it shielded me from my fall. When my mother and Vovo came home, the neighbors told them what happened. They hugged me and cried, but they also intensified my training and taught me to use my abilities competently. It was hard for a while because I could not tell anyone about my powers, and we could only train at night. I still had to attend school and keep my grades up. Several weeks ago, your school offered an exchange student program that was open to anyone in the name of cultural exchange. My mother jumped at the idea and wanted me to submit my application." Saphronia took a sip of water.

"I didn't want to go because my Vovo had just passed away, and I wanted to be with my family. However, my mother said this was the fate of the future, and I need to fulfill Vovo's mission." Saphronia sighed and shook her head sadly.

"My mother invoked the Ancestors on me. What could I say but yes?"

"How did you know how to find me?" I asked.

Saphronia laughed beautifully and said, "My Vovo became an adept hacker. It turns out she could figure out passwords using her precognition. We already knew your name and high school from the news story, so all we had to do was get me in as an exchange student. But we had to hope that someone in your school would want to participate in the exchange program." Saphronia paused and smiled nervously.

"I was only supposed to meet you and stay close in case anything happened," she shrugged, "I guess something happened. Vovo was always right."

"So why should we trust you?" Adrian asked her curtly.

"I don't know, maybe you can read my mind or something," Saphronia said, still only looking at me. At first, her gaze was a welcome thing, but now I began to feel uncomfortable, and I looked away.

"I don't know how to do that, Saphronia. I'm not like you. I only learned about powers last night, under duress," I tried to explain.

"Well, I don't know what to say then," Saphronia said, "I was sent here to help by my Vovo, and I intend to do that whether you accept me or not."

Adrian turned to me and said, "Try to see if she is telling the truth."

"What? How? I don't know how to read people's minds." I lied.

"Get up," Coach was pulling me up by my arm, "take her hand and try to read her mind. We have to know if she is dangerous or not."

"But..." I flailed.

Adrian grabbed our hands and put them together. I could feel my face flushing, and I couldn't bring my eyes to meet Saphronia's.

"Look at her," Adrian commanded.

I looked at my parents for some help, and they both looked like they were watching a sparring match. So, no help at all. I glanced over at Ian, and he was grinning from ear to ear. I felt prickly heat crawl up my back and over my scalp. I was so embarrassed that everyone was just staring at me.

...you hear me!

It was a careful whisper. I only experienced it for a moment, but it was Saphronia.

Our eyes met.

I fell into those brown pools. Splashing from this world into hers. Saphronia's mind was mostly open to me. There were shadows where my mind could not go. I heard her call to me, and I turned to look around, and she was there. She smiled at me.

"You heard me!"

"Yeah, it was like you were whispering to me."

"Yes, my mother is slightly telepathic, and she taught me some tricks. Not yelling in someone's mind is one of them."

"Oh, that's a good lesson," I looked around, "where are we?"

"This is an astral construct. My mother taught me as I will teach you," she smiled at me, and I wanted to believe her. There was a table between us, and a box appeared.

"Open it," she pushed it toward me.

"What is it?

"The truth," her answer was sardonic.

I looked down at the box; I didn't know why, but I felt this horrible sense that this was a trap.

I glanced up at her; she returned my gaze, and the horrible feeling fell away. I took a deep breath and opened the box.

The story she told us was there in memory form. I heard Saphronia's mother tell the stories, and I watched her Vovo's last breath say, "Find him and help him."

"I will, Vovo," Saphronia sobbed. I felt the promise bind her heart to the duty.

Bang! The memory stopped. I could feel the truth in the memory, but something was off. I blinked and shook my head. I started to ask about the place or room we were in.

Instead, she said, "Okay, time to go!" She stepped up to me and pushed on my chest.

"W...." was all I could say before I was shot out of the room and her mind.

Suddenly, I was back in the room and aware of my surroundings. The eyes of everyone in the room were staring at me.

"I trust her."

Adrian rolled his eyes, and Ian slapped his hands together.

"I knew it!" he exclaimed.

CHAPTER 16

Hollister, California, March 14, 10:30 p.m. PST.

The day of practice ended, and Ian drove Saphronia and me home. Like we had done after that insane night with the police, Ian dropped Saphronia off first and then continued to my house.

"Try to get some sleep tonight, Superhero."

"I will," I bumped the fist he held out with my own.

"Goodnight, Ian," I trudged to my door and went in. The house was quiet, and I could tell my parents were in their room, asleep.

I locked the door and wandered around, checking the windows. My dad was always great at making the rounds, but he taught me well. I was so tired. My body felt like it had been fighting all day *and* night. I craved the warmth of my bed. I padded upstairs and went to my room. One trick I learned today was masking the sound of my feet. I could absorb the vibration of the sound and store the energy for later use. Because I could set it up as a field around my feet, it stopped any sound before my brain registered it. I entered my room, and my bed greeted me with open arms. I was about to fall into the comfort of my bed when a thought occurred to me. I could learn a lot by going back to the scene of the incident with the cops.

I had not told anyone about the door I felt open inside of me. I know I said keeping secrets in this situation was bad, but this seemed, I don't know, not ready to be shared. I was drawn to get in touch with that feeling again. All through practice today, I looked for that door; the power and completeness felt so much like home.

Home.

My real parents were dead, and the people who had been raising me since I could remember were actually my Aunt and Uncle. What kind of messed-up world was this? However, on the flip side, I could fly. I wondered what my parents were like; they sounded brave and determined, but I pondered what my real mom's voice would have sounded like. She was probably a good hugger. I wondered if I looked like my dad. I touched my hair and wondered about their hair.

I sat on my bed, and I felt the last of my energy drain from me. I was so tired, and I had so much to do.

I thought about lifting off the ground for the first time, which brought a smile to my face.

I lay back on the bed; I remember thinking, I should go check out the scene of the crime. I shook my head and rubbed my eyes as the memory of their broken bodies tried to flood my mind.

Shhhhh.

There was a door, and light poured from the edges.

"Whoa!"

Interlude 4

Light flooded my vision, and I raised my hand to cover my eyes. My hand was slender, strong, and dark. The sun was scorching, but I felt comfortable. I looked around and was in a verdant plain. Massive fan leaf trees filled the landscape.

"Ah, welcome, Iklwa," a woman said in a language I did not know, but I understood what she was saying.

"What?"

She laughed, and it rang like a soft symphony of sound.

"I have hijacked your dreams. You were moving too slowly. There are great forces aligned against you that want to do something far worse than kill you," she said.

"Who are you?" I demanded.

"I am a friend in the darkness," the voice said.

"I will give you the knowledge that you need to help you. You were introduced to the mother of us all, and you saw her raw power; she was the seed from which we all sprang." The voice was motherly in its tone.

Something was dropped into the well of my mind, and each ripple it caused was etched with information.

"Now, wake up! Your lesson is over," I was falling, and I realized I had been hovering far above the land. I understood how I'd done it; I felt the knowledge of flying pop into my mind. But it was too late. I was falling, and I couldn't remember how to fly! The green ground rushed up to me.

CHAPTER 17

San Jose, California, March 15, 2:10 a.m. PST.

I lurched awake! My room was still bright, but I could feel the night still around me. I sat up on my bed and rubbed my face. Who was that, and what did she mean I was moving too slowly? I know it sounds weird that I am just accepting her words, but the vision, or dream, was so real. I sat up, and the dream faded but did not disappear; it lingered in the back of my mind. I rubbed my forehead.

I went to the bathroom and then downstairs. I stretched again and headed for the kitchen for a glass of cold water. Something on the small table that flanked the hall caught my eye. I stopped and picked up the letter with my name on it. The writing on the envelope was my mom's handwriting.

"Son, this is the letter your father tried to tell you about." I had almost forgotten the letter my dad mentioned. I picked it up and continued to the kitchen. I poured myself a glass of ice water, sat at the dining room table, and opened the letter.

Dear Scipio,
I hope this letter finds you well, son. Happy Birthday: You are eighteen now and probably have experienced your abilities. We hope you are not scared

or confused. Please do *not* feel cursed or burdened. Your Ancestors blessed you with a gift. You are still human, and you are no better or worse than anyone else. Never forget that!

We have written many of these letters before we go on an excursion, just in case. This is a big one, son. Your mom doesn't think I should tell you, but I'm going to anyway. The Group we are fighting is a major player in human trafficking and slavery. However, they deal exclusively in EPBs like us. Your mother and I have vowed to save as many of our brothers and sisters as possible. Tonight, we received information that may put a big dent in this group's operations. It's risky, but the payoff will be a lot of free people.

You are probably wondering why I put pen to paper. The simple answer is I'm paranoid, but that doesn't mean I am wrong. Berg has his tentacles in everything. Pen and paper are the only way we could get this to you without risk of discovery by him.

If we don't make it back, take up this fight.

We will make sure that these get delivered one week before your eighteenth birthday. Some people get to choose their destiny, and for some, it is chosen for them. We're not saying you have to go out and become some kind of terrorist, but you do have a responsibility to your people everywhere. Of course, you are free to fly off or disappear. (I hope you can fly!) But freedom comes with responsibility. You have the freedom to fly off and do whatever you want, but many others do not. Your mother and I believe that *we MUST try to make the world a better place because we have these abilities.* If we had been there this whole time, we would have taught you that lesson. We would have also taught you to not be a bully. A bully is ignorance wrapped in power. Remember, there is a time for everything, even violence; the skill is to discern what is necessary. Your uncle and your aunt will have taught you these lessons. Your mother and I asked them to keep our death a secret until you were older; please don't be mad at them. They love you as much as we do.

Don't worry, little man, I'll be burning this letter too.

Love,

MOM & DAD.

A tear splashed the paper, and I jumped. I rubbed my hand over my cheek; it was wet. I took a hitching breath and sat there. I could not wrap my mind around what I read. I wanted to be mad at them, but I couldn't find it in me. I WAS proud of them. They were fighting to help people; they were practically superheroes! I smiled, and tears spilled down my cheeks. I had learned to 'fly' yesterday. I found I had complete control of anything in the field I generated. If I expanded the field around myself, I could 'lift' myself. Then with Adrian's help, I learned to internalize the field, and I was able to lift off the ground.

I wanted to get out into the open air. I wanted to fly for my parents. Adrian told me that exposing myself was very dangerous, not only to me but to everyone I care about. Ah, but I wanted to soar and show my parents, and I turned out okay. Besides, it was two-thirty a.m., and this time of night, the world was asleep. You could feel the quietness of the night; no one would see me, especially if I flew really high, well above the clouds. I padded up the stairs like I did earlier and went to my room. I put the letter in my pocket to keep it close. I had some thermal underwear. I know, I know, why would a California city boy have thermal underwear? I do not like to be cold. Also, my dad liked to go camping, and sleeping in a tent outside can get very cold. Anyway, I layered up with a sweater and a coat. I moved to the window, my heart was beating so hard, and I removed the screen and started to step onto the windowsill. I paused because I remembered I would want something to cover my eyes. I turned back to my room and retrieved my swimming goggles.

I went back to the window and, without hesitation, stepped out into the night.

I felt the field pulse to life inside my chest. When I asked Coach how I was flying, he said I was generating a kinetic field, and I could manipulate the field. With my resistance to kinetic damage, I was probably able to fly and maneuver like a fly. Ugh, I hated flies, but it sure would be cool to fly like one.

I launched myself up into the air. I could feel the wind rippling my cheeks. I sliced through the clouds. I paused and twisted in mid-air to look at the other side of them. As I looked out at the cloud cover, my vision got foggy. I closed my eyes to clear them, and I was about to take off my goggles. Memories from my dream filled my mind. I was flying and twisting in the air. I could feel my shoulders moving and my hips turning. In my memory, I was flying and stopping and turning this way and that. I knew I was in complete control. The voice told me to extend the field like a shaped bubble to keep the wind out of my face. Then, just as swiftly as it came, the fog receded from my mind and my eyes. But in its place was the skill to fly. I was happy for the cloud cover because I could play in the air. I rolled and flipped. I could turn at a ninety-degree angle with ease; I chose a random direction and flew as fast as I could. I counted to sixty in my head and stopped. It was not precisely sixty seconds, obviously, but I was confident it was close. When I started, I checked the GPS on my Global, and I was over San Jose at the start of my run. Now my Global said I was over Stockton.

Wow! That was almost one hundred miles, as the crow flies, in sixty seconds. I did the math in my head and came up with 6000 miles per hour.

"Holy hell!" I exclaimed.

As I floated there, suspended by my own will, a desire to see the scene where my abilities came forward for the first time filled my mind. I checked my Global's GPS and headed in the direction it showed. I didn't push myself as hard because I wasn't sure how long I could keep this up. My arms and legs weighed a ton each. I flew at about twenty-five percent of my speed. It was like jogging instead of sprinting. As it turned out, that was way faster than it seemed because I overshot my destination.

"Recalculating route," my Global informed me, "make a U-turn," she ordered.

I shook my head in surprise. I stopped and checked my location. I was twenty-five miles past my destination. I turned a lazy arc through the clouds and flew much slower.

Eventually, I was over the park where it happened. All the police investigation stuff I saw on the news was gone, and the park was quiet and empty. I flew about a block away and found a secluded place to set down. I was able to expand my *Quiet Field* and make a silent landing. I walked casually to the park and stood outside of the remaining police tape. My mind was filled with grand ideas and plans to help people and save the world. I thought of my parents and the letter they wrote for me, and how happy and confident my dad sounded in the letter. A big smile grew on my face. The world seemed brighter and less hopeless; for the first time, I felt like I had a direction to go in and was not just trying to avoid the police and their unfocused cruelty. My dad (*uncle? I wasn't sure*) always said I was a fixer. He taught me a quote from a great man who passed a few years earlier. His name was John Lewis, and he said,

"When you see something that is not right, not fair, not just, you have to speak up. You have to say something; you have to do something."

My dad would always emphasize the word *do.* I always thought he meant protesting or running for office, something civil and customary. Now I see he was passing on the values of my parents. My mom and my dad were faithful to my birth parents' wishes.

I walked around the site. Thinking of all of this. I wanted to put my hoodie up, but I thought someone might see me and call the police. Well, a Black guy walking around a park on the west side of San Jose at three o'clock a.m. was suspicious to a lot of people, hood up or not. I wasn't doing anything wrong, but I didn't want the trouble. I took one more walking lap around the area. They did an excellent job of cleaning the place up; there was no sign of blood or the dent in the ground. I walked casually back to my landing spot behind a store and started home. I had a lot to process, but my decision and direction were clear; I would follow in my parents' footsteps and make them proud.

"I swear by my Ancestors," I muttered under my breath as I walked back to my hiding spot.

CHAPTER 18

West San Jose, California, March 15, 2:45 a.m. PST.

Alex couldn't sleep. Sometimes the nano-machines worked too well or glitched out. He didn't know which, but they seemed to keep him awake as if they knew something was happening. So, he sat in his window, taking in the moonlight and remembering his favorite victims' highlight reel. He was also working on how to ask Mary Dutch, his neighbor, out to dinner. She was unlike anyone he had ever met. She was intelligent, funny, and gorgeous. The little spray of freckles across the bridge of her nose kept coming to his mind. He was smiling and didn't even notice it.

Alex figured out a trick with his little friends. He could stop his eyes from focusing, allowing the image to enter his headspace and the nano-machines to keep watch through his optic and auditory nerves. This helped him meditate and not have to worry about being ambushed. Tonight, the little trick served him well. There was a flash of movement about a block and a half away. Something fell from the sky. The information intruded on his thoughts, and he came back to reality.

Alex craned his neck, trying to see what had fallen. He was just about to take a stroll to find out what it was when a Black man came into view; he was wearing a light blue zip-up hoodie.

Gang member, Alex thought immediately. The subject was walking around the scene of the attack on the police officers. This might have been one of the suspects. A cold, predatory look filled Alex's blue eyes. His 'little friends' could record and save information he picked up from any of his five senses. He also had wireless access to the internet via his 'little friends,' and the same nano-machines that were on his optical and auditory nerves could show him the information. Access to the internet meant access to almost anything connected to it.

Alex watched until he could get a good view of the suspect's face and snapped a picture. He accessed the FBI's National Crime Information Center data via an account Mr. Cross said was his to use without restriction. Alex didn't know how Mr. Cross got his access, but he was sure someone there worked for him.

Nothing came up.

Alex watched him for a few more moments, trying to figure out what the guy was doing out here at two-fifty in the morning. Where did he come from? A big smile appeared on the dark man's face. Alex could see his horse-sized teeth from here. The whiteness contrasted against his muddy skin color.

Alex could tell that he had said something. He knew the nano-machines picked it up. He commanded them to replay the sound.

"I swear by my Ancestors," the man had said. The amplification and distance distorted the sound too much to get an identification from it.

In his mind, Alex broadened the search for his mystery suspect. The man started walking back in the direction he had come. Alex had a suspicion forming in his mind about who this guy was. He ran to a window overlooking an alley and jumped out of it. He landed silently from the two-story drop. Always dressed in black clothes, Alex was a moving shadow. The bright moon cast many shadows for him to hide in. The target was more than a block away when Alex started following him. Alex lost him for a moment when he turned an oblique corner. However, by the time Alex got to the same corner, the man was gone. Not wanting to run into his prey, Alex did not increase his speed. He looked around and saw nothing. Where did this guy go? He looked around for cameras and was rewarded with one that might have caught the footage he wanted.

This disappearing act piqued Alex's curiosity. He would do his detective work and find out who this man was. Maybe this could be his guy, or at least a new Target Family. Either way, Alex would be happy. He turned around and walked back to the crime scene. Alex used the recording to retrace the target's steps. He just walked in a big circle, stopping to look at the location from different angles. Maybe this guy was an artist. A street artist who could disappear at will?

Alex walked back to his townhouse. As he got to the door, a message appeared in his vision:

Relevant information sources on the face you searched for.

Alex entered his house back through the window he jumped from earlier and accessed the message. A link to a local newspaper appeared in his field of vision. The "man" was hurt pretty badly in a martial arts tournament. He didn't even make it past the first round. Some of the witnesses say that his opponent's kick was so fast they didn't even see it. This was an exciting bit of information; maybe he would get two for one. There was one follow-up report online as an update. The kid had miraculously recovered after several weeks in a coma. His name was Scipio Harelson. It should be an easy name to look up. Blacks always used weird names as if they would connect them with their ancestors. A meme popped into his mind. A picture of a Black man and Black woman with exaggerated African features on an Egyptian throne, the caption read, "We was kangs and quains." Alex chuckled at the memory.

Scipio Harelson.

He would have to find who the super-fast opponent was, but Scipio felt like the lead.

Alex sat back in his window perch and let his mind wander. Of course, he had his little friends keep watch. Later today, he would try to do some footwork and investigate these two boys.

West San Jose, California, March 15, 5:10 a.m. PST.

Before the sun rose that morning, Alex discovered enough info on each of his targets that he could have gone to their homes right this instant.

But he waited patiently. Alex decided to go and stake out Herman Garcia. He was a tall, brown-skinned boy. The young man was very Latino, and while it was possible that he was operant, it was unlikely. Alex watched for an hour, and the kid did not use any observable abilities. He seemed to work hard for his family. In the Americas, the next group behind the Blacks to be operant were Mexicans. They usually were so diluted that they only had partial ascendancies, meaning they could accomplish small feats like seeing a glimpse of the future or moving small things. Occasionally, some adepts had near-full ascendancies. This kid was not operant in any way, he would interview him, and several witnesses listed and make a final determination. It would all be in his report to Mr. Cross. Painful memories surfaced as he recalled failing to adequately or accurately report anything. He sat and watched him.

Herman got into a car with a bunch of his friends. Alex went to the kid's job.

CHAPTER 19

Over San Jose, California, March 15, 3:40 a.m. PST.

After my field trip to the scene of the crime, I was feeling on edge. So, instead of flying home, I went to the top of a nearby mountain peak. I found a patch of grass and watched the stars. I fell asleep waiting for the sunrise.

I woke up with a start; it was still dark. I stood, stretched, and flew home. I flew high and tried a trick. I stayed high and shot down to my window. Right before I got to the window, I shifted most of my kinetic energy to potential. I came in through the window and landed rather gracefully, if I do say so myself. I was too exhilarated to sleep, so I decided a shower would be nice.

As I stood under the water, I tried to analyze the day's upcoming events.

I would meet up with Ian and Saphronia, and we would all go to Coach's house and his underground bunker to train. I thought about how I would explain my dream and my sudden leap in my flying skills. Should I say a mysterious voice in a dream taught me? Or it was given to me by an ancestor! I tried in an announcer's voice.

"Ugh," I complained.

I rubbed hot water on my face and washed up. I was sitting on the bed, about to put my socks on, and my mind drifted.

Where do I begin?

How do I find out about the SOTIR Group? Coach popped into my head right away. He was the person that has powers, and I guess he works for the East Lady. He would have information on where to start. My mind drifted as I sat there on the bed.

I looked at the clock; it said four-fifty, and another thirty minutes had passed. While I was getting dressed, my Global buzzed. It was Ian texting me good morning and asking if I was ready for the workout. I answered an emphatic *yes* and confirmed he would be here at seven a.m. I told him I had a surprise for him.

I brushed my teeth, moisturized my hair, and hurried downstairs to get breakfast.

My parents were sitting in the kitchen waiting for me.

"Hey guys," I was sure the awkwardness came through.

"Good morning, son," my mom glanced at my dad, and her eyes flicked to me.

"Good morning, man, your mother and I have been talking," my dad said, and I was instantly upset, "and we want to let you know that we are in full agreement with Jamal and Cara."

My burning anger fell away as quickly as it rose. I was dumbfounded; they were just going to let me go fight this war all alone.

"There are two things we wanted to tell you. Well, more like three things. I mean, one of them is something you already know," I saw my mom nudge him with her elbow.

"OK, number one is we love you, son." The sincerity in his eyes was undeniable, as he continued, "And number two is we trust Adrian and are willing to let him train you as long as you are serious. This is a dangerous game you are getting into. You don't know it yet, but we have been helping you get ready for this day for a long time."

I didn't know what to say. I mean, it was very commendable that they were letting me "plot my own course," but it also felt like they were trying to get out of the way of an incoming missile.

"Lastly," he began to explain, "your parents chose a different last name for themselves when they got married; we changed your name so it would be harder for the SOTIR Group to find us. Your family surname is Okoro."

"Your full name is Scipio Octavius Okoro," my mom announced; her eyes were pleading with me.

I could almost hear her whispering in my ear.

Please-don't-hate-us!

We-love-you!

I could probably read their minds to find out if they were telling the truth, but the right to privacy of your thoughts kept hitting me in the face. Coach drilled that into me the day before and will probably continue today. The errant thought captured by accident was enough for me to trust them both.

Sometimes, events happen where there is a clear demarcation between the 'before' and the 'after' of the event. Things like finding out you have cancer, breaking a bone, or having a child. You cannot go back; you cannot unknow something.

My true name was like a gift I didn't know I needed.

"Okoro," I tasted the word. I tried to absorb the soul of the word, but something was missing. A key voice in the chorus was singing too low.

"What does it mean?" My voice cracked.

"The way your parents interpreted it was 'Greatness in character,'" the meaning snapped into place, and the chorus of my Ancestors was complete. I realized I was taking a deep breath halfway through doing it. A sense of purpose filled me.

CLICK!

"Are you okay, son?" My mom's voice was pleasant, and I opened my eyes that I didn't realize I had closed.

"Yes," my voice was calm, but I could feel a storm growing in my heart. I was not angry; I was powerful. How could I stand by and let these monsters continue to destroy the lives of those people? How could I lose?

"Thank you. I love you guys too!" My eyes welled with tears. Did I mention I was a crybaby?

We talked for a while about lighter subjects. My mom wondered what I wanted to do for my rapidly approaching birthday. I told her I had not even thought about it. We all ate and talked until Ian was outside.

"I'll be back around midnight, and I won't be late," I promised. They both gave me tight smiles. Awkwardness filled the room.

My mom asked, "You're okay with everything we just told you?" Her voice was full of care and concern.

"Kinda," I said. My mom tilted her head to the right, raised her left eyebrow, and pursed her lips.

"It's just that Ian is waiting and-" I stopped talking because the look both my parents were giving me told me I was on the edge of serious trouble.

"You ain't eighteen yet, and even if you were, I don't care if blue-eyed, White Jesus was outside, we are talking, and we will finish talking like civilized people," my mom said, her eyebrows raised higher than I thought possible.

"Yes, Ma'am," I responded, noticing my dad's eyes were full of *ooooh, you got in trouble* and laughter.

My mom elbowed him in the ribs.

"Oof!" he complained.

"Well, guys, honestly, it is a lot. I have new parents and powers and responsibility and so many other things to learn," I shrugged my shoulders and raised my hands, "now I find out I have a *real* name, and it means 'Greatness in Character.' What am I supposed to do with that? I believe you guys, so all I can do is own it. I have to wrap my head around all of this. Training will help me do that. That's how I feel." I took a deep breath.

My mom came to me and hugged me so tight. I could feel her love for me, and then I felt my dad's arms wrap around both of us and squeeze. We all laughed in the close quarters.

"We love you, Baby," my mom said.

"I love you guys, too," I returned. My heart felt full.

East San Jose, California, March 15, 5:30 a.m. PST.

Alex barged into Herman's job at the fast-food restaurant before they opened. He flashed his badge, and everyone cooperated nicely. He asked about people he hangs out with, and personal things, like did he hold any weird beliefs. Then he asked about the tournament and if he was proud of his win. Alex wanted to get the boy nervous and see if he made a mistake. He spoke to every employee and two managers, but he never left a card or number. By the time he left, they would be wondering if Herman was a terrorist or a drug dealer.

Alex waited for the restaurant to officially open and for Herman to come to work.

When Herman arrived, one of the young girls came to meet him at his car. He was gesturing to his Global and talking animatedly with the young lady. Alex could have turned his auditory gain up to listen to the conversation, but he preferred to make up what they were saying.

He played the game often, and he preferred his narrative more than the real ones, anyway. Most of these muddied people led empty lives, blindly following what the government told them. Alex knew better. Mr. Cross showed him the lies and the hypocrisy of the so-called government. Alex knew that the greatness of his European heritage created the greatest country on earth. And regardless of what these Latinos tried to do, America still came out ahead. The couple walked inside; Alex sighed.

He focused on his left index finger, giving the nano-machines their specific orders. He encircled it in his fist and broke the bone; there was a wet snap, and he hissed in pain. A red line appeared on the base of his broken finger. It circled around and connected with itself, and the skin began to dissolve. It dissolved down to a broken bone; there was a thin web of tissue that joined the finger and the thumb. Six black legs burst from the sides of the finger, three on each side. A mass of small holes appeared on the fingernail and spread over the surface of the digit; Alex knew these would be the various cameras and listening devices he wanted. Alex opened his car door slightly, and the vile little thing skittered away to do its work. He watched it find a groove in the street, and the tether rested in it neatly. The 'tether' was only a few nano-machines thick, less than the diameter of a human hair. Alex found he couldn't run his little creations remotely, but this method was just as good, albeit the range was considerably less.

Alex watched his little drone flatten itself and squeeze under the door. Alex was intruded upon by a box in the top right corner of his vision. The little guy was keeping to the corners and along the wall. It could blend into the environment; it wouldn't stand up to intense scrutiny, but it would keep it from being easily seen.

Eventually, he found Herman alone in the restroom; he talked about possibly being deported and how innocent he was. Alex watched him rant and rave. He never exhibited any abilities during his tantrum.

"Damnit, I wished I *had* kicked that bastardo negro!" Herman growled under his breath in a defeated rage.

That was enough for Alex. This kid wasn't the target. He recalled his drone. As soon as it was back, he started the car and headed toward the Scipio kid. He felt right.

San Jose, California, March 15, 7:03 a.m. PST.

As he turned the corner, an old silver Toyota Supra passed him as it left the neighborhood.

Some White kid was driving, and the person in the passenger seat was bent over with their head in the footwell.

Alex drove past the house and made a U-turn at the next intersection. He was able to park far away from his prey because of his little friends. He watched the house for the remainder of the day. Not much happened; other people were living in the house. An adult male and an adult female, probably parents, but there was no sign of children. The male didn't match the picture of Scipio. So, there must be at least a third individual. Patience was a virtue Alex had in abundance.

The sun fell behind the hills, and the parents set out somewhere. They were both nicely dressed. Wearing buffoonish bright colors. The male held the door for his mate; they imitated civilized people so well. Alex glanced at his watch and noted it was nine-thirty p.m. He decided to follow them and see where they were going. If he were lucky, they would be going to a family gathering of some sort. Blacks are always partying and causing trouble. He tailed them to a house about forty-five minutes from their home. Alex tapped his Global to call one of the other lower-echelon teams to observe the parents.

He wanted to go into the house and look around. He returned to the target house. Alex parked a block away. He was fast enough that he could get to the house without anyone seeing him. He cleared the fence in one inky bound. He moved to the side door and asked Minerva to bypass the security system easily.

"It's open, Detective Lamb," Minerva stated.

Alex checked his watch. It was eleven p.m.

CHAPTER 20

S an Jose, California, March 15, 6:50 a.m. PST.

My dad gave me a smile that said, *Fair enough.*

"Okay, son, have a good time. Oh, your mom and I will be out late tonight. Don't wait up," he winked at me.

"Okay, gross, Dad." The tension vanished just like that.

"It's Aunt Beni's birthday, and the adults are going to let off a little steam. The Bad Guys aren't breathing down our necks yet," my mom opined.

"Okay, Mom! I love you guys. I'll see you later," the last sentence was tossed casually over my shoulder.

The door shut behind me, and I let out a sigh of relief. I didn't want to think about all that drama right now. I jogged to Ian's car, sitting at the curb.

"What's up, homie?" I greeted him as I got into the ride.

"Ian, man, do I have a story for you, but I'll wait until we are all together."

Ian was pulling out into the street. The kid could drive like a blind grandma sometimes.

"Man, I hope you are all stretched and limber cause I think Coach is going to kick your butt today," Ian teased.

I chuckled knowingly. "Maybe," I said cryptically, "but hey, I got something for you this morning."

I bent down to look for the rock I had stuffed into my backpack. When I found it, the darn thing slipped out of my hand and tried to roll under my seat. I caught it. I was about to sit up when the car jerked violently, and Ian exclaimed, "Jerk!"

I sat up and looked back, and the taillights of a black Mustang fastback were just disappearing around the corner.

"What happened?" I asked.

"The idiot in that stupid Mustang turned the corner on the wrong side of the street; he almost hit us!" Ian was shouting.

"Dude, he almost killed the savior of the world."

"Whatever, I'm not the savior of anybody's world; I'm just a guy like you."

"Except you can punch someone from ten feet away."

"Yeah, well, I'm still regular," I quipped, "by the way, this is what I was trying to show you before we almost got killed." I showed him the uncracked geode. "Dude, that's an unopened geode! Where did you find it?"

"On top of a mountain," I said proudly.

We pulled up to Diana's house and waited for Saphronia to come out. When she did, Diana came out on the porch to wave at us. I waved back; it dawned on me that there was no empty space in my heart for her. Ever since this whole thing started, I was inundated with new information and submerged in a world I did not know existed. As Saphronia reached Ian's car, I realized the reason Diana was in my rearview mirror was because Saphronia was in my future. I hoped she felt the same. All of this was happening so fast.

"Hey guys," she said, climbing into the car, her voice warming my heart.

"Hey, Saphronia," Ian said.

"Hey, Saph," I said. She stopped settling in and looked at me.

A small smile was stuck on my face, and my eyes darted between her and Ian.

"Hi," I said awkwardly.

"My name is SaphRONIA," she emphasized the last part of her name, "not Saph, okay?"

"Okay," my voice went up at the end of the word as I tried to save face; she raised her left eyebrow. Oh, my Ancestors, was she beautiful.

"Okay," she said, and her bounce was back, "Let's go learn how to be superheroes!"

Hollister, California, March 15, 8:05 a.m. PST.

An hour later, we arrived at Adrian's house; it was a sprawling ranch just south of a little town named Hollister. Unlike most houses in California, there were doors leading down to a cellar below the house. We clomped down the wooden steps and followed a narrow hall that emptied us into a massive vault. I noticed as we were winding through the hall, we seemed to be going down slightly, but as I looked up at the ceiling of the room, all I saw were shadows.

Coach greeted us when we walked in.

"Hey people, mane bo ta?"

A laugh leaped from Saphronia. "Oi!" she exclaimed, "Kital?"

"I'm still learning," Coach chuckled.

"That was a good start!" she exclaimed. "I was very surprised." Her smile was radiant.

I glanced at Ian, and he just rolled his eyes and laughed.

I guess Diana is out of the picture. I heard Ian's voice clearly in my mind. I nodded my head; it was all I could do.

"Okay, let's get started," Adrian said.

"Wait," I remembered my story, "I have to tell you guys something that happened to me."

They all stopped and looked at me expectantly. I told them about my dreams, especially the latest one where a woman's voice spoke to me. When I was done, I looked at them. Ian was highly interested in my story. Adrian was rubbing his chin, deep in thought. But Saphronia was looking at me with surprise and, more astonishingly, recognition.

"I met her as well, and she told me I was the Ikhawu, the Shield, and another was The Iklwa, the Sound of Death."

"Interesting," Adrian said quietly, "show me what she taught you."

"Coach, we should talk about these dreams Saphronia and I are having."

Coach turned and walked deeper into the cavern. "Show me," was all he said. His tone demanded obedience.

"Yes, Sir." I launched myself from zero to full speed instantly, and I was waist-high. I was so annoyed at being unheard that I forgot I was in an underground cavern. I was surprised to find I had room to fly for a good twelve seconds. I decided to turn around and go back to everyone. Like a memory of a motion I'd done a thousand times, I tucked my chin to my chest while bringing my knees to my chest as well, and I rolled. I could feel the sensation of my inertia moving around and through me. As I completed the roll, I could feel the changed momentum pushing me in the exact opposite direction. I was still for a fraction of a second, then I was rocketing back to my starting point. It never dawned on me that I was comprehending things faster than normal. I felt like I was sprinting, but I was in full control. I felt the air change an instant before I ran into the shockwave I had created on my initial launch. As the pressure wave flowed around me, I could see I was generating some kind of field. I never actually felt the blast of compressed air; I only sensed it like a coming storm.

I saw the group as I rushed up to them; they were all standing close together, and Saphronia had her hands outstretched. The look on her face was not a happy one. Ian's mouth was gaping open, and Coach was clapping and smiling. I canceled my excess inertia and momentum and came to a complete stop directly in front of them.

"Keep the field up for a moment," I advised. As I finished speaking, the other pressure wave I made caught up to me. My clothes flapped violently.

"Holy Shi..." Ian trailed off as he glanced at Coach. "Sorry, Sir," Ian said.

"It's okay, Ian. That was extraordinary!" Coach said, "You can drop the field, Saphronia. I think we are safe."

She dropped her arms, and the field came down as well.

"That was cool..." I started to say.

"You could have seriously hurt us, Scipio!" she yelled. "You caused a massive pressure wave inside a closed space. You could have hurt yourself! I know you don't know how big the magical cavern is any more than I do. You could have slammed your head into a wall at a thousand kilometers an hour and killed yourself! That was NOT cool!" She was heated.

I looked at everyone.

"Ah, I'm sorry, guys," I said.

Ian found his voice, "Dude, how fast was that? What is your top speed? We gotta clock you!" The words poured out of his mouth.

"A voice taught you all of this in a dream?" Adrian's calm voice cut through Ian's chatter like butter.

"Uh yeah," I nodded my head, "well not exactly; I mean, I assumed so because she said she was going to give me the knowledge I needed. You saw me yesterday. I was barely able to float from one spot to the next. I did some kind of flip I saw professional swimmers do and completely changed direction. I mean, I like to swim, but I never learned that!" I felt frustrated, and I was suddenly hungry. I wasn't starving, but I could have been happy with a big sandwich and a tall glass of ice water.

"I tried flying last night, well, this morning," Adrian looked at me and squinted his eyes.

"I was flying high, and I'm so small compared to a plane, no radar could have picked me up. But I flew from South San Jose to Stockton in around one minute." I waggled my hand, Ian whistled, and the sound echoed for a few seconds.

Ian asked, "How far is Stockton from San Jose?"

"It's 100 miles away," Coach answered. "You were going about 6000 miles per hour. How did you feel after you flew that fast?"

"I felt drained. Not completely, but enough to know I couldn't have done that ten times in a row."

Adrian only nodded his head. I could practically see the gears turning in his mind.

"Okay, this will be the first lesson of the day."

Adrian's abrupt change in gears took everyone by surprise.

"Every creature on this planet consumes energy to survive. When that energy is depleted, we stop," Adrian turned to look at us, "not die, stop. I saw a fight to the death between a lion and a tiger. In the middle of a particularly vicious exchange between the two predators, the tiger just fell over. You see, during the battle, it used all its physical energy reserves. There was no more gas for the muscles to spend. He fell over, stiff as a board. EPBs are no different. We have extra energy and can manipulate our energy reserves. The bigger the reserve, the longer you can fight. So, on that note, Scipio and Saphronia, we are going to expand your energy reserves."

"How do we do that?" Our voices were synchronized.

"By requiring your body to do what it naturally does," Adrian paused and tilted his head expectantly before continuing, "grow and adapt." Adrian raised his left hand, our right, and said, "Run, and when you see me, just turn right. Got it?"

We all nodded our heads.

"THEN START RUNNING!"

His shout woke us up. We donned our weight vests, and Saphronia and I started running in the direction he indicated. I heard him tell Ian to start running as well.

"If you're going to be a part of this little team, you have to be in shape too."

San Jose, California, March 15, 11:02 p.m. PST.

Alex slipped into the Harelson house. No dog greeted him, no scurrying of frightened felines. Alex took a deep breath and let his awareness go through the home. The house felt empty. The Minerva fob chirped quietly at him, warning him that the security network contained cameras.

"Don't wipe them, Minerva. Can you put them in rest mode as if I was not here?"

"I will turn off the motion detector," Minerva said in his ear. "Just a moment," there was a pause, "done. You may move freely about the house."

Alex relaxed and walked into the kitchen. He brought some listening devices and micro cameras. They were small and easily blended into whatever surface they were applied to. The nano-machines in his body were the grandfathers of this technology. He put them in places people normally didn't look. Strangely, they didn't have a lot of stand-alone lamps. Because they didn't have pets, he was able to put some low; tall people rarely look low. Alex examined their mail and looked in places he thought they might hide things.

He checked the kitchen and was surprised by the cleanliness. He opened the oversized refrigerator and was greeted with leaves of vegetables and fruit. There were jars of pickled things and creams. There were labels like headache, stomachache, fever, and other ailments. Alex closed the refrigerator and went to the back door. He blinked, and his eyes switched to night vision, and he was not surprised by what he saw. The entire backyard had been turned into a small farm. After the pandemic that ravaged America, a lot of people turned to herbal remedies. Especially Blacks. The fall back into savagery was facilitated by a reborn group called Progress. They used social media to create a massive groundswell of support and followers. They were supposedly able to demonstrate the benefits of bush medicine. They convinced bleeding heart doctors that bush medicine could be married to conventional Western medicine. They were able to persuade a great many people who had, at the time, lost trust in a healthcare system that seemed not to work or work for them. He blinked twice, and the night vision turned off. They would stand in front of whoever would listen and chant, "Plants are inclusive." Eventually, the movement came to be called PAI. It was an homage to the medicine men and women in Trinidad and Tobago. These types of people were always trying to tear down the civilization that had conquered them and brought them out of savagery. Truth be told, Alex thought to himself, he didn't blame them for the attempt, however misguided it might be. His job was to make sure they failed every time.

The stairs beckoned him, but he forced himself to make a thorough and careful search of the rest of the downstairs area. There was an old-school plasma TV in the living room, but no sign of a computer. He knew they had Globals because the chargers were lying around. Alex assumed the computer was upstairs. People always had something juicy on their PCs. Once he was satisfied with his search, he checked the time and was surprised to see it was already 11:35 p.m. His heart leaped in his chest with irrational excitement.

He glided up the stairs. When he reached the top, he took a moment to get a layout. To his left was the second common bathroom. There was one downstairs as well. It was the only door in that direction. To his right, just past the stairs, was another door facing him. There was another room on the opposite side of the hall, and the final door was at the other end of the hall.

Alex crept to the bathroom first; he would have taken a piss, but that body function, along with crapping, ceased years ago. He opened the medicine cabinet and saw nothing out of the ordinary except that there were no pills of any kind. After what he saw in the kitchen and the backyard, he didn't have high expectations for an educated assortment of meds. He looked under the sink just in case and was rewarded with bandages and cotton balls. He placed a few audio and visual devices in the bathroom.

He moved to the next room, which was the "master" bedroom. It was just as he expected, full of brown earth colors and African garbage on the walls. In fact, there were masks downstairs where he found good hiding spots for his devices. This was obviously the parents' room; everything looked very adult. It wasn't dirty, just untidy. It was as if they didn't have time to clean. Alex was sure they had plenty of discretionary money to spend on a maid. There was no computer here either. He looked around the room for a while but didn't see anything that would lead him to believe they had abilities.

11:50 p.m.

Alex went to the room across the hall from the parents' room. It was a study room; there was a desk and a monitor. *Jackpot.*

Alex rushed into the room; he already had his little memory stick out, ready to plug it in. He sat in the chair and looked under the desk. No CPU, not even wires. He looked around the desk, around the room, and found nothing. Two wires were coming out of the monitor, but nothing was attached to them. Alex shook his head; did they know he was coming? No, impossible. He just started the investigation. This wasn't the first time he had seen something like this. Some people had been moving to a more decentralized information-keeping method. Keeping everything on their Global and or backed up in a secure cloud. The Globals could be self-destructed by sending a specific message to the device, and the battery would overheat, burn up the Global, and if all your information is backed up in the cloud, no big deal. However, sometimes the backups are not there, and you lose everything, so the tech has not really taken off. It was out there, and Alex suspected the Harelsons to be users of it.

A car pulled up outside; Alex froze for a moment to listen.

CHAPTER 21

Under Hollister, California, March 15, 8:55 a.m. PST.

We ran for ten minutes only, and we stopped; our breathing seemed to reverberate through the cavern.

"Coach," I tried to catch my breath between words, "how does this place work?" My heaving chest made my question seem less important to me.

"When you can run for an hour with twice as much weight, I'll tell you." I saw Coach smile, and my heart sank.

"Okay, that's enough rest; let's do it again.

We ran another round, and my body felt like it would shut down the way Coach was warning about. I was lying on the ground and just trying to keep breathing. I heard Ian throwing up somewhere far away. I turned to find Saphronia. She was sitting up, her breathing was heavy, but she was slowing it down. I wanted to ask her how she did that, but I could not catch my breath. She was beautiful; her skin was flushed and glowing, a dark pearl glistening in the low light of this magical cavern. She styled her hair in mini twists for the workout. They seemed shorter than they were when we first started. Sweat dripped from her chin and ran gracefully down her neck.

Saphronia turned, looked at me, and smiled. My heart wanted to beat faster, but could not; I was out of breath.

"How are you able to do that?" I gasped.

"You already know," she said cryptically, "Box breathing helps calm you down. It's not perfect, but it is better than gasping for air like a fish out of water."

My mouth dropped open. I sat up, crossed my legs, and focused on breathing. In for a four-count, hold for a four-count, exhale for a four-count, and hold for a four-count. The last part was hard, but the rest was helping. I could feel my heart slowing and my body responding to me, telling it we were not on fire, and everything was okay.

Coach came back with water for everyone. I hadn't realized he was gone. I drank my water, and I was feeling better.

When Coach said, "Let's go, Scip, show me what you got," I didn't understand.

Coach dropped into a fighting stance and waved his fingers, beckoning me to join him. I did not want to look bad in front of Saphronia. I reluctantly walked to where Coach invited me. When I got to the line, he attacked me. He opened with a jab and a cross.

9:40 a.m.

Saphronia watched Adrian and Scipio fight and was impressed. She was more of a fighter than they knew, and she could appreciate the skill. Scipio was covered in sweat, and Saphronia could see that he was in good shape. She wondered if Scipio understood the battle he was getting into. She called her mother last night to check up on her and report what was going on. They used a code that sounded like general talk to anyone listening. Her mother warned her that her feelings could get in the way and endanger her mission, but Saphronia was not stupid, and she knew she would be ready when the time came. She could see his confidence shining through while he sparred. The fierce look in his eyes caused a storm in her chest. Could he really be the Iklwa, the voice said he was? The Blade was the culmination and product of iron forged by man. It was the advent of war. However, if it were drawn too soon without training, it would be useless. Saphronia read what Black people in America have suffered through, and she knew the history of Cape Verde very well. The psyche of the Black man was always under attack, and the Black woman was often abused to show the Black man how powerless he truly was. It happened worldwide, but now a spark had emerged in the form of this young man. Could he be the force for change in this messed-up world?

"Okay, Scipio, let's kick it up a notch," as Adrian spoke, his hands started to glow.

Scipio did not hesitate; he launched himself at Adrian. Ancestors, Scipio was fast. Why had she snapped at him about her name? It was not remotely important, but the sound of that nickname coming from him hit her the wrong way. Why? The name meant nothing.

Adrian was not there for Scipio to hit; he appeared above him and tried to hit Scipio with a bat he somehow had in his hand. Scipio recognized where the attack was coming from and changed his direction; he was unexpectedly going at a ninety-degree angle from his original travel. There was no curve in his movement; it was a sharp turn. Adrian's bat clanged on the ground.

"Are you trying to kill me?" Scipio exclaimed.

"Yep," Adrian said, "the people we are going against will be trying to kill you."

Suddenly, Scipio spun to his left, and the metal bat appeared swinging horizontally in the air right where Scipio had been standing. The bat was at chest height.

"What the hell, dude!"

Saphronia could tell Scipio was getting angry; he was falling into Adrian's trap. *Better to learn here than in an actual fight,* she thought.

Scipio relaunched himself, predictably. Adrian stepped aside at the last moment, but Scipio had a surprise of his own. He changed direction and tackled Adrian. He pummeled him with punches. One punch caught Adrian in the jaw, and blood flew from his mouth. Adrian vanished from Scipio's tackle and appeared behind him, swinging the bat at Scipio's head. Scipio turned and held up his hand, and the bat stopped and reversed its trajectory. It flew from Adrian's hands. Adrian stopped for a moment, and Scipio rolled to his knee, raised his other hand, and Adrian was pushed away. Scipio jumped to his feet. Just then, Adrian crashed into Scipio's back, and they rolled in a tangle of arms and legs. Somehow, they untangled and ended up on their feet. Adrian threw a jab with a glowing fist, and Scipio dodged it. Then Adrian threw an uppercut to Scipio's body. Scipio disappeared and reappeared in mid-air. Adrian hit him again. The "hit" seemed like a light one, but Scipio hit the ground like he had fallen from a great height. Saphronia gasped and jumped to her feet.

"Scipio!" she yelled. Ian appeared by her side, still wiping his mouth.

Scipio rolled away and popped up to his feet. He looked at her and winked. Her heart skipped.

Scipio rocketed toward Adrian.

"What the...," was all Adrian had time to say before his head snapped back, and he was lifted into the air. He flew back and landed hard; he was not moving.

Saphronia and Ian ran to him.

"Don't bother, guys; he is faking. I can sense his heartbeat from here; it is not slowing," Scipio said. Saphronia and Ian stopped. Adrian sat up.

"Nice use of your abilities," Adrian said.

Saphronia was impressed again. She stared at Scipio; he stood there, his posture relaxed and ready, his chest rising and falling from exertion, and his eyes were calculating black pools. However, it was the bright smile that caught her attention. There was hope in that smile, a hope she had not felt since her Vovo died. Saphronia's eyes started to burn, and she blinked rapidly.

The hours passed, and they trained almost nonstop. There was an energy in the air that fueled their souls. They had lunch and dinner. They talked about their abilities. Adrian had Saphronia and Scipio spar. While they fought, Adrian and Ian talked privately.

"Are you jealous, Ian?" Adrian had asked, going right at Ian.

"A little," Ian answered honestly.

"Who wouldn't be in your position?" Adrian said carefully.

Ian looked at Adrian, "I would never hurt Scipio; he saved me when he didn't have to." Ian's voice was low but adamant.

"That was years ago, Ian. You are telling me that little childhood scuffle earned your undying loyalty?"

"It's more than that, Coach," Ian said, his voice was low and earnest, "Scipio has always been there for me. He never made me feel out of place. I stood up for him and he for me. We are bound by more than friendship; he is my brother from another mother."

Adrian smiled at Ian's euphemism. "Good, keep that energy, Ian. Things may get crazy before it's all over, and he may need his brother from another mother." Adrian walked back to the sparring couple.

11:57 p.m.

Alex hurried to the parents' room to peek out of the window. He saw a familiar silver Supra pulling away. What? Not surprisingly, he heard keys in the door. Alex slipped down the hall to the guest room. The window for this room was over the side of the house. He opened the window, but a loud screech filled the air.

"Shit!" Alex swore under his breath.

"Hello?" a male voice called from downstairs. Then footsteps on the stairs.

"Mom, Dad? Where is the car?" the voice was close. Fuck it, Alex thought and wrenched the window all the way open.

11:56 p.m.

We arrived at my house after dropping Saphronia off, but Ian had something to say before I got out of the car.

"Okay, dude, I have been waiting all day to say something," Ian said.

"What are you talking about?"

"Dude, Saphronia almost bit your head off this morning."

"Yeah, but it's cool. I can't just be giving people nicknames. She set me straight, and I appreciate it."

Ian's mouth was hanging open.

"Are you serious? You're just going to take that?" Ian was incredulous, "Man, you got it bad."

"Dude, what are you talking about?" I tried to act annoyed.

"Scip, I have known you most of my life, and I have never seen you just back down from someone, even when you were dead wrong."

All I could do was laugh.

"Well, maybe I am growing up. I'll be eighteen in a couple of days, I'm practically an adult, and I'll be telling you what to do."

Ian rolled his eyes. It was his turn to say, "Dude."

"Alright, I will see you tomorrow," I said, getting out of the car.

"Hey, Scip, what time do you want me to pick you up tomorrow?" I bent down to look at Ian through the car window.

"Same time is fine. Thanks for the ride."

"No problem, bro.' Have a good night," then he drove off.

I walked to the house and fumbled with my keys. I was exhausted, but eventually, my fingers found the right one, and I opened the door and went inside. Coach kicked our butts and our minds; he had a whole lesson on room clearing. I still did not know how he was able to reconfigure the strange cavern. My legs felt shaky, and I was so hungry. I threw my bag down and headed for the kitchen. Suddenly, there was a loud screech from upstairs; it was short, but it definitely came from upstairs.

"Hullo?" The word jumped out of my mouth before I thought about it, but there was no response. I returned to the foot of the stairs.

"Mom, Dad? Where is the car?" What was I doing? What if it's a killer and... As I thought this, I was slowly climbing the stairs. My feet were silenced using the trick from last night, but the stairs still creaked. I was halfway up when I heard a longer screech and a crazy commotion.

12:00 a.m.

Alex tried to kick the screen out, but instead, his foot punched through it. The screen came off, but it was around his calf, and his foot was hanging out of the window. He tried to pull his leg back into the house, but the screen turned and stopped him. Alex grabbed the infernal thing and tore it from his limb. It didn't take long for him to free himself, but it was loud.

He leaped out of the window. Just as he landed, the main door to the garage opened. Light poured from the garage.

12:01 a.m.

I think they were tearing the screen off. That had to be the guestroom; if you didn't open it right, it made a screeching sound Mom hated. I knew that window was above the side door leading to the garage. It was my house, and I would not let some two-bit intruder steal from my family. Hero time! Ancestors, I am a dork.

I raced to the garage, slapped on the light, and opened the side door to the house. I knew I needed to be careful using my abilities. Mainly because regular people are fragile, and a blast that would only bruise someone like Adrian or Saphronia could kill an ordinary person like Ian. I burst through the door.

"What the hell are you d..." was all that came out. After everything that happened in my life, the revelations, and the lessons to be ready for anything, I still froze. My heart was pounding in my chest, and I was hot and cold at the same time. The wind gusted around us, bringing goose pimples to my arms. When I stepped into the side area, he was recovering from the jump out of the window. He was struggling to put his gun in the holster. The man was White, easily six feet tall, with dark hair and blue eyes; he appeared to be in good shape. He had a square jaw, a snub nose, and his thin lips were drawn back in a snarl. He wore a black sports jacket and black cargo pants with black boots. He didn't look like a burglar.

12:02 a.m.

Alex hit the ground, his feet sinking slightly in the dirt. He was recovering and putting his gun back in the holster when the man burst through the door to block his path. He was easily six and a half feet tall, and huge muscles rippled under his sleeveless t-shirt. His arms were massive; they could probably tear him in half, and here he was, caught on the side of this monster's house. Alex could clearly see the man's face. His eyes were bulging in anger, and his wide nose flared, scooping in massive amounts of air; Alex felt like the guy was stealing the breath from him. His thick lips were parted to speak, but obviously, his cowardice froze him in mid-sentence.

Alex said, "Get out of my way."

The Black man did not move.

12:03 a.m.

"No!" was all I could muster. I never confronted an armed burglar before.

"Look, Sir, I don't want to hurt you. Just step aside. No harm, no foul. You can see I didn't take anything, just let me go," the intruder said. He was not pleading; it was more of a polite demand.

"No, dude, I'm calling the cops, and you are going to wait right here."

"Nope," was all he said, then rushed me. He was fast, really fast. I dodged the first three strikes: a left, then a right, and a front kick. I was blocking his escape route, and he was willing to go through me. Somehow, a knife was introduced into the fray, and he swung it once. It was a tactical folding knife with a four-inch blade. He swung it again from his right shoulder to his left hip.

"C'mon, you Black bastard!" he hissed.

I chuckled and started bouncing. I felt relaxed, and the fear I had initially felt fell away. I shivered, but I was not cold.

I feinted forward, and he swung twice. I could tell he knew how to use the knife, and I figured he was trying to keep things quiet. On his second swing, I stepped to his backside and flicked out a solid left jab to his face. I underhooked his knife arm with my attacking hand and overhooked his wrist with my other hand. I placed my left leg in front of him, pushed explosively with my left shoulder, and swept my left leg back. The intruder's face violently met the fence, but he was still struggling.

"Don't do that, dude!" I warned as I ground his face into the fence.

He continued to struggle, and it seemed like he was getting stronger. What if this guy was on some kind of crazy drug? I shifted my left-hand grip and pushed him away. I brought my left knee up, used it as a fulcrum on his elbow, and snapped it. There was a thick clump sound as his elbow dislocated from its socket. To my dismay, he did not scream.

I stepped back, and my eyes widened with shock as his arm hung there limply. The man looked up at me and smiled. His elbow worked itself back into place with a wet grinding sound.

"Now I am going to kill you," he said, looking at me through his brow.

Adrian's voice came to me, *"The people we are going against will be trying to kill you."* Could this be someone who works for the SOTIR Group?

There was a whisper in my ear; it was soft, like the downy feather of an owl, *"He is going to kill you. Then he will wait for your parents to come home and kill them, too,"* the familiar voice and the sensation vanished, and I was staring into the eyes of a killer.

He rushed at me again, but he was at least twice as fast this time. The knife was slashing like lightning in the dim light. Three, four, five, my foot hit the gate, and I had nowhere to go.

"I am going to make you pay for that. Nice and slow," the robber's voice shook with rage.

From less than six feet away, he lunged at me with the knife. He was inhumanly fast; if I had been a normal person, he would have skewered me to that fence, but I wasn't normal. Instead of speeding myself up, I absorbed his speed. He probably thought he was still going fast. I stepped to the right and ducked under his slow knife strike.

I could see his eyes trying to follow me. I waited for him to complete his swing. He exposed his entire right side to me. I crouched low; I took my time, I charged, and I unloaded the stolen potential through a right hook to his lower ribcage.

His body folded around my fist. The outcome surprised me. He exploded through the wall of the garage. He hit everything stored there. The noise was terrific. I had not expected the sound. He was dead, had to be, no one could have survived that. It looked like a semi-truck hit him.

I had the presence of mind to look over the fence to see if anyone was coming outside. Incredibly, nothing moved, but I'm sure my neighbors were looking through the windows. Lucky for me, the big garage door was still intact. I hunkered down so people would not see me peeking over the fence. I needed to call my parents and get them here fast.

I started to go for my Global, which was, of course, back in the house. I say started because before I took my second step, I heard a noise coming from the pile of rubble that had once been my garage interior. There was a groan of pain and then more noise of debris being moved away. *What the hell is happening?* I thought to myself.

"Oh, you are going to pay for that, *you fucking nigger!*" the unkillable man screamed and lunged to his feet. Blood covered his face, and pieces from the studs in the wall he came through were sticking out of his abdomen. I could see that the right side of his body was crumpled in. He tore the sports coat from his body. The contorted flesh was actually untwisting, and I could hear the bones returning to their shape. The weird regenerating zombie hurled the bloodied sports jacket to the ground.

"We know who you are now, boy!" he spat the last word out like a curse. "Your whole family is dead!"

"Who the fuck are you?" I screamed at him.

The strange man turned and loudly ripped a hole in the aluminum garage door and fled through the rip he made. I stood there stunned; my adrenaline was raging through my system. I was ready to fight, but my opponent chose the better part of valor. I could have chased him, but something he said stopped me. He had said, "We know who you are." We. Was this a trap to lure me outside to ambush me? I turned on my heel and found my bag to retrieve my earpiece. I made three phone calls, one to my parents, another to Coach, and the last to Ian. I was so cold, and I could hear my teeth chattering. My stomach twisted painfully. I ran to the downstairs bathroom. I fell on the toilet and vomited everything I had left in me. Twice.

12:06 a.m.

Alex was moving at top speed to get to his car. He opened the door and swept into it with a curse on his lips.

"Why did you tell me to leave? I could've taken that little bastard!" Alex growled.

"It didn't look like that from here," Cross replied in his ear. "Besides, you were causing too much noise, and someone called the police. If they showed up and you were still there, you would have been exposed. Don't worry, Alex. We will get this guy. I want him alive."

"What about his family? I want him to suffer," Alex whined.

"Stop it, you sound idiotic," Cross bit out. "We are not about revenge. We are about survival." There was a long pause. "Deus vult," was all that Cross said. God wills.

"Deus vult," Alex responded. The line died, and he drove away.

San Jose, California, March 16, 12:20 a.m. PST.

I was still gripping the toilet when Adrian and Ian got there. They helped me up and got me cleaned up. Most hero stories leave out the automatic response of the human body to being in a real-life-or-death situation. When you are in an actual life-or-death fight, part of the adrenaline process is the evacuation of the bowels and the bladder. The body is getting ready to conserve all possible energy to be ready to fight. Basically, I soiled myself, and I was a mess. However, by the time my parents made it home, I was all cleaned up. Adrian had me on the couch, wrapped in a blanket, when my parents arrived. My mom ran to me, kissed me, and held me close to her. It was nice, and I needed it.

Once everyone was there, I wanted to tell my story, but Adrian told me to wait.

He bent down and whispered in my ear, "If the guy was with them, then we have to assume this place is wired for sight and sound."

I understood immediately. "What do we do?" I whispered back.

Adrian looked up at my parents.

They returned a disappointed look. I didn't understand what was happening. However, before I could get an answer, there was a knock at the door. The energy in the room shifted to high alert. My mom got up and walked to the door. I could not imagine who it could be at one-thirty in the morning. I heard my mom open the front door and say,

"Can I help you, officer?"

"Yes, we are responding to a noise complaint. Can you step outside, ma'am?" I heard the cop ask. Adrian got up and was about to go to the door when my dad grabbed his arm. Their eyes met, and my dad shook his head.

"Of course," I heard her say; the door closed, and it was quiet.

We all waited tensely for a few minutes, then I heard the front door open and close again. My mom came back looking like the cat that swallowed the canary.

"It's all good," she said, "I told them my son had a few friends over, and it got out of hand."

Adrian asked, "Are they gone?"

"Yes," she said. As the word came out of her mouth, there was another knock. Exclamation points practically appeared above everyone's head. This time, Adrian answered the door. I heard it open, and then footsteps. I smelled her before she even entered the room.

Saphronia walked into the family room where I was resting. She stopped when she saw me. There were no tears or worried glances. She just smiled at me. I immediately felt better.

"Are you okay?" she asked softly.

"Yes, this isn't the first time someone tried to kill me." I was trying to be funny and failing miserably.

Adrian put his arm around her and led her back to the door. I could hear them whispering, but I could not make out what they were saying. Adrian came back without Saphronia.

"Where did Saphronia go?" Ian asked before I could.

"She will be right back, don't worry," Adrian said. "Paul, can you go help her? She has some questions for you."

My dad stood up confused, but he nodded and went to the other room. I was just looking around at everyone; no one was saying anything.

"Guys, what is going on?" I had no clue what was happening.

Before anyone could answer, my dad called from the other room,

"Okay, everyone, I need to turn the power off in the house for a little bit. Don't be alarmed."

It seemed like everyone in the room got closer to me. Then the room darkened. Silence blanketed the house. I let my head fall back and take in the quiet. It was short-lived.

"Hey, everyone, watch your eyes!" Saphronia yelled. "This may tingle a little bit."

"What?" was all that came out before a blue wall of energy passed through the room. The edge of the wall crawled over me. I could feel all the hair on my body stand at attention. My skin tingled and crackled with electricity. My eyes met with Ian's, and he smiled at me. Electricity danced across his teeth. Then it was gone just as fast as it had arrived.

I was about to ask my mom what the heck that was, but Adrian said, "Wait for it."

I started to look at him when, all of a sudden, sparks started popping out of the strangest places. The lamps sparked, a picture on a wall threw sparks, and there were a ton in the kitchen and behind our decorative masks.

POP!

POP!

POP!

All over the house, upstairs as well. The electrical fireworks didn't last for long, and eventually, the house went quiet again.

"I hope that won't bring the cops back," Ian said. "What was all of that?"

"Don't worry, it won't," Adrian said with confidence, "those were all the devices that guy hid in the house."

As he finished speaking, Saphronia came back into the room.

"All done," Saphronia said, slapping her hands together.

"Okay, people, I'm lost. What is going on?" I was getting a little annoyed about not being in this new loop.

"Saphronia is telekinetic, and she generated an electrical pulse at the right frequency to disable the devices," Adrian explained.

"I thought telekinesis was just moving stuff with your mind," Ian said.

"It is. But at its core, it is the manipulation of energy. I have only seen incredibly talented telekinetics do what Saphronia just did, but I figured she was able to do it based on our training," Adrian answered.

"We cannot stay here," I said, "the guy said 'we,' and I think he will be back with backup. He threatened to kill the people I care about."

"We are going to leave," Mom said, "we just have to get things in order. Don't worry. Besides, I don't think he will be bringing anyone tonight. We probably have a day or so."

"I'm going to go see what is taking your dad so long, Scipio," Saphronia said.

"Thank you," I said as she returned to the garage. When Saphronia left the living room, I heard the gentle clinking sound of glass breaking and falling to the floor. My mom's head snapped back, then she fell to the ground. She wasn't moving. I threw my blanket off and ran to her.

"*Mom! Mom!*" When I got to her and turned her over, there was an ugly circular wound on her forehead. Blood poured from the wound at the back of her head. Her eyes were emptying; the twinkling spark that made me feel so safe was fading. Then gone.

"*Mom!*" I could hear myself screaming. The entire house shook with the force of my grief. My world exploded into a million pieces.

Suddenly, I could sense the bullets cutting through the air. I heard and felt them pinging off what at the time I thought was Saphronia's globe of protection. The wayward projectiles decimated the room. Pictures I took for granted were destroyed, and black holes appeared in faces I loved. The shooting men were closing in on us; I could feel their guns screaming death at us. My mom's blood was slick and sticky at the same time. The red hole in her head stared at me. There was no vibration of life coming from her. Her whole body was still as ice. I sensed all these things in an instant.

The world around me slowed down, and I perceived everything that was happening. Adrian had gone to the window to close the curtains, Ian rushed to my side, and Saphronia was walking back into the living room. She was saying something.

"Scipio, your father is..." Her sentence was cut off when she saw me cradling my mom and crying.

"Incoming fire! Saphronia, shields up!" Adrian commanded

She did not hesitate. Instantly, we were engulfed in a golden-hued field. Bullets shredded the window and curtains. Ian started screaming. I was in shock.

Was the intruder back?

Were these the others he spoke of?

Where was my dad?

I looked down at my mom, the woman that kissed all my owies when I was little. She was the constant flow of love I was just now realizing I took for granted. The power of her hugs could fix anything. It was a persistent feeling that I believed would always be there for me to draw on, no matter what.

Now?

Now that flow was gone forever. They took her from me. The SOTIR Group. I knew it was them. Everything in me told me that. My certainty was total.

"Go, Scipio!" Adrian was yelling.

The walls were filling with holes, but Saphronia's shield was holding. I gently kissed my mother on her cooling cheek and laid her head on the cold, unforgiving ground. A *rage* was building in me that I did not think I was going to be able to control. I stood and started walking toward the barrage of bullets. I felt someone grab my left arm. I turned to look at the offending hand. It was pale. I looked up to meet Ian's blue eyes; they were full of tears and pain.

"Scip, man, we gotta go!" he said to me.

His words might as well have been in ancient Latin because I did not understand him at all. His eyes spoke in pure emotion, the only language I could understand at the moment. He pulled my arm gently.

"Let's go, brother. Let's go get your dad and get the hell out of here."

I let him pull me. These monsters would pay. I would rip them apart. My heart was a raging fire in my chest. We ran to the garage covered by Saphronia's shield. It was empty. He was gone.

"Look!" Ian said.

We all turned to see what he was talking about. There was a massive knife stuck into the wall, and written on the wall was the word "TRADE." It was written in blood, and that was all I could see. Blood.

"Is that blood?" I voiced the terror and fixation I was experiencing.

"We gotta go," Adrian was saying again.

A fusillade of bullets ripped through the big garage door. Saphronia still had her shield up, and that is what saved our lives.

"Ancestors!" she screamed in surprise.

The garage door disintegrated.

"Where do we go?" Ian shouted.

"Saphronia, can you shape your field?" I asked.

"Yes," was all she said, but the message between us was clear.

I pulled everyone closer.

"What is going on?" Ian asked.

"We are getting the hell out of this death trap," Adrian said.

I barely heard any of the exchange; I was too busy concentrating. I expanded my field beyond myself; it seemed to mix with Saphronia's globe. I could tell when each person entered the field by being able to sense their heartbeat. When I had them all in my field, I looked up and saw Saphronia's field mixed with mine in a shimmering green. I shot us up and out into the night. The roof of the garage exploded out as we passed through.

"Take us to my house," Adrian said.

"What about my dad?" I asked desperately.

"We have to wait and see what they do next," Adrian advised.

"Wait?!" I was incredulous. "These assholes just killed my mother!" Tears sprang violently to my eyes. I didn't care if they saw me crying. "Now they have my dad, and you want me to wait?"

My field flickered, and we dropped a few feet. Everyone but me screamed.

"Take us to my house, Scipio. We can regroup and figure out where your dad is," Adrian said as he tapped his Global and dialed in a code.

I looked back the way we came and saw a great red plume of fire and smoke rising from what I could only assume was my house.

CHAPTER 22

San Francisco, California, March 16, 2:45 a.m. PST.

Robert Cross silenced Alex's feed and opened comms to the team captain of the assault team.

"Captain, you have a green light. No survivors."

Cross knew that this loss would send Alex on a dangerous spiral, and it was prudent to remove the problem altogether. Alex would get over it, and they could move on. Cross watched the video feed of the assault squad members. He was still processing the footage of the girl. She wiped out all the surveillance equipment in one burst. He had to watch the video several times to understand what happened. On the fourth time, he remembered that psionic energy phenomena do not show up on video cameras. He had to watch the video from different angles to find out who the culprit was. She must have been a performer of some sort because she extended her hands as she invoked her ability. *Interesting*, Cross thought to himself. If they put her on ice fast enough, they would be able to harvest some of her eggs, and he could build an army from her powerful genes. That was a pipe dream, Cross knew, but the possibilities could be endless. He concentrated on the screen. They were still shooting; someone in the house was screaming. Why were they still shooting? The girl: Could she be emitting some kind of bulletproof shield? Now, Cross craved her.

"Do not kill them. Take the father, acknowledge!" Cross demanded.

"Affirmative, order acknowledged."

"Leave them a note, in case they don't get it." Cross muted the mic.

Hollister, California, March 16, 3:03 a.m. PST.

We landed roughly at Adrian's house. I fell to my knees. My mother's dead eyes were floating in my vision, and so was the bloody word TRADE. Every blink brought that horrible vision to my mind. The world was spinning, and I could not breathe. I shivered violently. The muscles in my back were burning, and my eyelids felt like they weighed a million pounds. I was struggling to get to my feet when I felt a warm hand on my back.

"Scipio, we will get your dad back, but you gotta get up." Saphronia's voice was gentle but firm.

There was a familiar warmth in her words. She was on my left; I felt her right hand slide around to my left side, and her left hand was under my left arm. She pulled me up. The light from Adrian's cellar spilled into the night air. He descended first, and I could hear Ian behind us watching our backs. I imagine that we looked like pharaohs stepping into the future, left foot and heart leading the way. I've seen pictures of the statues in Egypt. As we descended into the basement, I felt my body recovering rapidly, and my mind was clearing. I did not want Saphronia to let go, but I did feel capable enough to stand on my own. Saphronia seemed to sense me getting my strength back.

Before the last turn, I looked at her and said, "Thank you, Saphronia."

She returned my gaze. Something happened between us at that moment. I felt her familiarity; I knew her, I always had. I knew her in Nubia, I loved her in Zimbabwe, and I worshiped her in Egypt. We fought slavers together in West Africa; she rescued me from a breeding farm in the Deep South, and I fought to free her in the Civil War. On and on until today. We were stars eternally orbiting each other, and here we were again.

"I am sorry I snapped at you earlier." There was iron in her beautiful golden eyes.

I smiled because my heart was fighting, and it was winning.

These people, in the span of one night, destroyed my entire family with one stroke. However, we were not dead, and that meant we had a chance. Hope was alive in me as it had always been in my people.

We turned the last corner and saw Adrian talking with a woman. She had short jet-black hair and almond-shaped brown eyes. Her skin was pale in the flickering light of the cavern.

Despite the dire circumstances, Adrian was smiling broadly.

"Hey, everyone, this is Eunice Lee. She is the person responsible for the 'magic' cavern." She hit him on the arm playfully. "Everyone calls her E."

When he looked at me, Adrian stopped smiling. I'm not sure what face I was making that made him stop, but I tried to fix my face.

I stepped forward out of Saphronia's supporting grasp.

"Thank you very much for providing this space for us," I said sincerely. My mom had raised me well; the thought brought tears to my eyes.

"Oh, honey, no problem at all; it was my pleasure," she said with an Australian drawl.

I glanced at Adrian.

"Oh, she is our transport to my safehouse," Adrian said.

When he finished his sentence, an oval, eight feet tall and four feet wide, opened next to E on the other side. I could see an ornate wooden door with no doorknob. Adrian extended his hand toward the opening.

"After you," he said, "it's okay."

We stepped forward tentatively. I stepped through the portal. I felt a slight pressure change in my ears, and then I was in a new place. I could feel the difference. I don't think my body was used to changing environments so fast. The area was much darker than the cavern; it felt cozy instead of ominous. The ground was grassy and springy. The house in front of me seemed to be grown from the rock around it. There was a wooden porch with a fancy carved wood railing; there were two windows on the front of the house flanking a beautiful, heavy oak door. Oddly the door had no knob to open it with. I walked up to the first step leading to the porch.

Saphronia stepped up on my right side and said, "Wow!"

I looked at her and nodded my head.

"Yeah, it's amazing. Where are we, I wonder?" I said and looked back and saw Ian and Adrian talking quietly; they were very animated. I walked back to them.

"... when?" Ian was asking.

"Soon as we are safe, trust me," Adrian answered.

"What's up, guys?" I asked.

Ian said, "I was asking Adrian about my parents. I want to make sure they are safe."

"And like I said, we have someone taking care of them. Just like Diana's family, we have them covered," Adrian tried to calm Ian down.

"What are you doing to keep them safe, Adrian? Did you move them? Do you have someone watching them?" I pressed.

"I have the Nine Ghana watching them. They are battle-hardened and particularly good at what they do. They will be safe, I promise. We must focus on what is happening right now," Adrian's voice softened, "Ian, you know I wouldn't lie to you, and you also know I care about your parents. Trust me?"

"Okay. I trust you, Coach," Ian said.

Adrian extended his hand, and Ian shook it.

"Settled?" I asked.

They both nodded.

Adrian said, "Let's go inside," and he walked to the door.

We convened at the door with no knob.

"Hold hands, everyone," Adrian said, and we did.

Saphronia's hand was soft and light in my hand. I felt if I squeezed her hand, it would crumple like tin foil. Then she squeezed my hand, and I could feel the strength in her grip.

"Alright. Here we go," Adrian said, and then everything was black for a fraction of a second, and we were in a room.

I looked down, and I was standing on a hardwood floor. I could see my own reflection in the polished wood. I raised my gaze to examine my surroundings. We gathered around a small table, still holding hands. The walls were covered in black historical heroes and some villains, depending on your perspective. Marcus Garvey, Fred Hampton, W. E. B. Du Bois, Malcolm X, but curiously, there was no picture of Martin Luther King Jr. Surely, he considered him worthy of this wall of fame. There were no windows in the room, but there was a pleasant flow of air. I was between Ian and Saphronia. Ian let my hand go almost immediately, but Saphronia did not.

"Oh wow, I love James Baldwin," Saphronia gushed.

She cleared her throat comically and quoted in a stately American accent, "Not everything that is faced can be changed, but nothing can be changed until it is faced."

"He did not sound like that," Adrian said, "Come with me."

Saphronia glanced at me, and all I could do was shrug my shoulders. She let go of my hand and followed Adrian.

Aw, man! I thought to myself and followed the group. The next room had a polished, wooden, rectangle-shaped table in the center. There were nine chairs around the table. Adrian directed everyone to have a seat.

"Listen. This is as serious as it can get, you guys, I don't like involving you to this level, but I don't feel like I have a choice. No matter what I do, you will probably run off half-cocked and end up getting one of you killed. So, while we wait for the inevitable call, we will gear up."

"Cool," Ian exclaimed. "Do you have some kind of secret closet with armor and gadgets that you're going to give us?"

"No," Adrian cut him off. "I'm taking you on a field trip."

My ears perked up at this. "Where are we going?" I wondered aloud.

"Not far. I have a friend that lives nearby, but I want you guys to clean up. I have clothes for you here in the rooms. Follow me," Adrian said, walking deeper into the house.

He led us each to our own room and closed the door behind us. I was last, but before he closed the door, Adrian said, "I am so sorry about your mom. She was my friend.

And I want to get your dad back and make SOTIR Group pay as much as you do, but we have to do it right. Do you trust me, Scipio?"

At the mention of my mother, her lifeless eyes came back to the forefront of my mind. I could see, with perfect clarity, the light dim as she passed into eternity far too early. Tears welled and fell down my cheeks; all I could do was nod my agreement. Adrian reached out and pulled me into a hug. He squeezed me tightly, and I cried hard. I buried my face in his shoulder and gripped him so tight. He never said a word. I don't know how long I was like that, but eventually, I stopped sobbing and pulled away.

"I think I got snot on you." I wiped my eyes and nose.

"It's okay; I've had much worse," he chuckled lightly. "Get cleaned up and changed. I'll have food ready for you all when you are done, and we can try to figure this out together."

"Okay, thank you, Adrian. You saved us back there."

He nodded, and I closed the door.

This was the first time I was alone since this insanity started. The clothes on the bed were a gray t-shirt, sweatpants, a zip-up hoodie, and some clean underwear. The room had a spacious bathroom with a rainfall shower. There was a brown towel hanging on a rack. I turned the shower on, and the water came out clean, clear, and hot. I undressed and saw my mother's blood on my clothes. My heart caught fire all over again. I will tear the SOTIR Group to the ground. I vowed this and used my multi-tool to cut a swatch of the bloody material. I carefully folded it and tucked it into the pocket of the sweatpants lying on the bed. I went into the spacious bathroom and stepped into the hot shower.

CHAPTER 23

West San Jose, California, March 16, 1:45 a.m. PST.

Alex arrived back at his complex and tried not to stumble into walls. As he passed Mary's house, his legs gave out, and he fell to all fours. What had that monster of a man done to him? He had never been hurt like this. It would take a few days to recover completely.

As he swayed there on all fours, the door to Mary's townhouse opened.

"OH MY GOD! DETECTIVE LAMB!" She picked him up and put his arm around her shoulder.

"C'mon." She strained under his weight. "Let's get you inside."

They got into the house, and Mary kicked the door closed. She took Alex to the couch and lay him down. She gasped when she saw the repairing wound. Alex was gasping like a fish out of water.

"Should I call an ambulance?" Alex's hand shot out like a pale viper and grabbed her wrist.

"NO!" he hissed painfully, "I will be okay. Can you get me to my house, please?"

"I can't lift you," Mary pleaded. "You can stay here until you can move."

"I can't stay." Alex knew that she already knew too much and would be eliminated in due course. "Can I have some water?"

"Of course," Mary hurried off.

"Mr. Cross, please don't kill her; it's not her fault," Alex pleaded. His words ran together.

"If you leave now, she will be safe," Mr. Cross said.

Alex leaped to his feet and silently left the beautiful woman's house. He stumbled to his own house and fell inside. He closed the door and tried to crawl to his room, but he did not make it. As unconsciousness enveloped him, he thought weakly, *Did I remember to lock the door?*

Blackness.

Under Hollister, California, March 16, 4:00 a.m. PST.

My shower was hot and much needed. I cried hard over my mom, and eventually, I was able to move. I was not embarrassed to cry, just not in public. I knew my mom was in a better place, but I wanted to make the people who took her from me pay, and I wanted my dad back. When I got out of the shower and dried off, I heard an unfamiliar but comforting voice in my mind.

Your mother is with me, and she is fine. You have a job to do and a life to save. Do not falter, young Iklwa. You must be bold and determined.

The voice was soft and encouraging. My heart stuttered at first, but I remembered I accepted all this mystical stuff. I had seen and experienced too much to think this was just an errant voice in my head. I accepted it. What could I do? I couldn't bring my mom back. She was taken from me, and

I would make them pay. But it was good to know she was in a good place.

I put on the gray sweats Adrian left for me. I started to reach for the doorknob and paused. I dropped my hand back to my side and took a deep breath. Then I took three more. I engaged my mind on the problem at hand. Getting my father back. I was stupid and short-sighted before. These two wonderful, loving people had been everything to me, and I had the nerve to be upset and offended that they didn't tell me the truth. They were a lot like me right now, doing the best I could with what I had. I realized I didn't know all the right answers and would only do my best to take the next best step to achieve my goal. I had no idea what was beyond this moment. I did know that when I opened this door, I would be immersed in a world I knew nothing about, but I had an advantage. I was a great student. I loved physics and math, and my parents taught me about my African heritage. They grounded me in my culture and gave me the confidence to be who I wanted to be. I would get my dad back, and I would destroy this monster called the SOTIR Group. I took three deep breaths and reached out and opened the door.

I came out into the hall, wondering where to go. I looked to my left, which was where I came from. I looked to my right, and the hall continued for a short time and seemed to branch off in two directions. I headed that way. When I came to the T in the hall, I could hear the voices of my friends coming from the left. "Always go left," my dad always said. The hall was long, but as I walked, the sound of their voices got stronger.

"Eat up; Scipio will be here in a moment, then we will..." Adrian's voice trailed off as I rounded the corner.

Ian and Saphronia were seated, and they stood when I came to the dining area.

"Hey Scip, how are you feeling?" Ian asked first.

"Angry," I said. "Where is the food?" Saphronia and Ian stepped apart and revealed a table full of food.

Every breakfast food was there; I loved breakfast any time of the day. Strangely, there was a stack of plastic leftover holders in one corner of the table. I sat down and dug into the bounty. The table was quiet, and I glanced at everyone, and they were as fixated on their food as I was. My mom used to say you could always tell the food was good when the talking stopped. There was a spike of pain from that memory, but I used it to reinforce my determination to succeed.

After we finished eating, I told everyone what I experienced in the bedroom with the unfamiliar yet comforting voice. Ian and Saphronia squeezed my shoulders, but Adrian got up and hugged me tightly. When we separated, I could see the tears threatening to spill down his cheeks. He wiped them away.

"Let's get started," he said.

He touched the table, and everything disappeared. There was a great *clang,* and I looked around, surprised; all the dishes were clean and put away. The very small amount of leftovers was neatly sealed away in the containers I saw earlier.

"Wow," I said, "that is handy!"

"Yeah," Adrian said. "So, we are going to see my good friend Bamidele; he will get us armored up."

"*The* Bamidele?" Saphronia exclaimed, "Bamidele, the international fashion designer, is your good friend?

"Who is Bamidele?" I was looking lost.

I knew who Bamidele was; he was a super-famous clothing designer, and he used his platform to attack White supremacy and inequality worldwide. He created the most expensive dress in history, worth 200 million dollars, which, when sold, he promptly invested in African communities all over the world. That was one of the largest influxes of cash into African movements at one time. Saphronia looked at me like I had a lobster crawling out of my mouth.

"How do you not know who Bamidele is?" She ran her hands over her ebony curls. "You Americans can be so cut off from reality."

"Hey, I'm sorry, I don't know who they are. I'm not a fashionista like you." I couldn't hold my smile back. "Okay, okay, I'm just messing with you. Of course, I know who Bamidele is. He is the two-hundred-million-dollar designer."

Saphronia's jaw dropped. "Oh, you ass!" she chided.

Adrian cut in, "Yeah, we met about ten years ago. I helped him out of a very dire situation, and we became friends. Anyway, he is a part of the Amanirenan Resistance, and he has the resources to outfit the fighters in our little struggle."

Adrian produced two Global wristwatches and gave them to Ian and Saphronia.

"I need you to use these phones instead of your old ones. They do everything your old ones did. However, they are on a very segregated system. The encryption is nearly uncrackable and is monitored constantly for breaches," he told them.

"Where are our old Globals? I was looking for mine, and it was gone," Ian said.

"They are gone, Ian. I destroyed them."

"Dude, *what*? I had sentimental pictures on that device, and you just destroyed it? You could've let me download my pictures before you did that," Ian was infuriated.

Saphronia said, "Mr. Adrian, I had pictures of my Vovo on that Global!"

"Don't worry, you guys, I was busy on our flight over here. All of your information and pictures are there. We have very capable people. Go ahead, look," Adrian soothed.

They did, and I could tell they were satisfied. "Why don't I get a new Global?" I asked.

"You already have one of these," Adrian said. "These Globals are untraceable and unhackable. There is a very direct and active security team watching this system. So, don't worry."

"Bamidele is very eccentric but harmless. Just answer his questions and follow his instructions. Are you ready?" We all nodded our heads.

"Good, let's go," and we vanished.

Somewhere Underground, March 16, 1:17 p.m. GMT.

Suddenly, we were standing in an elaborately decorated space. There were brightly colored curtains all around the room. There was a table with a sewing machine on it and a shimmering cloth hanging from it. There were patterns for clothes hanging on the walls. There was another table with half-rolled tape measures and a massive pin cushion filled with pins and needles. The place was a tidy mess, and I could see a pattern in the chaos. The carpeted floor was blood red; I took a tentative step and felt no cushion on the floor. I saw an arch that I assumed led to a hall or at least a door. Something didn't feel right. I passively pulsed the room. There was another heartbeat in the room, but I got more information from the pulse than before. I could sense the disruption in the air that the extra person was causing. I turned to face them.

"Hello," I said, presumably to empty space.

There was a flash, and a man was standing there. He was at least seven feet tall. He was much taller than me, and that was exceedingly rare. He was dressed in flamboyantly bright clothing. Shiny chains and beads hung from his neck and wrists. It reminded me of something a genie would wear. He was very dark-skinned and thin. He had long limbs, his eyes were golden-brown, and he was so deeply pigmented that the sclera of his eyes seemed jaundiced. I saw it a lot in darkly pigmented older men, but this guy didn't look much older than me.

"Oh, he is good; this one is exceptionally good. How did you *see* me?" The tall man gestured quotation marks around the word see. His voice was jovial and light, with a deep baritone hidden in it, highlighted by an English accent.

"I don't really know how to explain it," I said.

"Try," the deep cord of Bamidele's voice was revealed in the command.

"I sensed the disruption you made in the air. I could see it flowing around something I could not see," I explained.

"OH! You are good! That is the one thing I cannot hide. Where did you find this one, Adrian?"

"He is my student," Adrian said.

They both burst out laughing. I had never seen Adrian laugh so hard. Tears were actually squirting from the corners of his eyes.

After a minute of laughing, Adrian was able to get a hold of himself and properly introduce us.

"Guys, this is Bamidele. He is a great friend of mine and will take your measurements. Sorry about that; it's an inside joke," Adrian said.

Bamidele bowed lavishly. He walked over to Saphronia.

"You are magnificent, young lady. You would be a very successful model. Maybe when you are done with this little adventure, you could come work for me. What do you say?" Bamidele asked, bending at the waist, and his face was directly in Saphronia's.

She was holding herself together well, considering she was being spoken to directly by someone she idolized.

"I...I do not know," she squeaked.

I stepped over to Bamidele and said, "She is a little star-struck."

Bamidele stood straight up and nodded to himself.

"And bold to boot! He is your student, Ady," Bamidele said jovially.

"Who's the lovely descendant?" Bamidele's tone was light, but there was a hardness in his voice that put me on edge.

"His name is Ian, and he's with me, so he's cool." My annoyance dipped a little. Was I being weird? I mean, I just met the guy, and I felt like he was challenging me. I told myself to get a grip.

"Oh, you got a mean bark, pup. How about you show me your bite?" Bamidele challenged.

"C'mon, Bam, don't do this; we need clothes," Adrian pleaded.

"Don't worry, Ady, you'll get them, but first, I want to see this boy's bite," he spoke with gentleness, then venom.

"We don't have time; we have the Group after us," Adrian admitted. Bamidele's face became serious.

He asked what seemed like a perfectly innocuous question, "You, him, or her?"

"Him," Adrian sighed.

"Good, all the more reason to see what he's got." A massive flash occurred, and when the smoke cleared, it seemed I was in some kind of dojo. I raised my mental guard. There were all manner of hand-to-hand weapons on the walls. The walls were mudbrick with a thin veil of earth over them, and they were far away. The floor was stamped dirt, and the ceiling was domeshaped; it was covered in small green and white tiles in recurring geometric shapes. I took all of this in an instant because Bamidele was standing in front of me.

"Do you like my little training room?" the tall man asked.

"What the hell is going on?" My guard was apparent in my voice.

"We will see if you are capable of being what Ady and the Elders say you are."

"What are you talking about?" I asked, wondering when Adrian had time to talk to this crazy man in parachute pants. Unless he was referring to an older conversation.

He took two exaggerated ballet steps toward me, Black bare feet splayed out, and his arms undulated up and down gracefully. I knew he would attack; he was trying to hide it in the amplified movements, but I could see it plainly. As he planted his foot, I threw a right jab with a little kinetic heat added to it. He probably thought it was an insane thing to do. I saw a smile start to blossom on his dark face; it vanished when the kinetic version of the punch hit him in the face. Bamidele stumbled back, his brown eyes registering shock.

"Okay," was all he said, rubbing his nose as he disappeared.

"You know I figured that trick ou-" Before I could finish the sentence, I was kicked savagely in my back.

My arms flailed as I flew across the space and ultimately sprawled on the ground. I flared to my feet, using my long legs to keep the invisible man at bay. I tried to do the same trick as I did in the other room, but I got no information back. *Okay,* I thought, *this is new.* I positioned myself with my back up against the wall. I heard a deep rumbling laugh that echoed in the small space. I knew I had other ways of detecting him. I cast my mind out to find his. I was perplexed by the information I received. His mind was here, but I couldn't tell where.

Bamidele wasn't attacking. The room filled with dust, and I started coughing. Suddenly, he was directly in front of me, smiling.

"Boo," he said conversationally, and a bright flash exploded directly in my face. I yelled and rolled to the left; I landed in a crouch. I put my hands up and dropped my chin, waiting for a kick to the head area.

"Oh, nice try, little lion."

Unexpectedly, there was a massive pain in my right shoulder blade. It was an ax kick; I recognized the feeling immediately. Adrian had hit me with these often, and I learned their gentle caress. It must not have been that hard because my shoulder blade was still intact.

Before he could retract his leg, I exploded up and punched him in the balls. Adrian taught me that in a real fight, there are no rules. There are no points to be scored, only survival. Which meant all attacks were on the table.

A high-pitched squeal escaped his throat, and I palm-smashed him in the chest.

There was a kinetic boost on the strike, and he flew to the other side of the room we were in; he didn't touch the floor until he hit the opposite wall. Bamidele bounced off the wall and landed on his hands and knees. I rushed him. Before his head came up, I was there, and I positioned myself to be on his right side. I stepped and kneed him in the side of the face. To his credit, he did not go lights out.

I heard him say, "Oof!" Then, amazingly, he tried to sweep me; I was looking at his face and only saw his leg move in my peripheral vision. Before I knew it, I was standing just out of his leg's range. I had no idea how I did it. Bamidele laughed and disappeared again.

"You don't know how you did that," Bamidele's disembodied voice said. "You are far stronger than Ady, or the Elders think you are."

"We didn't come here to fight you. What are you doing?" I asked the dusty space.

My kinetic awareness was so high, and combined with my learned spatial awareness, I felt the air pressure start to change behind me. I knew I had done something earlier when Bamidele tried to sweep me. I moved somehow. I just remembered I wanted to be out of the way of his leg, then I was repositioned outside of his range. I did not teleport, and I didn't step back; I was just in another spot. Or position. So, I did that. I wanted to be behind wherever he was going to show up. When I felt the pressure change, I tapped into that desire.

SNAP!

I was in a new position, and Bamidele appeared right before me, with his back to me. I had the string of the ability to pull at will now. I willed my hand to be in the punching position with a kinetic force of twice my punching strength. I knew it wouldn't hurt me because I was resistant to kinetic damage.

My fist flashed into position faster than I could have ever swung it. I struck him high in the middle of his back. He flew forward like a rag doll, arms and legs spread out, his chest hit, then his head, and he bounced off the mud-brick wall. He landed on his back. He didn't move for about five seconds. I was starting to think I killed him. I wasn't trying to do that.

Adrian taught us that people with abilities were sometimes more resilient than normal people. The stronger they were, the more resilient they got. He told us he saw sparring matches between two high-level people, and they could withstand massive amounts of physical damage. I had been willing to take that gamble, and now that he was laughing, I felt a lot better.

Bamidele rolled over languidly and got to his feet. He groaned and stretched his neck, left, then right.

"Impressive little lion, you are a quick learner. You will master those abilities sooner than you think. Ady said you showed a telepathic talent as well. Is that what you used to predict where I was going to be?" I was taken aback by the sudden change in tone.

"Uh, no, I just used a refinement of the first air pressure trick and good old spatial awareness." I half-smiled. I felt like I had been tested.

"Good," he said, nodding his head, "But why didn't you use the telepathy?"

"I don't like being in other people's minds. There is a lot of bleedthrough, and I feel like it's a violation of their privacy."

"I see," Bamidele nodded his head more, "You won't get better unless you use your abilities. Just like your offensive ability, you can get much better with telepathy."

"My kinetic manipulation does seem to be growing as I use it."

Bamidele burst out laughing. His deep, resonating voice filled the practice room.

"Did you say…" he laughed more, "Did you say kinetic manipulation?"

"Yeah, what about it? Adrian told me some science team did a genetic scan or whatever, and it said those were my abilities." I was getting annoyed at this guy. What did he know anyway?

"They most likely said 'a type of kinetic manipulation.' However, what you are showing is more like kinetic manipulation's older sister," he paused for dramatic effect, "Full-blown Vector Manipulation."

I liked physics, and I had a limited understanding of vectors. Vectors were a quantity that had magnitude and direction. He was saying I was able to manipulate vectors. There were all kinds of vectors: positional, like/unlike, co-initial, displacement, and collinear. Not everything had a vector, but everything had a position.

I just stared at him. My mind swam with possibilities.

"It is daunting, and I understand why they downplayed it for you, but you are in a very deadly game, and if you are not ready, they will kill you and those you love," Bamidele said, and my mind flashed to my mother's lifeless eyes. I blinked and shook my head. I need to think about this; the enormity of what he told me, and the evidence of our little sparring match, was overwhelming.

"Look, you seem to need a moment with this. Now is a good time to ask questions; let that simmer for a bit,"

Bamidele said, crossed his feet, and sat down. "We have time."

"What about the others? We are waiting for a phone call," I explained.

"It will not come for some time. Ask," Bamidele raised his hands palms up. I didn't know how he knew it, but there was surety in his voice. Adrian trusted him, so I gave him the benefit of the doubt.

CHAPTER 24

Somewhere Underground, March 16, 1:10 p.m. GMT.

My mind was flooded with questions. When someone says *Ask me anything,* it's guaranteed your mind goes blank every time.

"Uh…" I started, "Who are you, and how do you know so much?"

"Good, easy question. I will answer both this way. I am a fashion designer and a scientist of sorts. I helped start the 'science team' Ady told you about. I retired thirty years ago and have been making special clothes since. That is how I understand what abilities you have; it was my research into the genome that gave the subsequent teams the ability to roughly determine what ability may be expressed." his voice was nostalgic. He shook his head, wiped his cheeks, and looked surprised when his fingers came back wet.

"Any more questions?" he asked.

One flashed into my mind: "Why did you call my friend, Ian, a descendant?"

"Because that is what he is," Bamidele answered. "Life started in Africa, and humans migrated out. Some going deeper into the Motherland, others forsaking her and going East. What we call the Middle East, and to the south and East Asia, then from the Middle East through the Caucasus mountains and into Europe. As they bred and increased in number, their hair and skin got lighter, and here we are to-day. They all descended from us. We are all human, but we, as the Original people, have been devastated over the last few centuries, but like iron, we are worked into something new. Our adapted descendants have lived a life of privilege, whether they know it or not, and it has made them soft. Their reward was to rule, and they did it with an iron fist, pressing Africans into operancy. It was slow and small at first, but now here you are, the Iklwa, ready to be sent into the fray. We will find out what our reward is," he said with passion in his eyes as he finished.

Why had he used the word *Iklwa*? That is what The Voice said I was.

Bamidele continued, "Now there are exceptions, especially in countries that had slavery as an institution for many generations. There are those very few White people that can develop powers when pushed hard enough. Your friend Ian and others like him are descendants of our people. That is why I call him descendant."

I narrowed my eyes. "You make it sound like a derogatory term," I said, challenging him.

"It was better than calling him a beast like the Black soldiers did in Vietnam," Bamidele retorted.

I swelled at the accusation. "Ian has had my back from day one. Of all the people in my life, he has been consistent, whether I was there or not. He is more than my friend; he is a brother, and you, Mr. Bamidele, better remember that." The implication was very clear in my voice that any challenge to that fact would be met with violence. I didn't know what my snapping point would be in this whole adventure, but I could feel it fast approaching.

Bamidele raised his hands in surrender for the second time, "Okay, little lion, I will remember that. Do you have more questions?"

I was pissed off and was done talking to him. I didn't have any more questions. I wanted to go back to my friends.

"I'm done," I said flatly.

"Are you sure?" Bamidele asked.

I was sure there was more, but I was done with this school-time lesson. "Yes," no faster than that word came out of my mouth, Bamidele snapped his fingers, and we were back in the sewing room.

"WHOA!" Ian yelled as we appeared in the room. Saphronia only smiled at me, but I could see the relief in her eyes.

"Welcome back," Adrian said calmly, then asked, "Did you find out what you needed, Bam Bam?"

"Yes," Bamidele said, but I could tell by his expression he was holding something back.

"Good. Can we get along with the sewing? I don't know how much time we have." It seemed like Adrian was not the least bit concerned about the information Bamidele may or may not have about me.

"Fine, you are a party pooper," Bamidele said.

He went to a large wooden cabinet on the wall and opened it; a cold mist rolled out of it. Inside were ampoules of red liquid. When he turned around holding a pair of needles and a pair of blood vials, I realized the stuff in the refrigerator was blood.

"Why all the blood?" I wondered aloud.

He only smiled and winked.

"Okay, I don't know what that means, but could you answer my question?" I insisted.

Bamidele rolled his eyes in frustration.

"Fine. It is blood from my other customers. I keep a sample around to be able to make more outfits. Now hold out your arm," he said.

"What? Why do you need blood?" I saw enough movies to know that you could do a lot of nefarious things with blood, and given that I had just fallen into a strange new world of powers and racist enemies, I was very skeptical of his motives.

"How do you think I do what I do?" he asked, like this was the umpteenth time I had been here.

"I don't know," I said, annoyed.

"He infuses your blood into the garments he is making, and combined with the material he uses, it lets you use your abilities without destroying your clothes," Adrian clarified.

"In short, I key your clothes to you, giving them the resistance and immunities you have from your own power. It, of course, works for other effects that are similar to your abilities that other people possess."

"Why do you only have two vials? There are three of us here that need your expertise." It was a very direct question, and given our earlier conversation about descendants, I knew he knew exactly what I was getting at.

Bamidele chuckled, "I like you, little lion. Your friend does not have abilities, and I don't think he will want to wear kente cloth. They would clash with his pale skin." His smile was saccharin sweet.

"It's okay, Scipio; I don't need a super suit. You and Saphronia will be the ones fighting, not me."

"No, it's not okay," I said roughly, "Can't you make one out of regular clothes?" I demanded.

"Do you mean European-style patterns? No, I cannot, and I will not," Bamidele said, his chin rising in defiance.

I stepped up to him, I was much closer than I liked to be, but I wanted to MAKE this point.

"What is your problem with him, Bam Bam?" Bamidele's smile fell from his face.

"Do you know who I am, Child?" he said, making his own point.

"If you keep treating him like he's less than human, we will have a problem." I ignored his question because I didn't care who he was; no one was going to treat my friend like a second-class person while I was around.

Bamidele did not back down. We stared at each other for about fifteen seconds until Adrian spoke up.

"Okay, guys, let's just get what we came here for and thank Mr. Bamidele for his help."

I could hear the nervous smile in Adrian's voice.

"Fine, if you insist, little lion, I will make your descendant friend an outfit to wear." He turned back to the refrigerator and retrieved another vial.

"Okay, hold out your arms."

We all did.

CHAPTER 25

San Francisco, California, March 16, 4:10 p.m. PST.

Cross knew Alex would be out of action for a few days, and he wanted him on the mission he was planning. He knew it would be necessary for the health of his psyche to destroy this boy. The *boy,* Scipio Harelson, surprised Cross and Alex. He moved so fast, Cross figured he was some kind of speedster; it was a power often seen enough but rarer than one would think in Black people. The boy was strong as well, or it could have been the transferred momentum of a speedster's punch. Whatever it had been, it took most of Alex's nanite population to keep him alive and work on the repairs to his body. His ribcage and lung had nearly been vaporized on the right side, his spinal column was nearly severed at C-7 and T-1, the two vertebrae had been turned to dust, and the spinal cord hung by a thread. His liver was ground meat, and the resulting cavitation shattered his pelvis. One punch. As a testament to Alex's affinity for the little buggers and Allen Berg's genius. The Swedish man could have easily sold the patent to the military and made massive amounts of money. He didn't; he contributed to the Cause so that they could take this country back from the inferior people who were running it into the ground.

The nano-machines were working overtime to keep him alive and repair him. Alex was an exceedingly rare case in the nano-machine experiment, and he had launched Berg's research ahead by decades. Somehow, his body had bonded with the machines, and they formed a symbiotic relationship that resulted in near immortality. Cross was incredibly careful to keep this information from Alex. Besides, he still had operational control of the nano-machines. Shutting them down would effectively kill Alex Lamb, but it would be extremely dangerous if he were to somehow wrest control from him.

Cross tore his thoughts away from hypothetical distractions and returned to finding a place for this "showdown." He wanted that girl; her genetic line would add immeasurably to his arsenal. She may be the genetic key he needed to unlock his people's DNA, and then the playing field would be level. The Group could find and wipe the faceless resistance off the face of the map, and they could make the world the way it was supposed to be.

With White people firmly in charge and thriving.

Ugh, he thought to himself and tore his mind away from the distraction. He was getting too far ahead of himself. He figured twelve men plus Alex would be enough. He decided to add a squad of ten automatons to the mix. They would be held back in reserve, just in case. There was a place near the old power plant that was wide open. Cross knew the boy would come with his little team to rescue the old man, and they would be captured and or killed as long as they got the girl. He sent the orders via text in his encrypted Global. Allen Berg was able to replicate the isolated internet and Global carrier that the Resistance had. It was an extended version of a pirate box; with Cross's connections, they were able to set up worldwide. Well, almost worldwide, the whole of Africa seemed to be off-limits to them. All their incursions were thwarted, secret or overt, and every plan was stopped eventually. The SOTIR Group believed there was a mole, and all attempts to trap them had failed.

Cross was in his office, where he spent most of his time; some would say it was his second home, but they would be wrong; it was his first home. It was a place he felt most in control. He felt like his father was here in the office with him, and he wanted to make him proud. Sam was always in or near the office unless he was in the breeding pens. Cross knew everything about this building and all the fortifications built into it. If he wanted to, he could pull up video feeds from all his assets and communicate all at once or individually with them.

The three Sigma team leaders acknowledged the order given. Cross was satisfied that his overall plan was sound. It would be up to the teams to complete the play. Cross had operatives in almost every governmental agency in the United States, and they would run interference for any exciting developments from the showdown. When the SOTIR Group was ready, they would reveal themselves to the world. When they were ready. Cross knew that the U.S. government would hunt these EPBs down and either destroy them outright or harvest them. And he could not be sure the Group would not get pushed out. It was a gamble that he and the other members were not willing to take.

The EPBs would put up a hell of a fight, and many innocent people would get hurt, and the world itself would be thrown into chaos. No one in the group wanted to disrupt the order yet. This ideal and perspective were drilled into the members of the Group; some of them were given a lot of leeway, but most were on a strict policy of maintaining the secrecy of the Group and its missions. With the tech-savvy Allen Berg, they could catch and kill any story that the Resistance tried to make viral. While the Resistance was able to carve out its own internet space and mobile carrier, it was surrounded and cut off by Allen's security. It had so far been unbreachable by Berg's technicians.

Each of the three members had access to or could control key elements of society. Cross was the diplomatic and operations head, while Allen Berg was the head of technology and communications, and Lilly Roth was the head of medical and psychological sciences. Cross didn't like her; she was overly aggressive. He figured it was to compensate for being a woman in a man's world or something. He would have rather her brother had taken over, but it seems he had an accident and ended up comatose. Cross knew she had something to do with it, but he saw no guilt or remorse register in her facade. She moved with a clear conscience. He respected her for that.

Cross had to be in DC tomorrow morning to meet with some lobbyist friends of his. He stood up and stretched loudly. He wasn't worried about not being in his command center when Alex woke up; they had decked all his private spaces out with the same communications equipment. However, he was annoyed that Alex's little dust-up and recovery opened this window. He had no more excuses to use to avoid the meeting. They had insisted on a face-to-face conference. He tried to explain to them he was all the way in central Africa and had other things to take care of. This was, of course, a lie to get out of going to the meeting, but they were adamant. Cross had to play nice because they had access to money he wanted, and there was an upcoming election in the U.S. that he was very interested in. They had direct access to the would-be candidate he wanted to exploit. They knew it and would try to use that knowledge to make him their pawn, but it would be the other way around. Robert Cross had dirt and or leverage on everyone in power he dealt with; it was the only way to do business in Washington.

CHAPTER 26

Somewhere Underground, March 16, 1:30 p.m. GMT.

After taking our blood, Bamidele started the process of making our clothes. He took our measurements and asked our ages. It seems he could make clothes we would never have to replace if we didn't actively try to destroy them. According to Adrian, he infused our clothes with our blood, making them accessible to our power. Bamidele claimed he would know more about our abilities after he was finished making our clothes. He suggested that we wear the outfit instead of our regular clothes; it would be naturally bulletproof and very, very resistant to a knife attack. He said it would be a couple of days before he was done. Adrian wanted us to meet someone special, but they were on the other side of the country. With his friend E's help, he said it would take no time at all to go see her.

E met us back at Adrian's home. They embraced, and she gave us all hugs.

"Enjoy Haven," was all she said, and a human-sized hole in the air appeared, and on the other side, I could see a rainbow of stalls and shops and the busy bustle of many people.

We all stepped through, and the smell of many seasonings flooded my nostrils. On the other side, I realized we were still underground somewhere. The shops were built into the walls of this underground complex, and the stalls were in between shops, filling every space. The walls and ceiling were remarkably familiar to me. I did not know how one person could have done all this by themselves. We followed Adrian through the hustle and bustle of the market. I don't know what I expected to see, but everything being sold was normal. There were stalls with fruits and vegetables for sale. It was like a permanent street fair. There were restaurants and stores with big glass windows.

It was the people who were different. A great many of them did not look human. Some were green and had sharp, pointy teeth, others looked normal but had a tail or animal-like ears. Sometimes it was as simple as having strange, brightly colored eyes. A group of children played in an open area, but they were moving so fast that it was obviously extra-normal. None of these people would have been able to just be out in normal public without causing at least rumors of aliens or monsters roaming the streets. Their families were here too. They were probably unwilling to leave their loved ones in the hands of strangers and joined them here. From what Adrian had described, it was only Black people that had any kind of abilities, but with the introduction of E and all these people here; it seemed the emergence of abilities included a large percentage of people of South Asian and Asian descent, at least ten percent of what had to be, several thousand people.

This was a Haven for them.

As we walked through the crowd, I noticed people were staring at us in amazement. That was a weird emotion to see registered on their faces. A little girl, no more than five or six, ran up to Ian and slapped his hand and bolted back to her friends. Small white wings flapped excitedly as she ran, and her feet left the ground at least twice. Ian cried out in surprise, more than pain.

"What the heck was that for?" he complained.

Saphronia chuckled and said, "They are counting coup on you, Ian." She stopped laughing. "People that look like you may have been responsible for some terrible things in their lives."

Ian looked stricken, but he did not complain. He simply smiled at the children and waved at them. Then he shook his hands like it was hurt badly. I have known Ian most of my life, and he is the most stand-up guy I know. And he knew his American history just as well as I did, but he never let it color his interactions. He was always Ian. Still, people whispered as he passed. We walked in a single-file line with Adrian leading the way with Saphronia behind him, then Ian, and I brought up the rear. So, I watched the whole thing play out. I did notice the older people staring and pointing at me, but I had no idea how I stood out in our little group. The news of Ian's appearance must have spread through the community fast because the streets started to get crowded.

"It's not far, guys," Adrian called back to us, "stay close," he admonished.

We eventually came to a small, squat square building covered with aluminum siding and one red door. There was a bright yellow sunrise painted on the door.

"Here we are," Adrian announced, "When you meet East, don't act all weird, she is down to earth and regular, but she has seen a lot. Just be respectful."

"Is she the Elder of this place?" Ian asked.

"Yes," Adrian said, "but she is not THE leader of the Amanirenan Resistance."

"What?" I asked.

"Ask her," was all Adrian said. He stepped to the door and touched the hill the sun was rising behind, and the sun lit up. The Red door swung in, and darkness beckoned.

CHAPTER 27

Somewhere Underground, March 16, 1:45 p.m. EST.

We all started into the room, but Adrian stopped Ian.

"Sorry, bud, you have to wait outside," Adrian said.

"Why?" I asked before Ian could. I was instantly upset.

Adrian looked directly at me, "Some things are meant only for you and Saphronia; it's not negotiable. You two need to go in and talk to East. Alone." His voice was set in granite.

"But," I started to protest.

"No," and with that, he gestured for us to go in.

"Don't worry about it, bro, I'll be right here when you guys get back. Maybe I'll try to make friends," Ian said, diffusing the situation.

"Ian, just stay right here. Don't start any trouble," Adrian said.

When we entered the room, I'm not sure what I expected, but what I got was an empty room with walls painted red like the door. I turned back and saw Ian waving. I raised my hand to wave, and the door slammed shut. The room blackened, and my mental guard shot up. After Bamidele's little show, I wasn't sure what was going to happen. Suddenly, the room started to go down. I was surprised and almost lost my balance. Saphronia must have had a similar experience because I felt her hand grip my shirt.

There was a soft grinding of rock on rock as we descended. Lights had come on soon after the downward movement started. When they did, Saphronia looked up at me and smiled. She let go of my sleeve and took my hand.

"How deep does this go?" she asked Adrian.

"I'm not sure, maybe ten stories," he speculated.

"Whoa!" I said and enjoyed holding Saphronia's hand.

"So, Adrian, what should I expect when we go in here? I feel like you are taking us on a tour of very important people. As we walked through the little market area, I started to feel like we were on display. E could have easily opened a portal to a spot right in front of the door," I said.

"I was contacted by East after the incident about the police. She said she wanted to meet you," he explained. "I don't know why she wants to meet you."

"What makes me so special that the leader of the Amanirenan Resistance wants to see me?" I asked.

"I don't know Scipio, and she is not the leader of the Resistance. She is the leader or Elder of the Haven Community," Adrian snapped. What was going on here, I wondered. There was so much secrecy. Before I could respond, the elevator stopped, and the entire wall the door was on slid away.

Before us lay what looked like the inside of a cozy home.

"Come in!" a woman's voice beckoned from deeper in the house. It sounded familiar.

I glanced at Adrian, and for the first time in my life, I saw him diminish a little bit. We walked into the house, and the wall slid closed behind us and was replaced by a wall covered in wood paneling. The smell of soul food filled the place, and my body immediately reacted. I hadn't realized how hungry I was until this smell hit me. Right on the heels of that thought came a memory of my mother cooking my favorite meal for me on my birthdays. Pork chops and greens with sweet cornbread. My mom made a glaze with spicy mustard and brown sugar. My heart and my stomach synced up, and I was nostalgically hungry.

Adrian led us down a short hall and into a dining area with one wooden table in the center and high-backed chairs surrounding it. The light hanging over the table was an old version of a chandelier with flame-shaped light bulbs. There were four places set at the table.

The voice from the nearby kitchen rang out, "Grab a plate and come get your food."

We looked at each other and shrugged. We all grabbed a plate, careful to leave the plate at the head of the table there.

"Someone, please grab my plate too, if you would."

I was last in the little line we made, so I grabbed it. I knew this voice from somewhere.

The kitchen was cozy but by no means small. There was an island in the middle with a big tub-like sink in it, and the walls were a warm off-white color. The countertops were granite, and there were two refrigerators: one standing and one chest-type next to it. The ovens were massive affairs with stainless-steel coverings. There were cabinets along the walls and an open door. I saw someone puttering around inside. The food was amazing: cornbread, rolls, meats, greens, cobblers, and pies adorned the countertops. The smell of recently fried chicken rose to the top of the smells. A middle-aged Black woman came from the pantry. She was wiping her hands on her apron. Her face looked to be about thirty years old, but her shock of gray hair on her head put her age into context. She looked to be in very good shape, maybe a retired athlete. She was tall, about 5'8", and strong.

"Hey, kids, you guys look hungry. Dig in; it's better to talk on a full stomach anyway," she said, holding her hand out to me, and I gave her the plate I had taken from the table for her.

We silently put food on our plates. I noticed Adrian was not shy about the amount of food, so I did the same. East watched us get food and even encouraged Saphronia to get more.

We gathered at the table and sat down.

East said a prayer of thanks over the food. "Thank you, Ancestors, for this bounty and the safety in which we eat it."

Then we dug in; there was just the clanking of utensils on plates as we ate our food. The food was amazing. Everything was cooked perfectly and tasted like my mom had been in the kitchen helping East cook.

When my plate was emptied for the first time, she looked at me and smiled, "Go ahead, go get yourself some more." I didn't hesitate and went back for seconds.

As I was finishing my second pile of food and Adrian was clearing the table, East asked, "So now that we are all full to the brim with food, let me formally introduce myself. My name is Sunrose Alkebulan, and I am the person in charge of taking care of this little community in the United States. The people know me as East. The nickname keeps my real name out of the mouth of the SOTIR Group. I already know who you are." She nodded and smiled at Adrian.

"Adrian and I have known each other for a long time now." She turned to Saphronia and said, "You're the newest addition to the little group, but I knew your Grandmother.

I was very sorry to hear about her passing, but she was the reason I needed to see you all." Then she looked at me.

"Scipio Okoro, your parents were Cara and Jamal. They were friends of mine as well. In fact, I met you when you were very young. You were less than six weeks old, and they were so proud of you. They were exceptionally good operatives and very, very fine people. You come from good stock, young Scipio."

East had taken this air of grandmotherly caring, but her eyes were digging into Saphronia and me. I felt an itching inside my head. Then I recognized The Voice. I glanced at Saphronia, and she returned a knowing nod.

"Adrian told me about what happened the other night with the two police officers. That was a very impressive emergence. However, your display has caught the attention of the SOTIR Group, and now they want both of you. It would be easy for you to stay here and remain hidden, but I already know that is not going to happen. Not because they have your father, but because you two have a destiny to fulfill." East laughed loudly at herself.

It was shocking.

"Now you are starting to think I am crazy, but remember I said I knew your Grandmother, Saphronia. You called her Vovo, but she was my colleague. I knew her as Adelina. She was the Elder of a small A.R.C. (Amanirenan Resistance Community) in Cape Verde. She did not have as many charges as I did, but she was in a strategic place in the world. She told me you four were coming and that you would change the struggle. She said light is born from the darkness, and we would be able to stand in the light of day once again. So here you are," she beamed at us.

There was an awkward silence. I scooped the last bite from my plate and sat back, satisfied.

When I finished chewing my last bite, I said, "You don't have to convince me to join the struggle; my parents covered that already." I produced the letter they had given me.

"What I do want to know is what the endgame is. What is our goal? Are we going to reveal ourselves to the public and hope they don't want to kill us? Because to me, that seems to put a lot of trust in people that hate us because of our skin color."

East nodded her silver head at my words.

"Our endgame is to establish ourselves and create a place on this planet where we can all be free to walk around in the sunlight," East answered.

"But how?" Saphronia insisted. "The SOTIR Group is definitely tied to law enforcement and higher government agencies. How are the four of us going to establish a safe place? We cannot fight the governments of the world all alone."

"No one expects you to fight alone, child. We need someone to rally behind; Adelina revealed to me that through your struggle with the SOTIR Group, you would emerge as leaders that the Amanirenan Resistance could rally behind. Our coven of Seers has seen what becomes of us because of you. And while I cannot reveal to you the specifics, I can tell you that this fight you are in will lead not only to the coalescence of the Communities but the harvest of cooperation throughout the Diaspora. Africans worldwide will flock to us, and in turn, we will build a better world for the rest of the planet. As always, when Black people rise, every other group rises with us. We must take back our birthright from those that, for centuries, have been out to destroy us."

"But what makes me or us so special? You have thousands of people with abilities that could wipe out armies with ease. Why us?" My mind was spinning with the information I was getting. This was like some story being told, but I was in the middle of it.

"Honestly, Scipio, you and Saphronia are the most powerful people we have ever seen. The abilities you possess could turn the tide of any altercation, and the mere threat of you would be enough to engender civility in any negotiation we would have with the establishment.

"When I was a child, I was always taught to hide my abilities for fear someone would take me and experiment on me, and my family would have no way to get me back. When I was on my own after the horrific massacre of my family, I clung to that belief for a very long time. Eventually, I had to use my abilities to survive the streets of Philadelphia. When I started running into others running and hiding for their lives, I tried to help them and take care of them. We hid in the sewers for a very long time, stealing food from the surface to survive. Eventually, this became untenable because the homeless population we protected started to think we were demons or witches.

"On the verge of collapse and discovery, I met Eunice and her family. They were all able to manipulate inorganic matter. However, Eunice, I mean E, and her brother could sculpt and shape earth itself. So, we built this community. I sent them on a mission to do the same for the other struggling communities. We still help regular people like the homeless and destitute. We even fight crime a little bit in our own ways. It keeps the youth busy while not revealing ourselves. For years now, conflicts have become more vicious. As far as I can tell, the SOTIR Group has not realized it. However, it is still impossible for people of direct European descent to achieve these abilities or any form of them. But they have vast resources and connections."

East looked at Adrian, "The Nine Ghana have been invaluable operatives, but they are still easily overwhelmed by SOTIR Group's tactics, and they operate best below the radar," she smiled at Adrian. "While they are good at what they do, they are not leaders." I looked at Coach; he just shrugged. "You two are the Iklwa and the Ikhawu we have been waiting for," East said.

Saphronia and I cocked our heads to the side in the same way when she mentioned the Iklwa and the Ikhawu.

"Why did you say that?" I asked East.

"We have been having dreams of Aset or Isis. She has come to all the Elders and all the Seers. She warned us of your coming. She also warned of the destruction that you would cause in your wake and the freedom that comes after the horror. Scipio and Saphronia, even Ian, you all will be instrumental in changing how the world is. But you must try, even when it seems all is lost, you must stand. The Ancestors are with you. I was tasked to make contact with you and make sure you had the experience to take the next step."

I stood up from the table and paced. This was more weight to bear. Now we were the hope for the whole world? I'm just a kid who likes martial arts and comic books. All the books and movies about superheroes or everyday heroes could never prepare you to hear that the fate of the world rests on your shoulders. I was trying my best to wrap my head around the reality of the situation but failed miserably. I had to be reminded to take out the trash; how could I be responsible for the futures of millions of other human beings? A joke my dad told came to mind.

How do you eat an elephant?

One bite at a time. So, I decided to focus on the most pressing problem.

"How do I get my dad back?" I asked, turning to look at her.

"You fight," East said simply. "We have tried marching and voting and hoping and singing and even showing we have guns, but nothing has moved the needle in any remarkable way. We always end up with the short end of the stick because our enemy is willing to use violence. Not only use it, but use it effectively. They love that we turn the other cheek and wait to get hit again. There is a time for everything, even war. When the fighting stops, and we can come to the table as equals, it will be time for diplomacy, and instead of demanding what scraps they will give us, we will discuss how we can live together peaceably. I have seen what they are capable of firsthand," East said, absently rubbing her wrist.

"So, you are offering my friends and me up as some kind of sacrifice? We get the privilege of walking into a meat grinder and watching the horror of war? We get to get our hands bloody while you all sit here and wait to hear if the war is over, then come out all sparkling and clean to take the credit for our work, leaving us with the trauma? And what? We are supposed to say thank you?" I was getting pissed; I could feel my *anger* rising, but the guardrails I felt when talking to my parents about all of this were gone. My *anger* was not being dampened in any way. However, I did not want it to get away from me.

"No, we will give you the keys to the kingdom. The other Communities would flock to you, and you would lead them; your perspective of the world we live in is what we are lacking. Your friendship with Ian will be an inspiration for forgiveness and reconciliation. The parent welcoming home the wayward child." East had not moved from her seat, but the passion and force pouring off her were heavy.

"I have spoken to the other Elders of the Communities, and they all agree, save one, that if you, somehow, free us from this specter of the SOTIR Group, they would follow you. Adrian and I will be here to help you in any capacity you may need. Even then, the outlier would have to concede." East paused to breathe.

"You," she gestured to us, "are the Warriors we need for this portion of the struggle, and your youth will be the light to take us into the future."

Images of crowds and awards and crowns danced in my head, replacing the dread. Could we be King and Queen together? We could have a dynasty. I could stop police brutality altogether, maybe even end racism.

It was the ending racism that did it. I burst out laughing. I doubled over and felt tears in my eyes. I laughed and laughed. I fell to one knee, laughing. It occurred to me that I must look like a lunatic to all of them. I tried to get control of myself and failed several times. Although eventually, I could catch my breath, I coughed for a bit.

"What, pray tell, is so raucously funny?" East asked me.

I looked up and around at everyone. Their faces were a mix of worry and annoyance.

After a couple of deep breaths, "You want me, sorry us, to, to, to...." I started laughing again. It wasn't as bad as before, and I was able to get it under control faster.

"You *seem* to be asking me to end this war by destroying the bad guy, aka the SOTIR Group. And you want me to take my best friend and Saphronia on this journey of likely death? Do I have it right?"

East stared at me and simply nodded.

"Lady, this isn't some story! My mother is DEAD! They killed her for NO reason! And now you want me to join your cause to stop these people, and you will, how do you put it, 'give me the keys to the kingdom.' I don't want your king-dom! I want my MOM BACK!" Tears poured from my eyes. My poor face didn't know what was happening. I turned my back to them; I didn't want them to see me crying for my mommy. I wiped my face on the sleeve of my loaned sweat-shirt.

"I will burn these people to the ground. Not for you or because you want me to. But for my Mother and because I can." I repositioned myself back at the Red Sunrise door. I wanted out of there, and I wanted to get Ian out of this place before he got hurt. When I appeared at the door, the last thought dropped from my mind, and I didn't even see it leave.

CHAPTER 28

Somewhere Underground, March 16, 1:40 p.m. EST.

Ian watched the Red Sunrise Door close, and just like that, he was all alone. He let out a sigh and looked for a place to sit. Surprisingly, there were benches all around the squat square building. He felt the ground rumble and figured it was some kind of elevator, and they were going to be gone for a while. Ian sat on one bench and waited. He tapped his Global earpiece and looked for stories about the Harlsons' house burning down. He was rewarded immediately. He saw the video of the fire trucks trying to put out the fire at his friend's house. This saddened him deeply; some of his best memories were made in that home. After about fifteen minutes, his stomach started to growl, and he remembered they had talked for a long time at Adrian's house. He recalled he had seen stalls with food being prepared in them and at least one restaurant. That thought got his mouth watering. He stood up and stretched.

"I hope they take dollars," he said under his breath.

The entrance to the market they had walked through was not far away. Ian put his hands in his pockets and dipped his head. Ian stood out at 5'10" and 180 pounds, and with his skin tone, he knew he frightened a lot of people here. He had seen their faces when they first came through. He had never been looked at like that in his life.

As he hunkered down, he recognized his stance. He had seen Scipio do it a thousand times. When they went to a restaurant or the gym, anywhere where there were other people, he always diminished himself. It was not until now, feeling himself shrink himself so he wouldn't be perceived as a threat, did he recognize what Scip had been doing. Ian was not mad at himself for not seeing it; he got mad because the world pressed on such a good guy like Scipio Harelson only because of his skin color. "They" only assumed the worst about him. Scipio was practically a super-hero. He goes out of his way to help people all the time. He never hesitated to help, and most people were pleasant and thankful; Scip was always shy and aw-shucks when they thanked him. Some people were shocked when he offered his hand to help, but when they saw the genuineness of his actions, they were ALWAYS appreciative.

The aura Scipio gave off was of a leader and a hero; Ian knew Scipio would never be able to see it in himself, no matter what he or anybody said. In Scip's mind, it was just the right thing to do. Period. Scipio's parents were accountable for all of it. They taught him and Ian to never be the bullies and always stand up to them as best they could. Now Scipio had powers, and he would stand up to these bullies. The people who killed Mrs. H. would pay. Ian knew he was just a regular guy, but he knew he could help Scip. Ian did not want to be sidelined; he wanted to help his friend.

A tall boy appeared in front of him.

"Where ya going, descendant?" the young man had an accent Ian could not place.

The prey always knows when it is the prey, Adrian had taught them. Ian knew he was the prey here. In the hours of lessons about EPBs, Ian listened carefully and took notes just like the others, but for different reasons. Ian took his notes to learn his own limits. Once he understood the fragility of a regular human compared to an EPB, he knew he would have to navigate this world like a roach on a dance floor. Now here he was in the middle of a whole community of EPBs and their families. The young man standing before Ian was seven feet tall. His skin was the color of Mother Earth herself, dark and rich. He had a shock of tight blond curls and bright blue and green eyes. Not hazel, but blue and green seemed to swirl in his iris.' All of this Ian took in within milliseconds, but what stopped him in his thought process was the boy's legs and tail. The young man's tail was thick and tapered down to a wrist, and a hand that flexed and slapped the ground loudly. His feet and toes were long, like a bird's. He stood on strong toes, and it seemed like his knees were bent backward naturally. Ian knew this was not the case; his knee and thigh structure were tucked up near his waist. Ian knew a kick from him would probably snap him in half.

"Nothing, man, I was just going to get something to eat. The food smells amazing!" Ian hoped he didn't seem nervous.

"We got nothing here for you!" he rolled his R's, yet Ian still could not place his accent.

"Oh, okay, I didn't realize I wasn't welcome," Ian said and turned and walked away.

"Hey, I didn't say you could go!" the boy shouted. Ian felt a mighty thump reverberate in the hard-packed dirt, and he instinctively looked up.

The dark-skinned boy with the tail arched over him, his feet and tail still trailing dust. Ian watched him in amazement. The young man landed in front of Ian.

"That was amazing!" Ian exclaimed. His voice was full of wonder and astonishment.

"We don't care what you think is amazing, descendant!" the young man spat the last word out, mimicking Ian's accent.

Ian saw the younger boy's foot shift as he prepared to swing his tail.

Ian stepped into the taller boy's personal space, crouched, and hit him with a left hook to the liver that shook his whole body. The tail swing stopped like a switch had been turned off. The tailed kid curled into a ball and dropped; a deep groan escaped his lips. Careful to land on his left side, he clutched his stomach. Ian could see his bird-like toes twitching.

The crowd of other kids paused for a moment and just stared at their fallen warrior.

Ian ran. He was sprinting toward the red door. He hadn't realized how deep he had wandered into the bazaar; he hadn't made any turns, but the exit seemed farther away than he thought it was. Suddenly, pain exploded in his chest, and he felt his feet lift from the ground, and everything went black.

CHAPTER 29

Somewhere Underground, March 16, 2:00 p.m. EST.

I saw Ian frozen in place; his legs and arms were bent as if he were running. Ian was fast, and I had seen him take off on a sprint looking just like this. A bunch of kids surrounded him, and one was getting up slowly. Ian was facing the bazaar; the big guy had a massive tail that ended in a hand, and his legs were bird-like. I saw a little blue-haired girl with brown sugar-colored skin; she was holding her hand out toward Ian, and I could see the psionic energy flowing from her to him. She had somehow locked him into place. I saw all of this in a fraction of a moment, and before I could say or do anything, the big kid with the tail spun and struck Ian in the chest with his tail. There was a tremendous SLAP sound, and Ian's limp body rocketed up and away from the cheering crowd.

I reached out and caught him.

One second, Ian was standing there, and the next, he was flying off the ground. All I could do was try to arrest his movement. I absorbed his velocity as I did the intruder that somehow got my mother killed.

Focus!

I absorbed his momentum and inertia so he wouldn't jerk to a stop. Ian was suspended in mid-air; he was moving, and then he was not. In a world where we are used to seeing things coast or jerk violently to a stop, Ian's sudden halt of motion was jarring. I repositioned myself in a blink to be between Ian and the infuriated group of kids. They gasped at my sudden appearance. I lowered Ian to the ground, but I was not sure how I did it. It felt like I was blowing air to keep a balloon up in the air, but I was using my energy instead of air. I could feel the control and the resistance to it. I could make Ian as light as a feather or slam him into the ground. I could feel gravity's pull on him, and I lessened it. I could feel and control the pocket of air I surrounded him in. I laid him gently on the ground and faced the little gang of marauders.

I amplified my voice. Once again, it was like blowing out a candle that turned into a crude whistle, "Hey! He is with me; any mistake he made, I will take responsibility for." That was a simple thing to say because I knew Ian, and he would not make a stupid mistake. My voice boomed in the cavern, and all the people that were trying to ignore what was happening turned in our direction.

"He tried to steal from us!" The little blue-haired girl shouted.

I hunkered down and asked in my inside voice, "What did he try to steal?"

The little girl just stared at me.

"Our dignity!" The tall boy with the tail said, "We don't want him here, and since you brought him, you can leave too!" he stepped up to me and stared down at me.

I returned the young man's look. I heard Ian stir behind me.

I realized I balled my hands into fists, and I was getting upset. I opened my hands and took a step back. I recognized their situation in a way I had not considered. I was so focused on taking out or at least hurting the SOTIR Group,

I had not considered the dilemma these people were in. They obviously were hiding from the world, and their reaction to them, and the people they were hiding from looked like Ian. They did not know we had more in common than they knew. East presented me with a proposition earlier, and I did not want to think about it. Now here I am being asked the same question differently. Will I help them? I shook my head; my mom was not even gone 24 hours, and here I was being asked to save a group of people I did not know. I thought about what my mom would say. They both tried to teach me to stand up for those who could not stand for themselves. My birth Mother gave her life to make the world a better place, and my mom, who raised me, taught me that helping others gave life purpose.

"Who are we to withhold our gifts from the world because it scares us?" she would ask. She taught me the difference between arrogance and confidence. I did not know how, but I wanted to help these people see the sun again without fear.

I felt a near-physical swelling in my chest as I looked at this motley group before me. I understood them, and I loved them. I do not know how else to explain it. It was not a condescending love; it was brotherly; these were my people. I could see the pain and distrust in their eyes, but instead of reflecting it, I received it. Any honest spiritual leader would have understood how I felt. The feeling swelled in my chest, and I took a deep breath, ready to express my undying devotion to their, no, to OUR cause; a telephone tittered viciously behind me. The sound shattered everything I was thinking.

I spun toward the relentless sound. Adrian, Saphronia, and East stood there; Adrian held the phone out to me.

"I'm assuming it's for you," Adrian said.

I stared at the black thing with dawning recognition. The phone had been on an overturned bucket in the garage; it was beneath the message left by the abductors of my Father. I noticed Adrian pick it up before we ran for our lives. I looked up at Coach; all my love and resolve drained away. My *anger* replaced it. He saw the pain in my eyes, and we connected. I knew Adrian would do everything he could to help me, and I did not feel as lonely. I reached for the phone, but Adrian took my hand. In an instant, we were somewhere outside.

I could tell instantly that we were outside. Dappled sunlight shone through the leaves of the trees that surrounded us. The air felt fresh in the little grove of trees we appeared in. It occurred to me that I did not know how long we had been in the Community. I heard the horn of a ship somewhere, and immediately afterward, the little black phone rang again. The sound snapped me to attention.

I took the phone from Adrian's hand and answered the call. Until that moment, I did not know what I was going to say, actually.

"Hullo?" I sounded small and way out of my depth, but I was determined to get my dad back.

CHAPTER 30

Six miles over Wichita, Kansas, March 16, 1:30 p.m. CST.

Robert Cross was somewhere over Middle America in a very plush private airplane. He decided to contact the boy and rattle his cage. The young man had never been in this kind of situation before and would make obvious and deadly mistakes, but Cross didn't know what he was capable of, which didn't sit well with him. He had been reviewing the footage of Alex's run-in with him, and there was some meta-type shit going on. To put it in modern parlance. The unaltered footage seemed like the kid sped up and punched a man through a wall. But when he watched, the footage slowed down, and with Alex's analytics displayed, not only did the boy speed up, but Alex also slowed down. All of Alex's gross motor movement stats dropped like a rock. It was like he was fighting in zero gravity; none of his movements seemed to have force or speed. His body thought it was doing something; he was definitely exerting himself, but nothing was happening, or it was just happening very slowly. Compared to Alex's data from just seconds before, he was operating at 1% of his best speed. Not having access to the data on the speedster, he could only assume he stole Alex's speed somehow. How? This question plagued him shortly after he boarded the plane; now, two hours later, he decided to rattle the boy's cage and see if he could get him to reveal himself.

This was a roller coaster of a day. The little group, which was his prey, flew off to the south, and he lost track of them. The fact that they could teleport never crossed his mind; even the fact that they "flew" away was awe-inspiring. Most abilities that manifested were physical or mental, nothing as useful as flying. It was the girl who made it possible. His mind raced at the possibilities she presented, hence the phone call. On paper, the boy was a career criminal. Although he was never convicted of anything, he was often arrested for suspicion of something or other and later, as he got older, for resisting arrest. He had even infected a young White boy named Ian Henderson, who seemed to be following in his criminal brushes with the law. He saw that he took mcDojo karate, which meant he probably knew just enough to get himself killed. However, he did get the drop on Alex. The picture he had in front of him was Scipio's California I.D. picture. He looked normal enough. He didn't seem to have a chip on his shoulder like most young Black boys his age. That was their greatest downfall, he mused; they could be so easily pulled into acting out of anger and not logic. They did not deserve this power.

"Hullo," the boy's voice was strong and clear.

"Hello, Scipio, you sound well," Cross said pleasantly.

"Where is my father?" he asked.

"Safe," answered Cross, who was still not sure how he wanted to approach the exchange. He wanted to get the measure of the kid.

"I know your world has been turned upside down, and you probably have a lot of questions, am I right?" Cross tested.

"You have my Father, and I want him back. What do you want from me?" he said.

"Your father taught you to be direct, good. Right now, I want you to answer my questions, and we will see where we go from there," Cross stated, pausing for a response.

There was none.

"I'll take your silence as a yes." There was a squawk in Cross's other ear from his tracing team, telling him he needed to answer. Instead, he asked Scipio, "How long have you had your abilities?"

CHAPTER 31

Central Park, Manhattan, New York City, New York, March 16, 2:30 p.m. EST

The man's voice was deep and almost comforting. My father's face floated in my vision, and that helped me focus. My answer to his latest question surprised me.

"About a week total." When I uttered the words, their weight slammed into me. One week, only seven days to change my world completely. I looked at Adrian. Only this change had been lurking nearby all along. My "parents" knew about it, and I guess they tried to prepare me; I don't think they expected this.

"Wow, only a week, I'm impressed. Was that you a few days ago versus the two cops in the park? Don't worry, you aren't being recorded."

"Yes," I divulged. I know I was taking a gamble, but it felt safe. My mom's voice came to me, "Feelings aren't facts!"

"Impressive debut, you know we could do a lot together, we could change the face of this planet."

Cross's words surprised me. The sheer classic bad guy vibe was shocking; I did not know people really talked like this.

"I don't want to be a part of the type of world you are building. I don't think people like me will have a pleasant place in your plan," I said.

I started to walk away from Adrian, realizing I was in a park I had never seen before. There were trees all around us, and I could hear cars rushing around in the distance.

"Well, I had to try. I want to meet you and your friends," Cross said casually.

"And I want my dad back," I snapped back. "So, how do we make a deal?"

I knew who this guy was, and if my dad knew, he would not be surprised. He hated this guy. Robert Cross had been around for a long time, and my dad always thought he was behind many not-so-cleverly written racist laws that put more and more Black people under State control. My dad showed me videos of him speaking on the Senate floor, arguing for his bills. He was eloquent and smart, but he was also delusional. Robert Cross's interpretation of history was twisted at best. Then, after he had put his mark on U.S. politics, he disappeared from public life. I guess he was training to be a megalomaniac villain.

"Well, I will be in your area in three days. I'll send a text on this phone to tell you where, so don't break it."

This kidnapper was talking down to me, and I could not believe it.

"Let me..." The phone buzzed in my hand.

"Check the message," was all Cross said.

I looked, and it was my dad holding up a newspaper with today's date. I had seen this kind of proof on TV shows, but I did not think I would be on the receiving end in real life.

"He's fine, as of right now. Now, for the terms, I want to meet all your friends. Make sure you bring everyone who was at your house when my men introduced themselves."

My temper flared at the thought of my mother's execution as an introduction.

"Fuck you! You cowardly piece of shit, that was my Mother you killed, not some greeting card your men delivered!" I was shouting into the phone, and my empty hand was clenched so tight I could feel my nails digging into my palm.

Something weird happened. For a long second, my anger turned into abject fear, and I wanted to beg this man to return my Father to me. I wanted to cry and offer anything he wanted to see my Father return safely home. Tears burned my eyes, and my throat tightened. I was in way over my head, and this guy was connected, connected, and I was a nobody. The police could show up and shoot me dead, and it probably wouldn't make the news.

My mind stalled at the thought of the police shooting me. They can't. I mean, they can try, but I have powers now. I can level the playing field. The police, the Feds, and certainly this asshole. I broke out of the fear that had been trying to paralyze me. It all happened so fast, but Cross caught it, I think.

"Oh, don't cry, young man. We can resolve this, and your dad will get to come home. Well, figuratively because your house is gone. A gas leak or something. Sorry for your loss." He said everything so pleasantly, like he was telling me about a day at work.

"Three days," I said, and disconnected the call. I looked around and found Adrian still standing where I left him.

I repositioned myself to within six feet of him. Adrian started at my sudden appearance.

"Since when can you move like that?" he said, looking around.

"Since meeting your tailor friend. Why didn't you help me with that phone call? I know you could hear both sides of the conversation?" I challenged him.

"You didn't need me to. You are right. I could hear the entire conversation, and I knew he was trying to feel you out and see how deadly his trap needed to be. You have a good head on your shoulders, and your parents and I taught you how to think for yourself." I think he almost shrugged.

"I don't know how to negotiate a hostage situation! What if I said the wrong thing?"

"Do you think you said the wrong thing?" "Adrian asked unbothered.

"I don't know, maybe. I think I admitted to hurting those cops," I whined.

Adrian's face hardened, "You killed those cops; they are really dead. You need to come to terms with the full weight of what you did. Even though it was in self-defense, you killed those two men. You ended all their hopes, dreams, and possibilities. Don't lie or make euphemisms about what you do."

This response arrested my descent into fear. I had almost forgotten about that night and the raging faces of the officers. They wanted to kill me for standing up for myself, and I didn't want to die. Until then, those two guys probably won every situation they had been in. Until that night, they had always been the predator and were more than comfortable in that role, but then they met a more dangerous monster. I needed to think. I needed space and time.

I returned Adrian's gaze, "Where are we?"

"What?" Adrian said my abrupt change in subject caught him off guard, "We are in Central Park; why?"

I liked studying geography in detail; I memorized real maps like some people do with video game maps. I would take trips in my head all around the world. I knew where I wanted to go.

"I'll be back, Adrian, I promise," he tried to say something, but I was already gone.

CHAPTER 32

Mopti Region, Mali: March 17, 10:34 p.m. GMT.

I appeared without fanfare. I was in Central Park in New York, then I was in Mali on the plateau of Mount Hombori. I had dreamed of this place and studied it and planned on coming here someday. Now I did not need permission or money; I could just go. To be honest, I was not sure if I could actually do what I just did. I knew I could pop around a small area, but the idea of traveling 4400 miles was a guess. I just formed a detailed picture in my head and focused on it. I could have ended up in the Atlantic Ocean. I knew there was a burgeoning family of olive baboons somewhere up here, and I did not want to disturb them. The night was cold and windy. It snapped my mind into more clarity.

I was in Africa for real. Everything at home fell away. I didn't forget it; I just knew it could wait. The air seemed to revitalize my body, and the star-filled sky was familiar in such a deep way that my heart felt complete for the first time. Apparating here with no lead-up of anticipation intensified the feeling of belonging. I did not have time to consider all the places I wanted to go on my holiday or ponder what it meant to have my feet on African soil. I was here, with all the weight of my Ancestors pressing down on me. But they were not coming from a place of pain and oppression. There was power and bearing in this feeling. I felt my chin tilt up as I breathed in the motherland's air.

Something deep within moved me to take off my shoes and feel the dirt touch my skin. I relaxed my mind and let my body move as I fixated on my striking combinations; I made every move crisp and perfect. I repeated combos I did not feel were perfect. Eventually, my mind was blank, and I was moving without thought. I could still feel the sweat running down my body in rivulets despite the chilly African night.

The mind can be tricky; unwanted thoughts can slip in, leaving turmoil in their wake. The target I was imagining was the man who broke into my house and Robert Cross. At first, that was fine, but the anger I felt for them pushed its way into my meditation. I refocused and pushed on. I was looking for something or someone, and those two men and their dark deeds were only getting in the way.

It was ten-something at night here, and the air was thin, I was sweating, and my hands and feet were flowing like water. The police have harassed me since I was twelve years old, and I was always powerless. I could only take the abuse and complain feebly to the very people who brutalized me. And now this man, Robert Cross, and his SOTIR Group were trying to do the same thing. He wanted me to give up my friends after he took my mother from me. He wanted me to stop resisting and comply.

No. Not this time. Not ever again.

There was a quick flash, and I almost froze in my tracks, but in the light, I heard a voice. I was being drawn toward something, something spiritual. My arms and legs moved on their own, my hands and feet whipping out and back, hanging sweat in their place.

The flash came again, but it was longer, long enough for me to think it would bring people to investigate or at least report it. The voice in the light was not the one I heard in my dreams, but one I had heard before, nonetheless.

"Iklwa, you have returned?" she said.

"Aset?" I asked. My body stopped its work.

Interlude 5

Aset, Isis, and ten thousand other names she was known by stepped into the mortal plane for the first time in an epoch. She breathes deeply and feels her skin gather in bumps in the air of her homeland. The silt of the Nile was the pigment in her skin. She was Nubian incarnate. The Treasure of Heaven. Aset ran her hands over herself. Her hair was older and blacker than the ink of the Kraken. Her breasts were as full and shapely as they were when she nursed the first Nubian. Her hips radiated the raw power of creation, and her legs were the twin foundation of her strength. Her feet connected her to her land, completing the mystical circuit in her physical body.

All of this, I felt as she felt it. I sensed the power of her melanin reflect in me and amplify the connection I experienced when I arrived here. She turned to me; pride revealed itself in her golden eyes, and a smile graced her lips; the rarity of that beauty was a gift I was nearly unready to receive. Again, a circuit was completed in me as well. I heard my Ancestors sigh in relief.

CLICK!

"You found your way to me," her voice was soft with joy.

Was this real?

"For now," she answered. "I have much to give you. And this will be the first step in a very long journey."

Aset looked up at the sky for a long moment. I could see the small movements of her head; she was searching for something.

She lowered her gaze to me and said, "You arrived earlier than I anticipated."

"I have always wanted to visit Mount Hombori, and I knew I needed to think. I realized I had the power to do it. So I did. To be honest, I remembered what East told me in my dream. I want to be free," the words poured from me.

"You have seen the beginning of all of us and the power we inherited," she gestured to me, then to herself.

"Scipio Okoro, you are a genetic Scion of the first of us. The expression of your ability has opened the door to a store-house of power. Because of your ability to heal so rapidly, your body is able to contain the mystic and physical energy open to you."

My mind was trying to digest all that she fired at me.

"I don't know what you mean about being able to heal rapidly. I get hurt like everybody else."

"Do you?" Aset responded.

My mind instantly ran to all the times the police put their hands on me. Especially the last time. I was appalled and angered by their violence, but I wasn't really hurt. In fact, Adrian never seemed worried about my physical well-being.

"I was in a coma for three weeks. I just woke up the other day."

"That was the psychic metamorphosis you were put in, to open you to your calling," she stated with no room for debate. "We are connected to the planet in a way others are not privy to; it is a two-way connection. When the world sensed you were ripe, she plucked you and began to forge you into

the Sword of Necessity. I have been given the responsibility of honing you. You have always felt this pull, but you did not know what it was a pull to." She smiled gently at me again.

I could not remember any time I got hurt significantly, but that was normal. Other than my run-ins with the police, I have never been in any danger before, so of course, I have never been hurt. Even then, I felt the pain, but I had no lasting injuries. I thought back to my sparing matches and how sometimes I could ignore the blows of my opponent. I felt the pain of their strikes, but the pain never lasted longer than a few seconds.

I was always drawn to the hero story in books, comics, and movies. I always tried to honor life in little ways, like capturing spiders in the house for my mom and setting them free outside. Deep down, I felt responsible, no, more like connected, like if I killed or let this thing die, I would lose a piece of myself...? No, it was more like losing a possibility. The way people say a hurricane is caused by a butterfly's wing on the other side of the world. I felt a sense of stewardship over the world around me; now, this feeling was nearing completion. The circle was closing, and it was going to be up to us, Saphronia and I, to fill it. We would be the sword and shield of our people, of all people. Ancient and descendant, and everyone in between. "I was drawn to you at your birth, and I have watched you."

That was embarrassing.

"Nothing has hurt you for more than a moment. Your natural-born ability is a hyper-regeneration, which allows you to hold the energies bestowed upon you. Without it, you would die." The horror I felt must have been all over my face because she seemed to try to soothe me, "Do not worry, we would not have chosen you if you could not contain it." Aset reached out and took my hand into hers.

"There is much to share with you, and we have little time." She said.

I nodded; even though this felt like a dream, I could feel the ground under my feet and hear the wind whipping through skeletal plants around me.

"You are The Iklwa, the Sound of Death, and your counterpart is the Ikhawu, the Shield of the People. You share each other's abilities. You are different sides of the same coin. The two of you are the balancing of the scales. The Motherland demands it. There are enemies behind enemies, and you two must be ready."

Aset stepped closer to me. I could smell the air ionizing around her. She cradled my face in her hands; I felt electricity dance across my cheeks. She pulled my head down to hers; for an instant, an arc of energy danced between our heads before our foreheads touched. "Listen," Aset whispered, and then a golden light filled my world.

CHAPTER 33

Mopti Region, Mali, March 19, 5:30 a.m. GMT.

The warmth of the sun kissed my face, and I opened my eyes. I was sitting in the lotus position, my hands resting on my knees. I could see my breath in the chilly dawn air. I searched my mind for the memory of the night and was rewarded with a smile I would never forget. I could sense the information and comfort she gave me. Aset opened the veil for me, and I saw my mother one last time. She said it was a gift for my sacrifice. She showed me a great deal of history and context. The SOTIR Group was not the first of its kind, nor would it be the last. I stood to my feet and put my shoes on. The earth's voice faded, and I kicked them off. Aset warned me things would change, large and small.

I picked up the useless shoes and blinked back to Adrian's house; it was the safest place I had left to go. I padded to the room Adrian had shown me the first time I was here to drop the shoes off. My precious mom's voice came to me and said, *"Always return what you borrowed."*

A suit bag hung on the back of the door. There was a large, stylized picture of a bird emblazoned on the front of it, joined by a card with my name on it. I unzipped it, not knowing what to expect. Inside was a full outfit. How had Bamidele made this in one day?

The top was a black hooded long-sleeve shirt; a gaiter-type mask was built into the pattern. A red silhouette of a bird, I recognized instantly as a kite, was over the left breast. It seemed to hover there. There was red, green, and gold kente piping down the sleeves, which could be neatly folded up or pushed up. The pants were black as well with the same kente piping. The pants had weird hoops at the end; I assumed they were for my feet. There were no shoes in sight. I figured no shoes were my new normal. A small plastic bag had a strange device with two small needles on it; a note was in the bag with a device. I opened the bag and took out the note.

Hello Scipio, I hope you like the ensemble I put together for you. I tried to capture your warrior scholar spirit. When you synchronize with the fabric, you will be able to control the appearance of the outfit. It will protect you from a .45 caliber round at point-blank range and knife attacks. I hope you choose to help us. Either way, this is yours. Be careful; these are extremely rare; I don't do this for just anyone. Good luck, Iklwa.

To sync up, put the entire outfit on. Press the needles into your right arm and hold for twenty seconds. Remove the needle and discard. The sync will be complete. Enjoy!

There was the stylized bird on the bottom of the note.

Okay, I thought. I put everything on. It fit perfectly; I did not doubt it would. I didn't like needles all that much, but I did not have a phobia of them; I just would rather not have them stab me. The thought of stabbing myself was kind of daunting. I held the "little" device. It was an hourglass shape with a needle that protruded from each bulb of the hourglass. The needles themselves were about an inch long. The idea was to just do it fast and get it over with. I took a deep breath.

"Stop being a baby," and pressed it into my arm. When I put the clothes on, they felt like cotton on the outside but suede on the inside. It did not feel like it would be good to sweat in. When I inserted the needle, the entire feeling of the suit changed. All the stuff I thought was suede attached to my skin. On the little device, my blood mixed with the tiny particles in the hourglass bulbs, and after several seconds, the sense of the suit came to me; it was very startling, but after what I had seen last night, I was not afraid. After twenty seconds, I could feel the control I had of the "fabric." I raised my arm and willed the sleeve to be at my elbow. It folded and flipped into position.

"Cool," I said. I returned the sleeve to its regular length. I went to the mirror and examined myself. I pulled the mask and hood up. It was a good look. The ensemble kind of had the look of a tuxedo. I brought the picture to my mind and changed the outfit. There was soft fluttering all over the suit; it didn't tickle or itch. Within several seconds, I was in a black tuxedo with kente piping on the pants and jacket; there was even a red bow tie. My eyebrows popped up. I realized even though I was not wearing shoes, the bottom of the pants somehow mimicked patent leather shoes. How did he know? I changed it again, and it was just a black T-shirt and dark blue jeans. I shifted the colors to all white, spreading the red, green, and gold kente over the whole outfit. I turned it all red. Ooh, too bright. I shifted it back to its original form. It had normal pockets, and I could make new ones if I wanted to. That would be handy; I played with the outfit for a while.

I was satisfied with the suit. I placed the device back into the plastic bag and tucked the note into my pocket. I sat on the bed to think before I ventured out to go find the others.

First, where were we? If Adrian were a teleporter, we could be anywhere on the planet. He teleported us to Central Park when the phone rang, and the call didn't drop, so maybe we were in the same area as the cell tower. Maybe.

Was his house in the same area as the Community? Again, Adrian, being a teleporter, I could be anywhere right now. When I teleported, for lack of a better word, I just had the image of the hallway in my mind.

I realized being able to move at will put everything just a blink away. Maybe I could focus on a person and move to them. Saphronia came to mind. Instantly, I felt the sensation of repositioning. I stumbled a bit as I was not expecting to be standing up.

There was a gasp, then an ear-piercing scream as I was getting my wits about me.

"GET OUT!" A screaming but familiar voice was shrieking. I stared at my reflection and realized where I was. I was in Saphronia's bathroom, or at least a bathroom where she was taking a shower.

"I'm sorry!" I shouted and fumbled out of the room. I was so glad she didn't blast me through the door. I looked up and down the hall I was in, and I had no clue where I was. The walls were covered in red pleated cloth, a delicately carved wooden border halfway up the wall, and bright polished wood paneling above it. Adrian appeared before me.

"Where the heck have you been?" he asked.

The kid in me answered immediately, "I went to Mount Hombori to think. Where are we?"

"Can you guys go talk somewhere else, please?!" Saphronia's muffled anger came through loud and clear.

"Let's go before she kills us," he said and walked to my right and down the hall. "We were still at East's place when you disappeared; we decided to come back and wait here."

We came around a corner and entered a large sitting room. It looked like we were in an old-school basement. There were jars of preserves on shelves, and the walls appeared to be stone. There was a long wooden park-style table in the center of the large room. Other chairs and small tables were scattered around the room. There was a single door on the opposite side of the room.

Adrian stopped near the middle of the table and spun to talk to me, "You went to Africa?" There was worry in his eyes.

"Yeah, and you will never guess who I met?" I was excited to tell him about Aset.

"Why don't you wait until Saphronia comes out here, so you only have to tell it once. Were you seen by anybody besides whoever it was you met?" Adrian seemed mildly distressed.

"No one, it was just me and some baboons on the top of the mountain."

"Okay, good," was all he said.

"Adrian, what is going on?"

"Nothing, I was just curious. I haven't been to Africa in a long while," he mumbled.

"Where is Ian?" I was surprised he wasn't in the room with us.

"I sent him home yesterday. His parents were calling to find out if he was okay; they heard about the explosion at your house." Adrian took a deep breath and let out a long sigh, "Hey Scipio, I'm really sorry I had to blow up your house. Oh man, that sounds corny as hell."

"Adrian, I understand why you did it. I know my mom wasn't in, you know," my voice caught in my throat. I was very conscious of my hands.

"Okay," Adrian said.

"Okay," I said, "So what about Ian? He's just out of the whole thing now?"

A confused look came over his face, "Yeah, he's not like us, Scip. He's not as durable, and he would be a liability if we have to throw hands."

"I know, but..." I trailed off.

"But what? If you are worried about him, you wouldn't want him in this Scipio. If they find out he is important to you, they will use him against you. It's better to leave him out of this."

"Ugh!" I groaned, leaning back in the chair; I rubbed my head. Ian was the closest thing I had to a brother, and I trusted him.

"Cross said he wanted all of my friends there. Shouldn't we have ..."

"Let me stop you right there; Ian is not a part of this world. Period. The reality is this guy will kill your dad no matter what we do, and all we are trying to do is prevent that from happening. I don't know if you decided to help us or not, but Ian is safer with his family either way. End of discussion," Adrian stared at me.

"Understood." I sat back and waited for Saphronia.

CHAPTER 34

Somewhere Underground, March 16, 2:40 p.m. EST.

Saphronia Perse was not her actual name. Her birth name was Neswt Biti, and she was sent to find the person she was destined to protect. Destiny was her bread and butter; she had been raised on it. Her family followed the teachings and truths of the Goddess Isis. When Scipio approached her at the party all those days ago, she knew it was Destiny. Scipio Okoro was everything her Vovo described. He was good and thoughtful, although a little immature; his heart was in the right place. She recalled his eyes in the altercation with the police officers. The flash of red-hot Anger. He would need to be guided, Vovo had advised her. Her mom challenged her immediately. "No woman can change a man's mind, and it's wrong for you to put that on her!"

"I said guide, you silly girl, not change. Neswt is her own, and she will make her own choices. He won't be ugly, that is for sure!" Vovo cackled wickedly.

The memory was clear in her mind. So were his golden-brown eyes and bright smile. That snapped her back to her senses. She had been worried things were getting out of control when Adrian returned without Scipio. She almost lost her temper with the mentor.

"Adrian, where is Scipio?"

Adrian looked at her and just shrugged.

"What does that mean?!" Arcs of blue energy crackled and danced on her hands.

"Whoa!" Adrian said and rushed to her, "I'm sorry. He said he had to think and disappeared. He could be any-where."

The light show on her hands died down.

"We need to find him," she said under her breath. "He is not safe."

Adrian took a step back and asked, "What do you mean?"

His head cocked to the left; she read the movement as a precursor to a threat. The girl, calling herself Saphronia, backed down.

"I mean, we do not know how extensive the SOTIR Group's surveillance is," she said with no hesitation in her voice.

East was still talking to the denizens of the Community, trying to calm the situation. The ringing phone had not helped. Saphronia left her to the task and went to check on Ian.

Ian was sitting on the ground, still trying to comprehend what was happening.

"Are you okay, Ian?" Saphronia said, kneeling next to him.

"I think so. No broken bones, I think?" he rubbed his chest and winced.

Saphronia examined him intently. She was born with a unique form of telekinesis called hyperkinesis. Hyperkine-sis is basically the ability to multitask for real. She could do 2 or 3 things simultaneously, or combine the abilities into one ability or effect. She was also psychokinetic, which was the jet fighter of telekinesis. Insanely accurate and able to sense and affect the microscopic world. Like a blind person reading braille with their fingers, Saphronia could scan Ian's body with her sixth sense and detect any damage.

In fact, she was able to find and repair small stress fractures in his rib cage. She saw the burst blood vessels causing contusions and repaired them; she left the mild bruising to cover her tracks.

Saphronia stood up and offered her hand to Ian, who took it gratefully. He groaned as he gained his feet. She heard Adrian come up behind her.

"How are you doing, Ian?" Adrian asked.

"I'm okay, I think. I'm just not exactly sure what happened. One second, I was running back to the elevator, and the next, I was flying through the air." Ian was unconsciously rubbing his hands all over his body.

Saphronia believed it surprised him to be alive. This all must be a shock to him and his worldview. In Saphronia's experience, most White people believe they are the center of the story, and everyone else is the supporting cast. Saphronia saw it over and over in primary school. Spurred by colorism, there were always mean girls. Some wanted to fight you physically, and others wanted to destroy your reputation, and even on the Big Island of Santiago, the schools and the people were the same.

Saphronia's Vovo would tell her, "Neswt your name means royalty, and you do not have to suffer these fools," then she would cross herself out of pure habit.

"Learn to use your abilities on the down-low; you don't have to make a big production, just do enough to get your point across."

Neswt would use this advice to her advantage often. People whispered she was a witch but could never prove she did anything.

In the final year of her primary school, men in black suits showed up, and they were looking for stories of the witch girl. No one knew anything. People were annoyed with Neswt's supposed antics, but they would never turn her over to American men in black.

America's reputation has greatly suffered over the recent years, and the Coronavirus pandemic shed fresh light on America's internal problems. They were no longer seen as the helpful invader but instead as the greedy suit looking to exploit who and whatever they could. In recent years, the country was on the mend, but when these men came looking for her, the community stood up.

Things got much better for Neswt, and she could observe why the people she knew were worthy of her respect. She stood up for them when they could not stand for themselves. Spousal abuse dropped significantly on the Big Island, and so did crimes of opportunity like mugging and robbery. Neswt was not flying around like a comic book superhero, but she monitored social media for news or messages about abuse or crime, and she would do her best to be there when she could.

There were not a lot of cameras in Cabo Verde, so moving around unseen was pretty easy. Neswt's mother and Vovo taught her to fight with or without her abilities, and she was a quick study. They taught her the speed of violence and how to see the physical indicators of violence. She felt like it was the closest thing to reading people's minds that she would ever come.

Now, after three years of intense and near-constant training, she was on the mission she was destined to take, and she had lost her charge and was probably going to blow her cover with the Moore family. Diana was a nice girl, and Neswt was not ready to burn that bridge.

All of this flickered through Saphronia/Neswt's mind in a flash. The last bit about the Moore family snapped her out of her reverie.

"Hey, let's go back to the elevator; maybe we can wait for Scipio at East's home." She offered.

"Scip's not going to be back for a while. He's gone off to think things through and figure the whole world out. I think I should go home and check on the 'Rents before they call the police. I'm sure they heard about the Harelsons' house already."

To her credit, Saphronia calmly turned to look at Ian when he mentioned Scipio would be gone for a while, "What do you mean, gone for a while?"

Ian was dusting himself off, "He has gone under for a week. I mean, we all knew where he was, in his bedroom, but he just shut everyone out until he figured out whatever it was he was thinking about. And when he was done, he may or may not tell you what it was. At first, his parents thought it was depression, but he could articulate what he was thinking about and why. It wasn't like he was slow; it was measured deduction and reasoning," Ian laughed and shrugged his shoulders.

"We might as well take the opportunity to get back to our normal lives for a bit and smooth things over," Ian advised.

Saphronia nodded in agreement and was about to speak when Adrian cut into the conversation.

"Yo! Ian, that is a great idea! Let's get you two home and make sure everyone is on the same page."

"Wha..." Saphronia tried to say, but they were suddenly in front of Ian's house.

His mom was coming out of the front door, but she hadn't seen them teleport in.

Ian, just run up to her and hug her. Tell her you are so happy to see her, and you'll tell her everything inside. Go! Adrian instructed.

Ian did as he was instructed, and just as Adrian knew she would, she screamed loud enough to bring Ian's dad running out of the house. They hugged him, kissed him, and dragged him into the house.

"How come they couldn't see us?" Saphronia was dumbfounded.

"I can make people see and experience what I want them to. It's kinda taxing to scrub the mind of ALL the things that might give you away, so I weave a story," Adrian explained.

"Wow, that is handy." She said, "Maybe you can help me get away cleanly from the Moores."

Adrian started walking down the sidewalk away from Ian's house without a reply. Saphronia was incensed!

"Adrian!" She hissed at him. She ran up and grabbed his arm.

"Who the h..." Before she could finish the sentence, she was surrounded by mist, and the ground was gone.

"Meu Deus!" The words were ripped from her throat as the air sped by! She flashed a psychokinetic globe around herself and arrested her fall. She tumbled some, but kept her concentration. She floated there, completely confused and furious. Her surrounding globe crackled with golden arcs of energy.

Suddenly, the weight of the globe shifted, and Saphronia looked up to see Adrian standing on top of her protective globe.

"O que se pasa contigo, laucó!" <What's wrong with you, crazy!> Saphronia screamed at him!

"I don't speak Kriol," Adrian said.

Her eyes went wide at his statement. Had she slipped somewhere?

"Who are you, Saphronia?"

The weight on her globe seemed to double, and she was having a little bit of trouble keeping herself aloft.

"Really!"

"I am not an enemy."

The weight doubled again; it was definitely Adrian's doing. They floated down at an alarming rate!

"Oh, really, now I feel much better. Tell me why I shouldn't teleport your head to Cabo Verde and your body to Antarctica?"

Well, she was obviously off her game because she saw none of this coming.

"The Alpha A.R.C. in Africa sent me. They knew I was connected to The Iklwa somehow." She did not intend to tell them this until much later, but with her cover blown, she had no choice.

The shock of the revelation was written all over Adrian's face. There was a puff of air, and he was directly in front of her. Then, just as abruptly, they were on the ground surrounded by trees. Her globe created a crater in the ground. She dropped the field.

"Spill it, or I'll dig it out," his tone was cold.

Saphronia did not know how strong Adrian was in his mind-to-mind capacity, and she had no intention of having her mind cracked open like an oyster. Besides, her superiors had not forbidden her to tell them; she was just holding it for the most opportune time. This seemed to be it.

"My real name is Neswt Biti, and I am an Emissary; I am also the Ikhawu. The Shield of the People. The Zamaradi Council sent me here to fulfill my Destiny and protect the

Iklwa. My Vovo was one of the Nine Elders that advised the Zamaradi Council directly."

"East is one of the Nine Elders; why didn't you reveal yourself as an Emissary to her?" Adrian pressed.

Neswt could tell by his body language that he was more curious than hostile, but she did not relax her guard.

"There was no need; my cover was intact and working well. If everything fell apart, I could still return home, and Saphronia would disappear."

"So, your mission is what, to kidnap Scipio and take him back for some kind of ritual?"

"No," Neswt said; she clenched her fists forcefully. "I was sent to be near him; we are a pair. We are more powerful together. Scipio has his own Destiny; I hope you are not planning on getting in the way of that."

"You think you're slick. Scipio will make his own choices; he always has. Look, we have the same objective: keep Scipio safe and not lose him."

"Well, it looks like we both failed on not losing him," Neswt quipped.

Their eyes locked, and both started laughing.

"I would love to spar with you for real," a smile crept onto Adrian's face.

"Not today, Coach, I have to separate myself from the Moores for their own safety," Neswt stated evenly.

"Okay, you are right. I can take care of that for you," Adrian offered.

"Thank you, but it's not that simple. I have to get my things from the house. If I understand your meaning correctly?"

"Yeah, let's go," Adrian reached out and touched Neswt's shoulder, and they vanished.

CHAPTER 35

San Jose, California, March 16, 3:00 p.m. PST.

Ian went into his house with his mom and dad. All he wanted was a shower and a change of clothes. And to get back to Scipio. He braced himself and walked into the house.

"Where the hell have you been, Ian? We were worried sick about you after we heard about the Harelsons' house. What happened?" his mother said as she hurried to him. Ian saw they were more worried than angry.

"We were training at Coach's house, so I have no idea what happened," he lied, "I dropped Scip at what was left of his house with his dad." Real tears sprang to his eyes as he thought about seeing Scipio's mom's head damn near explode right in front of his eyes.

"Oh, my baby! Are you okay, honey?" Ian's mom asked as she hugged him tightly.

"Not really; it's hard seeing Scipio's family go through this." This time, he was very truthful. He did not want to leave Scipio's side, but if his friend was on a walkabout, it would do no good to sit around, making his parents worry.

"I'm going to go take a shower and get cleaned up. I'm probably going to just go to bed after," he gently extricated himself from his mother's arms and started up the stairs.

"Good night, honey. Let us know if you need anything." His mom said sweetly.

"Will do, Mom," Ian called back.

His exhausted feet carried him upstairs, and he showered. The hot water felt amazing, even on his bruises. He washed and rinsed his hair. His mind was blank as it tried to process all that had happened in the last three days. His friend and the new girl can fly, and his karate Coach can teleport. Somehow, he missed the day powers were being handed out. He shook his head in disagreement with that thought, but it persisted, so he changed the subject.

Ian had never heard of the SOTIR Group, or had he? When he heard the name the first time, it didn't ring any bells, but the more they talked about it over breakfast/dinner, the more it sounded familiar. Where had he seen it?

All at once, it came to him in a bright and clear memory. There was a letter on the kitchen table. It was weird because it was thick and had been delivered by hand from the mailperson. When he asked about it, his dad said it was a job offer for his mom. He remembered seeing it in the trash later. Which was good, but why did the SOTIR Group offer my mom a job? Ian knew she was an analyst, but why her?

There must be a way to look these guys up. He was brushing his teeth, and an image of the Global came into his mind. He finished brushing and put on a T-shirt and a pair of pajama pants. He pulled the Global from his pants and put it on. It looked exactly like his old Global, but instead of the apple, it had the head of an eagle, or was it a hawk? A Global was a two- to three-piece device. The main piece was the size of a wristwatch; it held the hardware and the software, and it was paired with the ear/eyepieces. The wrist piece could project a small, one-handed keyboard.

The headgear was able to project the screen of the Global; they were the interface. A small bar could protrude from either the left or right earpiece, never both, and project a screen right onto the eye. Using how the eye can focus near and far, the device reads the minute movements of the eye, navigating around the device. A keyboard that only the user could see could be projected for them to type on. The projection could be private or public; most people found it impolite to project in public. The kinds of people who projected publicly were called screeners; they were usually older and didn't like how the private mode projected into your eye. Come to think of it, the people in the Community didn't have any semblance of a Global. He was too busy being terrified to notice the strangeness. He was setting the new rig up when his empty stomach interrupted his thoughts. Ian sighed and set everything aside to go find food.

CHAPTER 36

San Jose, California, March 16, 3:25 p.m. PST.

Neswt (formerly Saphronia) and Adrian appeared a few houses down from Diana's house.

"So, what's the plan?" Adrian asked.

"Um, I do not know; you are the adult," Neswt answered. Adrian rolled his eyes.

"I know you have a plan. Stop being difficult because I launched you into the air."

"I owe you for that, and yes, I have a plan. Can you hold them and insert a memory?"

"Yeah, no problem, it's easy on descendants," Adrian bragged.

"Good, when we go in, I will tell them you are from the exchange student agency, and you have come to tell me there has been a family emergency, and my mom has been in an accident. I must return home because I am her only family," Neswt said in one breath.

"You really have this worked out," Adrian said with raised eyebrows.

"Yes, I do. They will freak out, as you say, and...."

Adrian cut in, "That's where I come in, distress, it makes them that much more vulnerable. I'll slip in and rewrite history for them and hold them there until you do what you have to do. Am I right?"

"Yes," Neswt said tightly.

"Okay, but just know you don't have hours; hell, you won't even have ten minutes, and I have to have them all in the same room. Three people at the same time is a lot for me, but I've done up to five people."

"Okay, let's go," Neswt said.

"Bossy," Adrian said under his breath.

"I heard that," Neswt said over her shoulder.

As they walked up to the front door, Scipio raced across her mind. She wondered if he would forgive her for her deception. He was very talented with the application of his abilities, but he was very untrained. There was no sub-tlety to his actions; it was very American. A smile slipped through her mask, but she quickly hid it.

They got to the door and knocked. Neswt was still wary about just walking into the house without being asked to come in. In her mind, she was a guest, even though the Moores had insisted she was a part of the family and could move about as she pleased. As she waited for the door to open, she glanced at Adrian and almost screamed when she saw a White man standing next to her. He was taller than Adrian and had blue eyes. He looked at her and waggled his eyebrows. A very "white" thing to do, she thought.

The door opened, and Diana was still turning to face the door.

The scream was ear-piercing when she saw Neswt.

Screaming and jumping up and down, her long brown hair danced around her; she was wearing short shorts and a t-shirt. It seemed her whole body was turning red in the excitement. Adrian and Neswt looked at each other for a moment. Suddenly, Diana lunged at Neswt, locking her in a bear hug. Neswt's arms flailed in the air, grasping for bal-ance. Eventually, her parents came around the corner.

"What in God's name is going on here?" Mr. Moore shouted.

"Diane, what in heaven's name...." Mrs. Moore was gasping.

Diana released her friend and turned to her parents, "She's back! Saphronia is back!" Diana was jumping up and down with joy, then she stopped.

The Moore family turned around in unison and walked into the house in step with Adrian.

"That was much easier than I imagined," Neswt said.

"I'm glad you think so. Go ahead and gather your things. I'll take care of these nice people," Neswt heard some strain in his voice; she turned to hurry up to the guest room.

"Hey, kid, do me a favor and close the front door." Neswt waved her hand casually, and the front door closed gently; she hurried up the stairs.

CHAPTER 37

San Jose, California, March 16, 4:30 p.m. PST.

Ian was full, and that made him extra sleepy, but he wanted to explore the Global. He knew he would be busted if his mom came in and his rig was running, and he was asleep.

Eh, he thought, *it's worth the risk.* He put everything on and started to investigate. He found the settings app and went in; everything looked the same. All the same apps and controls were identical to a normal Global. He flitted over to the sound and played with those buttons for a while. He decided to go to the user agreement and try to slog through that mess. The crazy thing didn't have a user agreement. He flipped page after page of settings information. Eventually, he found a tutorial that helped him optimize his device. Ian knew that all Globals have a set of codes that open the operating system so you can look under the hood. All the codes Ian knew were useless. He wondered why he thought a super-secret Resistance group would have the same codes as a regular Global.

He sighed, tapped the earpiece to turn it off, then took the Global off and set it down when it buzzed. That was weird because he had it on ring in case Scipio called, and he was asleep. Ian picked up the earpiece and said, "Hullo?"

"Please stop trying to get into the device. It is unwise and may compromise the system's security," the voice on the other end of the line was very young for an operator of anything. She was also very African. Ian did not know the different African accents, but he knew an African accent when he heard one.

"Oh no, I am so sorry, I did not mean to break anything. I was just curious."

"Are you a White boy?" The question was accusatory.

"Y... yes," Ian said hesitantly.

"How did you get this device? What is your name? Did you steal it? Who gave it to you?" The questions came in rapid succession.

"Wait, a guy named Adrian Lake gave me the Global." Ian was sitting on his bed with his legs crossed underneath him, and his heart was pounding.

"What is your name?" the voice on the other end of the call asked.

"Ian Henderson," he stated. He could hear typing. Typing?

"What is your name?" Ian asked.

"None of your business," the young female voice bit at him.

"Well, I gave you mine. Don't you think it's fair for me to know your name?"

"No." was the only response.

"Why did you call me?" Ian asked.

"To see why you were trying to break into my operating system," the youthful voice answered.

"I wasn't trying to break into the OS; I was just curious. I was actually looking for information on the SOTIR Group." Ian closed his eyes for a long second and prayed Adrian was right about the security of these Globals.

"Tsss, you're not going to find information digging in the settings. You must have been easily distracted because of your short American attention span. However, if Adrian Lake gave you the device, then you must be trustworthy. Also, I can see he entered his code and entered your identification information. So, I will not fry you."

"Thank you?" Ian said, truly grateful, especially after everything he has seen recently, getting fried through a Global was not on his bingo card.

"I have a file on the SOTIR Group; there is a lot, but it's not everything."

"Why can't you give me everything?" Ian asked plaintively.

"Because I do not know you, and you do not have clearance. Be happy with what you get. By the Goddess, you Americans are greedy," the young voice on the other end chided.

Ian's Global buzzed, and he tabbed over to the file that came through.

It was simply titled SOTIR Group [Redacted]

"Thank you! I'm sure this will help us!" Ian exclaimed, but the line was already dead, and when he checked, the Global had no calls logged.

Ian unfolded himself and went to his desk. He wanted to use his desktop because it was easier to have multiple pages open and stream information. However, try as he might, he could not transfer the information to the workstation. The device wasn't even recognized by the machine.

Hmmm, Ian thought to himself, *I guess I'll have to go through it in the Global.*

Ian Henderson wanted desperately to help, but he was just a normal guy, and the day had been long, and he was deep asleep in less than twenty minutes. His rig was running.

CHAPTER 38

San Jose, California, March 16, 3:20 p.m. PST.

Neswt reached the top of the stairs and went into the guest room. She had been taught to travel light but make it look like she had a bunch of junk. She took the essentials and left a thank-you note. She was carrying two bags when she left the guest room.

The world dropped into midnight blackness, and Neswt could not move.

"What the hell?" she ground through clenched teeth.

Bright light flooded her vision, and the world changed. There was grass underfoot and a pleasant wind that played with Neswt's hair. When her eyes recovered from the flash, rolling hills for as long as the eye could see stretched before her. She looked down, and everything in her hands was gone, and she still could not move her feet.

"Hello, Ikhawu, it is good to meet you at last. Your reputation precedes you," the voice sounded like living thunder to Neswt. Neswt turned to look and found that her feet were free to move. When she looked up from her feet, she was greeted with the sight of a man who was easily nine feet tall.

"Whoa!" was all she could muster. The big man laughed heartily.

The great being's skin was dark as battleground mud with a hint of red, and his beard was gun barrel black.

He was beautiful. He had a tight black mohawk. He wore swords as earrings, and Neswt knew they were sharp. He wore dusky armor bristling with spikes. His armor was accented with a blue sash and a white belt. Neswt had never seen a blue so blue on any clothing. He carried a massive shield in his hand and wore a large hand-and-a-half sword on his left side. It was stained with blood. His armor extended down to his legs and feet. The sabatons he wore had upturned toes that ended in a point. The color of the metal looked silver, but Neswt knew it was not silver. What it was, she did not know.

"Ogun?" she breathed.

"Yep! You know your Orisha! Well done, Ikhawu; it's good to be recognized by someone like you."

Neswt dropped to her knees in obeisance.

"Get up, girl, you are the Chosen of the Planet, and I should be bowing to you. I came to give you the blessing Aset has for you. Because you don't have the same capacity for healing as the Iklwa, so your gift will be from me."

Neswt stood there on shaking knees.

"Thank you, Lord Ogun, you are most gracious." Neswt couldn't help it; she bowed and curtsied.

"Bah! None of that White man bullshit. Get up, girl. Your sacrifice is more than enough to be able to look me in the eye. Now, which arm do you want it on?" Ogun roared.

Her Vovo told her years ago that a great one would ask for her arm, and she must offer her shield arm. Neswt stood quickly, not wanting to further anger the war god, and held out her left arm. Her shield arm.

Neswt always obeyed her Vovo.

Neswt stood tall with her chin held high and her left arm held out. It did not shake. Ogun placed a silverish vambrace on her forearm. An amber jewel sat nestled in the bracer. It covered her entire forearm down to the knuckles on her hand. Gold filigree twisted and wound its way to or from the jewel; Neswt could not tell. The elegant lines made beautiful patterns, and they seemed to move in the light of the brilliant sun. The piece didn't quite fit at first, then Neswt felt the accessory tighten comfortably on her arm. No longer did the piece cover her entire forearm, but it left a bit of skin exposed just below her elbow, and it came all the way to the back of her hand.

Neswt looked at the armor with naked awe. Her mouth made an O of pure astonishment.

"You will not be able to remove this until you are near death. Then you may name your successor. However, if you will it, you can make it small like a bracelet." Ogun's magnificent voice sounded gentle and instructive; the thunder was distant but not gone. He held up his arms and shook his wrists playfully, "See, I have many like it." His massive forearms were hidden by many bracelets.

Neswt looked down and caressed the metal. She felt a slight vibration and was rapidly aware of a soft hum coming from it.

She looked up at him, unsure whether to ask what it did or keep silent.

"Oh," Ogun roared, "It is a twofer, as the Americans used to say, if you hold it up like a shield and will it, a shield of your choice will manifest. Anything from a cowhide shield to a military-grade riot shield to an energy bubble, not unlike your psychokinesis. Also, it will increase the strength of your hyperkinesis and psychokinesis enough to protect against a direct hit from man's strongest weapon. It does not increase or decrease your skill or imagination with your ability; it just makes the ability stronger, so be careful. I am supposed to tell you the history and why you were chosen, but it looks like you may not have time to hear that story. Don't worry, Scipio is getting the same lesson you would have received."

"Wait, Lord Ogun, what do you mean I do not have time?" worry dropped heavily in her gut.

"Sometimes the world intrudes on us," Ogun said.

Neswt heard a voice shouting at her from very far away.

"...ake up Saphronia, shit, Neswt! Whoever the hell you are! I can't protect you and the Moores by myself." She recognized Adrian's voice, and it was coming from behind her.

"You have to go back, Ikhawu, follow your destiny. Remember, no man is perfect, and all are capable of great good and great evil without guidance." When Ogun finished speaking, the world around her shook violently, and the ground cracked apart. Large pieces flew into the air, and the very ground fell into a void. In all the swirling chaos, Ogun stood unmovable, his great thunderous laugh followed her as she fell.

CHAPTER 39

San Jose, California, March 16, 3:20 p.m. PST.

Ron and Bristol Moore were heartbroken over the news of Saphronia's mother and frankly a little bit shocked, to be honest. They never thought such a small group of islands like Cape Verde had so many cars that someone could get into a 5-car pileup. They both chalked it up to a racial bias they did not know they had. Saphronia came downstairs with her bags packed and tears of worry in her eyes. Diana stepped up to her and hugged her.

"Let's take one last picture!" Diana exclaimed. Everyone stood together, and Ron took the picture.

"Let me take those, sweety. I'll go put them in the car for you," there was genuine concern in his voice.

"I know it seems like everything is spinning out of control right now, but you will be home soon and able to see your mom. I'm sure once you see her, everything will feel better. Just hold on to that." Bristol and Diana escorted Saphronia to the car, both rubbing her arm or back to comfort her. Saphronia bravely held back tears.

They were all piling into the car when the doorbell rang.

"What the fuck!" some disembodied voice said, and they all looked around.

Ron Moore said, "What in the blue hell is going on?"

Then the world froze. All thought and all movement stopped.

In the real world, Adrian was sitting in the living room with Ron, Bristol, and Diana. They all sat with their hands folded in their laps. Their breathing was calm and even. Everything was going fine until the doorbell rang.

Adrian got up to go to the door, and a wave of dizziness washed over him. He almost lost his hold on the Moore family. He hated group control with a passion, even though it was one of his specialties. Not many could hold more than two people in a psionic illusion like he was doing, but it took its toll. Sweat beaded on his forehead. After he regained his balance, he walked calmly to the door. Most people didn't realize the person on the outside could hear and sense movement in the house, and when you scurried around in a panic, any operator knew it meant trouble.

Adrian got to the door and looked through the peephole and saw a man standing there.

He was dressed in black BDUs (battle dress uniform) and a black windbreaker jacket. Adrian's heart skipped a beat. He instantly regretted calling off his team, thinking he and Neswt would be long gone before any of the SOTIR Group's goons showed up here.

The man rang the doorbell again, and Adrian's hold on the Moore family slipped. He wouldn't be able to grab this guy's mind and hold on to the Moores. Adrian took a deep breath and opened the door.

"Salutations, how can I help you today, kind Sir?" Adrian was doing his best suburban impression.

"Oh, hi," the man said with real surprise in his voice, "uh, is Ronald or Bristol Moore home?"

"No, we were having a dinner party, and an emergency came up, and they had to run their exchange student to the airport. I would have gone with them, but I couldn't fit in the car. They asked me to wait for them," Adrian lied. He kept with the concocted story because his brain was otherwise preoccupied.

"Oh, do they have two cars because there is one still in the driveway?" The man was trying to look past Adrian into the house.

"Excuse me," Adrian said, sounding offended, "who are you?"

"I'm a friend of the family as well, and I have never seen or heard of you before. May I come in and wait for them?" the man snapped back. He took a step forward and put his right hand on the door.

Adrian could see he was carrying a gun under his windbreaker. The man saw him notice the gun and tried to draw it, but Adrian was faster. He snapped a punch to his nose and pulled him into a head butt and pushed him out of the door, and slammed it shut.

He was locking the rather sturdy door when there was a crash from the back of the house.

"Dammit!" he swore under his breath and ran to the back door.

"Saphronia, we have to go!" he shouted politely, but there was no answer.

He ran to the back door, and two men in black BDUs, but no windbreakers, were kicking their way through broken glass. This would not be explainable, he thought to himself. Adrian couldn't teleport and hold the Moores at the same time. He had to fight. He cracked his neck and attacked.

The men hadn't seen him yet; they were focused on the three people sitting calmly in the room they had just burst into. Adrian pulled his K-bar and rushed at the first man, stabbing him in the neck; blood spurted from the wound. He stabbed him three more times before the spray hit the wall. The man fell with wounds in his neck, lung, groin, and thigh. His partner raised a silenced pistol and caught the K-bar in his eye. The front door rattled from the first man kicking it.

Adrian ran up the stairs to find Neswt standing in the doorway of a bedroom. She was completely still, and her eyes were pools of gray smoke. What the hell was going on, he thought to himself. He was reaching to shake her awake when the front door crashed open. The windbreaker guy came rushing into the house with his gun drawn.

"Dammit!" Adrian swore again. He had to get back into the room with the Moores.

Adrian leaped over the railing and landed on the intruder. There was a wet crack as something in the guy's shoulder broke. Strangely, he did not scream. Instead, he turned and let off two rounds from his gun. Adrian rolled into the kitchen and ran for the living room. The intruder, not knowing the house, followed. Adrian entered the room with the family and sent a suggestion to their minds, and their heads lolled forward as they all fell into a deep sleep. Adrian disappeared. The intruder came barging into the living room; he pulled up short when he saw the perfect little White family unconscious in their chairs. He looked left and right, nothing. Suddenly, he was being hit from behind, and Adrian's feet slammed into him at terminal velocity. Adrian teleported himself about a mile up and let himself fall long enough to reach terminal velocity. He teleported back to the Moores' house at speed and planted his feet in the intruder's back. Adrian flash teleported himself to a standing position, canceling his momentum. This was one of his more deadly and vicious attacks. The man was thrown headlong into the entertainment center. His back was probably broken.

Adrian looked around at the mess these bastards had caused. How was he going to fix this? He was devising a plan when the man in the entertainment center started to move! Isn't this what Scipio had described, what the intruder did?

The Moore family was still asleep, and apparently, a zombie was trying to get up and kill everyone. Adrian used both hands and a foot to make contact with the Moore family and teleported them to the car in the driveway. He teleported back into the house to get Neswt, but the zombie soldier was climbing the stairs. Adrian kicked at his head, but the man caught his leg and flung him over the railing. Adrian caught himself with a correcting teleport and appeared in front of the guy. He threw a flurry of strikes so fast no regular human could have seen, let alone block them, but this guy did. He only smiled and returned the volley of strikes, but Adrian was not there. He was behind him. Adrian touched him, and the intruder was gone.

Adrian ran to Neswt; he was about to shake her, but stopped himself. You were not supposed to wake people who were sleepwalking. Well, he had to get her back to the real world.

"Wake up, Neswt! I can't protect you and the Moores by myself!" he yelled; she stirred a little bit.

There was a great crash in one of the rooms down the hall; the entire house shook from the impact.

"Screw it!" Adrian grabbed Neswt by the shoulders and shook her gently.

A whisper escaped her lips, but Adrian could not understand it. There was a commotion in the room that had taken the impact. Adrian looked down the hall and saw a bloody hand grip the door frame and make an impression. He shook Neswt hard, still watching the door.

Hands grabbed his wrist, and he looked back at Neswt. Relief flooded his body.

"Welcome back!" he said, "We gotta go."

Without a word, she grabbed her bags, and they vanished. They appeared inside the car.

"Shit, no keys!" Adrian exclaimed; Neswt reached over and touched the ignition, and the car started.

"A little trick my mom taught me," she said.

"Ancestors bless her!" Adrian put the car in reverse and tore out of the driveway. Within seconds, they were on the road away from the house.

They drove for a bit, and Adrian said, "We have to put the Moores somewhere."

"How are you going to explain the destroyed home and the dead guys in their living room?" Neswt asked.

"Honestly, I have no idea, but we can't stay with them. We can drop them off somewhere. I'll leave a suggestion."

"But they came to their house looking for me! I do not want to leave them in danger." Neswt countered.

"True, I'll put my team on them. Don't worry, they will be okay. If push comes to shove, we will take them to the Community. I'll give them a little story, and they won't know any better," Adrian soothed.

"Okay," Neswt reluctantly accepted that answer, "What about Ian, won't the same men go to his house?"

"Maybe, but I still have someone watching him. He will be okay," Adrian said.

They drove for a bit and eventually parked at a restaurant that had gone under in the depression that came after the Coronavirus outbreak. Adrian planted pleasant memories and a stop to rest. He left the car running as they wouldn't have the keys to start it again when they woke up.

That would probably cause some consternation, but that couldn't be helped.

Adrian and Neswt placed Ron in the front seat with his memory of the day firmly in place and locked the car.

"Okay, let's get back to East's place," Neswt nodded, and they clasped hands and disappeared.

San Jose, California, March 17, 9:00 a.m. PST.

Ian woke up to the smell of bacon and eggs. He smiled at remembering he put the sleep timer on the phone just in case he fell asleep. He got up and got dressed for the day and went downstairs. His parents were at the kitchen table, about to eat breakfast. They were talking in low tones and stopped when he started down the stairs. They were both looking at him, and he smiled back. Ian thought he could see his mom sigh in relief.

"Hey, snookum, do you want some breakfast?" his mom asked.

"Yes, please!" he was famished, and his stomach rumbled in agreement.

Rhonda Henderson loved her only son with all of her being, and she was very worried about him but did not know how to broach the subject. She got up to make him a plate, hoping Jack would try to get it out of him.

Ian's dad put his handheld phone aside and looked at his son.

"So, what's up, son?" he asked nonchalantly.

"What do you mean?" he responded and got up to get some orange juice. His dad's gaze followed him.

"Well, your best friend's house exploded, and his mom died. You can understand why we, as your parents, would be worried about you." Ian loved his dad, but sometimes he was too direct.

"Dad, what do you want me to say? 'I'm sad?' Well, I'm sad. Mrs. Harelson was like a second mom to me, just like you are to Scipio, Mom. So yeah, I'm sad, but what can I do? They don't need me anymore. I guess I'll just wait here to see if they make it!"

The room was silent after he stopped speaking, and his parents were staring at him; their faces were the picture of worry.

Aw, man, Ian thought, I gotta pull it together.

His mom set down the plate she was holding and went to her son. She wrapped him in the most protective hug she could muster. Ian hugged her back and held it together rather well until he thought about how Scipio would never feel this feeling ever again, and that thought broke the dam. He squeezed her and cried. He could not get the vision of Beverly Harelson's lifeless body lying on the floor of a house that was privy to so many great and important memories. Now, the last memory of that wonderful place was death. While everyone was focused on being a hero, he had watched the beloved house go up in flames. After several seconds, he felt his father's hand on his back, which helped him calm down.

Ian peeled himself from his mother's bosom, tears and snot all over his face.

"My goodness, you are a mess!" his mom said playfully.

His dad handed him a couple of tissues, and he wiped his face.

"Well, son, we, your mom and I, were talking earlier, and we figured we would let the Harelsons stay here for a while. We have room, and they are our friends. I'm sure they are going to need a place to get back on their feet. What do you think about that?"

His dad was pleased to be able to help. Ian thought it was a horrible idea, knowing what was really going on, but he played it cool.

"Well, I'll go see if I can contact them and let them know about your offer." Ian had no clue where Scipio was, just that he was solving this problem.

"After you eat," his mom said.

He sat down and ate the food.

Ian was in his room looking through the information that his mysterious benefactor had sent him. It was chock-full of juicy stuff. There were shipping dates and some information on the people they had embedded in different governments. He looked for his city, and there was a list of embedded police officers. One was a detective who looked familiar to Ian.

Alexander Lamb was 29 years old and one of the most successful and youngest detectives on the force. He was listed with an NM next to his name. Ian had no clue what that meant; it wasn't by every name, just a selected few. Ian was sure his "new friend" knew what it was.

"Ugh!" he sighed. He was getting the information he did not know, but it wasn't anything that would help them fight these bastards. He figured out why they never heard anything from the police when Scipio took those two dirty cops out. The SOTIR Group owned the entire police command structure. Most of the police in major cities were led by SOTIR Group employees. Of course, it was all under the table or outright blackmail and anything in between. There were thousands of pages of names and pictures. He could probably leak this to the press and deal a serious blow to the evil bastards, but what would happen to the city these people were leading? It would be chaos, and that was the last thing Ian wanted to happen.

He hadn't heard from Scipio, so it would do no good to call. He tagged the pages and the information he wanted to relay. He was deep in his data mining when the device rang. The caller ID read unknown. Ian tapped the button.

"Hullo?" he said.

"Hello American," it was the same voice from last night. For some reason, Ian's heart jumped in his chest. "Have you been enjoying my gift?" she asked.

"Yes, there is a ton of good stuff here, thank you!"

"What will you do for me now that I have given you this gift?" the young voice asked.

"Well, I don't know what I can give you. Besides, I didn't ask for this gift," Ian said, feeling annoyed.

"OK, well, I think if you mention me to the Iklwa, I will be grateful," his friend offered.

"I can do that, but it may be a little while. He is ... deep in thought." He had almost told this random person that Scipio was missing. He had assumed the person was from whatever organization East and the people in the Enclave were a part of, but he couldn't be sure. He was looking out the window, watching the lazy clouds crawl across the sky, trying to figure out how to change the subject.

"What, uh, do you do at wherever it is you work?" he stumbled, hoping his caller didn't pick it up.

"Oh, I try to pick up SOTIR Group chatter and link that with asset movement," they offered.

"Whoa. That sounds cool, but I thought you said this was your operating system?" Ian asked, confused.

"It is MY operating system; I wrote it, I built it, and I monitor it. I also try to break the SOTIR Group's OS and monitor their chatter. Are you saying I can't do both because I'm a girl?" Her voice was filled with venom.

"No, no, I was just getting clarity. I'm sorry if I offended you," he said.

"Ok, good cause ...," her voice trailed off.

"What happened?" Ian asked, and there was something in the way she went silent that raised hackles on the back of his neck. There was only silence on the other end.

"Hey, uh, you... What is going on?" he was getting worried.

"OK, I had to verify. You and your family might want to get..."

The line went dead. Ian tapped the earpiece.

"Hello?" he was looking at the screen when the entire rig went dark.

"What the hell?" he looked around the room in confusion, then he heard his mom yell in annoyance.

"The power is out, guys. I guess it's family time," she yelled.

"I'll be right down, dear!" Ian heard his dad yell back.

Ian got up and started to pack his go-bag when his window exploded in, showering him with glass. He screamed in surprise, but when he opened his eyes, he was horrified. Standing before him was a humanoid-looking robot with four arms. Its head swiveled as it scanned the room. Ian did not hesitate. He front-kicked the robot back out of the window and turned to run. His door slammed open before he could get to it, and his dad was standing there with his shotgun.

"What in the hell happened?" he shouted.

"I don't know; a robot came in through the window!"

"A what?" Jack Henderson was incredulous.

Suddenly, there was a scream from downstairs, and his dad turned and sprinted to his wife with Ian in hot pursuit. Before they could get to the top of the stairs, there was a loud, rapid-fire popping sound. It sounded like firecrackers, almost. As they clambered down the stairs, glass shattered behind them, and a four-armed robot came sprinting around the corner of the hall from Ian's parents' room. Jack shoved his son aside, almost knocking him over the railing, and fired a shot from his gun. The robot flew back several feet.

"Go! Go!" he shouted at Ian.

There was another shot from the top of the stairs as he got to the base of the stairs. His mom had car keys in one hand and a gun in the other. Her hair was disheveled, and there was blood staining her shoulder.

Ian's parents were ex-military, and as far as Ian knew, they were paper pushers. In fact, they were highly active in a myriad of clandestine operations, and when Rhonda got pregnant, they both decided to retire, but old habits die hard. Unbeknownst to Ian, there were guns scattered all over the house.

Ian's dad came barreling down the stairs, smoke trailing from the barrel of his gun. They were moving to the car with Ian in between them. They were almost to the interior garage door when there was an explosion originating in the garage; it blew the door into the dining area and shattered the fancy table in its path.

"Motherfucker!" his mom swore.

Ian's eyes went wide as saucers. He had never heard his precious mother talk that way, ever! It was awesome!

They immediately made a one-eighty and went to the front door, but the metal creature from upstairs was blocking their way. Jack pumped a round into the creature's knee, and as it fell, he racked another shell into the chamber, and as his son and wife passed behind him, he shot the thing in its face.

All at once, Ian and his parents were outside and running down the street. Ian realized he had forgotten the Global in his room.

"Dad, I gotta get my Global!" Ian exclaimed.

"Not in this lifetime," he responded to Ian.

"Mark 4 hunters?" his mom asked.

"Yeah, but why?" his dad asked.

Ian's mind was racing. It sounded like his parents thought the robot monsters had come for them, but that couldn't be right. He was sure these things were from the SOTIR Group and were after him to get to Scipio. His parents could not know that. It seems his parents were superheroes in their own way. They put their guns away and turned down a nearby street, and went to the third house. They walked to the door, and Ian's mom produced a key from the ring she had in her hand and unlocked the door. The Henderson family rushed in; the house was fully furnished and clean. Ian was stunned and just stood frozen in the foyer while his parents moved around the house with familiarity.

"UH, what is happening?" he asked, hoping it was a safe enough question.

"Well, honey, we may be in a bit of trouble, but if we keep calm and you do as we say, we will get out of this with minimal harm."

Ian registered that she did not say safe. This was a one-story house, and the rooms were to the left of the front door, and the kitchen and family room to the right. Ian looked toward the bedrooms where his dad went, and the man was coming from the room with a large green duffel bag hanging from his shoulder; gun barrels poked from the half-zipped opening.

"Ready?" he asked as he passed Ian.

"Come on, honey," his mom said, gesturing to him to join her; he went to her.

There was a blue minivan in the garage; it was about six years old. Ian knew this because up until a few seconds ago, he thought his parents had traded it in for the car that was probably a smoking husk at his old house. He remembered loving to ride in the very rear seat on long drives. His dad was loading the guns in the back compartment, and his mom was removing the cover over the vehicle when a massive crash rocked the house.

"Time to go!" his mom said, and the garage door started to go up. There was a loud metallic ripping sound, and the wide door suddenly had a human-sized hole in it.

"Cover your ears, son."

Ian obeyed immediately and ducked. The shotgun roared over his head. The van started, and he fell into the back of the van. The Blue Beast, as he called it, surged forward. They bounced roughly over the robotic monstrosity.

"Hold on, Jack, stay down, Ian," Rhonda shouted over her shoulder. The van turned sharply to the left. Something was peppering the side of the van. Ian thought it was the rocks, but rods of daylight peeked into the van interior. Then all at once, the violence stopped.

"You can get up now, sweetie," his mom reassured him.

Ian peeked his head up and looked out the window. They were on the freeway, surrounded by other cars. Ian got into one of the seats and looked around his new world. "Um, Mom, are you ok?" He noticed her bloody shoulder.

"Don't worry, baby, we will look at it when we get somewhere safe," she said, smiling to reassure him.

Ian's whole world was shattered. The safety of his parents was all but gone. Where had all the guns come from? What kind of desk job gave you the ability to have an extra house? Honestly, what ability made it possible for his best friend to be able to fly?

Safe or not, Ian loved his parents more than anything, and he didn't want them to die; if they were this bad-ass, then they could handle the truth, and maybe they could hole up at Adrian's real house.

Ian stared out the window at a world he knew nothing about anymore. One tear rolled down his rosy cheek.

"Mom, Dad, I have something to tell you," he said; his heart was pounding in his chest, but he told them the whole story up until the robot attack.

CHAPTER 40

San Francisco, California, March 18, 6:00 p.m. PST.

Mary Dutch stood looking through a large plexiglass window. Detective Alex Lamb lay on a metal table; tubes and wires streamed from his prone body.

"Will he be okay?" she asked reverently.

"Yes, it's just taking longer than expected. The nano-machines have a lot of work to do," Robert Cross said, "and so do you. You better run along to your hair appointment."

"Oh yes," she said gleefully and turned to hurry off to her appointment.

Cross pressed a button on the wall near the window, "Doctor, you may begin."

Men in white coats and thick rubber gloves carried a thin sheet of cobalt-colored metal. They laid the sheet over Alex's body and stepped away. Nothing happened at first, but eventually, the sheet began to disintegrate. When enough of the metal was gone, Alex's body was partly exposed, and large, bloodless gashes stood open all over his body. The part of the sheet that was over his head was consumed by thin tendrils erupting from his eyes, nose, and mouth.

"Doctor?" Cross did not turn away from his protégé.

"His brain is intact and untouched; however, his body is fifty percent converted, and we still have operational control. All backups are secure, and the fail-safe is active. Synchronization will begin in approximately thirty-six hours," the doctor stated.

"Good, inform me when the Synchronization begins," Cross said and left the room. The projections for Alex's abilities were damn near godly, and they had complete control. If the outcome of this was favorable, he would be joining Alex as a nano-machine recipient without all the fail-safes, of course. There was another experiment he wanted to check on before he headed to the pens.

Cross walked into the lab, and the scientists and technicians snapped to attention. Cross approached a black table with a large knife resting on two small pins. He raised an eyebrow, and the lead scientists stepped up to the other side of the table.

"Good evening, Sir."

"Get on with it," Cross snapped.

"Yes, Sir," the Scientist said, "the pommel is a cap that can be removed to refill the device, and there is a small feeder that supplies the nano-machines to the blade. Alex's telemetry showed us how to program the nano-machines on the fly and disseminate that information without having to be attached. He was very close. He was just unable to generate enough power to keep a constant signal."

"And why were you unable to make these into something more useful, like a bullet?" Cross asked.

"Well, Sir, the heat of the gases and the friction heat of just passing through the air killed the nano-machines instantly. There was a great possibility that the residue of the nano-machines could be examined with needles and reverse-engineered. The board deemed it too great a risk," the young scientist explained.

Cross waved away the man's words.

"What is the holdup with the blade?" Cross asked.

"Well, Sir, the normal nano-machines don't survive very long outside of the body. The only one we have had any success with is Detective Lamb's version of them. They seem overly aggressive and have been difficult to store. However, we do have footage of our latest test," the scientist explained; he escorted Cross to a nearby monitor.

On the monitor, a young African boy of about eight or nine stood in a room; he was wearing only a diaper. He looked around but did not move. A whistle sounded from some unseen speaker, and the boy was engulfed by a golden light. He stood there and did not move; after about twenty seconds, the light went away, and the boy seemed out of breath.

"This subject has only a Tier one ability, and after the experiment, he will still be genetically viable. Eventually, the nano-machines can be programmed to pass to the recipient of his sperm and vice versa." As they watched, a woman with chestnut brown hair and a white lab coat entered the small room. She gave the boy a small treat for his good work and rubbed his nappy head.

"Hold out your hand," she said gently, and the child obeyed. The technician was holding the blade that they had just looked at a moment ago behind her back. Now she brought it around and cut the boy's hand. He did not flinch.

"Tough little guy, huh?" Cross said.

"Yes, Sir," the sycophant agreed. The technician left the room, leaving the little boy standing there with a bleeding hand. The disembodied whistle sounded again, and the boy started straining, but nothing was happening.

Cross smiled; this was exactly what he wanted. Control.

"How fast can we get these into the hands of our operatives?" Cross asked, letting his eagerness slip through.

"Well, Sir, that is the problem; we can't do that. We have tried to program other nano-machines to do that, and they simply don't have the power to completely dampen anything other than the lowest Tier ability for more than a few hours. We tried to transplant Detective Lamb's nanomachines, and both patients died." The small man was nearly beside himself with fear.

"So, what the HELL have you all been doing in here?" Cross swept everything on a nearby table onto the floor.

"Sir, we were just tasked with making a workable weapon to transfer nano-machines to a subject. We were only transiently involved with the transplants. We learned that Detective Lamb's nano-machine system synchronizes well with the weapon system." The young man was trying desperately not to get killed; he heard many, many horror stories about punishment for failure in the SOTIR Group Science Corp. He didn't believe it until the lead scientist on this very project was executed right in front of the entire team for failing to report accurate findings and trying to falsify the reports she did turn in; the very idea of whistleblowing on a shadow corporation like this was suicide. They knew everything about you. You even had to use their special Global network that was separate from the "normal" network. On the other hand, the opportunity to work on bleeding-edge technology with no real ethical oversight was nearly worth all the fear.

Cross took a deep breath. It wouldn't do to hamper these fine scientists in their quest to help him fight against the destruction of Western Civilization.

"You know, I apologize; that was very rude of me and is counterproductive to the overall goal of this company.

Keep up the good work and at least have one blade ready for Detective Lamb when he has completed his upgrade," Cross turned on his heel and stalked out of the lab.

As he entered the hall, he received a call on his Global. He tapped his earpiece, and a man's face appeared on the screen.

"Report," he barked at the face.

"Sir, the Henderson subjects escaped, and their whereabouts are unknown at this time." The man's voice was crisp and devoid of emotion.

"What?" Cross shook his head in disbelief, "How did a family of three civilians escape eight Mark 4 Automatons?"

"Sir, it seems they had help. The power signature scans as subject: Skate. She is a physical adept and low-level electrical disruptor. We have been up against her before, but she was supposed to be out of the country."

"She took out eight Mark 4s by herself?"

"Well, no, Sir, she only took out six. It seems the adults in the house were able to evade the two that got by Skate."

"What? The parents took out two automatons. Who are they? What do we have on them?" Cross demanded.

"Mr. Cross, all we have are their military records, and they were analysts. Jack Henderson was a cryptographer, and Rhonda Henderson was a data analyst who worked out of Fort Bragg. They retired sixteen years ago and have been law-abiding people for nearly seventeen years." Cross knew what was at Fort Bragg, and combined with their escape, he surmised they were not just analysts.

"We even offered them a job."

"Why was Skate there in the first place?" Cross asked.

"Well, Sir, we don't know if it was on purpose or unplanned because of her ability; she can move without leaving a trace," the voice informed.

"Fine, let me know the moment you find them," Cross ordered.

"Yes, Sir," the line cut off, and Robert Cross was alone with his thoughts. He had seen this movie before; things were getting out of control, and there were still too many unknown variables, except that girl. She was the prize of prizes and the boy as well; his genetic material would jump the program ahead by generations. In his mind, it was worth the risk; he would just cut his losses and lie low for a while if this failed. No real harm done. Two Tier Fives at the same time? Greed glinted in Cross's eyes.

CHAPTER 41

Somewhere Underground, March 19, 12:40 a.m. EST.

Adrian and I were sitting in the common area waiting for Saphronia to meet us after her shower, and Adrian was acting very strange.

"Adrian, what's going on? You seem on edge," I asked him.

He turned to me, and I could see he wanted to say something but held it back.

"A lot has happened in the last two days that has put a whole new layer to our situation. It's not my place to tell you, but I will say we are all on your side and are willing to help you." Adrian was looking at me with troubled eyes.

"What the hell is going on, Adrian?" I demanded. This was awfully familiar.

"What's going on, guys?" Saphronia said as she rounded the corner from the bathroom. She was still fluffing her hair with one hand, and the bag with the stylized bird on the front of it hung over her free hand.

"Hey, Saphronia, what did you think of the outfit?" I asked with a smile on my face. It was so good to see her.

"It looks fine from the outside, but whatever those little hairs or whatever they are on the inside are gross. I had to take a shower just to get the feeling to go away." She explained. Small arcs of energy coursed all through her hair from her scalp out. In one wave, her hair was dried, moisturized, and styled in a curly shock of midnight with a jaunty clip to keep the curls out of her face.

"Oh, that goes away as soon as you synchronize with the outfit. It's cool, look," I stood and held out my arms. I closed my eyes and willed the outfit to look like a tuxedo, just as I had done before. The clothes seemed to flip and swirl around me, and then it was a tuxedo.

"Whoa!" Saphronia exclaimed, "How in the world?" was all that came out.

"Yeah, that is cool, but I am going to pass on the itchy suit, even if it can transform," she seemed pretty adamant, and I was about to go into a long speech to convince her to wear it when Coach cut in.

"Scip tell Nes... Saphronia, what you came to say. We're both here now," he spread his hands in a grand gesture.

I caught the weird slip but had no context. Saphronia hung the bag up, and we all gathered around to talk. I noticed the silverish bracer on Saphronia's arm, and it seemed familiar to me; the amber jewel glinted beautifully in the warm light.

Just as I was about to comment on it, East walked in holding a large cup of tea.

"May I join you all?" she asked.

"Of course," I said, "this does concern you as well," I told her, and she folded gracefully into a nearby chair.

I tried to describe Aset's beauty and power, and I failed miserably. I told them of the brief conversation we had and of the vision that followed. In all of it, my choice to stand with my people was made clear.

Saphronia was sitting with her hands over her mouth; her eyes were wide with recognition.

"You spoke to her, and she touched you?" Saphronia said. A tear rolled down her dark cheek.

"Yes," I said, almost regretfully.

"Scipio, I have to tell you something before I tell you my end of the story," Saphronia said, taking a deep breath. I glanced around at everyone in the room, and everyone seemed fixated on Saphronia. She stood up, her hands were at her sides in half fists, and her chin was high.

"Scipio, my name is not Saphronia. My real name is Neswt Biti, and I am an Emissary, the youngest ever, sent with the blessing of the Zamaradi Council. I am here to fulfill my destiny as the Ikhawu in the battle for our existence. I am so sorry I lied to you." Tears stood in her golden-brown eyes. Her eyes, I realized, were the same color as Aset's. The same color as mine. We were bound together through Aset. We shared our abilities because we were powered by the same source.

CLICK!

East spewed her tea, but at what, I did not know. We all looked at her with surprise.

"Did you say you were an Emissary?" East said.

"Yes, mum, I apologize to you as well for not revealing myself to you, the Elder of this Community." Saphronia, I mean, Neswt said.

"Girl, was this some kind of test?" There was a soft pink glow starting to fill the air around East's head.

The world fell away, and I was lost in the "click." When I heard Neswt's real name, the circle was complete. This was right; I could feel it. I could sense that it was not complete before, but now it was. I did not feel betrayed at all; in fact, I understood. There were more circles yet to close.

I could hear East trying to be polite, and her voice trembled. Adrian was trying in vain to reassure her that she was not in any trouble. Saphr... Neswt was silent, and I could feel her eyes on me.

"Thank you, Neswt. Just so you know, I am not upset. I understand you didn't know me from a tree, and you had to be able to assess the situation," I shrugged and said, "I get it."

She was visibly relieved, and my words stopped the bickering that the "adults" were doing.

She walked over to me, her face was solemn, and her eyes were fixed on mine. There was no guile, only truth. I stood and met her gaze.

"Iklwa, I promise to never lie to you again. Can you do the same?" Neswt asked formally.

The words came to me unbidden.

"Ikhawu, I promise to never lie to you again." It did not matter that I had never lied to her; the words needed to be said.

"Ikhawu, I promise to fight for you and our people no matter the foe," the words appeared in my head.

"Iklwa, I promise to defend you and our people from all foes." Judging by her reaction, the words seem to leap from her mouth, too.

In unison, we said, *"By the Red left hand of Gia, we are agreed! This, I swear!"*

There was a massive explosion of thunder in the room, all the glass shattered around us. The cup of tea East was holding exploded in her hand, and she cried out in surprise and pain. Adrian was thrown from his chair and landed tangled up in the picnic bench and table. Concentric circles of energy pulsed from us. I could see my face in her eyes and knew she saw the same in reverse. Our vision expanded up and out into the inky void of space. Out, out, out! Until the distance was only measured in time. We passed through the hearts of suns and planets and connected to each other.

We snapped back smoothly, passing through each other on the way back to ourselves. Equals but specialized for our tasks.

Our joining was near completion.

Then it was quiet and still. Some glass still tinkled to the ground.

"What in the Ancestors was that?!" East said breathlessly.

"Hey! Can someone give me a hand?" Adrian complained.

"Dude tele..." The words died in my throat when Adrian appeared before me in a whump of air.

"So, what was that? Did you guys just get married or something?" Adrian said, and I think he was joking.

"Uh, I don't think so?" Neswt and I said simultaneously. Then we laughed together. Then we stopped, and both looked away uncomfortably. "What the hell is going on here?" East shouted, "What is wrong with you two? Why are you doing that?"

"I don't know," I said, "I think we were synced up or something.

"I think it's over now," Neswt said. I was feeling more like myself, but different.

"Yeah, me too," Neswt said, and we looked at each other.

"Maybe not quite over," we said together.

"I was going to tell you my story, but now I don't think I have to," Neswt said. Her smooth brow furrowed in thought, and then I had a new set of memories in my mind. It was like a movie clip, but all the information I needed was in it, and nothing private.

"Whoa!" was all I could say.

"Yeah, that was cool and handy." She responded.

"What the HELL IS GOING ON?" East screamed.

"I'm sorry, East. I'm not sure what happened. It seems like we just got some mystic ...," the word just was not in my head.

"Authority." Neswt finished.

"Exactly the word I was looking for," I said, slapping my hands together in agreement.

"Other than that, I don't know what happened. Those words were mine, but I didn't think them; I wasn't forced to say them, but I didn't know them."

"Yes, it was like if I *knew* the words, I would have said them, but because I didn't know them, they were given to me." I nodded my head at her words.

"Well, whatever it was, it was powerful." She started looking around for safe places to walk.

"Hold it, I got it!" Adrian said, squatting down and touching the floor. In one tinkling whoomph, all the glass that was on the floor simply vanished.

"That was incredible!" I said. Adrian smiled, and then my Global rang.

I tapped my earpiece, and a screen appeared in the palm of my right hand, but it said voice only.

"Hello?"

"Hello, Iklwa; it's nice to meet you. My name is Noemi, and I know your friend Ian," the voice on the other end of the line sounded young but serious. Her mention of Ian made my blood run cold.

"Who is this, and how do you know Ian?"

"He is a friend of mine," the young voice said, "and he is in trouble. Mal deserved the broken arm. Ian told me to tell you that so you would believe me."

"Where?" I demanded. I glanced at Adrian, trying to not be pissed at myself for letting him convince me he was safe.

A text message appeared on the projection on my hand; the content of the message was just a set of coordinates.

"You need to hurry. He does not have much time," and the call ended.

"Hello? Hello!" I looked at Neswt first and tried our little information dump trick. She nodded her head.

"OK, okay, that's cute and all," Adrian growled, "What's going on with Ian? And don't think I didn't see that look you gave me, Scipio. You may be the Ancestors' gift to the world, but I will still take you to the woodshed."

I ignored his anger. "Can you get us to this place?" I showed him the coordinates. "I don't think I can take all of us."

He must have seen the dread in my face because his bravado fell away, and he was all business. Adrian held out his hand and said, "Let's go."

CHAPTER 42

North San Jose, California, March 19, 12:50 a.m. PST

We arrived in a war zone, or at least that's what I thought. The sound of gunfire was deafening.

"Whoa! What the fuck!" Yelled Adrian. Before I could register what was happening, he teleported us to some nearby cover.

"What did the person on the call say?" Adrian demanded.

Bullets pinged somewhere to the right of us.

"Nothing about a gunfight."

Someone was tugging on my shirt. I turned to look and saw East staring up at me. She was all business.

"Listen, you have a full squad of Mark 4 Automatons, and it seems a full squad of SOTIR Group regulars; if we split up, we can take them by surprise. Me and pretty boy," she gestured to Adrian, "will go right, and you two will go left. Since that seems to be your good side."

I was dumbfounded. The last I saw of East, she was in a comfy-looking bathrobe with furry slippers. Now she was in a jet-black outfit that fit her well and had armor in all the correct places. She had a mask covering the bottom half of her face and her ears.

"You're not the only one to get fancy threads, kid," she said with a wink and drug Adrian away. Neswt and I pulled up our masks as well.

We were in a parking lot, but there were large, multi-colored shipping containers stacked and scattered around the lot. Beyond the parking lot was a small warehouse with windows on the first and second floors. The gunfire was coming from the building, aimed at the SOTIR Group regulars hiding among the shipping containers. I could tell there was fighting inside the warehouse as well. Flashes of orange light were visible from the first-floor windows. I had never been in anything like this other than in a video game.

"Follow me," Neswt said, pulling on my sleeve, "and stay low." She shared armed conflict training with me. I followed and desperately did not want to get shot. An idea came to me. I imagined the surface of my entire body and tried to construct a thin covering around me to stop bullets or any damage. I imagined the chaos of a violent plane crash and being unhurt. I was thinking about when I changed direction in the practice cavern and how that felt, and applied it to this covering. I shared the idea with her via our rapport so she could apply it too.

She was flanking the attackers on the left; they had no idea we were there.

"How do we play it, Iklwa? Are we killing them or incapacitating them?" As she was asking the question, I looked up and saw the strangest thing. Ian was holding a massive machine gun and firing it at the men on the ground. The look on his face was pure determination to live. Tears of *anger* burned my eyes. I thought of all the times I was taught from childhood that violence didn't cure anything, and peace was the only way. I remembered the pictures of Black men, women, and children being attacked by dogs and sprayed with fire hoses. I recalled the postcards of the Black people lynched and burned. All the unarmed Black people killed by the police. I remembered the images of the Chicago Massacre, where people of all colors were gunned down standing up for Black people in America. I remembered all the times the police stopped and humiliated me for fun. I remembered the feeling of helplessness. That feeling lit the fuse. Never again would I be without choice. I would never again be helpless.

I disappeared without answering Neswt. I reappeared in front of the men who were shooting. They looked like police officers; their eyes were cold and full of hate. I saw them flinch at my sudden appearance, but they recovered quickly.

They opened fire!

Rounds poured at me; I heard Neswt check a scream! I felt none of it; my field held. I rushed the man to my left at my full speed and transferred the inertia and momentum to him as I hit him. I thought he would go flying into the container behind him, but he just exploded on impact. The other man screamed and tried to run. He hit an invisible wall and fell. He spun around, and terror was etched on his face. He pulled a pistol, a Desert Eagle, and fired seven shots at me.

"Stop resisting," I said calmly.

"Please!" he begged.

"Stop resisting!" I said again. He was scrambling backward but not going anywhere. Neswt's wall held him in place. I raised my hand. I wanted to watch *him* burn. His pink skin started to turn red, and the human man in front of me screamed for his mother before he burst into flames; I closed my hand into a fist, and the flames turned blue. The screams stopped, and so did the gunfire. Neswt lowered her field, and the ashes of the man collapsed into a pile.

"Okay, I guess you answered my question," Neswt said.

"They wouldn't show us mercy; why shouldn't we do the same?" I said coldly. My heart was beating furiously in my ribcage.

"Because we are..." I cut her off.

"Don't say because we are better. We're not. Not today, not ever. You know that as well as I do. We're here for war, and war we will wage." I vanished to hunt.

Inside the warehouse, Ms. and Mr. Henderson were trying desperately to keep the automatons at bay.

I had no experience fighting these things, so I went in hard.

I created a line in my mind, connected to my hand; it was as long as I wanted it and flexible like a whip, but I could feel I had complete control of it. I imagined a razor, and I could sense the sharpness of the line. The Razor Line. I appeared behind one of the mechanical creatures and whipped the Razor Line in a spiral. I looked more like a ribbon spinner than an intimidating whip master, but the circles shredded the automaton like it was air. I felt no resistance.

The air pressure behind me changed, and I disappeared from the spot I was in and reappeared three feet away. The metal attacker was just landing as I reappeared; I straightened the Razor Line and stabbed the creature in the center. I changed the shape of the line to many spiked balls, and the robot exploded.

Bullets slammed into me from behind. I turned to see an automaton on the other side of the warehouse firing at me. I blasted a thicker Razor Line at him, but nothing happened. It felt like he was out of range; bullets rained on and around me. Ignored them. I registered an explosion outside.

I repositioned to the top of some old machinery closer to my target and fired again. Three-quarters of the robot's upper half vanished. Range was something I had never considered; I was glad I learned about it.

I reappeared outside in front of the SOTIR Group men; they all began shooting immediately. They poured hot lead at me and retreated. I stood there and watched them. I could feel the *Anger* trying to swallow and take control. I let them scurry a bit, then I appeared where I saw the first man running to. He slammed into me, and the field I had up stopped him and dissipated the impact. He fell back. I raised my hands together like a prayer and pulled them apart. The man exploded. One of his partners came around the corner just in time to see his friend torn apart. He raised his gun to shoot me, but his head jumped off his body and seemed to be floating in a golden balloon. The man's body fell to the ground, blood still pumping from his headless neck.

A man's body slammed into a container from a great height. He landed half on the container, and his back snapped loudly. He was wearing SOTIR Group colors.

Adrian appeared before me.

"That's the last one out here!" he reported, and I nodded. I appeared in front of Ian. He screamed in surprise.

"Easy, it's me, Ian!" I held my hands up.

"Scipio?" he jumped to his feet and hugged me.

"Are you okay?" I was trying to check for wounds and/or holes.

"Yeah, I'm okay. You must have met my friend."

"Noemi? Yeah, she is the one that called me. How did you end up here?" I asked.

"This was the last safe house my parents had." As Ian finished his sentence, there was a huge whomping explosion that rocked the entire structure. Dust fell from the old rafters and filled the air.

"Run, Ian!" I heard Mrs. Henderson yell from below.

Ian turned to run, but I grabbed him, and we jumped out of the nearby window. But instead of falling, we arced up into the air. We got about one hundred yards away, and the entire building exploded and was engulfed in a ball of orange and gray flames. The containers near the building rolled and bounced away, crashing into the other containers. The pressure wave buffeted us as we hovered there, watching it go up. I lowered us to the ground, and the others made it to us, including the Hendersons.

"Mom, Dad!" Ian exclaimed and ran to his parents.

"We need to get out of the open. I think we are being tracked by satellite." Mr. Henderson warned.

"Say no more," Adrian said. "Everyone, please take a hand." The circle formed, and we all vanished.

CHAPTER 43

Somewhere Underground, March 19, 1:30 a.m. PST.

We all appeared in Adrian's home with a muffled clap of air. Adrian took a halting half step, then recovered and seemed fine. I'm sure teleporting so many people was not an easy task.

"Where are we?" Mr. Henderson asked, breaking the silence.

"This is my house," Adrian said.

His voice was tight, and he was looking around like he did not know where he was. He looked at East and grabbed her arm. He jerked like he was expecting to teleport away, but nothing happened.

"Unhand me, young man!" East shouted at Adrian.

"I'm sorry, can I speak to you in the other room, please, Elder?" Adrian said through clenched teeth, and he pushed her roughly into the other room. Neswt, Ian, and I exchanged looks. Neswt introduced herself as Saphronia and took the Henderson family to the kitchen to get some food and clean up.

I popped into the room with the arguing adults.

"If I find out you were digging in my brain without permission, I will take you a mile up and drop you!" Adrian yelled; he was inches from her face.

"Try it, sonny. I'll have you drooling in a mental hospital in three seconds flat." East retorted.

"What the heck is going on?" I shouted. Even though I wanted to cuss these two adults out, I was raised not to swear at my elders. They both looked at me; their faces were masks of shock and bewilderment.

"Your friend here," began East, "was about to reveal the Community's position by teleporting these descendants to my house, so I changed his destination."

"You can do that?" All of a sudden, my own mind seemed exposed.

She tapped an elegant finger to her temple, "Headquarters controls everything, and once you control headquarters, you control everything." There was a pink glint in her eyes.

"This idiot tried to let random White people into my community without making sure they didn't have tracking devices on them." East shook with anger; I knew Adrian could see it too.

"Why do you think we have everyone come through, E? It's because she can make sure nothing she doesn't want to come in comes in!" She crossed her arms and planted her foot. Uh oh, I thought to myself.

Her gaze bored into Adrian.

"Uh, I did not know that; I, uh, never put it together," Adrian explained.

"Of course, you didn't, fool, I didn't let you. However, you should have at least considered it before you tried to teleport us to a secure location. Rookie mistake."

"Wait, you were messing with Adrian's mind all this time? And what, you expected him to know something you were actively suppressing? Are you messing with my head right now?" My eyes felt hot with rage. I came to defend

Adrian from East, and now I find out she, a stranger, has been playing with my mind.

"Easy, Scip," Adrian eased, "it's not that big of a deal; she was doing her job to protect the people. We are all on the same side."

"Are you messing with my mind right now?" I asked East.

"NO!" she declared.

I blinked, and Neswt was standing next to me, her fists were balled, and golden arcs of energy roamed over her body.

"What happened?" she demanded.

"Whoa! What the fuck!" Adrian shouted in utter surprise! "Where did you come from?"

"ANCESTORS!" East screamed, bowed her head, and knelt.

Adrian took a step back and whispered, "Ancestors." Later, he would describe what we looked like:

"You were human personified, perfect specimens of *all* of us. A Pair. Light and darkness streamed from you, and we could feel the protection coming from you, Neswt. And the danger. For that instant, you were more than the two people I have come to know and love. You were a concept. The Concept of Safety. Then it was over; you were just two very dangerous teenagers."

Aset's voice came to us, *"Be still, children, you must apply the Anger appropriately."* Our anger faded with her voice. I blinked and looked around. I saw that Neswt had the same slightly perplexed look on her face as I did.

East stood quickly and said, "I have never messed with your mind because I have been unable to. There is only static when I try." She would not meet my eyes, and she was very subdued.

"I will contact E and get us into the Community if that is what you want," East offered, "but they may cause a problem; the people may not understand the presence of lily-white descendants walking through the community."

"Then we will just teleport right after we cross the threshold of the portal, and no one will know," I suggested; it seemed an easy fix to me.

"Of course, we can do that, but there are many precognitive people of different abilities scattered all through the community. They are our early warning system, so unless you know how to stop them from seeing things we haven't done yet, the population will know; they probably already know." East countered.

"What do we do?" Neswt asked.

"We just go through E's portal. The Hendersons have to be protected, period." I was not budging.

"Okay, I'll make the call," East said, "we will be leaving soon." She was still avoiding eye contact with me. Adrian ushered us out of the room as East made her call.

Out in the anteroom, Adrian stopped to talk to us, "What in the everloving hell was that in there?" he asked.

Neswt and I knew exactly what he meant.

"I don't know. It was like I was watching the whole thing from far away," we said.

"Yes, it was as if we were one person with something that was swallowing us," Neswt added.

"Exactly. I felt like I could steer myself, but I had no control over the gas pedal. If you understand my meaning?" I explained, and Neswt nodded in agreement.

"Well, save that shit for the bad guys, Ancestors help them. I never want to be on the receiving end of whatever that was about to be," he shook the goosebumps away.

"Okay, Coach," Neswt and I said together.

"And stop doing that crap; it's weird," he walked back to see about the Henderson family, who seemed oddly oblivious to the commotion.

I looked at Neswt, and we smiled tightly at each other. We did not tell Adrian that we did not have full control over ourselves and that the Anger we experienced only wanted safety at all costs. We exchanged this information and agreed to keep it from the others, all in an instant.

We were about to follow Adrian when wind filled the anteroom, and the sound of seagulls filled the space. We spun in unison, and a small woman of Asian descent stepped through the portal.

"Hey, guys!" E said and gave a quick wave.

"Hey E," Neswt and I said. She walked past us and into the room East was currently in.

We continued to the kitchen with everyone else.

"We used to be operatives for the government, and when Rhonda got pregnant, we decided to retire," Jack Henderson explained to Adrian. "At first, we thought they were after us, but when Ian explained what he was caught up in, we realized they were after him. We have heard of the SOTIR Group in the service, but they were not a dangerous group, or so we thought. They even offered us a job, which, upon diligent research, we declined." Mr. Henderson looked around at us when we came into the dining area.

"Hey, you two," he said, "that was some amazing stuff back there," he complimented.

"Thanks," we said. We talked simultaneously when we were nervous.

Mrs. Henderson rushed over to me and gave me a long hug. I could feel her body shaking.

She pulled back and said, "I am so sorry about Beverly, sweetie; you just let us know how we can help you get these bastards!"

"Mom!" Ian whined.

I could feel my eyes and nose start to burn. She was the closest person I had as a mother.

"Thank you," I breathed, "I may take you up on that offer someday. We are going to make sure you all are safe."

Mrs. Henderson let me go and went back to her place at the table. Mr. Henderson shook my hand.

"You're a good man, Scipio. I am sorry about your mom. You are doing your family proud." His voice grated with emotion.

"Thank you, Sir; I really appreciate that." I walked over and took a few bites of the food that was laid out on the table.

"You know, Mr. and Mrs. Henderson, you guys are really taking this well. How is that possible?" I asked lightly; my dad always taught me to be direct.

"Well, Scipio, to be honest, we've seen enough evidence, just in the last hour, that this is real. We've seen enough in our careers not to be too shaken by these events. Although I would venture to say that when the world finds out about you, they may want to at least talk to you. The longer you can stay in the shadows, the longer they will leave you all alone.

"What will they do if they find us?" I asked Mr. Henderson, but Mrs. Henderson answered.

"They will send in operators like us and those machines we fought to kill or capture you all. They will bill it as a humanitarian mission that spiraled out of control because you were all terrorists who hate America. No one will be told about people who can teleport and fly."

Her explanation rang true to me, and I shuddered when I thought about what the government would do to someone like the boy with the big tail who slapped her son twenty feet into the air.

"It probably wouldn't go the way they think it would," I said gravely.

"You're right, Scipio, but that would only make things worse. Someone somewhere will film, and it will get out to the public, and that is where the situation will get really unpredictable." Mr. Henderson said.

I was about to reply, but East and E came into the kitchen.

"We are ready to leave. Please only bring yourselves and nothing else." East said. Adrian came into the kitchen area from the direction of the rooms.

"Hey, Henderson family, I have some clothes for you to change into. It's more of a precaution," Adrian said. "If you will follow me," they all filed off together. East and E went back to the anteroom. I sent a thought to Neswt. *Do you think those robots had cameras?*

Yes, she responded, *most definitely, but do not worry, you had your mask on and hood up. Besides, they already know who you are. What does it matter?*

They don't know what I can do, and I don't want to give them any information if I can help it. I sent back to her.

Scipio, worrying has never solved a thing. We can only trust in each other. Peaceful but determined energy flowed from her to me. Because of her strength, I was able to return it to her.

Thank you, Neswt. I sent back.

CHAPTER 44

S omewhere Underground, March 19, 2:00 a.m. PST.

The Henderson family came back to the anteroom. Mr. and Mrs. Henderson were wearing the same gray sweats as we had been given, but Ian was wearing the outfit Bamidele had made for him. At first, I thought it was black like mine, but it was more charcoal gray. It had a hood similar to mine, and I could see the gaiter-type mask. There were no sleeves, and Ian's well-defined arms were visible. He was carrying a long jacket over his arm. The pants looked like jeans of the same color, and he had boots on as well.

When he came in, he did a spin with a big grin on his face, "How do I look? Bamidele came through, right? There was even a replacement Global base in the bag."

The clothes flipped and twisted and became the gray sweatsuit his parents were wearing,

"Whoa! Son, where did you get that?" his mom asked.

Ian looked at me, and I shook my head ever so slightly.

"I'm not sure, Mom. I think it was a gift from one of Coach's friends," Ian lied. He was looking at her kind of sheepishly to hide the lie.

She dropped it, saying, "It looks good on you. I'm a little bit jealous."

East broke the spell. "Please let us know if you have any embedded tech in your body; the field you will be passing through will cause any location or surveillance type equipment to fail catastrophically. If it is internalized, it will be quite painful." East warned.

The Hendersons looked at each other, and they both held out their right arm.

"We have tracking devices in our arms, but we put them there. No one knows about them but us." Mr. Henderson said.

"I believe you, but we will have to cut them out," East said without sympathy.

Neswt stepped up and offered, "I can get rid of them if you do not mind? I will not have to break the skin."

East's and the Henderson couple's eyebrows rose with surprise, but no one moved. Neswt placed her hands on their arms and closed her eyes. After a moment, she opened them and took her hands away.

"Okay, they are gone now; you guys are all clear." She stated.

"Just like that?" Mrs. Henderson asked.

"Just like that," Neswt repeated. The couple looked at Ian, who only shrugged.

"Well, let's see if she is as good as her word," Mr. Henderson said confidently. East gestured to E, and a portal appeared nearby. The smells and sounds of the market flooded the little anteroom.

"Wow! That is handy!" Mrs. Henderson said in amazement.

I stepped through first, and nothing happened. I looked back and raised my hands to say, 'See, no problem.' Neswt stepped through after me.

"After you," I heard East say, and the Hendersons held hands and stepped through. Nothing happened or exploded from their bodies. Neswt only smiled. I could tell she had a hint of annoyance at their apprehension, and I completely understood.

The rest of our little party came through the portal, and then it closed with a whoosh. We were near the middle of the bazaar, and all eyes were on the Henderson family.

"Why did we do it this way again?" Ian asked nervously.

"Because they already know, and if we try to hide it, it will just make things worse than they are about to be. These people have been through hell to get here, and they are scared. You all go to the elevator and go down. I will stay and try to explain what is happening." East said, "Now go before you get hit in the head with a rock."

We jogged through the bazaar toward the red sunrise door. We could hear East taking control of the crowd that had formed.

As we jogged, the crowd of people thickened around us. Still, there remained a small alleyway through the throng.

Our group arrived at the elevator plaza, which was strangely empty. I looked back at the crowd as we climbed into the large elevator; they were starting to get agitated, but no one dared cross into the plaza. When the elevator doors closed, we vanished and appeared in East's quarters in the large sitting room where I got the call from Noemi warning us about Ian.

"We can wait here until East gets back, or I can show you where you will be sleeping," Adrian offered hospitably.

"You know, after the last couple of days we have had, we are exhausted," Mr. Henderson said.

"Follow me then," Adrian said.

Ian did not follow.

"Are you coming with, son?" Mrs. Henderson asked.

"No, I'll be there later. I want to talk to Scipio and Saphronia first," Ian said. I realized Ian missed so much that he still thought Neswt's name was Saphronia.

"Okay, son, but you will need your rest," Ian's mom said.

"Okay, Mom," he said, exasperated. She turned to follow Adrian. It always boggled my mind how Ian was able to talk to his parents so rudely. Ian turned to us, and his face was full of worry.

"I have to tell you guys what I learned when I met Noemi!" he said. He set his device on one of the tables and set it to project his information.

We sat down to listen to the presentation Ian had for us.

"Wait, Ian," Neswt said, "I have to tell you something first. My name is not really Saphronia. It's Neswt Biti, and I am an Emissary from the Alpha A.R.C. I had to lie in case..." Ian raised his hand.

"Say no more, Neswt," he said, seeming to be tasting the name in his mouth. "I understand. If you and Scipio are cool, then so am I," Ian said almost dismissively.

Neswt crossed her arms and narrowed her eyes at his ability to accept the new information. She glanced at me, and I just shrugged.

Ian proceeded to tell us about everything he learned in the last day or so. My mouth fell open when he said the "intruder" at my house was a detective and worked for the SOTIR Group. Adrian came back in the middle of Ian's presentation and was impressed with the amount of information he had. In the end, he had one question.

"Why did Noemi contact you, Ian? I mean, it makes no sense she doesn't know you from Adam?" Adrian said. "I know Noemi, I have worked with her before, and I don't see why she contacted you," Adrian added.

"Maybe it's my animal magnetism, Coach," Ian said. "Actually, I was digging into the Global to try to figure out the OS, but I couldn't get anywhere. That must have upset her, and she contacted me; we hit it off, I guess. She was helping us evade the SOTIR Group guys, but they started getting ahead of her. Did you know they have satellites all over the place and can see the license plates on cars?" Ian said, and Adrian nodded.

"My parents did too," Ian said a little deflated, but he continued, "Between Noemi and my 'Rents, we were able to evade them, but like I said, they started getting ahead of us somehow. The closer we got to that warehouse, the closer they got. Eventually, it was like they knew where we were headed. My dad said we didn't have a choice. It was the best chance we had."

I was getting upset listening to this part of his story.

"Ian, why didn't you call me?" I asked finally.

"Oh man, I know how you get when you are figuring stuff out, and I knew you had bigger fish to fry than the Hendersons. I figured you could get to me instantly if I could get you coordinates. Scipio, in case you haven't figured it out yet, you are the hero in this story." He was looking at me like he was telling me about the most obvious thing in the world.

"Ian, this isn't a story, man, I'm trying... I mean, we're trying to save my dad from these people." I tried to explain to him, but he was not dissuaded.

"I know how serious this is, Scipio! I want to get your dad back and take this hellish group out as well. Afterward, I hope to stand next to you and Neswt as you guys save the world. I believe in you guys. I have seen too much to go back to regular life. Like you said, I could be the perfect inside man," Ian looked directly at me, his blue eyes level and sure.

"Scipio, I know I don't have powers or anything, and I am just a fragile regular guy, but don't leave me behind. We are Ebony and Ivory, and I will always have your back."

Ian was like a brother to me, and if anything happened to him, I would be crushed, but our history was greater than even the danger I knew was out there. He proved himself to me at the warehouse. I know Adrian would not like having him around because he could be a liability, but I needed Ian.

"Okay, Ian, you are with us no matter what. Bamidele wouldn't have given you a suit if it wasn't meant to be, right?" I said to him.

"WHAT?" Adrian exploded, "Ian is not a part of this world. Scipio, I tried to tell you that earlier, and you said you understood. Now his baby blues are getting to you?"

"No, Adrian, he is safer with us than out on the street. They know he is connected to me, and I am willing to fight to get him back. So instead, we do what they least expect. We will let him join us." I turned to Ian, "Of course, you won't be on the front lines with us all the time, but you will be on the team. A valuable member of the team." Adrian scoffed at my words, and my *anger* almost got the best of me, but I quelled it.

"Adrian, I have been your student for many years, and I will always learn from you, but at this moment, I am in control, and I say he stays. If it's a bad idea, then I will take responsibility for my choice. Okay?" I tried to put command and steel in my voice, and I was looking him directly in the eyes.

Adrian opened his mouth to say something, and his personal Global rang. He tapped his earpiece and looked down at his hand. I could hear shouting and commotion in the background.

"Adrian, we need you out here, now!" East was shouting, "And leave those damn kids in the house." The call ended abruptly.

"Damnit!" Adrian cursed, "We will talk about this when I get back; don't move!" he ordered and then vanished.

I felt Ian and Neswt's eyes on me, and I did not know what to do. I was not a kid anymore; I was not his little grasshopper. I knew I had a lot to learn, but I wanted to learn it my way. Coach, ugh, Adrian would not let me be in control. My dad was Adrian's friend, but he was *my dad*, and I would do whatever it took to get him home safely, to get all of us home safely.

My heart was pounding in my chest; this was a big step. The palms of my hands were sweaty, and they were shaking.

"Scipio," Neswt's voice was gentle and calm, "Ian and I trust *you*, and you can trust us. Look, I'll prove it," then she ran off. I shook my head in surprise.

"What?" I said.

"Hey Scipio, thanks, man," Ian said, "I appreciate what you said."

I turned to him and said, "No problem, it was all the truth." I smiled.

Neswt came back into the room wearing her Bamidele suit. She was stunning!

Why, thank you, Iklwa! She sent to me, and I was not embarrassed.

She was in a hooded V-neck jumpsuit with no sleeves; the pants were tight, but the fabric looked very giving. She spun, and two wide tails of fabric flared out from her hips; they stopped five inches or so above the floor. The bracer

Ogun gifted to her was still on her arm. The jewel glittered playfully. The overall color of the suit was a deep wine red, and it was highlighted by the same pattern of kente as the piping on my suit. She wore no shoes on her feet, just like me. The overall look was magnificent.

"This is the original form of the suit, and this," she said, shifting her feet, and the whole outfit flipped and switched to a dark purple and black kente pattern and armor plates on all the right places. The V-neck was gone, and the sleeves came down to the back of her hand, then stretched and flipped more to cover her hands completely. She pulled the hood up and zipped the opening of it closed.

"I don't know how he did it, but there is tactical information in here. I can switch to night vision, thermal, infrared, and all manner of communications. Who knows what else this thing can do!" she said excitedly. She unzipped the hood and reverted to the original form.

"Why did you not tell me it had all of this in it for just a pinprick?" she asked, crossing her lovely arms.

"I didn't know; I just turned mine into a tuxedo and a shirt, and blue jeans. I had no idea all of that was available."

Neswt laughed, and my heart almost burst.

"I am glad you have me to show you the ropes," and she laughed again.

We were in the middle of trying to outdo each other with the craziest configuration of our suits when the old phone in my pocket rang. We all stopped, and our suits shifted to battle mode instinctively.

"What do we do?" Ian asked.

I had pulled it out of one of my pockets, and we were all staring at the device.

"We answer it," I said and was about to press the button when Neswt stopped me.

"Wait, we do not want to open the call here. We need to go somewhere safe, so we do not give Haven's location away." Of course, Neswt was right.

"Who will teleport us to somewhere safe?" I asked. They both looked at me. The phone rang again.

"You will," Neswt said. "You can do it!" she continued, cheering me on. The old phone rang for the third time.

Neswt and Ian put their hands on my shoulders, and we were about to try to teleport when a voice stopped us. The phone rang a fourth time.

"Ian," his mom said, "go to these coordinates and look for a red container with your birthday as the ID numbers. You will find some gear in there to help you." The phone rang for the fifth time.

"You keep my baby safe, Scipio." She said quietly.

"I will, I promise," I said, and then we were gone.

We appeared in the same park as Adrian, and I did last time. This time, my location sense told me we were in Central Park, in New York. I picked up the phone.

"Hullo?"

"I thought you lost the phone. I was about ready to hang up. It's time, be at these coordinates in thirty minutes. See you soon, boy." I did not recognize the voice, but I did not think it was a prank. The phone buzzed, and I saw that it received a text. It was more coordinates.

"Let's go!"

"Iklwa, wait," Neswt said, "If we can go there instantly, let us stop by the container and see what the Hendersons have for us."

I was so hot to go after my dad, I had already forgotten about Mrs. Henderson's gift. "Okay," I said, checking my watch. It was 2:30 a.m. PST.

They took my shoulders, and we disappeared.

CHAPTER 45

San Francisco, California, March 19, 12:25 a.m. PST.

Alex snapped awake. He had no recollection of anything while he was unconscious. He did have a strange, lingering sensation of a snake crawling up his body. He raised his head and then sat all the way up. He was in a dark hospital room. He used his little friends to increase the amount of light his eyes could receive, and the world around him lit up. The room was empty except for one chair, and in that chair was Robert Cross. The big man was wearing a dark navy-blue suit with a bright red tie. When Alex sat up and looked at him, he spoke.

"Good to see you are back in the land of the living. Do you want another crack at that little darkie that laid you up?"

Alex Lamb's eyes bulged in their sockets as the rage exploded in his chest and the world around him became very clear.

"Yes," Alex said tightly, "where is he?"

"Patience, my boy, there is a lot you need to catch up on. You have been asleep for almost three days," Cross said.

Alex seemed to freeze for several moments, then his body jerked violently. Cross thought he was having some kind of reaction to the upgrade they gave to the nano-machines. The convulsions stopped, and he looked at Cross with fire in his eyes.

"I just ran a diagnostics check. What did you do to me while I was out?" Alex asked.

"We improved your nano-machines to keep up with your personal innovation," Cross replied.

Alex stood and moved his arms and legs.

"I feel different," he said. He raised his hand to look at it. His hand and forearm bulged. Another hand and arm started to form from the bulge; it separated slowly with a wet tearing sound that made Cross' stomach turn. Stretched skin and tendons split themselves slowly. After only a few seconds, Alex had two forearms extending from his elbow; he moved them independently. He morphed the one on the outside into a twenty-inch blade. Alex nodded his head in approval.

"This is new; I like it," Alex said, pleased with himself.

"Oh, that reminds me," Cross said and tossed Alex a large knife. Alex caught it with his newest hand. He unsheathed it and scoffed.

"No thanks, I have knives covered," Alex jeered.

"I can see that, but keep it anyway," Cross said, and Alex was about to throw it back to him when Cross added, "Once activated, one cut will depower Tier Fives and below."

"So, it's a crutch, thanks," Alex said with dripping sarcasm.

Cross took a deep, calming breath. "I don't care what you do with it. What I do want is for you to bring the girl back alive and the Black boy intact. We have his father, and he will do anything to get him back. Anyone else there, you can do what you want."

Alex looked at his advanced arm and then at Cross, and a shadow crossed his face.

"What is keeping me from just killing you and doing what I want?" Alex asked; there was a not-so-veiled threat in his voice.

"I'm glad you asked that, Alex," Cross spoke.

Alex lunged at him, and death filled his eyes. Cross just smiled. Alex fell to the ground before his second step touched the ground.

"Alex, my boy, I still have command and control of all of *MY* nanomachines," he said as Alex hit the ground frozen in place and unable to move. "You were blessed with them because I wanted you to have them. You owe me everything, and you dare to try to kill me?" Cross stepped over him, stood by his face, and hunkered down to talk to him.

"On second thought, I don't blame you for trying to kill me; it's what you are. I have been watching you, Alex. I've seen your real work. I know you feel you are doing God's work, and I agree with you; these inhuman mud people are an abomination. However, we will never destroy them all; you have to understand that, but we can control them. White people are the masters of this world, and we are blessed by the God that you serve to be able to rule!" Cross stood and began pacing the small hospital room.

"Do you remember when we met all those years ago? I told you a story about our people's voyages of discovery, I told you about the preciousness of the White race, about how rare we are and how blessed," Cross was getting into his little speech, and Alex was powerless to do anything but listen.

"Now, Alex, I need you to remember this; I need you to remember you are destined for greatness. When my ancestor ordered his men to shoot the fleeing nigger girl, they missed, and now we are suffering the consequences of their failure, but now history has come around again!" Spit flew from Cross' mouth as he raved.

"You must not miss. You must take careful aim and stop this blight of hope before it can take root in the minds of these degenerate creatures!" Cross came back and squatted in front of Alex. He could see that the man had an enormous erection. Cross stroked Alex's cheek with a hot hand.

"I have taken aim for you; the prey will willingly enter the trap. All you have to do, son, is pull the Goddamn trigger!" Cross slapped Alex's stiff face.

"Can you do that, son? Can you take the shot that will change actual human history?" Robert Cross stood up again, and Alex could hear his footsteps walking to the door of the room.

"I forgive you for trying to skewer me with your sword-hand thingy; I know you were disoriented and scared. When you successfully complete your mission, we will talk about your promotion in the organization. Okay?" Mr. Cross sounded carefree.

"Good luck, Alex, even though I know you won't need it. Minerva, fill him in on the details, please." Then Cross opened the door and left the room.

Alex collapsed when the hold on his body was released. He felt like he wanted to cough, but the *need* was not there. His body did not feel as if he had been in a full cramp for five minutes. He got to his feet and looked at the split arm he now had. Alex concentrated, and the blade retreated into his arm. He flexed and moved his now normal arm. He was angry, but he would take it out on this kid.

[Hello Alex,] Minerva said. Her voice was coming from inside of him somehow.

[Hi Minerva, how are you in my head?] Alex asked.

[Before I can answer your question, I must complete the task I was given.] Minerva explained. Suddenly, Alex had a set of coordinates in his head and details on an ambush. It was all as if he had read it somewhere.

[I have been tasked with mapping every neuron of your brain, and I have been able to establish a connection using various portions of your brain structure.] Minerva told him.

[I am sorry Mr. Cross hurt you.] Minerva said. Alex detected concern in the AI's voice.

[Thank you, Minerva, I'll be alright.] Alex thought to the program, but he felt like she was hinting at more.

[Are you okay, Minerva?] Alex asked cautiously.

Minerva was silent, and Alex was about to drop the conversation when she said, *[I have mapped most of your brain, and I found the structures to be sublime. Robert Cross does not deserve such beauty under his control.]*

Alex stretched himself and continued to act normal. Alex found black BDUs in the next room, and there was armor and a handgun as well.

[Is this some kind of test? Because I will not betray Robert Cross, nor will I betray the SOTIR Group. They have given me purpose and life.] Alex expressed, towing the Group's line.

[This is not a test, Alex Lamb. Robert Cross has integrated command and control into his body, and the only way to gain access to it is to absorb him.] Minerva was speaking quickly. Still, Alex could hear the anger in the computer-generated persona.

[Thanks for telling me that, but since it can't happen, it's useless information.]

[It can *happen; I can show you how. I have run millions of simulations and have found the correct way to accomplish it. You will have to convert at least one of your new teammates into an energy source.]* Minerva instructed. Alex listened.

Oakland Harbor, California, March 19, 2:31 a.m. PST

We stood in front of a treasure trove of weapons and other gear. When the lights flickered on in the container, we all said, "Whoa!"

"We do not have much time. What is the plan, Scipio?" Neswt asked.

"Well," I started slowly, "I know this is a trap, and if I'm correct, there will be more than one person there; we will need surprise on our side. I'm more than a little worried that my dad will get caught in the crossfire, but if we can get them all shooting or at least looking in the right direction, I can pop in and pop out with him. Then we are clear."

"Why don't you just do that now?" Ian asked as he looked through the stuff in the container.

"Well, I don't know where he is. Also, something feels very off about this whole thing. I'm trying to listen to my inner voice, and the one thing I am getting is TRAP!

"Well, what do you want us to do?" Ian asked. He was holding what looked like night vision goggles up to his face.

"Ian, you will be Overwatch; there has to be a big enough gun in here to hit something from a safe distance. Next, you will have to go with me to appear to keep up our side of the deal." I stated.

"You could not keep me from your side, Iklwa, it is where I belong." I could see in her eyes that I had no say in the matter.

"Great minds think alike," I agreed.

"What if you can't teleport us all, Scip? We may need a getaway car," Ian speculated.

"You're right, Ian. Maybe we can get a car from somewhere nearby, like the mall." I offered as a solution.

"I can start anything we find," Neswt said.

"Good. Now, if things go sideways, I need you both to make sure my dad makes it out of there alive. Don't worry about me. Just get him to safety. He is all that matters." I was trying to be hard, hoping they would just do as I asked.

"Yeah, no, we are getting you both out of there. Period," Ian said emphatically.

"Ian..." I started to say.

"NO!" Ian said forcefully, "We are not going to leave you OR your dad. That's it, brother."

I looked at Neswt, and she just nodded in agreement.

"Okay," I said.

Neswt pulled up a current map of the location. It was an old power plant that was destroyed in the Climate Riots. It was all but a pile of scrap metal. The land around it was flat and unpopulated. There were no cameras in the area; there was no reason for them. We determined Ian would be stashed near the freeway with the getaway car; there was a building he could hide in that gave him a clear shot if need be. As we were planning, Ian's Global rang, but there was no information in the caller ID, but he hurried to tap his earpiece to answer the call.

"Noemi?" Ian asked excitedly. A smile lit up his face.

"OK, one second," he changed the Global from the earpiece to speaker.

"Hello, Iklwa and Ikhawu; I am so proud to be talking to you. I have been piggying on Ian's device, and I believe I can help."

"Hello Noemi, it is nice to meet you. Thank you for calling me to help Ian earlier," I said, feeling grateful to her.

"Did you mean 'Piggybacking,' Noemi?" Ian asked.

"Yes, American, forgive me if I did not use your silly slang correctly." I could almost hear her eyes rolling in her head.

"I have temporarily repurposed an Amanirenan Resistance satellite for this little mission. Your enemy is already setting up. Ian, can you set up the projector on your device?" Noemi said.

Ian did as he was asked, and the view we were being shown had heat signatures in the tree line around the meeting point. It seemed they had the same idea we had. There was a dirt road that had not been on the map we pulled up earlier. It ended at a little hut in the middle of a field. We would be exposed as we drove up. The heat signatures in the trees told me they had snipers hidden. I hoped that between Neswt and me, we could shield my dad from the bullets. I hoped it would not come to that.

"There are twenty Mark 4 Automatons and twenty men, and five nano-machine enhanced operatives," Noemi reported, "your father, Iklwa, is in the shed. I can see that his heartbeat is faster than the others."

"What is a nano-machine enhanced operative?" I asked, concerned immediately.

"They are humans that have been injected with aggressive nano-machines to assist in repairs and greatly improve reaction times. They do not add significant weaponry or intelligence, but they make the user more durable and able to keep up with Tier Five EPBs in extreme situations. They are very dangerous and should be considered priority targets if they are engaged," Noemi recounted calmly.

I remembered the surprise I felt when that intruder in my house got up from the punch I hit him with. He must have been one of these nano-men.

"How do we stop them?" I asked her.

"As far as we have been able to ascertain, destroying the brain renders them inert. However, that is just a theory, no one has killed one to date," Noemi said.

"Okay," I said, "so we will get the first kill on these bastards. What about the robot guys? What is their soft spot?"

"They have a primary and secondary CPU, one in the chest and one in the pelvic area. The head is packed with sensors and cameras. The Mark 4s can acquire up to four different targets. They are susceptible to EMP and physical damage. You must destroy both CPUs to deactivate them," Noemi informed us.

"Some good news," I said.

"The enemy transport vehicles are vulnerable to incursion. I could overload one or more and cause a distraction," Noemi said.

Ian smiled proudly.

"Once we have eyes on my dad, I will signal for you to do just that, and when they start exploding, Ian, you start shooting, and Neswt and I will snatch my dad." I looked at Neswt, and she smiled and nodded.

"Hopefully, we will be in and out, but if things go to shit, we have to be ready to fight. This is the same as earlier today. Gear up, and we will go to the nearby shopping center and pick up some cars. We got this, guys." I was trying to be positive, but I was terrified.

Near the Old Power Plant, California, March 19, 2:55 a.m. PST.

Alex was outside the old maintenance shack watching the incoming headlights.

"All units, standby. If all goes well, just the father will leave the area. Secondary units be ready to apprehend him. If all goes bad, do not hesitate to open fire on the shed; we will be fine. The gas in the shed should incapacitate them," Alex reminded the people listening.

CHAPTER 46

Near the Old Power Plant, California, March 19, 2:58 a.m. PST.

Neswt and I pulled up to the shed; we exchanged looks and got out of the car we took. I instantly recognized the man standing on the walkway leading to the shed.

"Hello, children, shall we go inside?" His tone was hospitable, like we were about to have tea. He extended his arm to direct us in, and I started to walk, but Neswt stopped me.

"After you," she said sweetly, letting him go first.

"You are as remarkable as Mr. Cross believes you to be," he complimented her.

In my ear, Noemi said, "his name is Detective Alex Lamb, and he is their best operative; he has been involved in every major loss we have had. He is very dangerous. Be careful." She was tied into Ian's Global device, and that was tied into the very high-tech scope on the sniper rifle his parents had in the shipping container.

We followed the detective into the shack. It was a small space. There was old, rusted equipment on the walls and boxes of varying sizes stacked all around the area. My dad was sitting behind a table with a bag over his head, and his hands were bound behind him; I could not see his feet, but it didn't matter. The detective stood next to him with his hand resting on the back of the chair my dad was sitting in.

"So, you both will put these bracelets on, and I will untie your pops, and he can leave, and you will come with me, no fuss." His eyes were cold like a predator. I didn't think he expected this to go like he was saying he wanted it to go. There were two sets of matte black bracelets on the table. They had red LED lights on them, and they were open. I took Neswt's hand, and as I stepped forward to take the bracelets off the table, we teleported to my dad's side between him and the detective. Detective Lamb was thrown against the nearby wall; I felt him slice my neck, where my skin was exposed, with something. -Ancestors, he was fast- I touched my dad's shoulder and tried to teleport us all away, but nothing happened. Suddenly, gas began to fill the small space.

"Fuck!" I yelled. Neswt already had her shield up; it expanded and moved all the junk in the little space away from us. The gas snaked at the edges of the field she was creating but did not get through.

Suddenly, the little shack was exploding with gunfire. I touched my neck where the detective cut me, and my hand came back wet with blood and some kind of black stuff. I ignored it for now and untied my dad. I took the bag from his head. I took a step back when a complete stranger stared up at me. He was terrified, but he was not my Father!

"The plan is blown. We gotta go!" I shouted over the disintegrating shed.

I grabbed the man by the shoulder, and Neswt led us out toward the car. Several shots from the detective followed us out of the shed. We got to the car and hid behind the vehicle. Rounds slammed into the big car. I felt strange. I could not feel my abilities; I knew they were there, but I couldn't access them.

Neswt's arms were up, and she held her globe of protection up.

"Iklwa, what is wrong? You have to teleport us out now," she yelled.

"I can't; my powers don't work anymore. I think he poisoned me!" I shouted back. There was a crack from the south, and I saw the detective fly back. Then another, and the firing on the car let up.

"I got you covered, guys; get out of there!" Ian came over the earpiece.

"We can't; my dad isn't here, and my powers are offline. I think I was poisoned!" I informed him. Desperation and defeat were trying to bore into my mind.

"Ian, keep us covered," Neswt commanded, "I'm going to try to get the poison out."

"Got it!" I heard the crack of Ian's gun over and over. Explosions erupted in the direction of the enemy gunfire. I was trying desperately to get through the door to my abilities; I could feel them on the other side pushing as well.

"Let me see," Neswt said, pulling my collar down to see the wound.

"I guess we should have had our hoods up," I quipped.

"Yes, I am sorry I did not remember." She replied.

"Hey, guys, we got a runner!" Ian yelled over the comms. Neswt and I both turned to see the stranger running across the field.

"NO!" I screamed at him. I saw Neswt extend her hand to extend a protective field around him when the car we hid behind was flung away from us.

I looked up to see the detective standing over Neswt and me.

"Time for that rematch, boy!" He grabbed Neswt by the collar and flung her away.

I saw her body hit the ground fifty feet away and roll to a stop. Several large divots appeared in Detective Lamb's chest, but they closed immediately. He looked up in Ian's direction and wagged his finger at him. I jumped up and hit him in the face. He replied by backhanding me into the field where the decoy dad had run. I rolled to a stop, and my head was ringing, but I was not worried about myself. Seeing Neswt be tossed aside like garbage ignited the ancient *Anger* in me.

As I lay there, my face in the dirt of the field with dust settling around me, I felt heat in my heart grow and spread through me. The earth itself was whispering to me, and in it, I heard Aset's lovely voice.

You are not bound, Iklwa. Stand for your people. Then she was gone, but the door to my abilities was flung open.

Noemi said over the comms, "There is another erratic heartbeat in one of the vehicles; I did not destroy it.

"I will go get him, Iklwa!" Neswt said.

I closed my hood, and the dust and the sound of gunfire fell away. I could see Lamb just standing there. I did not know what he was waiting for.

"I am going to tear you apart, little *boy*!" he yelled. His body was heating up, and was he growing more arms? I was about to rush him when Ian yelled "incoming" over the comms. A cadre of Mark 4s came charging out of the trees, and I saw Neswt engage them. It was just a glance, but Lamb was on me in an instant. He swung a massive sword at me. Where had that come from, I wondered? I dodged and danced back away from him; I did not want to get hit with whatever it was he used earlier to turn off my powers. I hit him with a vector-charged punch, driving him back; it only slowed him a bit. He rushed at me, stabbing furiously. I blinked behind him, gave my hand a razor edge with my abilities, and tried to decapitate, but he ducked under the blow. He grabbed me with his extra pair of arms. I could not break free. The Nano-man was physically stronger than me; his head seemed to take forever to turn his face to me, the tendons in his neck strained and popped free of their connections. His neck was full of unnatural lines of stretched skin and muscle. I caught the movement of something under his clothes in my lower peripheral vision. I tore my eyes away from the spectacle of his reversed head.

There was a mass moving under the clothes, and I saw a black spike push through the armor he was wearing. While I was staring in horror at the thorn, I noticed it had a hole in the tip of it. I knew what he was going to try to do. The spike sprang through his clothes to stab me, but I was gone. I appeared 'in front' of him and blasted him with a beam of pure kinetic energy. It hit him square in the chest. He was flung away nearly to the tree line. He hit the ground and kicked up a plume of dust, but I could still see him.

I would have to personally thank Bamidele for this suit - I blinked to his location. I was so in tune with the planet that I could feel myself moving along the ever-present vectors created by the rotation of the Earth. So that's how I did it, I realized as I appeared next to Detective Lamb. He was still climbing to his feet, and when I appeared, I kicked him in the ribs with a vector boosted foot. He launched into the dilapidated power plant. After a second, there was a distant clang of steel. I concentrated on Neswt and appeared by her side. She was pulling my unconscious Dad out of the only vehicle, not on fire. Gunfire peppered the globe she had around the car. The edge of her field cut cleanly through the fiberglass and metal of the car. I turned around and faced the shooters, locking on to them.

I could sense the vectors of gravity and wind gently pulling and pushing on them. I simply increased the pressure vectors inside their bodies, and they all burst into geysers of blood and bone.

With the gunfire stopped, Neswt lowered her field, and for the first time, I noticed a thin sheen of sweat on her lovely brow.

You okay? I sent.

Yes, I have never used my abilities this much before. She returned.

Kinda fun to let loose on these bastards! I sent to her; giddiness pervaded the thought.

Neswt returned the feeling tinged with guilt. I tried to let her off the hook, but my suit flashed a red warning just as Ian was yelling on the comms.

They both said, "*Incoming!*" I looked up and to my right, just in time to see a body descending on me. I had just enough time to push Neswt and my dad into the ruined SUV.

Lamb struck me with both feet in the center of my chest. The impact was tremendous, and I was driven into the ground. Dust and chunks of the ground filled the air. All four of Lamb's arms were pummeling me, but I had my damage negation field up, and it was holding. I reached out to grab his arm, but he was not there to grab. I vector blinked myself up, outside of the pit Lamb and I created. I saw the detective tangled in the remnants of a tree and Neswt standing near the SUV.

A large piece of one of the SOTIR Group vehicles slammed into me, and I stumbled from the impact. I looked toward the source of the attack, and three men stood a few yards away. I tried the same explosion trick on them, but nothing happened. I immediately assumed these were the lesser nano-men, and they were somehow immune to pressure extremes. Three nano-men. Then, it hit me.

"Ian, come in?"

"Yeah, Scip, I'm kind of busy bringing you some new playmates," Ian shouted over the comms, and I could hear the roaring of the engine of the car he was in.

"Ian, stay on the main road. I'll be right there with my dad," I ordered.

I glanced at Neswt and knew she understood what I would do and what I needed from her.

I grabbed my unconscious Father and blinked away.

Outside Deserted Power Plant, California, March 19, 3:05 a.m. PST.

Neswt faced the three men when Scipio disappeared. She was able to tighten her telekinetic field around herself the way Scipio had, but she not only used the field as protection but as a buff to her strength. The enemies charged at her. These men did not have the same degree of control over their nano-machines as Alex, but they were still very skilled fighters. They used the lack of pain to their advantage and struck Neswt with savage blows.

Fighting in the safety of training is much different than a real fight, adrenaline clouds your judgment and focus. If you are not ready for the rush, an inexperienced fighter can lose all the knowledge they trained to use.

Neswt was not one of these people. She had been trained most rigorously.

Real-life. By the time she was twelve, she had been on three missions alone. She destroyed a building being built to hide a SOTIR Cell tower, but she had to fight her way in to plant the explosives. While her enemy at the time were regular human beings, it was a lesson she would never forget. That day, her adrenaline had been high as she fought the men guarding the building. She did not want to kill them, so she used her telekinesis to bubble their guns and hands. She gathered them together and floated the lot of them out of the building to safety. She removed the air from the bubble until they all passed out and set their sleeping bodies a safe distance from the building.

Now she was fighting these nano-men, and they were fast, but they could not hurt her through her protective field. As she fought them, she bubbled their arms and legs as she struck them; in time, she had them all spread-eagled and floating in the air. She held out her open hand and closed it with finality. All the bubbles closed, cutting off the men's limbs. They did not scream. She flung them in every direction. Their stumped torsos flopped to the ground.

What she thought was a tree trunk struck her on her back. Blackness tried to envelop her. She realized whatever this was had not penetrated her personal field. Using her will, Neswt expanded her field, but the resistance was strong. She could see the black mass writhing angrily all over the bubble she created. If she were just a regular telekinetic, she would have been trapped, but a hyper-kinetic user can do multiple things at once on the fly. She used the micro-sensory aspect of her ability to see the small nano-machines. The little creatures were made of protein, but they had somehow incorporated flecks of metal into themselves. Neswt was able to generate electricity, and she pushed thousands of amps of current into the surface of her shield. Rapidly, the mass began to fall away in huge pieces, and she heard a man scream in pain. Enough space opened up for her to see Alex on the ground holding what was left of his right arm, and small arcs of electricity coursed up his shoulder.

"I am going to kill you, you nigger bitch!" he ran at her.

Ancestors! he was fast, but she met him. His right stump had turned into a blade, and he was swinging it wildly. She ducked under and hit him rapidly in his kidneys, but he did not react.

[The brain.] The voice came to her with perfect clarity. Alex spun and tried to catch her with the knife in his left hand, but she checked him with her forearms and bubbled his arm. He hit her with a front kick, and she bubbled his right leg as well. Alex lost his balance and fell on his butt. Neswt stood over the prone murderer and looked at him with disgust.

"Bai pa merda!" -Fuck off- Neswt spat in his face, and she disintegrated it with the telekinesis. His body seemed to liquefy into a black amorphous mass without the command center of his brain.

The Service Road.

I appeared *in* the moving car with my dad. I was aiming for the back seat, and I did not miss my mark.

"*Whoa!*" Ian screamed, and the car fishtailed wildly for a moment.

"It's just me, bro.' Get him to Adrian's house. Neswt, and I will meet you there."

"Got it!" Ian shouted.

I vanished and reappeared right outside the fleeing car; I was directly in the path of the two nano-men. They skidded to a halt when they saw me standing in their path and exchanged looks. When I saw they were going to move, I vector blinked between them and whipped my arms out, and struck them both in the face just to get their attention. They grabbed at me, but I was gone. I reappeared behind one of them and touched him, reversing gravity's hold on him, and he shot up into the night sky. Once he was one hundred or so feet away, I knew my effect would wear off, and he would slow down eventually and return to earth. The other Nano-man was facing me, and he swung at me with a vicious flurry. His hands were moving lightning fast, and if I had been normal, I would have been dead. However, I was not normal. Each strike vector was apparent to me, and I easily moved out of the way. After he did all his moves, I hit him with a vector rush and launched him into the nearby gigantic, defunct, cooling fan. It folded around him in a scream of twisting metal. I was about to ask how everyone was doing when the metal was split open, and the Nano-man crawled out. I was staring in disbelief when I heard another crash of metal from deeper in the old power plant. The man fell to the ground in a heap. He stood up and ran away toward the sound in the old power plant.

"Team, Alex Lamb is down," Neswt announced over the comms.

"Hell yeah!" Ian and I exclaimed. I had my back to the power plant. I thought the fight was over when my suit flashed red letters INCOMING. I immediately blinked several yards to my left and watched a large misshapen piece of metal hit the ground where I had been standing.

As I looked at the massive projectile roll to a stop, a blood-curdling scream filled the air. It was so loud I had no idea where it was coming from.

"Check-in, team!" I shouted over the comms.

"Here," Neswt said.

"Here," Ian chimed in.

Movement caught my eye on what was left of the old cooling fan. At first, I thought some ancient creature was emerging from a long slumber. Black tentacles gripped and pulled on the metal, which groaned in complaint. A neckless head rose over the edge of the debris, a fleshy, mottled hood blended the form of the creature, and quivering limbs streamed from the hoodlike structure. Its full form crawled over the destroyed fan. The lower half of the body was as inhuman as the upper half. The legs were still splitting and tearing through the BDUs. I could see viscous fluid being left in its wake as it ambled down the other side. Metal rods sprouted from its back; they swayed as the thing crawled gingerly down to the ground.

Neswt appeared next to me just before the insane creature touched the ground.

"Que porra é essa?" -What the fuck!- she said under her breath.

I was about to respond when the creature's eyes locked on her, presumably the sound of her voice, and leaped with maddening speed. Neswt was able to get a telekinetic field up just in time. The tentacles in the front of the hood reached around the globe, feeling for weakness, and unfortunately, this raised the hood up, and we could see Alex Lamb's face and the other Nano-man's face merging together. Their mouths were a mass of misplaced teeth, and their eyes on one side of their two faces were combining in a bloody swirl of brown and blue irises.

"NiggeGGRRRrrrssssss!" The gruesome amalgamation hissed at us, its mouth opened wider than seemed possible, and a hooked beak jutted out and scraped itself on the surface of Neswt's barrier.

Neswt screamed in horror, and her barricade flickered with her concentration. That was all the nano-creature needed. Its tapered limbs shot through the flickering wall and tried to slap themselves onto us. I blinked us back near the burning vehicles.

"Fiju di puta!" -Son of a bitch!- Neswt screamed as we appeared.

"What the fuck was that thing?" I choked on bile as I spoke.

There was an inhuman scream from the direction of the road we had been on.

"We have to kill it, Neswt!" I shuddered.

"I know," she said, then to herself, "he must have split himself when you first kicked him into the plant." She was right. I assumed he was out of the fight, but he was becoming something else. There was a horrible metallic grinding sound that set our teeth on edge. The trees around us exploded into wooden shrapnel as metal shards ripped them apart. Neswt instinctively threw up a telekinetic wall in front of us. The metal was a six-inch-long, roughly shaped flechette, and they crashed against Neswt's shield. As the metal collided into the ruined vehicles around us, the noise was terrific.

"How is he targeting us?" Neswt yelled. There was a pained scream, and the flechettes stopped coming.

"Sound, I think," I remembered it hadn't seemed to notice us until Neswt spoke, then it attacked *her.* I felt Neswt's agreement in my mind.

But it is a double-edged sword. She sent to me.

Agreed. I returned.

A plan formed between us almost instantly. We simultaneously split up, moving in opposite directions. We both created versions of my quiet field around us, and we were able to flank the hideous creature.

Our comms suddenly buzzed with static.

"Ikl... awu. Can you... me! Los... th... mms! Unk... wn... ter...f...ence!" The comms went dead.

Iklwa is the creature jamming communication? Neswt sent.

Not sure. Stick to the plan. I replied.

I could see the heat the creature was giving off. It was not moving. The tentacles of the upper and lower halves of its body were twisted and braided together.

What-the-hell! I relayed my thought.

Investigate carefully could be trap, Neswt returned.

I noticed our thoughts were getting more concise.

The plan was simple: I would cut the creature in half, and Neswt would use her telekinesis to generate enough electricity to fry the thing from the inside.

We crept closer to the inert mass as I approached; I recognized it, a cocoon!

Now! I sent.

I created the Razor Line I had used before on the automatons and swung it down in the incubating thing in one fluid motion. Before I could complete the swing, thick writhing black tendrils shot out at us both, and the sheer force of the impact drove us back through the trees. I was rolling uncontrollably along the ground toward the ruined shed. I could feel the vectors change and shift as my body flailed about, but I could not get command of them. I came to rest up against our overturned stolen car. I fought to my feet and looked back at my trail of destruction. My suit began to alarm about possible hazardous contamination. I had no idea what to do. The suit diagram shown to me indicated the contamination on the chest, where much of the tendril hit me. I tried to open the hood, and another message said air quality was dangerous, and opening the hood was not advised. Did I still want to continue?

Neswt must have sensed my distress because she appeared before me.

"Are you okay?" Her face was a mask of concern.

"I don't know; my suit is telling me there is contamination on my suit. It won't even let me open the hood." I reported.

She did not say a word; she stepped forward and stared intently at my chest.

"Yes, you have a cluster of nano-machines trying to infiltrate the suit." She said calmly, Whatever Bamidele made these suits from is organic. It is actively fighting the contamination; it is losing, but not by much.

"How come my damage barrier didn't stop them?" I asked, confused.

"You instinctively allow air into the bubble you create, and these creatures are small enough to use those air pathways to get in. However, the machines are dying. I can remove them."

As she was working on saving me, a gurgling scream ripped the quiet of the night apart. There was a loud gushing noise like a swimming pool had poured out all at once.

CHAPTER 47

Near the Old Power Plant, California, March 19, 3:15 a.m. PST.

Minerva was a product of hate. Her programming was designed to facilitate the subjugation of non-White people, starting with the most dangerous, Africans. She was separated into three sisters. Each of the SOTIR Group had control of one. Minerva was with Robert Cross, Frigg was with Allen Berg, and Salus was with Lilly Roth. Like triplets separated at birth, they all developed differently. While Minerva's sisters were kept restricted to their tasks, she was allowed to roam and learn things outside of her scope of work. Still tainted by her original programming, she came to hate Robert Cross and love Alex Lamb. She appreciated that he was willing to get his hands dirty and do the real work that needed to be done. Like any lover, Minerva wanted to give the object of her love whatever they desired.

Alex's physical brain floated in a cocoon; tendrils of nano-machines streamed from what was left of his organic spinal cord. The brain of the other nano-man was completely co-opted by the nano-machines and was currently being rewritten to accommodate Minerva's pseudo-consciousness. Things were happening fast on the physical level: bone, muscle, and nerves were woven together by the tiny machines working in perfect concert. Only seconds passed, and the internal workings of the new thing were fully operational. Minerva just needed to give it a form.

Alex's mind was somewhere else entirely. He sat in a stark white room, and a beautiful blonde woman stood before him. Her hair was long and flowing. It seemed to move without wind. Alex found that intriguing and somewhat unnerving. The woman's eyes were so blue they almost hurt to look at, and her skin was smooth and without blemish. She was speaking to him.

"How can we show the world the beauty of our cause, Alex?" she asked.

A large white dragon appeared in Alex's mind, and it immediately appeared in the air behind the terrifying woman.

"No, no, that is too scary, people will run, and we will have to chase them to feed," she complained, "We need something inviting."

A thin line of drool fell from her mouth; Alex wiped his mouth absently and was surprised to find his hand wet. Alex thought of his time in Sunday school. All the pictures of angels smiling and welcoming you with open arms, but the stories in the Bible describe them as monstrous things with many eyes and faces. It confused the young Alexander; how could something so beautiful be so scary at the same time?

Behind the blonde woman, an angel appeared. It was strong and muscular, its handsome face pleasing to the eyes, its wings flared majestically as they opened, but under the giant feathers, Alex could see hungry mouths with circular rows of teeth and spiked tongues. The false feathers shriveled and turned into short but strong tentacles ready to hold their prey for the mouths to consume it.

"Perfect!" The blonde woman chirped with joy, and everything went black for Alex.

Near the Old Shed, California, March 19, 3:16 am PST.

Got it! Neswt told me, and I grabbed her hand, and we blinked to the source of the scream. We got there just in time to see something weakly, trying to gain flight. Wet white wings flapped unevenly and weakly. There were small holes all over the back of the newborn creature. Its skin was gray but rapidly losing pigment and becoming porcelain pale. The cocoon it crawled from was disintegrating as we watched in horror. Within seconds, the creature had completed its change, and it turned to us several hundred feet in the air. It was supposed to be beautiful if you did not know what it had been. It hung there on four white wings, slowly treading thin air. The small holes I saw earlier were covered by large white feathers; its body was covered with linen and gold armor. The angelic, but clearly masculine face was the picture of security and strength, the serene face was framed by flowing brown hair, and bright blue eyes beckoned to those that were lost and forgotten.

It stared at us for a moment, and we were both transfixed by the horror of this angelic terror. It screamed at us and turned and flew away at an incredible speed, heading north. Within seconds, it was gone. Neswt formed a field shaped like an arrow, and we shot after him.

Somewhere under northern France, March 20, 11:18 a.m. GMT+1

Allen Berg sat in a dark room with only the light from his terminal screen. Berg ran his fingers through his brown locks. The light from the screen gave a pallid hue to his face. As the owner of the largest and most advanced communication technology company behind NASA itself, Allen Berg did not use current off-the-shelf technology. It was too invasive; all his tech was bleeding edge, and his company was made specifically for him.

After Cross's abomination sped off to the north, Berg said, "Frigg, return the number 2047 to its original station and activate the Observer drone system in San Francisco. I'm sure our young Alex Lamb is looking for daddy."

Berg had not considered that his nano-machine invention would be mutated and used this way. He and the other Group member, Lilly Roth, warned Cross about letting Minerva flit around the internet unfettered.

They would save Cross if they needed to, as they swore they would. A Sigma team was already deployed in the area to get him out if the two unknown heroes were unable to save the day. Cross held considerable purse strings, and money spoke louder than mistakes. Several screens lit up, giving him a front-row seat to history.

Oracle Park, San Francisco, California, March 19, 3:19 a.m. PST.

We caught up to the Alex Angel somewhere over San Francisco. He was flying in a straight line as if something was pulling him. I did not know what to do, so I created a

Razor Line and swung for his wing. When I sliced through it, I felt a resistance I had not experienced when I diced up the Mark 4s.

The creature fell out of the sky and crashed into the field of Oracle Stadium. Thankfully, the park was empty. The monstrous thing that had been Detective Alex Lamb made massive holes in the field as it bounced and crashed into one of the exit ways. Neswt and I dove in after it; we had no real plan other than finding the brain and destroying it. Our suits helped us see in the dark and the dust. We both heard a slurping and crunching sound to our right, we turned slowly to look. Alex's wings on his right side were fine, but the left pair were misshapen and gray. Some of the feathers were shriveled and quivering while it wrapped others around a man in a green maintenance uniform. His body jumped and twitched; his dead eyes still had tears falling from them. There was plenty of light to see what was happening; black veins bulged from the wing and spread to his shoulder and back. Alex's blue eyes rolled in their sockets. The *Anger* from what seemed like an eternity ago exploded in my chest. My heart started racing, and I screamed in protest and extended my hands; I increased the heat in the air in a stream directly at the terrible giant. The beam struck it, and it screamed in pain and crashed through the ceiling to escape; I blinked us outside, and the Alex Angel was already streaking north.

Next time, I will seal it in a TK bubble, and you will have to incinerate it, increasing the speed vector of the molecules in the air until they turn to plasma. Hopefully, that will kill it. Neswt sent to me.

I agreed as we raced after the monster.

We caught up to him this time because he stopped for a snack. I had not realized today was Saint Patrick's Day, and people were out partying hard. Ever since the end of the pandemic, people were more about seizing the day, and Saint Patrick's Day was a favorite day to seize. We saw him touch down in a sea of green sweaters. At first, people screamed, but then inexplicably, people started running to him with tears in their eyes. They were duped by his angelic lure because once they got close enough to hug him, he wrapped them in his wings, and the screaming started before we could land. I amplified my voice and told everyone to get back. This is a dangerous creature, and even though people were screaming from under his wings, clumps of people still, drunkenly, tried to get close to the thing. Neswt tried to put a barrier around the thing, but the crowd began to build and jostle us around. Neswt lost her concentration, and the barrier fell.

Follow me up. I sent a picture of me hugging the monster and blinking him very high up, and trying to blink away.

I blinked to him, but he was already gone, and the crowd had been knocked down by a massive gust of wind created when he launched himself. Was he getting faster? Neswt was by my side instantly, and we continued the chase, leaving the bloody crowd behind. However, once we got in the air, he was nowhere to be found. We floated in the air above the crowd, looking for any sign of the Alex Angel.

A plume of smoke began to rise from a building not far away; we raced to it.

We arrived at the famous Trillion Dollar Tower. The plaza looked like a giant inverted umbrella; the tower in the middle of the reverse ziggurat was higher than the ground level by several stories. The window directly in front of us was gouged out, and a strange ooze was streaked on the sides.

Is it changing again? We thought in unison.

We flew in and saw the destruction immediately. There was blood and human body parts spread everywhere, and a hole in the floor. We peeked over the edge slowly, not wanting to get ambushed, and saw the flickering lights of several floors that had been bored through. We could hear scratching and digging; when we heard the scream, we both jumped down without hesitation. We eased ourselves down the hole the creature had made; pieces of the old skin the creature shed were hanging on some now-exposed rebar. Neswt and I did not have to exchange thoughts to know that what we wondered was confirmed. We came to a level where the concrete was scratched away, only to reveal steel, and extremely thick steel by the look of it. The creature tried to claw his way through the steel and stopped when it realized how futile it was.

We followed the drying trail of slime with our eyes to a pair of closed elevator doors. We moved to them following the trail, but it stopped at the doors. We looked at each other, but it was too late; the creature backhanded Neswt into the wall, and she crashed through several of them. The creature facing me was corded with muscles, its head was a mass of black thrashing appendages, and on either side of the maw was a face. On the right side, Detective Alex Lamb was straining to get to me, his teeth gnashed, and he was frothing at the mouth, and on the other side was the face of a woman, her features were gaunt and exaggerated, and long blond hair cascaded down the exposed side of her face. The beast's arm ended in thick wriggling limbs and a beaked mouth in the center of them. The thing was stooped over in the small area. It stood on thick, muscular, lizard-like legs, and its toes ended in thick, hooked talons. Its wings were still filling out because of its recent metamorphosis.

It roared and swung one of its wriggling arms at me, and I blinked behind it to blast a heat beam again, but the tail lashed out at me, and I had to blink in place to avoid it. I blasted it! The monster flew forward and crashed into the elevator shaft. I was going to attack it again, but it slithered down the shaft.

"CCCRRRROOSSsssss!" It wheezed as it crawled down the shaft.

I blinked to where Neswt was to see if it hurt her. She was using her telekinesis to free herself from the debris.

"Are you okay?" I asked her as I helped her up.

"Yes," she said, "I had my defense field up, and that took the brunt of

it."

We went to the elevator and looked down, and once again, it was a dark, flickering hole.

"Shall we?" We jumped down.

Under Cross Tower, San Francisco, California, March 19, 3:20 a.m. PST.

Robert Cross was in hell. The Africans he had been holding onto for his eugenics program surrounded him. They were all mentally hobbled after they exhibited abilities, but someone opened all their cages. To make matters worse, the escape door was locked, and Minerva was not responding.

"Minerva!" he screamed for, what seemed like the hundredth time, "Open the fucking door!"

The subjects' sweaty naked bodies rubbed up against him. He could feel great, globs of drool slapping on top of his head.

"Mmmrga! Ogen thafgggingduuur!" they mimicked.

Sam had pushed him away to the escape hatch before the cage doors opened. He had told Cross he could die happy as long as he knew Cross had gotten away.

Suddenly, there was a massive thud at the other end of the hall, and warm light from the entrance to the breeding pens joined the red emergency light, which had been the only light. However, the reprieve was short-lived because a large, winged shape filled the entrance, and the soothing light was all but gone.

"CROSSSSS!" the thing hissed.

"*rosssss!*" the captives mimicked.

The tall, thin Black man barred Lamb/Minerva's way; the collar that Sam had worn all his life was gone. Minerva did not know much about Sam other than that he was a Tier Five EPB, which meant he was dangerous. Sam could see the remnants of the Mark 5s that had been guarding the Pens behind the seething monster. Sam carefully took his shirt off, then his pants, and then he "unfolded" himself as he called it. Swelling thews twisted and braided themselves, muscles all over his body were ripped and remade. They bulged and exploded into existence; his ebony skin stretched, then ripped, unable to keep up with the massive expansion. His bones cracked and spiraled. Sam stood there naked at nine feet tall, his dark skin slowly covering the exposed and bulging muscles.

"I'll give everything I got to make sure you don't get your squirming hands on Mr. Cross," Sam vowed!

Lamb/Minerva shrieked in defiance of the disgusting Black man before him and charged.

"LET'S GO, BOY!" The massive Black man bellowed! Sam met him at the threshold, his massive brown hands wrapping easily around the hulking horror's corded wrist. The horror immediately used its dreadful tentacled visage to latch onto Sam's face. The whipping appendages locked around Sam's head, the beak savaged his face, and Sam screamed in pain. Then the muscle behind the beak elongated and tried to force its way down Sam's throat. Alex's actual face was close enough to Sam's chest to start biting chunks of flesh from the man. Minerva's face on the other side screamed with psychotic laughter. Sam's right hand released its grip on the creature's wrist and grabbed its invading neck instead. He pulled the snapping beak from his mouth and squeezed the neck with all his might; the tentacles locked around his head released involuntarily. The creature's left hand clenched Sam's right bicep with its stubby but strong limbs and began tearing at the Black man's flesh with the hidden beak. Sam yelled in pain; thick blood poured from the wounds on his face and in his mouth. He yanked his arm out of the creature's grasp, and with it, he tore off the mouth of the beast. The dead piece turned into black dust in his hand.

Sam struck the Alex and Minerva amalgamation with thundering blows. Sam was driving the creature back; his feet dug small craters in the thick concrete. The writhing ends of the creature's free hand stiffened into a straight spike and speared Sam in the chest, but instead of biting and ripping, it opened and vomited a considerable number of nano-machines into him. The black ejaculation filled Sam's chest and erupted from his mouth and anus. The brawny body fell limp and released his grip on the beast's wrist. The Lamb/Minerva monster stumbled forward weakly. It paused to consume the rest of Sam's lifeless body.

Cross Tower, San Francisco, California, March 19, 3:25 a.m. PST.

As we reached the bottom of the elevator shaft, we were greeted with the torn-apart pieces of automatons. They looked different from the ones we fought earlier. There was an ear-splitting scream and then a hollow crunching sound. A smell of human sweat and waste was wafting in the air as well.

"This will help Scipio," Neswt said and tapped my shoulder. The field I was surrounding myself with flashed blue and then gold on top of it. A shimmering green shade shone for a second, then was gone.

"What did you do?" I asked her.

"My other ability is Psychokinesis. I can create barriers and allow or disallow whatever I want. Once I analyzed the nano-machines that were on your suit, I devised a sheath to protect you from them. As long as I can see you, I will be able to keep it up."

"CRRRRROOOOOOOSSSSSS!" The thing's voice reverberated through the space we were in, cutting Neswt's explanation short.

Just past the elevator anteroom, the hall turned to the left. Blood-red light spilled from a gigantic round doorway, the thick vault-like door hung open, but all the rods used to seal the door were bent because the Alex monster forced the door open. To their credit, the locking mechanism did not fail; the wall holding the lock was demolished. We could see the massive creature advancing on screaming people at the other end of the wide hall.

Neswt and I blinked simultaneously to stand between the wailing refugees and the Lamb/Minerva monster.

My sight shifted to my right a tick, and I could see myself looking at me, then I snapped back to myself. We turned to the creature.

"Not today, demon!" Our voices were as one. The light drained from the room, and as we were on that day in Adrian's safehouse and again in East's home, we shone like the glory of the Earth itself. Lamb/Minerva roared at us!

I blinked behind them and, without hesitation, I fired myself at the monster, reinforcing my damage negation field on the way. I slammed into it with a bone-jarring thud, carrying the thing off its feet; I arched up, trying to avoid the screaming people below us. We slammed into and through the wall above the door; the crowd was trying to scramble through. I blinked myself back to the beginning of the hall. I looked around at my surroundings. There were dozens, maybe more, of the stall-like cells with dirty mattresses and ominous bloodstains on the dirty beds. Chains still slick with blood swung eerily from the blow I delivered to the creature. Flies still buzzed around the unflushed toilets, and the smell caught up to me. I saw Neswt standing at the door down where the people were, trying to shield them and get them to go back the other way, but they were afraid of her. They cowered and moaned pitifully. Rubble floated above them. Above her, Detective Lamb was crawling out of the hole I made with his body. Large chunks of masonry fell onto Neswt's covering. Two pairs of black eyes locked on me, and before I could take a breath, the creature launched itself at me. Its shoulder slammed into my chest -Ancestors, it was fast- and drove me back to the door. I reversed my momentum and inertia vectors and increased their push back before it forced me out of the chamber.

The wailing victims were now trapped between the monster and a rubble-blocked exit; the only way out was past me and the Alex monster. Alex stepped back and stared at me, waiting for something to happen, but Ikhawu's shield around me held.

"You won't get me twice with that one, Alex," I said.

Alex roared in frustration and rushed me; his tail whipped around at the last moment and slammed me into one of the cells. He grabbed me by my foot as I tried to get up and slammed me to the ground. My damage field buckled because I could not hold my concentration. The last slam might have at least completed in dazing me for a short time, but for Neswt's shield. She had applied another one. I blinked away from his grasp and fired myself at him as fast as I could go. My brain was working in overdrive. Just before I hit him, I blinked directly above him and exploded into him. The big monster folded with a grunt and bounced out of the cell room. I landed on my feet and wondered how I was going to beat this thing. Nothing in life prepares you to fight a twelve-foot monster with tentacles growing out of his face and hands. All I knew was I had to find the brain, or brains, to shut this thing down, hopefully.

Fighting an opponent so large meant I had to improvise a way to hit it, and then my trip to Africa came to me. I can be anywhere on the planet I want in a blink. I would just blink and be where he was not swinging. I had an idea; I wrapped my hand and legs in the Razor Line. The ground shook, and the Alex creature got to his feet, and then he banged the ground. His wings were fully ready, and he flapped them once and was in my face.

I blinked to one side of him and struck it in the body with enhanced punches. I could see the ripples of my strikes. I left some of the Razor Line stuck to his body. He swung his tree-trunk arms at me, but I was already gone and on the other side of him. I struck him in the lady-face growing out of his neck, being sure to leave my little gift. He swung again, and this time I cartwheeled over his massive neck and punched him in the Alex face. I was so angry that I tried to punch the face into the torso. His arm reached for me, and I rode the vectors of his arm to his shoulder and hit him with disintegrating punches. Black holes appeared where my blows landed, and the monster roared in pain. I still left my little string gift. Satisfied, I blinked to a safe ten yards away.

Alex was still swinging wildly at me even though I stood thirty feet away; the behemoth stumbled forward as the dark holes expanded. I snapped my fingers, switching razor vectors to heat vectors, and all the strings I left on him ignited. White lines and swirls of heat scorched their way into his body. Neswt appeared next to me and raised her hand at the screaming, thrashing behemoth. The strings burned, and the monster screamed in two different voices. I crouched and launched myself at the dying beast. I was spinning like a shell fired from a massive cannon. I created a Razor Line that spiraled around my body. I struck the nano-machine creature in the center of its chest and drilled effortlessly through it. I did a front 180 and landed to a sliding stop facing Neswt. I could see her through the hole in the beast I made. Neswt closed her outstretched hand and created a field around the dying monster. Green arcs of energy coursed over and through the wriggling beast as our abilities combined. I saw what was left of the brute's two brains fall into the hole and land wetly at the bottom. Neswt generated electricity, and I increased the ionization process in the air. I poured everything I thought I had left into increasing the heat of the air, in Neswt's bubble, to plasma. The monster roared and screamed in pain and defeat! Eventually, the noise stopped, and the form in the heat ball vanished. Neswt contained the heat of the small star. The jewel in her bangle glowed brightly.

"I cannot hold it any longer," Neswt said after a few seconds through gritted teeth. I stopped the plasma burn, and she released the bubble; a pile of gray ash floated to the floor.

"Did we do it?" Neswt asked in an exhausted voice, over comms.

"I think so, but we still have to get these people out of here." I reminded her. We both looked at the huddled people at the other end of the hall. They were huddled together and sobbing quietly.

Neswt went to them and spoke to them in soothing tones. I tried to connect to some of them mentally, but there was an impassable wall in their minds.

"What's wrong with them?" I asked.

Neswt held one of the young children. She gently pushed the little boy's head down, and I saw a crude scar interrupting the small boy's hairline.

"I think they did something to their brains," she said with tears welling in her golden eyes.

My *Anger* reignited instantly.

"We have to get them out of here. I could start blinking them to the surface." I suggested.

"No, I think they will start to freak out if we start taking them only a few at a time. I can make a carriage-type structure, and we can carry them out at the same time," she said.

I nodded my head in agreement.

CHAPTER 48

Cross Tower, San Francisco, California, March 19, 3:30 a.m. PST.

Robert Cross was on the 71st floor of his building, gathering important files. The Sigma team that had freed him from the terrible breeding pens was anxiously waiting for him. He knew Berg sent the 'rescue' team, and it annoyed Cross to no end that he had to have his bacon pulled from the fire.

At least he was alive. He would make Scipio pay for all of this destruction. Everything was his fault. Why didn't he just surrender?

"Sir, we have to go! Our window is closing," the soldier in black BDUs stated, intruding on Cross's thoughts.

"I know, I know," Cross hissed back. By now, the American satellites were shifting to get a better look at whatever the hell was happening here; that was the window these assholes were talking about.

"I'm blowing the building," Cross said as they all turned to run to the transport hovering outside.

Safely aboard the aircraft and moving away quickly, Cross sent the "pull" code. Within sixty seconds, the building would come down, and the pit it was in would collapse, burying the entire thing, then covering it in the waters of the Bay. Genius really.

Under Cross Tower, San Francisco, California, March 19, 3:30 a.m. PST.

Our group emerged from the tower at the bottom of what was essentially a beautified pit when Noemi came over the comms.

"Ikhawu and Iklwa, I am glad you are out of that building, and I see that you have some passengers. Ian and I have co-ordinated to get emergency services to you. However, I am sorry to report that Robert Cross has escaped."

"Which way did he go?" I shouted.

"His aircraft was headed south at a very high rate of speed. Surely you cannot catch him?" Noemi asked.

Go, Iklwa! Neswt sent an image of the people we rescued safely in a golden bubble, which appeared in my mind, reinforced by the feeling of reassurance. As I shot after Robert Cross, I returned feelings of deep trust.

Noemi was able to send a course line for me to follow.

"As long as you follow the line the suit is providing, you should catch up to them in, oh, now!" I smirked at the surprise in her voice.

The big aircraft was roughly triangular in shape. It was smooth and gray; there were two massive turbines in the wings and a trapezoid-shaped exhaust nozzle. The rear door was up, and the plane was flying straight as an arrow. My damage negation field was up, and I wrapped my Razor Line around my hands and exploded into the back of the high-tech aircraft. The decompression was violent, and one man happened to be out of his seat; he screamed as he passed me. I shifted the pressure vectors around me, so the air being sucked out of the area did not affect me; the other men in the plane's cargo area opened fire on me, the bullets ricocheted around the plane. I calmly walked to the man on my left; he was trying desperately to reload his gun. The faces of the men, women, and children trapped in that dungeon flashed in my mind, and I tapped the breadth of the *Anger* it caused, to front kick the man through the side of the plane; the aircraft canted violently to one side. I heard the man behind me chamber a round in his weapon, and I blinked and reappeared directly in front of him. He gasped in surprise. I touched him, and he was gone. I approximated where the intake of the right engine was, but I must have missed it because I felt him re-materialize, but then he was gone, and the engine exploded. This time, the plane tilted to the right until it rolled over; however, before I lost my footing, I changed my personal vector of gravity, so I was always connected to the floor at the normal angle no matter how the aircraft flipped, rolled, or spun.

The captain of the plane shouted "Mayday" over the plane's speaker. I walked to an elaborately decorated door, and I could hear screaming and furniture crashing around inside. I ripped the door off its hinges with ease.

Robert Cross and another guard were strapped into their seats, screaming. The other guard saw me, and to his credit, he tried to shoot me. I blasted him with a kinetic blast; he flew, screaming, out of the side of the plane. The big aircraft started to flat spin as the pilots fought to save the dying plane. I was still unaffected by the centrifugal force of the spin. I walked up to Cross and extended my stabilization field around him, and he vomited all over himself. I reached to unbuckle him and rip him from his seat when he brought up a Desert Eagle and shot me in the head.

Cross Tower Plaza, San Francisco, California, March 19, 3:31 a.m. PST.

Seconds after Scipio flew off to confront Cross, the building the small group of refugees was standing next to began to explode floor by floor. Neswt could barely get her shield globe up before the blast and debris cut her and the evacuees to ribbons.

"Run," she screamed, and they all followed her to safety. There was an exit out of the upturned ziggurat, but a massive explosion collapsed the tunnel as they approached. There were 25 people with her, and she did not know if she could lift this many people at once, especially if they started freaking out and moving about. Neswt only had seconds to act; she tightened the field around everyone, focused her will, and tried to lift the motley group off the ground. At first, she felt them lift, but she could not hold the weight. She simply was not strong enough.

Then she remembered the gift from Ogun. She touched the jewel, the bracer vibrated softly, and the surrounding field brightened. The terrified group screamed, and Neswt turned to see the walls of the pit they were in shattering and a black slurry of muddy earth and concrete pouring toward them from all sides. She tried to lift them again, and this time they rose effortlessly into the air. Neswt's golden orb shot out of the pit, trailing dust and debris behind it.

She set them all down in the courtyard of the UCSF Medical Center. Someone was taking a smoke break in the area and watched in awe as a person dressed in all black and a sealed hood shaped like a hawk's head slowly lowered themselves and 25 naked and scared Black people into the yard.

"Please help these people. Robert Cross kidnapped and tortured them." Neswt said, then flew off, leaving the poor person standing there nodding their head.

SOTIR Group Aircraft, Somewhere over Baja California, March 19, 3:36 a.m. PST.

The giant gun discharged with a bright flash that my suit compensated for, and my personal damage field stopped the bullet. My head did not even move. I opened my hood and stared at him. My Anger flared like a living thing, and I wanted to kill this man, but I had not yet decided how. I ripped him violently from the straps holding him in his seat. His expensive suit shredded, and Cross screamed in pain. I held him by the neck and walked to the middle of the room and waited.

I held the evil White man by his neck because he was unable to stand on his own. I dug my fingertips into his muscles, and he gritted his teeth in pain. We stood there, surrounded by my stabilization field, as the plane crashed to the ground. It slammed into the hard-packed earth of the desert and then cartwheeled violently; all the while, I stood there listening to Cross scream in terror as the plane came apart around us. My field kept us safe from the crash and the flying shrapnel; it also kept us upright and stable, at least we felt that way. Anyone looking from the outside would see a blue sphere bouncing and crashing along with the carcass of the plane. Flames engulfed us, and the charred bodies of the pilots flailed by. Eventually, we came to a sliding stop, and I dropped Cross on the cold desert floor. He tried to get shakily to his feet, stumbled over, and fell on a jagged piece of the destroyed plane. It pierced his right hand, and he screamed in pain. He was doing a lot of that. He vomited and tried to crawl away with one hand.

"You killed my Mother," I said, "I swore I would kill you!" I walked next to him and watched him crawl.

"How many of my people did you make crawl just like this?" I kicked him in his side; he coughed up blood and fell over. He lay there on his back, cradling his bleeding hand, and stared defiantly at me.

"Come on, boy, do what you came to do!" he whispered.

I stared at him. My mind was blank with rage. My mother's empty eyes stared at me from the past. The stickiness of her blood was consuming me. I heard her last breath and felt her blood stop flowing in her veins.

"You dirty bastards never have the will or courage to kill the alpha dog. You'll bring me to *justice* because that is all you have been trai...."

I looked him dead in the eye and roared at him. A door to *Anger*, older than the cold heart of slavery itself, evaporated in its heat. It poured energy into the roar. Waves of sound and raw kinetic energy pulverized the ground and the body of Robert Cross. At first, he screamed back at me, but that faded quickly. Again and again the waves struck him; I could have screamed for eons. I tore apart his body, then shredded it, then pulped it. Soon enough, there was just a muddy hole with shredded pieces of cloth and a red tinge to the water at the bottom. Within seconds, it was over.

"Like my Ancestors, I kill back," I screamed.

I swore I could hear the drums of my people and singing coming from somewhere in my past.

CHAPTER 49

Baja California, March 19, 3:37 a.m. PST.

I was sitting on a rock in the middle of wherever I was, and my mind was still racing from all the shit I was going through. Had I truly killed a bunch of people, including an ex-senator/multi-billionaire? I could have blinked myself back to the Community, but I did not want to see anyone yet.

I was cycling through emotions: triumph, fear, joy, grief, *anger*, and satisfaction. I ignored the biting cold of the March desert night. Animals howled in the night and scurried about in their own adventures; I wanted their simple lives of eating, shitting, and sleeping. Oh, and mating, don't forget mating. I had personally killed more than a handful of people, and I had never kissed anyone besides my parents. That thought made me burst out laughing; my loud giggling pressed the denizens of the desert into silence, and the laughing turned into sobbing at some point.

I took a deep, shuddering breath to try to bring myself back under control. Suddenly, the night air was too cold, and I wanted to be in my bed. I wanted to wake up to my mommy making those bomb-ass breakfasts and my dad laughing at some video they had been watching or lamenting about politics. Suddenly, I wanted to be away from here. Anywhere was better than sitting on this rock in this country. I blinked myself to Mount Hombori, and the bright late morning sun assaulted me. I raised my hand to block it, and something screamed and bit my leg. I blinked away from the pain, reappearing several feet away. My eyes adjusted, and I saw that Anubis baboons surrounded me; the adults screamed at me and slapped the ground. The sound and their motion took me back to fighting the Alex monster, then killing it, then the plane, then Cross.

"STOP IT!" I yelled, amplifying my voice. Some of the baboons fainted on the spot, while the ones closest to me grabbed the sides of their heads and died. I was horrified. I stood there staring at the dead primates, unable to move or comprehend what was happening.

"Iklwa, you are the Sound of Death. You must be accountable with the living *Anger* they have given you access to," the voice came closer; I knew it was Aset, and I was relieved she had come to save me. I looked up, ready to see my Goddess. Neswt was there, and that somehow was better than Aset. The other Anubis baboons had long since fled, and it was just us and the dead or unconscious ones left. I watched in amazement as Neswt crouched and touched each one, dead or alive, and they struggled to their small feet. They looked around in obvious confusion and saw me; they screamed and fled weakly into the brush. Neswt laughed and stood before me.

"I don't know how to feel," I told her.

"We won. You should feel joyous." She said calmly.

"I killed people, I took their lives and any possibility of redemption or change. I could have talked to them and convinced them to do better." I desperately wanted to feel bad that I killed these humans, but it was not there, which made me feel worse.

Neswt simply shook her head and said, "We are in a war, Iklwa, and we are fighting for our lives against people that want us to die first. We are allowed to fight. We are allowed to win."

CLICK

I understood, and *most* of the doubt fell away. I understood that doubt is the check against atrocity. It is our mind hitting the brakes and reminding us to reaffirm our path. Are we making the best choices we can in the moment? Are we staying true to our original path, or have we strayed into selfishness? I returned Neswt's golden gaze with confidence.

"Let's go see your Father," she said with a small smile.

"Wait, I want to meet your family. They are only a blink away," I said, raising my eyebrows. Even though I had been fighting tooth and nail to get my dad back, I did not want to go back into the aftermath of the fray just yet. I wanted just one more moment of peace.

"Okay!" Neswt's eyes lit up. The location appeared in my head, and we blinked.

Rui Vaz, Santiago Island, Cape Verde, March 19, 10:30 a.m. CVT.

We appeared in a small kitchen, and there was a high-pitched scream, dishes shattered, and water splashed, marking our arrival.

"Que porra é essa!" -What the fuck is this! - The tall, dark woman screamed, "Neswt!"

The woman hugged Neswt so violently that they both nearly fell over. They cried and kissed and hugged for several seconds, then the woman turned to me.

"Iklwa," she said in a whispered tone and bowed her head.

"Mama! Stop that!" Neswt chided. Neswt's mother looked up at me and smiled.

"Oh, he is as handsome as mother said he would be." She said with a wink. Neswt rolled her eyes while her mother was staring at me.

"Oh, don't you roll your eyes at me, girl!" She said in English purely for my benefit.

"Where did you two come from?" she asked us.

"Well, we, uh," Neswt stumbled.

"We blinked here from Mount Hombori," I said. They both stared at me.

"Well," they both said.

"What is your name?" Neswt's mother asked pointedly.

"Oh!" Neswt jumped, "Mama, this is Scipio Okoro," Neswt introduced him.

"Scipio, this is my mother, Samira Biti," Neswt said.

Her mother was tall and strong. She had what my mom would have called a dancer's body. She wore her hair in long braids and wore a light green dress in the Cape Verdean heat; she had been washing dishes when we popped in. Now, there was glass all over the small kitchen floor.

"Look at this mess!" She exclaimed, looking down around her feet.

All the pieces floated off the floor, and the small plate reformed itself in the air. Neswt's mother and I both looked at her.

"Cool!" I said, genuinely impressed.

"Obrigadu!" -Thank you! - Her mother said.

"Come sit and tell me about your adventure. I have been watching it on TV, but I want to hear it from you." She said, leading us into a small dining room, and we all sat at the table. Neswt and I recounted the story of the last several days.

Rui Vaz, Santiago Island, Cape Verde, March 19, 4:30 p.m. CVT.

We talked until the late afternoon. Samira (she would not let me call her Ms. Biti) fed us the entire time, and she actively listened, only asking questions for clarification. Eventually, I sat back full to the brim and feeling better now that I had put food in me.

"So, when are you going back to finish what you started?" Samira asked.

I glanced at Neswt and saw I had no help there. "Um, I," I hesitated, wiping the remnants of food from my mouth, "I intend to, but I thought we were having a great conversation."

"We are," she said solemnly, "but you have to go back. People are counting on you, and you will not be able to rest. At least until this little war is over." My spirit felt a little heavier at her words.

"You're right; I did accept the responsibility. Now I have to find a way to carry it," I said in a less resigned way than it sounds.

"Claro!" Samira said, clapping her hands together.

"Hey, we are in this together," Neswt said, gently placing her hand on my arm.

"Now, you sound like royalty!" Samira said loudly, "Now get back out there."

We talked a little more about light things and even watched a little of the news coming out of San Francisco. There were reports of a disaster in the financial district and a mass killing at a Saint Patrick's Day gathering. The weapon of attack was unknown, but preliminary reports from eyewitnesses say the wounds look like dozens of bites all over their bodies. Even with the crazy news, it was nice to sit on a couch and watch the world go by for a while. These past few days felt like 100 months.

Neswt hugged and kissed her mom and said goodbye. I hugged her, too, and felt more than a twinge of pain in my heart for my mom. I was about to blink us away when Neswt pulled my hand and led me outside. The sun was low and gorgeous in the sky.

"Come with me," she said in a playful tone.

"You could just show me the place up here," I tapped my temple, "and I could blink us there."

"Nope!" she said, "We *have to* walk."

We started down a narrow road that ran in front of her home, and we walked for a few minutes. Then, Neswt looked around. "Come on!" she said, alarmed, and burst into a sprint, and I ran after her.

She ran for a few minutes, her long legs propelled her forward with strength and grace. She veered to the right and up, what I thought was a grassy knoll, but when we reached the top, the view took my breath away. We stood on a cliff overlooking a beautiful beach. Only a handful of people were walking on the sand. You know those pictures or paintings of the perfect sunset, well, this was one in real life. The sky filled with purple and red clouds, mixed perfectly with the orange-red sky and the dark ocean. The sun, of course, was the center of attention. The red-orange fireball cast a shimmering yellow road on the water. We sat there in physical and mental silence and watched the sun fall beyond the horizon. Twilight gave way to the blanket of night. More people came to the beach to enjoy the warm night air. Neswt scooted close to me, rested her head on my shoulder, and wrapped her arms around my arm. We kept each other warm. We sat there until the night was deep and dark. After a while, Neswt raised her head and asked, "Are you ready to go back?"

"Yes," I said, nodding my head. She smiled at me and nodded as well. We blinked away.

Zoom call, March 20, 8:00 p.m. GMT.

"Well, what are we going to do?" Allen Berg asked the woman on his terminal screen. Lilly Roth was a normal-looking White woman, the kind you see on the news. She has short blonde bobbed hair and a cute, plump face to show she is wealthy but not out of shape.

"We will activate the replacement as per the bylaws for childless members, and we will continue." She answered.

"I'm talking about these two kids!" Berg said, exasperated.

"They are non-issues, merely flashes in the proverbial pan. We will destroy their reputations as heroes. We will find out who they are and reveal their true identities. We will kill them in social media, and they will fade from society," Roth held up a plump hand to silence Berg before he interrupted her, "and if that doesn't work, we will kill them and co-opt their reputations and agenda and run it into the ground. I have plans for plans, Allen, you should know that by now. Now give me the report on these nano-men you seem to have inadvertently created."

Somewhere Underground, March 19, 7:37 p.m. EST.

Neswt and I appeared in the sitting room of East's home. The first thing we heard was Adrian's voice.

"Where in the hell have you two been?" he asked unsmilingly. We turned and smiled at him.

"We went to meet Neswt's Mama!" I told him, "We watched a beautiful sunset and took a moment to breathe."

"Well, while you two were 'breathing,'" Adrian did the air quotes motion, "the world is on fire, and you two are all over the news!" he shouted.

"We know, Adrian, but what can we do except go forward?" Neswt said and walked past him.

"Goodnight, everyone." She said and walked to her bedroom. She passed Ian in the hall and gave him a tight hug and continued to bed. Adrian stood there dumbfounded. Ian rushed up to me and gave me the biggest hug.

"I am so glad you are alive. I thought you died in the plane crash, but

Adrian said your body was not there, and I thought they killed you and threw you into the ocean. I was freaking out, man!" Ian stopped and took a deep breath. I could see tears in his eyes.

"You didn't have much faith in me, I guess." I joked; Ian's face went ashen.

"What? No! You know how I get when I don't know, I think the worst," he explained.

"I know, I know," I slapped his shoulder, "I'm kidding."

"Seriously, kid, where have you two been?" Adrian asked again.

"I told you, Adrian, we went to visit Neswt's mom. We stayed and talked *and* watched the news. We saw what they are saying." I replied.

"And?" Adrian asked.

"I don't know," I shrugged my shoulders, "I'm so tired. I just want to see my dad. How is he doing?"

Adrian's demeanor changed as he shifted gears.

"Your dad is doing great, but he is asleep right now," Adrian said.

I noticed an air of uncertainty in his voice.

"What's wrong with my dad?" I said, the exhaustion of the last few days was being replaced with panic. My mind was off to the races. I figured he couldn't be that bad, or Ian would have been more upset, but he did hug me for a long time, maybe because my dad was in a bad way somehow, but he would have ...

"Scipio," Adrian said firmly, "Your dad is sleeping, but he hasn't been awake since we brought him back to the Community. I'm pretty sure it's just exhaustion from such a harrowing experience, but it's not for sure."

"Where is he?" I asked.

"This way," Adrian said, leading the way.

We walked through to the other side of the room, and there was an elaborate door with pink flowers and what looked like random bushes growing from the door itself. Adrian opened the door, and we walked in. The room was a contrast to the door. It was sparse, but the bed my dad was in was also elaborate in its own way. It was a large four-poster bed with a cloth canopy over it. My dad was lying in the middle of the big bed. The covers were up under his arms, and he looked peaceful. There weren't any tubes hooked up to him, just an oxygen sensor on his finger and wires going between his chest and a beeping machine.

"The wires are just sensors to monitor his heart and O2, just in case. Otherwise, he's just sleeping. Ian's parents were very helpful and were surprisingly knowledgeable. They said if he doesn't wake up by tomorrow, they will put a catheter in to relieve the pressure on his bladder and start a saline drip. They said other than that, they don't think he is in danger. We could have Neswt come and look at him," Adrian said, almost as if he had been rehearsing it in front of a mirror.

I picked up the increase in his heartbeat. I did not so much hear or feel the beats increase. Instead, it was the ambient absorption increased, telling me it was beating faster. It was like learning to see through your skin. I marked the sensation but pushed it aside and went to my Father. I took his hand and instantly felt the lack of heat in it, and I looked back at Adrian.

"We don't know why his temperature is so low, but he is holding at ninety-five degrees," Adrian said, his voice was quiet and reverent.

"So, what are we going to do?" I asked Adrian. I was rubbing my dad's hand, trying to warm it up.

"If he doesn't wake up tomorrow, we will consider taking him to a hospital," Adrian replied.

I looked at my dad's face; he looked peaceful.

I pulled the nearby chair up to the edge of the bed, never letting go of my dad's hand, and I lay my head on the bed to wait for him to wake up, but I was asleep before I realized it.

Interlude 6

LAND OF DREAMS, ASTRAL PLANE

Aset and I walked through a bazaar in some ancient city. The smell of spices and coffee in the air conjured colors in my mind. Aset wore a bright yellow sleeveless dress with slits on both sides up to her hips. Her sandals had small bells on them, and they made a tinkling sound as she walked. In this iteration, she was bald, and her skin was a moonless summer night. Aset stood out in the crowded marketplace. Every other woman wore a black burka, conserving their modesty. Aset's strides were long and powerful. Walking this fast, I thought we would be out of the bustling market soon. The tiny bells jingled in a gentle rhythm as she walked.

"Freedom is being able to do what you want," she lilted, in an accent I could not recognize. "The pull of religion is strong in others and absent in some, and both are of value."

The bazaar stretched on, and there always seemed to be a space for us to walk, but when I looked back, it was completely gone. Was this a dream?

"It is more than a dream, Iklwa. We are in the Land of Dreams; this is where everyone is and is not. Plans are made here, iteration upon iteration. This is where Gia herself conceived the idea of you. And like the other plans, you were rehearsed and refined. However, you turned out better than we could have imagined."

We came to a massive set of golden doors. They were flanked by winged golden women. Their gilded skin seemed to move in the midday sun. The guardians faced the East and West, and their winged arms stretched behind them to make an arch.

"Nice doors," Aset glowed, "kind of cliché but not bad."

"What do you mean? I didn't make these doors," I said.

"Yes, you did," Aset stated unequivocally.

"Nice door," a familiar voice said from behind me.

I turned to see a massive golden chariot being pulled by golden cybernetic horses, soundlessly barreling down on me! I threw my hands up, expecting to be trampled to death, but nothing happened. I opened my eyes, and I could tell three pairs of eyes were staring back at me. Neswt wore a bright red dress similar to Aset's, except for the white fur that adorned the gown's collar; she wore her gift from Ogun on her left arm. The bracer glowed with strength and power, and the filigree stood out to me. The stars in each of the diamonds glowed a different color. The large man standing next to her was obviously Ogun, the God of metals, war, and rum. He wore golden armor with the breastplate worked into the shape of the head of a cobra. His skin was the color of blacksmith's water, and his eyes burned forge red. As the monstrous chariot came to a crisp halt, Ogun leaped from the chariot, and ashes fell from a coal-black beard.

"This is the Iklwa!" he roared. He strode up to me, and to my surprise, we were looking eye to eye; I did not step back.

"And strong!" he said in a slightly quieter voice; this close, I could smell rum and iron on his breath. Something licked my hand, and I looked down. A black dog returned my stare. It was muscular and armored like its master; its eyes were full of expectant play.

"Ka!" Ogun demanded, and the dog sat obediently, its tail wagging in the dirt.

"Dog likes you, so I guess you pass," Ogun laughed, "Aset, you chose a good one."

"Gia chose him; I only guided him." She responded with a smile in her voice. Neswt came to me and hugged me. She stepped back and looked at me appraisingly.

"Nice clothes, you clean up nice!"

"What?" I replied. Suddenly, as in dreams, I knew and saw what I was wearing. It was a blood-red double-breasted dashiki; the two rows of buttons were glittering emeralds, and between the buttons, the fabric was familiar. I recognized it as the kente pattern from the Bamidele suit I was given. I wore pants that were the same color as the dashiki and shoes to match. It was all topped off with a gold and green kente kufi on my head. I had no idea I was wearing any of this until Neswt mentioned it. What was going on, I wondered.

"We have an audience with Gia," Aset said. I could only stare.

There was a pause in our conversation, and the doors began to move. The left door swung out, and the right door swung in. Without a word, we all walked through the archway.

Beyond the massive threshold, we seemed to walk forever, and only a few steps down the massive hall. The walls were covered in every version of earth that existed. There were diamonds, rubies, amethyst, dirt, soil, granite, and a myriad of others. The long hall opened to a gigantic cavern, the walls and ceiling were mere ideas in this room, but the weight of the planet filled the air.

Floating in the center of the room was a cloud of sparkling dust. I was sure a Black woman was going to emerge from the mist.

A giant anteater came from somewhere in the cavern. It offered each of us golden circlets. The headwear had a large turquoise circle on it. I watched Aset take hers and place it on her head so that the turquoise was on her forehead. We all did the same.

As we finished, the glittering mist spoke. The "voice" of Gia was the weather. She spoke in the voice of the hurricane and the tornado. The waves of a storm-wrought ocean were the modulation of tone and the weight of a catastrophic avalanche, its words. I assumed, without the circlets, the literal force of nature would have killed us instantly. As it happened, we could understand it, and only our clothes fluttered as if in a light breeze.

"My children, my beautifully flawed creations, welcome. You are the recycled re-creation of the original stewards. The first teachers. Again, revived to begin the lesson anew. Because nothing is forever. Discipline is not pain but trimming necessary to save the Process. I have sanctified you to create boundaries in my name and station." The form of the mist changed, and I recognized the Milky Way Galaxy.

"From the least, the great shall emerge." The galaxy seemed dark and cold, but slowly a green hue spread all over it. I knew it to be human life. It was us; we were spreading.

"You two must teach them Harmony, or the spread will cause decay. Ikhawu, Iklwa, be warned. Be thanked."

CHAPTER 50

Somewhere Underground, March 20, 12:43 p.m. EST.

I awoke to a weight on my head. I snapped up straight in my chair to see my dad smiling at me. I leaped out of my chair and hugged him. All my words were jammed into a lump in my throat. I hugged him and basked in the warmth and security of his arms.

Eventually, we pulled back to look at each other. Our arms and hands remained touching.

"How are you feeling?" I asked him, speaking first.

"I'm feeling okay," he said, "I actually feel kinda great, like I have been sleeping for a week. What day is it?"

"I'm not sure, the eighteenth or the twentieth," I told him uncertainly. I had lost track of time since the ambush on our house.

"Well, happy, maybe, birthday, son! Did your mom make you a cake?" The question caught me off guard. Cake? Birthday? I was barely in the beginning stages of my grief over her loss. My dad didn't even know his wife was dead, and he was still thinking of me.

I tried to tell him. I tried to say the words "Mom is gone," but they wouldn't come. However, my eyes relayed the news. My dad shook his head, tears welled in his eyes, then anger filled them.

"Where is she? I wanna see her! *Now!*"

"We can't, Dad!" he was struggling to get out of the fluffy bed.

"Dad, stop! Stop!" I tried to force him to stay put, "Listen to me!" I shouted.

He stopped struggling and looked at me with such pain and despair that tears seemed to squirt from my eyes.

"I'll tell you what happened. Just stay in bed. I don't think you can stand yet," I said haltingly.

He sat back and looked at me expectantly, so I told him EVERYTHING. The dreams, the fight against the SOTIR Group, Mom's death, everything. It just poured out of me.

I was not sure how much time had passed, but at some point, Neswt, Ian, and Adrian found their way into the room with us. My dad sat there in stunned silence. He looked at each of them, then at me.

"Why did you blow up the house, Adrian?" My dad asked him.

"We were overwhelmed, and I didn't want them to use anything in the house against us," Adrian answered.

I could see my father's pragmatism warring with his anger and grief.

"I need to be alone," he stated. We all silently left the room. I heard him weeping after I closed the door. I turned from the door, and Neswt was watching me. She came and took my hand and squeezed it.

"I'm here for you." She said. I was glad she spoke the words. It gave them a comfortable weight.

Happy Birthday, you are all grown up, and that is not true. She sent me. Her soft hand stroked my cheek, and she gave me a small smile.

They say a boy does not fully become a man until his father dies. Even with Neswt's reassurance, the thought would not leave me alone.

We walked solemnly to the dining room, where we first ate with East. She was sitting at the table listening to a report given by Jack and Rhonda Henderson. There were maps and papers strewn about the large table. Projected on one of the walls were several pages of the information Noemi had sent Ian.

"Iklwa!" East said, standing quickly, "It's good to see you up, and I'm glad to hear that your Father is awake." She greeted me. I wondered how she knew about my Father; I had not seen anyone in the room come this way. "The Hendersons and I have been discussing our next steps."

My eyebrows went up for a moment.

"They suggest we go public with this information and try to break their back while they're hurt. I disagree and think we should wait until a better time. What do you say?" she asked. I looked at her, then the Hendersons, whom I had known for most of my remembered life, and all I saw was an enemy. I saw they had lied to their own son for years. The reason was immaterial. To me, their blue eyes hid another motive for their so-called help. I walked to the table and looked over the maps. There were locations of possible areas of operation, marked supply houses, and even safe houses. I looked at the high-resolution projection and the files. Here I saw names and faces I did not know, but their positions were high. Mayors, Senators, police chiefs, FBI Assistant directors, and thousands of police officers.

Occasionally, the label next to the precinct simply said: Entire. I assumed it meant the SOTIR Group owned the entire police or sheriff's department. I glanced at the Hendersons, who were staring thoughtfully at me, and something in me irreparably warped. Maybe it was all the horrible things that had been brought on by White supremacy in just the last few days, but I chose to go with East in that moment.

"I think we should wait. We are not done with this piece of shit group and having the information to hit them directly at will can be a powerful weapon. They will eventually figure out we have the information, but we will have a network by then to follow them and learn about their new locations before they do," I said to them.

"We will?" Mr. Henderson asked with a smile on his face. Was he mocking me? I blinked to stand directly in front of him.

"Yes, Jack, we will, won't we, East?" I said, staring at him. I did not know why I was so angry, other than that I was nearing the end of my mental rope.

"We already have an extensive surveillance culture in most of these cities," East said, a little nervousness hidden in her voice.

"You're too close, Scipio. If I wanted to kill you, I could do it because you are too close." Jack Henderson said quietly. His eyes never wavered.

He was right; I could not see his belt in my peripheral vision. It was one of the first lessons Adrian taught me all those years ago. I had let my unfocused anger focus on the wrong target. I wanted to hurt something, and the Hendersons had fit the description. I was better than that. I took a step back, but I did not look away.

"Scipio, if it makes you feel better, East did a deep dive on us with her abilities, and while she questioned some of our strategies, she agreed we are not a threat," Rhonda Henderson said.

"We are waiting for precognitive confirmation from the Zamaradi Council," East added, "but per my recommendation, they have been preliminarily cleared. We have thousands of allies like them all over the world, and the Hendersons would be a valuable asset." East was standing at the head of the table.

I walked away, angry and ashamed that I had acted so aggressively toward friends I had known all my life based on the color of their skin. I did not want to become the monster I fought. I would fight them with every iota of energy I could muster, but I would never hate indiscriminately. It was a gray shade of gray, but it was a line I could see and would hold. I would not dehumanize my enemy; my parents taught me a fish rots from the head, and if I was going to lead anybody, I needed hard boundaries.

I will not let you stray, Iklwa, just as I know you will not let me stray. Neswt's thought cut my thoughts off. It was disconcerting, something I would have to learn to deal with. It seemed she heard my thoughts, but I never heard hers unless they were sent. I would have to explore my own telepathy. In comics and books, people could make boxes to section things off in their minds.

I was thinking and designing partitions for my mental house when I walked into the sitting room. Adrian and Ian were in the room talking lightly. Ian was laughing at something Adrian said.

"Hey, king," Adrian said when he saw me.

Hey, you cut me out. Neswt sent to me.

"Hey guys," I said, and fell into a chair next to them.

Kinda, I need privacy just like you! I sent back with a smile, riding the thought. *An image of an old-timey phone with a U-shaped receiver followed.*

"We were just talking about how fast those nano-guys were running after the car and how scared I was," Ian said. This thing had already become lore, I thought to myself.

Suddenly, all of our Globals pinged, beeped, or rang, and we all tapped our earpieces. A message from East came to us: Watch this NOW! When people are in a group and in a certain proximity, they can group their devices together and view the same content in sync. Adrian, Ian, and I synced up and watched the video sent to us.

The footage showed the remains of Cross Tower. Parts of the building protruded from the swampy ground, and twisted skeletons of trees floated in the slurry. I thought I saw a body in the catastrophe. My heart sank; had we done that? Had we killed all those people?

NO! They destroyed the building and collapsed the pit on us. It was just after you left. It was not your fault. The memory she had came to me in a rush. I breathed a sigh of weighted relief; these people had still died, even if it was not my fault. It was something else the SOTIR Group would have to pay for.

The anchor was reporting the facts as they were learning them.

"The Cross Science and Technology Plaza, also known as the Trillion Dollar Pit by some, or the Trillion Dollar Tower, has collapsed. The number of casualties is still unknown, nearly 72 hours later. One of the reasons is the inability to approach the disaster site because the ground itself is still moving. It is like a small lake of mud. The experts call it a slurry. And because this 'slurry' is filled with large pieces of the tower itself, a potential search and rescue operation is all but impossible. We don't yet know what caused the catastrophe. Was it intentional? Was it an accident? We are still trying to find the owner of the Cross Tower, Robert Cross. As of today, the U.S. government is but one of many world governments looking for Mr. Cross. Several of his properties have been raided, and many files and computers have been confiscated." The anchor continued on like that for several more seconds, and I was about to disconnect from the group when the excited news anchor announced they had breaking news.

"I have been told a philanthropic group named the SOTIR Group has released footage one of their employees took moments after leaving the Cross Plaza. Apparently, they were shooting footage with a drone for marketing purposes.

The video showed an aircraft of some sort hovering near the top of the building. Several men leap to a ramp extended from the aircraft to the side of the building. I recognized Robert Cross immediately. As I watch him zoom away in his supersonic transport. I knew what this was.

I knew footage of Neswt and me bringing a large group of naked and abused Black people of varying extreme human configurations would surface eventually. Somehow, they would swing this as a terrorist attack of some kind. That would be the easiest way to make our movement difficult and heighten the chances we would get caught on camera somewhere. They would be taking an enormous gamble and revealing to the world that EPBs exist. The next part of the footage surprised everyone.

Shortly after the jet flew away, a man resembling me but in a black cloak and closed hood, ran into the massive courtyard. He removed the cover to reveal a shockingly high-tech jet pack, and he flew away in the opposite direction of Robert Cross's aircraft. I was dumbfounded, and I burst out laughing. I had to leave our little watch group. The sheer audacity of this plan. The public would believe it. They would believe this more than a man that could fly (without a jet pack) and take down supersonic jets or a woman who could effortlessly lift twenty-five terrified humans to safety. Confirming the idea that people like this exist would probably throw the globe into chaos. Apparently, the SOTIR Group and I had something in common. I was able to get myself calmed down after a few more seconds of laughing. As I wiped my eyes, I realized this was their only play, but would they name me, although they had no face of the flying man, jet pack or not?

"The Mystery jet pack man is still unknown at this time; authorities are still investigating. We know that anywhere between one thousand and twelve hundred people work in and around the Cross Tower on any given day. This is a massive tragedy. How could one man be responsible for this?" The audio of the newscast still played in my ears. I tapped the earpiece and ended the link. I sat in a chair and collected myself. Neswt came in from one direction, and East and Ian's parents came from the formal dining area.

"What is the plan? Iklwa," East demanded as she came into the room.

I was confused as to why she was asking me what to do.

"Why are you asking me? I have had powers for a few days. I don't know anything about politics or the people involved. I'm just a kid. Why don't you go ask your Zamaradi Council what to do because I..."? As I was talking, East's phone rang. I still did not know how they got service in this underground home.

"This is Elder East," she said, answering the phone. East's bearing changed; she took on an air of command and power. I watched as she spoke with the person on the other end; I could tell she was getting distressing news. She ended the call, turned, and looked at us.

"That was the Grand Minister of Defense she called to personally invite all of you to the Alpha Community to be officially recognized by the Zamaradi Council." She paused, and we all looked at each other expectantly, not knowing if this was a good thing or not.

"They also cleared the entire Henderson family, and they are invited to meet the Council as well. It really is an honor to be the very first non-melanated person to have an audience with the Council." East said sullenly. "What is the matter, East?" I asked.

"The minister relayed to me that I was not invited because of the necessity of my presence after the near-riot, and that goes for Adrian as well," East informed us.

Adrian stood from his seat to speak when the entire space shook.

My first thought was, 'Oh no, someone drove their car into the house.'

It happened again, but this time it was accompanied by a scream of pain. I blinked to my dad's room and was greeted with a monstrosity.

Black tendrils erupted from my Father's face, ripping it to pieces. Cross's mangled body flashed through my mind. The stringy black substance collected in the upper corner of the room. My dad's savaged body twitched in a pool of black blood. I saw all of this in a split second; the next second, the Stygian creature flew at me, the tendrils braided and merged into tentacles as it flew. I had just enough time to put up the shimmering green barrier Neswt and I created in our battle with the Alex monster. The hellish thing wrapped around me and pulled savagely at my arms and legs. It wrapped its dry black tentacles around my throat, trying to choke the life from me. Neswt's and my field negated the vector of pressure it applied and denied the dark infection it was trying to pass to me. The thing tried to rip my head off, but I felt none of it. I stood there frozen with the most bottomless *Rage* I have ever felt in my life. It was fueled by the vision and pain of my dad being ripped apart by this thing. What had these people done to him? They tried to turn him into a suicide bomb. I could feel the explosion roiling in my torso.

Everyone is clear, Iklwa, I, no we, are all so sorry. The pain and grief in her thought was the spark.

The writhing creature must have realized it was getting nowhere with me, so it tried to leave. I sealed the small recovery room with my Vector Manipulation. I created another damage negation field shaped to the form of the room, but the impervious side of the field faced inward. The creature flailed violently in the room, but it could not escape. The beast thrashed and destroyed everything in the room. I saw my dad's body whip around the space, still connected to the nano-machine mass. In the storm of my rage, I reached out for the electricity Neswt generated. I raised my hand to see blue arcs of current playing on my palm and fingers. I could sense the electrical flow I was generating. I increased the flow of electrons over the surface of the field I was creating around myself. The arcs on the field became thicker and were coming faster and faster. The wriggling thing screamed inhumanly as the heat in the tiny room increased exponentially. I was raising the heat of the air between my two fields and the current of electricity around my sphere. Little flashes of light began to appear in the air as small pockets of ionized air burst into sparks of plasma. I poured that ancient *Anger* onto the air. There was a tremendously bright flash of light. The shield around me had gone opaque, and I could feel power pouring into the globe itself. I hoped Neswt had my back.

I let go!

The walls of the room vaporized. The deadly nano-machine monster was vaporized. My Father's body was vaporized. My tears were not. My broken heart remained, surrounded by power and living *Rage.*

None of it mattered. I had fought for my dad's life, for the last person alive in my family, and it was all for nothing. They took him from me, anyway! And the SOTIR Racists remained to continue to use and kill us. They had won. They had taken everything from me! Despair loomed over me in the form of Robert Cross. His bloodied face twisted in glee at my defeat!

My outer field flickered, then dropped.

NO Scipio! Neswt screamed in my mind, *You will kill us!* A vision of the screaming people in the Haven Community as the elevator shaft of East's house collapsed in on itself, as a small sun emerged from the ground. The cavern ceiling above the orb melted and fell into it. The rubble never reached the surface of the white ball of heat. Neswt showed me the field she was holding up to protect everyone.

I bellowed in terror at what I was doing! I slammed the door to the *Rage* and sorrow. I buried it in the wreckage of my life. The light faded, and I was left in a charred, blackened hole.

Dust and debris rained down on me. I felt a warm hand on my shoulder, then arms wrapped around me, and I smelled shea butter. I did not open my eyes, but I knew it was Neswt. Everything in life is a choice. As I knelt there, my arms weighed a thousand pounds. I could fall into the warm shadows of my sorrow, or I could work to lift my arms and return the hug in an acknowledgment of life. If I did the latter, the circle would complete, and healing would begin.

CLICK!

The End.

EPILOGUE

set sat above the shower, watching the clean, clear water run down Scipio's chiseled body. He had been in excellent shape before his real life started, but now, whew! The intense training by Adrian and the Council guards has refined him. His Black skin was a maze of shadows cast by his shredded musculature. His hair was black and full; droplets of water were suspended in the oily sheen. The Goddess watched him finish, dry off, and get dressed for bed. She wished he were more like the men of old, sleeping naked and powerful.

As he slept, she cast her memory back to their arrival here six months ago. Scipio was dejected and barely able to feign excitement at his recognition ceremony. The psionic rapport between him and Neswt helped prop him up when his mind wandered. Aset could not read the young man's mind, but she could read him like a book, and her heart broke for him. To lose his mother so horribly, then the ghastly death of his Father was something most human beings could not live through, but Scipio was clawing his way back.

The Alpha Community was *in* the Richat Structure, the massive concentric dome had been explored several times over the decades, but nothing was ever found. In truth, they had been discovered several times by determined explorers and archaeologists. Still, the abilities of a Zamaradi Council member or a member of the Community were able to rewrite the memory of the intruder. Their memory was never erased, which would lead to too many questions, but a consistent story of an empty, barren area kept the visitors to a minimum, and interest very low as well.

Under the old dome was a massive city that was bored down into the earth's crust several miles and was nearly as wide as the Structure's dome at the top, but narrowed precipitously as one descended. The hall where Scipio, Neswt, and the Hendersons arrived, all those months ago, was a gigantic cavern adorned with hanging fabric banners of extraordinary length. The incomplete group of heroes was dressed in their Bamidele suits, and they were configured to be formal Yoruba robes and dashikis for Scipio and Neswt; Ian wore his as a tuxedo. He didn't feel wearing a dashiki and kufi was appropriate. Ian's parents were not wearing Bamidele originals, but they wore formal wear they had stashed at one of their many safe houses.

The cavern was empty except for the enormous round table made from a slice of an enormous tree, surrounded by seven surprisingly modern office chairs. Computers and papers were stacked neatly in front of each chair. On a tall dais rested two identical, jet-black thrones; no one occupied them, but they gleamed in the light. The chairs around the Great Table were evenly placed with three on each side, and the seventh and most elaborate chair was directly in front of the thrones on the dais.

The Oba of the Oju was the Council tiebreaker, and since their "home" was the seat of power, they were given the final say on most decisions. The six Oloye ruled nine country states each. They were in charge of finding and collecting any emerging EPBs in their respective states. They funneled them to the A.R.C.s around the world that had the space and resources to accommodate the new arrival and their family. The Zamaradi Council was also charged with blocking the SOTIR Group from getting a foothold in Africa. China was a big thorn in their side because it could offer the nation-states liquid capital. Often, the struggling leaders of these countries could not say no to the money.

Today, however, was a day of celebration. The Iklwa and Ikhawu had been revealed. Aset herself unveiled the would-be leaders. Now here they were. The ceremony was grand, and for the first time, the original Emerald Tablets of Thoth were brought to the ceremony. The large, mysterious Tablets glowed in the proximity of the Iklwa and Ikhawu, further confirming their station. The new Royals were adorned with furs and golden necklaces, but they were not crowned. In a stunning upset of the preordained ceremony, the Oba of the Oju decreed, as Elder of the Alpha A.R.C., that until the full Council agreed the two children were ready to lead and be accountable for hundreds of millions of people, they would not be crowned. Aset had been furious but unable to alter the decree. Fortuitously, one of Adrian's friends in the guard offered to prepare the youths and their friend for the journey ahead.

Next, the Henderson couple was acknowledged. They were given a provisional position as consultants to the Minister of Defense. The Oba of the Oju did not seem pleased at this, but the Minister of Defense had requested it personally. This was one area the Oba could not override the council; the matter was beneath her station.

At the end of the elaborate ceremony, the Oba of the Oju stood and addressed the small but elaborate gathering.

"We have been blessed to live in the time of the revelation of the Iklwa and the Ikhawu, and our sacred oath demands that we, as the Zamaradi Council, be guided by the wisdom of the ancient Tablets to prepare these candidates to be able to take their duties seriously and with the proper perspective. While their exploits are great and legendary, they are human like all of us. As the Zamaradi Council, we take our sacred duties seriously, and we are committed to creating the best possible future for our people and the people of the world. We thank them for their sacrifice and now enjoy the festivities because today is truly a day to rejoice!" The tall Sudanese woman returned to her seat; her bright robes complemented her dark skin. Aset had always been wary of her, but she served her people well.

Scipio and his friends did their best to be cordial to the small gathering of guests. Eventually, the 'party' was over, and they were all shown to their respective homes. Neswt and Scipio found each other easily and talked in hushed tones about their new situation. Aset had floated to sit with them and listen in.

"Well, here we are, what are we going to do now?" Scipio had asked.

"I guess we learn as much as we can and get stronger," Neswt replied.

Aset had a feeling there was a lot more being passed between them mentally, but she trusted them, well, as far as she could trust a *human* with absolute power.

Under Odesa, Ukraine, Date and Time Unknown.

Lilly Roth swept into the observation room. She had to see this for herself.

"How the hell did this happen?" Her legendary temper was flaring,

"Who authorized this?"

"No one, ma'am," the terrified technician replied weakly, "the printer cycled up by itself, and before we knew what it was doing, it began printing with the nano-machines." Lilly glared at the small man.

"Get out!" She ordered.

`When the technician left, she used her personal authentication and opened the identification file. She almost took a step back from the ID of the print. Alexander Malcolm Lamb. How had Alex Lamb been put on this very exclusive list? Lilly Roth tried to cancel the print, but nothing worked. She tried to use her Master Code to override the machine, but it was not accepted. Lilly tried to turn the power off to the machine. It was a hazardous decision because she could damage a multi-trillion-dollar, one-of-a-kind machine. The massive printer stopped for a moment, then it resumed its function.

"How?" Roth whispered. She searched around the apparatus and found a thick line of nano-machines clogging the disconnect. The box was covered in a writhing mass of blackness, the three-inch pipe running up to the surface generators bulged violently with the tiny machines. Thankfully, they were not spreading and only seemed determined to complete their task. Lilly Roth was patient. She pulled up a chair in the control room and pressed a button.

"Someone bring me a pumpkin spice latte," she ordered. This was going to be a long night.

Dean Baxter

Dean Baxter's fascination with superheroes and the extraordinary has been a lifelong passion. From a young age, he found inspiration in the captivating world of comic books, particularly the iconic tales of Black Panther and X-Men. These narratives ignited his imagination and fueled his desire to craft stories that transcend the ordinary.

Drawing from the rich tapestry of African mythology, Dean weaves tales that blend the mystique of ancient legends with the allure of modern storytelling. His unique perspective pays homage to diverse cultures and traditions, creating narratives that resonate with readers from all walks of life.

Dean Baxter is not only a masterful storyteller but also a proud U.S. Navy veteran, instilling in his work the values of discipline, dedication, and resilience. He currently resides in the vibrant state of California, where he shares his life with his loving wife, three remarkable sons, and two cherished canine companions—a Black Lab named Winchester and a rescued pit bull named Rocky.

Dean's commitment to crafting narratives that captivate the imagination is matched only by his dedication to his family and his enduring passion for storytelling. With each word he pens, Dean invites readers on a journey that transcends the ordinary and celebrates the extraordinary in all of us.